I AM TRAITOR

I AM TRAITOR

SIF SIGMARSDÓTTIR

Hodder
Children's
Books

HODDER CHILDREN'S BOOKS

First published in Great Britain in 2017 by Hodder and Stoughton

1 3 5 7 9 10 8 6 4 2

A CIP catalogue record for this book is available from the British Library.

ISBN 978 1 444 93447 2

Typeset in Berkeley Oldstyle Book
Printed and bound in Great Britain by Clays Ltd, St Ives plc

The paper and board used in this book are made from wood
from responsible sources.

Hodder Children's Books
An imprint of Hachette Children's Group
Part of Hodder and Stoughton
Carmelite House
50 Victoria Embankment
London EC4Y 0DZ

An Hachette UK Company
www.hachette.co.uk

www.hachettechildrens.co.uk

To Geir, for all the foolishness

To my parents, for always keeping a straight face

PART I

THERE IS A LIGHT THAT NEVER GOES OUT

PROLOGUE

I can hear Dad's footsteps as he paces the living room floor. Mum is crying. The sound is making my insides twist into a knot. I managed to block it out for a while by listening to some music, but now the battery on my phone is dead. A part of me wants to scream. Or hurl. Or lie down and fall asleep and wake up in the past. But I can't let myself think like that. I have to be strong. I can't be a burden. I can't be another thing to cry about.

Emma is slouching on my unmade sofa bed, using my pencil case as a chew toy and happily drooling all over my sheets. I envy her. She has no clue what her two-year-old eyes just witnessed. I wish I was a toddler and oblivious to everything that is happening – oblivious to how our world is falling apart in the most horrendous, unimaginable way possible.

The sky over Canary Wharf is quietly overcast. It's as if the heavens know they should look sad. As if they are overseeing a funeral. Clouds envelop the skyscrapers of London's swanky financial district. The glass, the

3

concrete, the steel – the sharp, clean lines – are softened by the fog. From my bedroom I can see the building where Mum works – or used to work. Usually, the light in the windows makes the area look like a forest of brightly lit Christmas trees. Now the skyscrapers look more like skeletons of the ghosts of Christmas past.

Mum's crying is dying down, the heavy sobs slowing into whimpers and then fading to nothing. Suddenly, I find myself wishing that she wouldn't stop. The events of the past weeks have taught me that the one thing worse than the sound of someone sobbing their eyes out is silence. Of everything that could get under your skin – the screaming, the crying, all the futile begging for mercy – it's the piercing sound of nothing that makes me feel as if I'm losing my mind. Because when everything goes silent, the voices in your head grow louder. The questions are deafening: Why are they here? What do they want? Are we – am I – going to die?

Until this evening, I had hope; I believed that something could be done. Things wouldn't always be this way. But now ... I don't know ... I'm already beginning to forget how things used to be. I'm beginning to forget that things used to be any different at all.

The electricity has been out for hours. Dark shadows twitch in the candlelight, looking like dead souls trying desperately to fight their way back to life.

No one has any answers to the questions that the silence arouses. No one knows why. No one knows what will happen. The only thing I know for sure is this: There is nothing I can do except wait for my turn.

They took my brother. My brother is gone. So is Matilda. I think I might be next.

1

A week earlier

I'd just finished a small bowl of cereal – the chocolate kind that I was only allowed as a treat at the weekend. Afterwards, Mum asked me to go and wake Andrew, my chronically tired older brother who would sleep for months if no one intervened. When I burst into his bedroom he growled at me like a hibernating bear being disturbed in the middle of winter. I picked up his dirty socks from the floor and threw them at his head. He dragged himself, half-asleep, into the kitchen.

The electricity was on – it was becoming a less frequent occurrence – so I went to my room, closed the door and opened my laptop. I couldn't wait to see if Matilda was online. Or Anita – although I knew she probably wouldn't be. She hadn't been for a while, but I would not allow myself to imagine the worst.

All of a sudden, Mum began shouting.

'I can't believe you did that! How could you? You weren't supposed to finish all of it!'

I crept along the hallway to the kitchen.

Sitting at the kitchen table, Andrew looked up at Mum,

bewilderment in his sleepy eyes. An empty cereal bowl was on the table in front of him.

'There's no more now,' Mum continued, her voice screechy and hysterical. 'There's no more bloody cereal.'

Dad came rushing past from the bathroom, leaving a trail of newspaper sheets behind him as his week-old copy of the Guardian gradually fell apart.

Andrew stayed silent and ran his fingers awkwardly through his ash-blond hair while Mum kept on howling at him. His usually sleek, side-swept fringe was sticking up in the air like a horn protruding from his head. Finally, a wave of recognition flickered across Andrew's face. For a brief moment I could see he was frightened. He had realised what he had done. But just as swiftly, the corners of his mouth turned down, his sea-green eyes did their roll of indignation and his expression turned hard and sulky.

Mum started crying then. So did Emma, who was sitting in her highchair, playing with spoons. The dummy fell out of her mouth.

I covered my ears. There is nothing like the sound of babies crying. It's like having a screwdriver thrust into your brain; the high-pitched noise is at a frequency only dogs should be able to hear.

'What's happened?' Dad shouted over the clamour, still doing up his trousers.

'The box,' Mum sobbed. She pointed at the packet of chocolate cereal. 'The whole thing is empty.'

The little that was left of Dad's paper dropped to the floor.

The muscles in his neck, which had looked as if they might burst out from under his skin at any moment, slackened, and his clamped lips parted in relief.

I knew what he was thinking. Sure, this was bad. But it could have been something so much worse.

Dad wrapped his arms around Mum and stroked her hair. 'It will be all right, Di,' he said, giving Andrew an apologetic hint of a smile over his shoulder.

Andrew wouldn't look at him.

'We'll figure something out.'

Without meeting anyone's eyes, Andrew got up and went back to his room. I noted that he didn't slam the door as he usually did when he'd been told off by one of our parents.

I knew I should have been angry at Andrew, but I just felt sorry for him. He didn't mean anything by it. He had just momentarily forgotten. I had read online that it was practically scientifically proven that the male of the species was not in full control of his brain. Especially sixteen-year-old boys. Lately, the reason Andrew acted stupidly seemed to be down to the one thing that took up all the space in his head: girls. So it wasn't his fault. I left the kitchen and headed back to my room.

Once she had calmed down, Mum invited herself in and sat at the foot of the bed.

'God, Amy, you shouldn't have had to see that,' she said, blushing through her foundation. 'I'm so sorry. I hope you know that at times such as these, it's okay to feel a little crazy, especially given the circumstances.' She hesitated. 'You can have a cry if you want to.'

8

'Mum!' I snapped. 'I'm fourteen, not four.'

She narrowed her lips, forming a hurtful pout. 'So? Crying at any age is allowed. It's not healthy to be so closed about everything that's happening.'

'I'm not going to cry.' *Or at least not in front of anyone,* I thought, but kept that to myself.

She sighed in that universal Mum-knows-best-why-can't-you-just-do-as-I-say way that always drove me mad. 'Let's just talk then. How are you feeling?'

I didn't have time for this. I needed to get on the computer before the electricity cut out again. And I certainly wasn't in the mood for one of her amateur psychoanalysis sessions. But I knew from experience the only way to get her out of my room was to 'share'.

'I'm a bit upset actually,' I said, hunching my shoulders for effect. I swear she wriggled as if she'd just won the lottery or something.

'Okay, go on,' she said, obviously trying hard not to sound too happy about it.

'I sent Matilda an email this morning about a pair of shoes I found online that I thought she might like.'

She was nodding far too enthusiastically, like the dog in that annoying car insurance advert.

'The S key on my laptop has been a bit dodgy ever since Emma and the apple-juice spillage incident ...'

'Go on.'

'I didn't realise until after I'd pressed send that the subject of the email wasn't the innocent fashion tip I'd meant, but an inappropriate proposition. It said: "hoes with your name on them".'

I knew that emotional turmoil caused by a keyboard wasn't what Mum was after. I knew I should have told her about my recurring nightmare about drowning in a big, black sea of muddy water; about how I woke up in the night, drenched in sweat, feeling as if the darkness was a big black pillow that someone – I didn't know who – was using to suffocate me. But somehow I couldn't put those things into words.

Mum was very understanding about my plight. She told me about a time she'd sent her boss at the bank a text which, thanks to the autocorrect function on her phone, said, 'Will get cracking on the raccoon as soon as I'm finished with the thong I'm working on.' She'd meant to say she would get cracking on the report as soon as she'd finished with the thing she was working on – although a place that made thongs from the skins of dead raccoons would have made so much more sense to me than Mum's 'Department of Symmetrical Hedging and Collateralised Debt Obligations'.

I thought I'd managed to sidetrack Mum regarding the issue of 'feelings' when she got up off my bed and headed towards the door. I'd already done a victory lap in my head when she stopped and turned around.

'Oh, Amy.' She was standing in the doorway. 'You're just like your father! The two of you always keep things all bottled up.'

I felt my chest deflate. I just wanted to go on the computer and check whether Matilda was online. I couldn't understand why she wasn't. Where else could she be? I hoped she hadn't done a permanent vanishing act from the internet like Anita seemed to have done.

'I have an idea,' Mum said.

I wanted to shout, 'Whatever it takes to get this awkward conversation over with,' but instead I nodded, pretending not to know that whatever she was about to suggest would be embarrassing.

'Remember that lovely notebook you got from Aunt Rosa on your birthday?'

'Umm, yes.'

'I think you should start keeping a diary.'

'A diary?'

'Yes, a diary.' Mum frowned. 'It's like what you kids call a blog, but you write it down with an instrument called a pen on a primitive version of the iPad called paper.'

'Ha, ha – very funny.'

I tried to remember where I'd put the thing. The notebook was pink with a heart-shaped lock on it. I hadn't even taken it out of the box. It seemed it wasn't only Mum who still thought I was four years old.

'I think writing down your story might be good for you. Especially during this ...' She broke off as she searched for the right word. 'During this experience,' she concluded. 'At least it will give you something to do.'

Although the idea of keeping a diary seemed as much fun as having every single spot on my forehead squeezed by a first-year beauty student armed with a pair of pliers, I agreed to it. Anything to get Mum out of my room.

11

That evening, when the electricity was out, which meant our router was out, which meant the internet was out, I tried to write an entry. I sat and stared at a blank page for half an hour. Nothing happened. Despite everything that was going on, I had nothing to say.

It wasn't until a week later that I tried again. Maybe it was the awfulness of our situation – when we thought things couldn't get much worse, they always did. Or maybe it was something else – a small seed of hope that had nestled itself somewhere deep inside my head or my soul or whatever. But suddenly the words just started trickling out.

Tuesday 23 August

Mum and Dad are fighting again. They think I can't hear them. They're supposed to be smart people, but sometimes they are just so stupid. You'd think that every rational being with half a brain would realise that screaming penetrates easily through hollow wood-laminated doors. Especially the two beings who used to order Andrew to turn down his 'God-awful screech of music' ten times a day. Noise travels both ways, people!

'We have to do something,' I can hear Dad say.

'Don't start, Dan,' Mum snaps at him.

'But we have to.'

'Don't you think I would if I could?' Mum is raising her voice now.

'There must be something—'

'There isn't anything we can do.'

'Don't say that, Di. You can't let yourself give up like that. That's what they want. That's what they're counting on.'

Now there's an unintelligible shouting match.

I'm trying to ignore them. Grief makes people angry. So does guilt.

I'm trying to stay strong. I guess that's my duty given that they have enough to deal with. Given that they have just lost their son.

I fear Mum is right. It's difficult to imagine we stand a chance. But I do see where Dad is coming from. He hasn't said it, but I know what he is thinking. I know he's thinking about what Mandira said. Mum doesn't want to hear it. She's just lost a child. She doesn't want to lose another one. But things don't have to be over. There is still one thing we can do.

2

It was the day after the incident with the cereal that the idea of death first entered my mind.

After a breakfast of an expired can of lobster bisque I finally caught Matilda online.

FrizzyAmy: Where the hell were you yesterday?!? Don't you know that your virtual presence is the only thing keeping me from exploding from boredom and thus, with my liquidated body, ruining my triple-core, 128-bit laptop which I've spent weeks enhancing with an extremely expensive custom-built graphics accelerator? How could you abandon me like that?
M-Girl: Sorry, babe.
FrizzyAmy: What could you possibly have had to attend to that was more important than chatting to your best friend?

The answer was so blatantly obvious, I couldn't believe I hadn't thought of it.

M-Girl: I met a really cute guy!

Of course she had.

M-Girl: His name is Tom.
FrizzyAmy: Tell me more.
M-Girl: He looks exactly like Harry Styles.
FrizzyAmy: Naturally …
M-Girl: He lives on the top floor of my building.
FrizzyAmy: Quite the coincidence. How did you meet?
M-Girl: It was during an air-raid warning. The sirens were going full blast and everyone was jostling each other, trying to get down to the bottom of Island Gardens station for shelter. I got knocked over and Tom was a few paces behind me. He elbowed his way towards me and scooped me up in his arms.
FrizzyAmy: Sounds quite romantic, if a little nauseating.
M-Girl: Oh, you and your wit.
FrizzyAmy: I try.
M-Girl: Sorry, babe – I've got to go.
FrizzyAmy: No, don't go!
M-Girl: I'm off to see Tom. He's asked me up to his.
FrizzyAmy: Traitor!
M-Girl: Speak to you later. Miss you!

And then she was offline.

The news wasn't really news. When it came to guys, Matilda had a gravitational pull comparable to that of a small planet. They revolved around her like moons around Jupiter.

Although we'd been friends since the age of five, I knew some people at our school (some people meaning Courtney and Louisa)

16

still considered it one of the biggest mysteries of the universe why tall, gorgeous, fun Matilda Matthews would ever be friends with average-heighted, geeky, slightly short-sighted Amy Sullivan. The two of us couldn't possibly have been more different.

Matilda had beautiful curves, a perfectly sculptured nose and sleek blonde hair. I, on the other hand, stopped growing at twelve, except for my arms, which almost came down to my knees. The only curves I had were the frizzy waves in my mousy hair, which not even a hair straightener with heat from the hottest flames of hell would be able to smooth out. And, whereas Matilda was always impeccably groomed and had the latest make-up, it was more likely I'd apply it develop the skills to build a robot and programme it to apply eyeliner in a straight line before I'd learn to myself.

But somehow we just clicked.

I was genuinely happy for Matilda and her non-news. Really. I was. She was my oldest and best friend. Why would I not have been happy for her? Happy, happy, happy.

Okay. I had to admit it. Maybe I was also a teeny-tiny bit jealous.

It was nothing personal, if that could be considered a defence. If it hadn't been for this one little thing, I would have been a hundred per cent happy for Matilda (even a hundred and ten per cent if this had been *The X Factor*).

I could never admit to the reason for my jealousy out loud. I knew what Dad would have said. He would have come up with some Darwinian explanation for my trouble rejoicing in my friend's conquests in the field of boyfriend-catching. As a geneticist he worshipped at the altar of Charles Darwin. You could hardly blink without him giving a speech on the origin of blinking. Mum, on the other hand, would have had me talk through the issue, a process that would have inevitably descended into a monologue on self-esteem and the importance of being yourself (like I could have been anyone else if I'd tried).

But I knew the real reason. It was very simple. It didn't take a rocket scientist – or the combined powers of a geneticist and an amateur shrink – to figure it out. It was shame. The reason I wasn't TV-talent-show happy for Matilda was that I was ashamed.

And what was I ashamed of? I guess you could say it was maths. While Matilda had already had seven boyfriends in the past two years – 0.875 per season – I myself had only had … oh, God, I can't admit to it … but I must … I must do it …

I'd had …

None.

Cringe!

My boyfriend count of the fourteen years that I'd lived was ZERO. A big, fat, embarrassing ZERO.

And the boyfriend shortage was not the only mortifying maths equation of my life. Not only had I never had a boyfriend, I'd never even kissed a guy! I was fourteen and I'd never been kissed!

Double cringe!

Deep down, though, I always had hope. I never truly believed I would go my whole life without so much as one kiss. I wasn't that bad to look at – Matilda said I could have the face of a C-list celebrity if only I plucked my eyebrows once in a while. And there was still time for my breasts to grow in – or rather out.

But when Matilda told me about Tom I realised that I actually might die without ever being kissed.

It sounds embarrassing, but the idea frightened me more than anything had since they had arrived; more than anything had since the whole siege began. I guess the seriousness of the situation had finally sunk in: I might not have long to tick things off my what-to-do-before-I-die list.

I have a secret. Well, it's not exactly a proper secret, more like a little light penetrating the darkness; a good thing that's probably not appropriate for me to think about too much given the circumstances. But it lives inside me and, when I desperately need a distraction from feeling guilty about still being here when Andrew and Matilda and all the others aren't, I let my mind go there. I wonder what he's doing. I wonder whether he's thinking about me. I wonder whether I'll see him again.

I realise it's not important in the grand scheme of things – I realise I'm being a bit stupid – but it gives me small pleasure to know that, whatever happens, at least now I won't die without ever being kissed.

I was thinking about him when the electricity finally came back on this morning. Dad made a stack of toast from some old bread Mrs Walnut-face, the old, wrinkly lady from downstairs, brought us. Mum called Granny Vera to tell her about Andrew being gone. I could hear her sobbing into the phone. Her words were mostly unintelligible, but I did detect 'leave here' and 'stay with you'.

After the phone call, Mum and Dad had a whispering session in the kitchen. I went into the living room and pretended I was watching reruns of old episodes, the only things that are on TV these days. But I wasn't. I was listening in. I had a feeling they were planning something and I was pretty sure I knew what it was.

Dad was saying he was sorry. 'You were right. We should have tried. We might not have made it, but we should have tried. Then maybe Andrew wouldn't have—'

'It's not important at this point who was right and who was wrong,' Mum said in a flat voice, the kind you use when you don't mean what you're saying.

Dad's devastation felt tangible in the empty silence.

Mum cleared her throat. 'We need to focus on what we do now. We have Amy to think about. I think we should try.'

More silence. Then Dad finally said: 'Okay. Let's try.'

I'm still in shock. They must be out of their minds. It's as if they have amnesia or something. It's as if they weren't there in the car park that day; the day my hope that this was all just a big misunderstanding had been spectacularly wiped out.

3

I was in my room looking at cat videos on YouTube. Nothing helps you forget like cat videos. Emma was pinching my leg in the hope I might pick her up and let her play with my laptop.

There was a knock on the door. It opened and Andrew's head appeared through the crack.

'They've done it again.'

I rolled my eyes. 'I'll fix it.'

My fingers skidded across the keyboard of my laptop as confidently as if I were a piano player who knew her song by heart. It wasn't the first time Mum and Dad had put some sort of parental control on our internet access so Andrew and I wouldn't google what was going on. It took me less than a minute to disable it.

'There.'

'Thanks.'

His floating head disappeared back through the crack.

They could have saved themselves the trouble. There was nothing to see. I did a bit of googling every morning when I woke up. No one seemed to know what was going on. I hadn't found any photos online except the one that was shown on TV the day it'd all started – and a few that were clearly fake. On the surface of things, everything seemed normal.

I spent about an hour chatting to Matilda about her roots. No, not her ancestry. Matilda's appointment to have her hair done had been booked for that day. She was really upset. She was of the opinion that visible hair roots were the root of all evil in Western society.

She said she hadn't seen any movement inside Anita's house for days. I wasn't surprised. Anita hadn't been online for ages. Her family must have made their escape despite the curfew. I knew that some people had fled to the countryside.

I really hoped they'd been able to get away. The alternative was too awful to think about.

When it was time for Matilda to go and meet up with Tom I watched some more cat videos: a cat snoring; a cat cuddling a baby; two cats fast asleep on a snoring dog.

Then, when the electricity cut out, I made binoculars out of empty toilet rolls for Emma. She didn't get the concept and chewed them to bits. I thought about tidying my room, but decided against it and instead sat down on my beanbag by my huge bedroom window and waited for time to pass.

When we first moved into our flat in Canary Wharf, the view from my room was the only thing I liked about it. It overlooked the canal, South Quay DLR Station and a few of the other skyscrapers. Out of habit my eyes were drawn down to the pavement below in search of movement: colours rushing over the grey concrete; people going about their day looking like tiny little ants from the tenth floor. Now, the streets were empty of course.

When the air-raid sirens sounded I wasn't even startled. I'd got so used to the hollow screeching that instead of sounding

23

menacing they reminded me of the noise of the CBeebies shows Emma liked watching.

I picked Emma up and met Mum, Dad and Andrew in the hallway. We took the stairs down to the underground car park – no mean feat when you live in a skyscraper, but we couldn't take the lift in case there was another blackout.

It began just like usual. Everyone from the building sat down in their spot – we'd done this so many times before that people were starting to become territorial about where they sat – and, without a word, we waited for the sirens to stop.

I wasn't scared at all. These dire meet-ups in the car park had become routine. With the cold stone floor beneath our bottoms we sat there and avoided one another's gaze just as if we were on the Tube. Five minutes later the noise would stop and everyone would hurry back to their flats.

But this time the sirens didn't stop after five minutes. And they didn't stop after ten. When more than half an hour had passed the woman from the flat opposite ours grabbed her head with both hands and started howling.

'We're going to die!' Her thin, nasal voice made me jump. 'We're all going to die!'

I didn't recognise her at first, sitting up against a sky-blue BMW with her knees pulled up to her chin, rocking back and forth. I only knew her as the stuck-up cow who never said hello in the hallway and always wore impeccable trouser suits in different shades of grey. But in the faint light of the car park she looked nothing like her old self. She had no make-up on. Her skin was pale. Clusters of freckles dotted her nose. She was wearing flannel pyjama bottoms and a grey T-shirt. Her hair was a sculpture of tangled mess.

'This is the end,' she continued, her voice shifting into a falsetto and hitting the exact note of the sirens.

'Get a grip, woman,' Mr Walnut-face ordered, poking his walking stick in her direction. It was Andrew who had given the old man from the ground floor the nickname and it had caught on. 'Can't you see there are children here?'

Despite Mrs Walnut-face joining her husband in protest, the woman just kept on going. And soon the panic spread.

'Do you really think so?' said a youngish man dressed in khaki trousers and a white shirt, his Ray-Bans pushed up and buried in his meticulously styled thick, brown hair. 'Do you really think that this is it?'

A woman holding a kid around Emma's age appeared from behind a Range Rover. 'I heard that large parts of Asia have already been wiped out.' Her child started crying.

'I heard Germany is completely gone,' someone else offered.

Soon everybody was talking at once.

'You're wrong – it's the States. It's the States that's gone.'

'We can't let this happen. We should be fighting back.'

'You must be kidding! As if we'd stand a chance.'

'We shouldn't just let them trap us in like this; like rats in a cage.'

'It's useless.'

'It's not useless!'

'I heard it took only a fraction of a second to reduce the whole of West China to rubble.'

The rational part of my brain told me that I shouldn't listen to them. What did they know? I'd spent hours and hours googling and had come up with nothing. And I knew the United States was still there. Dad had received an email from Grandma Stacy in Boston only two days ago. She and Grandpa Jack were shaken but fine. This was just gossip fuelled by paranoia. But it was hard not to let it get to you.

Dad put his hands over Emma's ears. Given that she couldn't even understand the simple sentence: 'Do not eat my pencil case,' it was probably an unnecessary measure.

He looked at Mum, his lips tight. 'If ever there was a time to legislate against mass stupidity, it would be now,' he grumbled underneath his breath.

'Shush,' Mum ordered.

'This silly irrationality should be punishable by execution. By firing squad.'

'Dan! They can hear you.'

'Why are these people not yet extinct?' With a jerk Dad shifted towards Andrew and me. 'Don't give what these evolutionary mishaps are saying a second thought. Everything will be fine.'

His eyes shimmered with anger. His jaw was clenched in determination. But there it was. Right in the middle of his forehead. It was shallow, but it could always be relied upon to reveal the truth when Dad tried to mask his uncertainty with exaggerated resolution: the wrinkle of doubt.

The sirens stopped ten minutes later. So did the frantic voices shrill with predictions of impending doom. I could hear the birds singing outside in the courtyard behind the building.

26

See, I thought as I got up. *Dad's right. Everything will be fine.*

We started making our way towards the small single exit door at the back of the car park. The sun pushed its warm light through the bars in the narrow windows up by the ceiling, level with the pavement outside. I was walking over the yellow stripes the sun's rays painted on the grey floor when I realised I couldn't hear the sound of the birds any more.

I stopped to listen. Silence. There was only silence.

The temperature cooled as the light in the car park suddenly faded. The faint yellow beams from the emergency wall lights did their best to penetrate the murkiness, but with limited success. The sunny stripes were gone from the floor.

I felt a blow from behind. A gust of wind swept the car park like a wave crashing on a beach. I saw people being knocked to the ground. I grabbed hold of a car-door handle and managed to stay on my feet. For a brief moment the air became still. Then, with a hollow whoosh, the wind started up again, now blowing in the opposite direction. Or so I thought. It took me a few seconds to realise that this time it wasn't actually blowing. It was sucking. Air was being sucked through the car park. I held on to the handle with all my strength, my clothes pulled up against my body.

A deafening metallic screech cut through the air, culminating in a crushing blast. Everything went quiet again as the wind stopped. I couldn't move. I couldn't look up.

'Amy!' I heard Dad call out.

I forced myself to raise my eyes. Everywhere people were scrambling to their feet, cowering in corners, leaning up against the walls.

27

Dad's head shot up from behind the back of a Mini. 'Amy, over here!'

I prised open my hand, let go of the handle and rushed over to him. They were all there – Mum with Emma in her arms, Dad, Andrew – huddled up together against one of the tyres. The relief made my legs go soft.

'Let's go,' Dad whispered as he got to his feet. He started towards the exit leading into the building. 'Hurry!'

My eyes were drawn to the windows by the ceiling. The bars were gone. Little piles of rubble lay beneath them. I tried not to think about what had caused the steel bars to be pulled out.

The crowd by the exit was dense. The single door wasn't designed for all the building's inhabitants at once. Some tried to shove their way through the horde of people. Most were unsuccessful. They would have to wait their turn.

'Stay low,' Dad ordered as we joined the throng.

We were moving at the pace of a snail in need of a hip replacement when some people at the back started screaming. The ones behind me immediately began pressing even harder at my back. Pushed up against Dad, I was like a piece of cheese stuck between two slices of bread. I couldn't move.

'Run!' someone shouted.

'Let me through!'

'Out of the way! Out of the way!'

I managed to turn my head slightly. The crowd was shuffling away from the wall with its crumbling holes where the windows had been. I looked up. At first I didn't see it. I guess it blended in with the grey of the concrete ceiling and walls. It was only when

I noticed how it reflected one of the wall lights like a small bolt of fire above the people at the back that I realised there was something there.

My eyes shifted from the light to the object casting it.

I dug my fingers into Dad's back. Entering the car park through the window, hovering in the air above, was what looked like a metallic hose. Long and thin, it crawled slowly through the air by flexing alternately to the left and right like a snake slithering through grass. Like an octopus's arm stretching through water.

'What the ...?' Dad pushed with his elbows at the people surrounding him, grabbed me and Andrew by the shoulders and shoved us in front of him.

'Did you see that?' I asked Andrew.

He just nodded, his mouth hanging wide open.

The screams pounded in my ears as the metallic arm slowly lowered itself into the crowd and started gliding in between the shrieking residents.

'We've got to get out of here,' Dad said.

People were pushing. Shoving. There were arms flying everywhere. Someone stomped on my toe. A shoulder crashed into my cheek.

The arm was getting closer. Its movements were smooth. Occasionally, it stopped for a few seconds, pointing its tip towards someone's face, before continuing its journey through the crowd.

'Someone open the gate!' Dad shouted. His voice was drowned out. He tried again. 'You at the back, open the gate. Open the car park gate so people can get out on both sides!'

'Do it yourself!' someone shouted back. 'I'm not going out there.'

It was no use. Everyone wanted to get to the exit leading into the building. No one wanted to go out into the street. No one wanted to be out there with whatever it was the flexible metallic arm was attached to.

'Dan!' Mum shouted. She was standing a couple of metres away, holding Emma close to her chest. 'Dan, look out!'

The arm was curving around Dad's head. It stopped in front of his face, level with his eyes. Was it looking at him?

'Kids,' Dad said to Andrew and me without taking his eyes off the arm, 'move over to your mother.'

We did our best to shuffle across but got stuck somewhere midway between Mum and Dad.

Relief flooded through me when the arm started sliding forward again.

But no sooner had it begun to move away from Dad than it halted. With a silent dip, the arm lowered itself deeper into the crowd and did a quick U-turn.

It shot forward. The tip was staring me in the face.

I held my breath as I waited for the arm to be on its way. To keep on crawling through the air as it had done all the other times. But it didn't.

'Amy, be perfectly still,' Dad called out, trying to make his way over. But it was like swimming upstream. He couldn't get past the people who were fighting their way in the opposite direction, away from me.

I felt Andrew pull at my arm. 'Amy, try to back away.'

It was as useful a suggestion as asking me to grow wings and fly. There was no room for movement in the packed crowd.

A hole opened at the tip of the arm. Cold air brushed my face.

'Amy!' Dad yelled.

The blackness inside expanded as the hole grew bigger and bigger, the tip forming the shape of a trumpet.

People kept kicking and screaming, trying to get out of the way.

The hole had become the size of my head. It looked like a big, toothless mouth. I stared into the vast darkness.

'Move over, Amy.' Andrew was trying to squeeze himself between me and the arm. I felt someone grab my shoulder. The next thing I knew, I was being shoved to one side.

'Get out of my way!'

I knew the voice. It belonged to the woman from the flat opposite ours.

I lost my balance and fell to my knees.

'Let me out of here!'

Her fingernails scratched at my face as she tried to clamber over me.

The hole was now the size of a human being. Kneeling, I could see the lower part of the trumpet-shaped tip of the arm touch the floor. I tried to back away but couldn't because all the people.

'Let me out of here!'

Pain shot up my leg. The woman was stomping on my calves, trying to get past.

But suddenly she started to wobble. My head was pulled back as she grabbed my hair. I could feel her feet scrambling for balance where she shifted on top of my legs.

'No!' she screamed.

Her other hand was flailing, trying to grab hold of the shirts and jackets of people around her. They did their best to shuffle away.

She was leaning towards the hole, one leg sticking out in the air, when she lost her grip on my hair. As if in slow motion, she started falling.

'No!'

I tried to grab her arm but couldn't move quick enough.

As soon as she disappeared into the blackness of the hole, it closed up with a muffled sucking sound. Her outline was visible as she travelled through the hose-like arm like a mouse being eaten by a snake. When the lump vanished through one of the windows by the ceiling, the arm itself slithered back to where it came from.

I held my breath. That deadly black hole had been meant for me. I was sure of it. The snake's mouth hadn't opened up for anyone else. But our crazy neighbour had accidentally taken my place.

Why me?

Mum and Dad had a huge fight when we got back up to the flat.

'We're not going down there again,' Dad snapped at Mum in the Neanderthal-like this-is-not-up-for-debate-and-my-word-is-final tone of voice that men used when they forgot that there ever were suffragettes along with the fact that they were not the bosses of the universe any more. 'We never should have been down there in the first place. I told you we shouldn't go down there.'

'But everyone else—'

'I don't care what everyone else does.'

'And the air-raid sirens—'

'Di, I told you, this isn't World War Three. We don't know what we're dealing with here.'

I could see the tears welling up in Mum's eyes as she shouted back at Dad. 'But we've got to do something next time the sirens go off. We can't just—'

'Di!' Dad snapped. 'I'd rather be toast in the comfort of our own flat than in the company of our idiot banker neighbours and their overcompensating cars. From now on we're staying put.'

Thursday 25 August

They haven't said anything. Mum and Dad haven't said anything about their plan. Maybe they changed their mind. Maybe I misunderstood.

Things have been surprisingly calm for the past few days. Eerily quiet. I miss listening to Andrew play his guitar through my bedroom wall. I miss the noise from his stereo and Mum and Dad shouting at him, ordering him to turn it down.

The air-raid sirens have been silent. There has been no sign of the visitors.

I mostly stay in my room. I can't take the quiet craziness that goes on in the living room. Mum and Dad are hardly speaking. Dad sits on the sofa reading. Reading! As if this is just a lazy Sunday afternoon and the weather is bad so we can't go out. Mum is like one of those clowns with two faces – one happy, one sad. She spends her day at the kitchen table crying. Except for when I come out of my room, then she turns into a bad comedian slash dinner lady who's high on too many Red Bulls and can't stop talking: 'Oh, I just remembered a really good joke Janine from work told me: Why did the chicken cross the road ... Or was it the cat? Why did the cat cross the road? Or maybe it was a dog ... Would you like some toast? I can make you some toast. We don't have much butter left but it tastes good with some olive oil and garlic powder. Would you like to play a game of cards? I read somewhere that it's meant to improve mental abilities and keep your mind sharp – or was that playing solitaire, or maybe chess? I think it was the chicken that crossed the road, not the cat ... or maybe it was a zebra. Would you like a glass of water? It's important to keep hydrated; the body is sixty per cent water, you know ...'

When I go back to my room she sits back down and keeps on crying. It's as if she thinks I can't see both of her clown faces.

I think Emma senses the mood. She sleeps a lot.

I've seen so many strange things lately. So many awful and unbelievable things. And I know they're all real. I mean, Andrew is gone, Matilda is gone. It couldn't get more real than that. But somehow what we're facing doesn't feel genuine. It's hard to explain. I think it's maybe because of YouTube and Photoshop and mobiles and special effects and the internet. Thanks to technology we're so used to seeing crazy things – flying saucers, dinosaurs and zombies created with CGI, fake pranks, fake stunts, Photoshopped thigh gaps and cleavages – that it's hard to buy into the unbelievable, even when it's the truth.

I think that if I hadn't seen it with my own eyes, a part of me would still think that all this was just a hoax; that somewhere someone was having a big old laugh.

4

The morning after the horror in the car park, I watched a video on YouTube that had gone viral during the night. It was of a metallic arm. Just like the one we'd seen the day before. The video was really fuzzy but it seemed to have been shot inside a Tube station. People were screaming and clambering over each other. Air-raid sirens were howling in the background. The arm stopped in front of a skinny, pimply teenage boy, opened up and sucked him into its black hole.

I'd tried my best to erase the day before from my mind. I'd tried to pretend it hadn't happened. But seeing that boy getting swallowed up brought it all back. A mudslide of cold, suffocating thoughts washed over me: *My neighbour – is she dead? And what about that boy? Is he dead? They must be. How can anyone survive something like that? Or maybe surviving isn't the key thing. If you survived, where would that thing take you? What would happen to you? Maybe death isn't that bad. Maybe death is the best you can hope for.*

I called out to Andrew, just to stop my thoughts snowballing any further and crushing me completely. I showed him the video.

'At least we know what we are dealing with,' he said after the third time of watching it.

'How is that a relief?' I snapped at him. 'I mean, it can hardly be any worse. What we're dealing with can hardly be any worse than this machine, this jaw of darkness that swallows people up like a giant snake.'

But it could be. As it turned out, it could be so much worse.

That same day I got the message from Matilda. I'd been waiting all day for her to come online so I could tell her what had happened down in the car park and send her a link to the YouTube video of the metallic arm. When she finally appeared she just said, 'I'm coming over,' and went straight offline again.

As there was a curfew in place and Matilda sometimes had a weird sense of humour I presumed she was joking. Last year, during a party at Anita's, Matilda decorated the house with 'balloons' that were helium-inflated condoms with pink ribbons tied around them. Mr Withers had been reluctant to let Anita throw a party in the first place – he didn't approve of parties, or any activity that didn't lead to a measurable end result, like cleaning or studying (having fun apparently did not count as an end result) – and he did not see the funny side of the party ornaments.

I was browsing the internet, waiting for her to come online again, when everyone was suddenly talking about the prime minster. There was a rumour circulating that he was going to be on TV soon. That he was going to give a statement or whatever.

I told Mum and Dad and they got really excited. Dad didn't once refer to him as the 'talking turd' like he usually did. Mum made scones from the last of the flour.

At last, we thought, *we might know something.*

37

The last time we'd seen the prime minister was when we'd found out. It was with a statement from him that it all began. It felt like ages ago, although it had actually only been just over a week. Mum and Andrew and I had been watching *EastEnders*, and Dad was sitting on the sofa holding his newspaper and pretending not to watch *EastEnders*, when all of a sudden the screen went blank. At first we thought a fuse might have blown. But the bright halogen lights in the ceiling above were still on.

Dad got up to inspect the TV. 'It can't be broken; it's barely two years old.' He was scratching his chin.

'Do something, Dan!' Mum cried from the sofa.

But with no buttons to push on our fancy flat screen, Dad just stood and stared at the TV.

'Maybe there's something wrong with the socket,' Mum suggested.

Dad bent down and started fiddling with it.

'There's nothing wrong with the socket,' Andrew growled. 'The power light is on which it wouldn't be if the TV wasn't properly connected to electricity.'

Still, Dad pulled out the plug and replaced it with the plug of the steel floor lamp next to the TV.

Andrew rolled his eyes.

The frosted glass shade lit up. The plug was fine.

'Just try plugging it in again,' Andrew barked, the impatience in his voice tearing at his throat.

At first nothing happened. Then, suddenly, a picture of an empty BBC studio appeared on the screen. The TV had been fine all along. There just hadn't been anything on.

It looked like a still photo. There was a big mahogany desk in the middle of the screen and behind it a red office chair. In the background was a black and white view of the London skyline.

It wasn't until a man dressed in a grey T-shirt and jeans suddenly ran into view that we realised this wasn't a photograph but a live broadcast. On his head he had a set of headphones with a mic attached. Still on the move, he slammed a piece of paper and a glass of water on the table before sprinting off-screen again.

We all looked at each other.

I gave a little laugh. I thought they were just having technical difficulties at the BBC and that *EastEnders* would resume in a moment.

Dad slumped down on the sofa again. He was reaching for the newspaper when the prime minister walked on to the set. Dad froze with his outstretched arm hovering above the paper.

It wasn't the sight of the prime minister per se that changed the atmosphere in the living room from oh-God-not-another-case-of-amnesia-in-Albert-Square to OMG-what-in-the-world-has-happened – William Davidson, or Wonky Willy as Dad sometimes called him, was on telly all the time. But that evening, there was something different about him.

During the first seconds of the broadcast you couldn't really see it. The prime minister looked normal enough. He walked calmly across the screen wearing his usual grey suit. His blue tie was carefully tucked under the collar of his neatly pressed, bleach-white shirt.

It wasn't until he grabbed hold of the red chair and pulled it out from underneath the table that I realised what exposed the fact that something was seriously wrong. It was his hair. It sounds stupid, I know. But I could tell that something was wrong by his hair. His ash-blond hair was usually immaculately combed back with its two grey sections running in a straight line from his hairline to the back of his head. And it always seemed to have just the right amount of product in it: just enough to keep it neat but never so much that it looked greasy. The media often made fun of how much pride he took in his hair. Dad said the prime minister considered the key to stability to be hairspray.

But as he sat down and placed his arms on the table in front of him I noticed that the edges of the grey sections were all fuzzy. And there was a parting visible on one side of his head. When he lifted his eyes and looked straight into the camera, a lock of hair came loose and fell across his forehead.

There was no doubt about it. This was serious.

His voice was steady. But his eyes kept wavering as he said:

'Dear countrymen. As I sit before you this evening, events are taking place of such magnitude that they have the power to alter the course of all our lives. My words will inevitably cause trepidation. But I ask you to keep calm.

'For generations, curious minds have contemplated life on other planets. This evening we have our answer. It turns out that we are not alone in the universe. And Earth has had a visit.

'It is not my intention to cause unnecessary alarm. It is, however, my duty as your prime minister to treat this nation with the honesty and respect it deserves. As world leaders everywhere announce to their people the arrival of an alien species, the only thing we can be sure of is that this day shall go down in history as the day that everything changed. For better or for worse, however, we have yet to find out.

'We know neither why they're here nor what they want. As prime minister it is my responsibility to do everything in my power to secure the safety of each and every one of you. That is my priority and my promise. I therefore declare a curfew with immediate effect which will remain in place until further notice. I ask all of you, the good people of Great Britain, to stay indoors, stay strong and wait for further announcements.'

The screen went blank again.

What followed is all a bit hazy. I can remember the swollen silence which descended on the living room and made my ears ring. I can remember the sickly sweet smell of cooking oil lingering in the air from the fish and chips we'd had for supper. And I can remember my heart jumping to my throat when the TV screen suddenly lit up again. This time it was a newsreader sitting at the desk. I can't recall much of what he said; something about the first unidentified flying object having been detected by a satellite a couple of hours earlier, hovering inside Earth's atmosphere somewhere above Greenland; that since then dozens more had been discovered – at least seven were thought to be placed above the UK. The only thing that really stuck with me was the photograph. It looked so … unremarkable. So unimpressive. It didn't look momentous at all. It was just a picture of the sky above some unidentifiable town. At first I couldn't even spot the flying object the newsreader was talking about. I had to lean forward and peer at the screen. I finally spotted it in the upper-right-hand corner. It was just a dot. Like a pinkish star in the early evening sky.

The newsreader was mid-sentence when the broadcast went off the air.

There was silence again.

'This is clearly a joke,' Mum finally said, her voice forced and sounding like a cartoon chipmunk. 'It's a prank. Like April Fool's Day.'

'It's August,' Andrew said. He was trying to sound all cool and cynical but the quiver in his voice gave him away. He was scared.

'I don't mean it literally. Just that this is a prank in the spirit of …'

Dad got up from the sofa.

'Where are you going, Dan?'

'I'm turning on Radio 4.'

'I'll check the internet,' Andrew said and pulled out his phone.

I felt I should be doing something, but I didn't know what. What was the right response to something that was so unimaginable it couldn't possibly be true?

'Shush,' Mum suddenly said even though no one was talking. She turned on the sofa to face the window. 'Are those … are those voices in the street?'

At first it only sounded like a couple of people, but soon it seemed the pavement outside was buzzing.

Dad forgot about the radio and ran towards the window. He pulled back the blinds.

'What are they …? Why aren't they …?'

All of a sudden he jerked back his hand.

'Shit!'

He turned on his heel and started running across the living room.

I dropped deep into the soft cushion of the sofa as Mum jumped to her feet.

'What?!'

'Shit! Shit! Shit!'

'What's going on?!' Mum hissed through clenched teeth as if she was trying to contain her panic inside her mouth.

Dad disappeared down the hall.

Mum rushed to the window. She made a small crack between two strips in the vertical blinds and peeked through it. 'What's everyone doing out? We're supposed to stay ins—' All of a sudden her face turned the pukey-beige colour of the blinds. 'Oh God.' She widened the crack. 'Food! They're getting food!'

Dad appeared in the doorway. He had on his suit jacket and running shoes.

'What do we need?'

Mum spun round.

'Everything. Milk. Juice. Chicken. Canned stuff.' She glanced out of the window. 'Just anything you can get your hands on.'

Forty minutes later, Dad returned with six shopping bags hanging off his arms bursting with food that only a man who never did the shopping could assemble including Spam (who ate Spam except people in their nineties with neither teeth nor taste buds?) and minced beef in a can (probably a code for minced My Little Pony). But we were lucky. Not everyone managed to stock

43

up. It wasn't long after Dad got back that the army appeared on the streets to enforce the curfew.

And not long after that, when Matilda turned up on our doorstep – over a week after the curfew had been put into place, I was so happy to see her that I hugged her.

'What are you doing here? How did you get here? You know we're not meant to go outside, right?'

She looked down at her toes. She was blushing and I immediately knew the reason she'd left her house despite the dangers.

She tried to laugh it off. 'It's Mum again. You know how bonkers she can get.'

'Are you okay?'

'Yeah, of course I'm okay. Don't be stupid.' She shrugged. 'You know Mum and her prayer group. They're annoying on a good day. But this situation with the alien invasion, or whatever this is, really set them off. There's like twenty of them gathered at my house and they're acting all loony, sacrificing food to the aliens on a makeshift altar on the balcony and constructing a flagpole in the communal garden that says: "Welcome! We're ready to be received."' She rolled her eyes. 'I just couldn't take it any more. I had to get out of there.'

'Did you walk here?'

'No, I drove my new BMW. Of course I walked. I tried to get here yesterday but I was stopped by a group of soldiers. They drove me home in a big camouflaged tank. Some of them were actually quite cute. I tried Anita's house but there was no answer.

44

This morning I took the footpath by the canal rather than the main road. And now I'm here …' She started to blush again. 'Do you think I can stay for a bit? Maybe sleep over?'

I asked Mum and Dad. They said it was okay for her to stay, as long as she called her mum to tell her where she was.

It was so great to have someone to talk to. We mostly managed to steer clear of the subject of the visitors, focusing on more practical things like whether we should each have a fringe and whether I should let her pluck my eyebrows.

'If this is the end of the world, do you really want to face it looking like a hairy gorilla?' Matilda argued.

I went and got Mum's tweezers.

The only time we talked about the visitors, like, properly was when we talked about Anita – Matilda could see her house out of her bedroom window and she hadn't seen them leave town and their car was still in the driveway – and when she borrowed my laptop to talk to Tom online.

'Tom says they're definitely after energy sources.'

'What?'

'The visitors. He says they're after energy sources.'

'What does he know?' I answered, not really wanting to talk about it. There really was no point. No one knew what they wanted. No one knew what they were after.

'He's really smart,' was Matilda's reply.

I wanted to grab my laptop and hit her over the head with it. She always did that. When she fancied a guy, he became this all-knowing, infinitely wise being who was under no circumstances to be doubted. In a way, she morphed into the guy she was dating. If he liked football, all of a sudden all her weekends were spent in front of the telly, following the score; if he liked swimming, she'd instantly buy herself a new bikini and brave the chlorine-filled waters of the local pool despite what it did to her hair.

'However smart he is, he can't know,' I said, trying to contain my annoyance. After all, I was grateful for her company.

'He's not only smart. He also knows what he's talking about. He's going to study international politics at uni.'

I took a deep breath. 'A: Unless he's going to study intergalactic politics at college, he doesn't know what he's talking about. And B: If I intended to study heart surgery in the future, would you let me conduct open-heart surgery on you this afternoon?'

She ignored me and continued typing away to her infinitely wise and oh-he's-so-cute-I-can't-help-mentioning-it-in-every-other-sentence boyfriend.

God, I miss her.

They've gone mad. Mum and Dad have gone completely mad. I have to do something. I can't let them go ahead with this.

But what can I do? I'm useless. I'm a 'nestling'. That's what she called me. Mandira. She said, 'She's like a little nestling, that girl.' She said I was mousy and timid.

Although I know she's right, it's still hurtful to hear that the thing you like least about yourself is the main thing other people see in you.

I've tried not to be 'mousy and timid'. I tried once to be more like Matilda — all legs and confidence. It went spectacularly wrong.

I remember September last year. When I decided that this was the year that I would 'bloom' (Mum's phrase, not mine). I was going to come out of my shell — or whatever it is you do when you stop being a 'little nestling'.

I was shocked when Damien from my class asked me out. I didn't even think people did that any more — asked each other out. But I was so geared up to try new things that I said yes without even thinking about it.

I should of course have suspected something. Damien was tall and strong and broad-shouldered and he played rugby. Why would he ask me out? And I definitely should have suspected something when I started to hear Courtney and Louisa snigger in their seats behind me. I blame Mum. She was always telling me to be open-minded. She forgot to mention that you should never be so open-minded that your brain falls out.

The whole week I was super-excited. I was going out with Damien! Mum and I went shopping and she bought me a new pair of trainers.

He took me to Haslam's corner shop. The same Haslam's corner shop where everybody hangs out all the time outside doing absolutely nothing. I stood there with Damien and his friends, listening to them bang on about boobs and bums and whether the Batmobile had automatic or manual gears.

When the night was over, Damien said he thought the date had gone well. I wondered whether we'd been on the same date. Then he asked if he could kiss me.

I flinched.

'I know I'm no Mr Farcy,' he continued, tossing his cigarette to the ground and grinding it with the sole of his shoe.

'No who?'

'You know. Mr Farcy. Mr Farcy from the Jane Austen thingy ...'

'Mr Darcy?'

'Yeah, whatever ...'

As much as I hated never having been kissed, I decided I would prefer to stay a kiss virgin than to be kissed by Mr Farcy. I'd simply turned around and walked away.

I found out later that it had all been a bet. Courtney and Louisa had promised Damien a six pack of beer if he asked me out and I said yes.

48

I was so humiliated I felt like crying every morning for weeks over the fact I had to go to school and be under the same roof as Courtney and Louisa and Damien. I could never wear the new trainers Mum had bought me ever again.

From then on I accepted who I was. I was mousy and timid and that would never change.

I wonder if Mandira has found someone. I hope so. I hope she has got her volunteer. It would have to be someone brave, of course. Someone strong. Not someone like me who gets nervous just thinking about Courtney and Louisa making fun of my shoes or my hair. Not someone like me who feels nauseated just thinking about the metallic arm.

Although, there are worse things than the metallic arm. I didn't think there could be. But then Matilda dragged me to the party.

5

It was one in the morning when Matilda woke me up.

'Get up, snore face. We're going to a party.'

Matilda ripped the warm duvet from me. The cold air washed over me like glacial water.

I curled up in a ball, my eyes still closed. 'This isn't funny, Matilda. Give me back my duvet.'

She turned on the lights. 'I'm not joking. Hurry up. We're already late.'

I opened one eye. The bright light was like a knife being thrust through my eyeball into my brain.

'Everyone is going to be there,' she said, squeezing herself into the new extra-skinny jeans Mum had got me from Topshop just before the siege. I hadn't seen the point in wearing fashion that felt like a medieval torture device just for the benefit of Mum and Dad and Andrew and Emma, so the jeans still had the tag on them.

'More than a hundred and fifty people have said on Facebook that they're coming.' Matilda tore open the drawers in my dressing table and began rummaging through them. 'God, do you have any tops that don't look like they came from the teen fashion catalogue approved by the nuns of the Convent of Banishment of Flesh on Show?'

I sat up. 'We're not going to a party. There's a curfew.'

'Oh, don't be such a goody-goody.'

'I'm not a goody-goody!'

'Okay, don't be such a wuss then.'

'There's no way Mum and Dad will let us go!'

'Duh! Why do you think I waited for everyone to go to sleep? We're not going to ask for their permission.'

I wasn't going. I didn't like massive parties under normal circumstances. I reminded Matilda about the terrifying metallic arm that swallowed my neighbour; that swallowed the kid in the YouTube video; but Matilda had never been known to take no for an answer.

We were putting on our shoes when the door to Andrew's room opened. His face froze in a startled mouth-open-eyes-wide grimace, but then he walked to the front door without looking at us. He was wearing his party T-shirt, the one that said 'Kill the DJ', and way too much aftershave.

'Where do you think you're going?' I asked with indignation in my voice that made me sound just like Mum. The realisation made me shiver.

He rolled his eyes. 'Where do you think you're going?'

We took the lift down to the ground floor. Matilda was wearing heels and refused to take the stairs.

The streets were quiet. The party was down by the warehouses. But Matilda had arranged to meet up with Tom on Reuters Plaza, so we had to make a detour. Andrew walked with us.

'I don't need a babysitter you know,' I said.

'Good. I don't have time to look after my little sister anyway.'

The street lights were out in most places and we kept losing our footing. We tried to use our phones as torches but with limited success. Why was I going to this thing? I'd never liked parties. I liked watching movies with Matilda and Anita on a Saturday evening, ordering in pizza and talking late into the night. Large parties had always made me uncomfortable. I suspected it was the boy thing. Parties seemed to be all about boys: talking to boys, kissing boys, finding boyfriends. I liked boys. But when I tried having a conversation with one, two things happened: 1) my excessively long arms seemed to grow even longer and 2) my vocabulary was reduced to that of a chimpanzee.

I wanted to turn around and go back home. But I didn't.

After a while we heard voices echoing in between the tall glass buildings. We turned the corner and Reuters Plaza opened up to us like a field of concrete.

Boxed in by even taller towers than the one we lived in, the area almost gave the impression that things were back to normal. As if this were just a normal evening in Canary Wharf. A group of teenagers sat on the wall by the canal. The big clock in the centre of the plaza was still ticking as if nothing unusual had happened.

'Over there,' said Matilda and pointed towards two guys sitting on barstools by a high table in front of a deserted All Bar One.

Matilda ran across the square and jumped on one of them, wrapping her arms and legs around him. Andrew and I made our way over.

It turned out Tom went to our school and that he was in Year 12 like Andrew. How old, I thought. Matilda and I were only starting Year 10. (Or were supposed to be starting Year 10.)

The other guy was Tom's cousin who'd been visiting from Suffolk when all this started and hadn't been able to go back home.

'Let's got to Waitrose on our way and pick up some drinks,' Tom suggested.

Andrew rearranged his fringe, which had fallen into his eyes – we'd run out of gel. 'Isn't it closed?'

'Technically, I guess. But the doors are wide open. Most of the food is gone but some people told us that there's still some booze left in there.'

We walked in silence through the darkened hallways of the shopping centre. The windows of some of the stores had been smashed in. Glass covered the marble floors. In Waitrose, the lights were on. But there was no one there. Usually, Waitrose was the nicest of all the supermarkets. But now the store was a complete mess. There were empty food containers everywhere. The floor was sticky from spilled drinks. The tills had been smashed open, the cash drawers sticking out of them like tongues from mouths. They'd been completely emptied.

Tom led the way. 'Let's split up and see what we can find.'

I headed for the dairy section. It was really difficult to get Emma to eat the expired canned food we'd been eating for the past few days and she loved diced cheese. The dairy fridge was empty. So was the bread shelf. And the sweets aisle.

On the floor, amid crushed crisps and leaking cans of tomatoes, I found a packet of sanitary towels and picked it up. The packaging was dirty, but otherwise it looked fine. I'd started having my periods six months earlier.

Suddenly, I heard something crunch behind me. I jumped and spun around.

'Hi.'

'Shit! Are you trying to give me a heart attack?' The first thing I saw was brown shoes grinding a pile of crisps. I looked up and was greeted by an unknown smile. It belonged to a guy, probably around my age. A word popped into my head: *CUTE*. My cheeks went red, as if they thought he could read my mind.

His smile widened. 'Shit.'

I couldn't take my eyes off his dimples. They were weirdly irresistible.

'Shit.' He chewed on the word. 'I like that greeting. It sounds so much feistier than hi. Shit. Shit, how are you?'

I stared. His dark hair was so thick I had to order my hands not to reach out and touch it. His hazel-brown eyes had a strange yellow tinge to them. I'd never seen him before. He definitely didn't go to our school. I would have noticed.

Then something unusual happened. I was standing in front of a cute guy, but I wasn't lost for words. Yet the alternative didn't turn out to be any better, as I found myself barking at him, 'What are you doing here?'

He shrugged his shoulders. 'Just having a look around.'

'Are you going to the party?' I asked accusingly, again sounding a little too much like Mum. Why was I being a total idiot? His dimples were as deep as the Grand Canyon. I'd seen it once when I'd gone to visit Grandma Stacy and Grandpa Jack. It was so huge I was afraid of falling into it. It wouldn't have taken more than a gust of wind. I felt the same about the dimples.

'Party? Sure. Why not?'

I didn't know what else to say, so I turned around and headed for one of the aisles in search of something edible for Emma.

I could hear jaunty footsteps behind me.

After a while I glanced over my shoulder. 'Why are you following me?'

He shrugged his shoulders. 'I don't know. Am I not meant to?'

I stared at him. 'You're weird.'

I found the others in the wine section. Tom was trying to convince Andrew to give up a bottle of orange juice he had found so it could be used as a mixer for the sherry, which was the only type of alcohol left in the store.

'C'mon … It'll make the sherry taste better.'

'Dude, don't be such an old lady,' Andrew scoffed. 'You'll manage it neat just fine.'

I knew he was saving the juice for Emma.

'Hey, guys,' I said to divert the attention from the juice. 'This is …' I turned and pointed behind me, towards the dimpled guy who was still smiling.

I rolled my eyes. 'That's the part where you say your name.'

'Oh, is it? Cool. My name is Caesar.'

Tom seemed to take an instant dislike to him. 'Like the salad.'

'Like the Roman dictator,' Caesar said, his smile only widening.

Tom frowned. 'Let's go. We're late.'

As we left the store I sneaked a tenner into one of the tills for the sanitary towels and the juice.

The party was down in the abandoned warehouse next to Millwall Quays. I'd been there only a couple of times during the day with Matilda and Anita. Andrew and his classmates hung out there all the time. It used to be a storage facility when the area served as part of the Port of London way back when. Dad said that the Port of London used to be the largest port in the world. But these days you couldn't see a proper ship on the canals that encircled the glass towers of Docklands. The water ways only served as decorations for the skyscrapers, a new building popping up as if out of nowhere every few months, cluttering up the skyline like extra teeth growing in an already crowded mouth.

We were almost there. If you listened really hard you could hear music in the distance.

Caesar was still following us. It made me excited and frustrated at the same time. Who had invited him along? I hadn't. Or had I?

'Have any of you heard of the Splinters?' he asked as we arrived at the warehouse.

'What's that?' Andrew asked. 'Is that a band?'

'Never mind,' Caesar said.

We climbed the stairs up to the second floor. The building was a hollow shell. The door was just a hole in the wall. There was no glass in the windows and the brick walls were crumbling.

Matilda, who was leading the way, stopped on the landing at the top of the stairs where a room the size of our flat opened up.

'Where is everyone?'

I joined her on the landing. Bollocks. Courtney and Louisa were there. They saw me and started to snigger, but I pretended not to notice.

There were only around thirty people inside the main hall of the warehouse, sitting on windowsills or trying to get comfortable on piles of bricks.

We all sat down on the cold stone floor by one of the windows, except for Caesar who had started walking around the room, introducing himself to everyone.

'Shit, I'm Caesar,' he said, shaking people's hands and giving me an amused glance every time.

I blushed and tried to ignore him.

The room was lit up by a candle. On the floor was an iPhone connected to small loudspeakers, which blasted some awful dubstep.

'Okay, now it's someone else's turn,' a guy shouted from beside a window the size of a door, which overlooked the street.

'I'll take the next shift,' said a girl I recognised as being in Andrew's class.

Andrew turned to her. 'The next shift?'

'Yeah, we're taking turns watching out for the army. There are soldiers walking past all the time. We don't want them to shut down the party.'

Andrew joined the girl at the huge window.

Tom took out two bottles of sherry from his Waitrose bag and screwed the cap off one of them.

Caesar was talking to a group of people playing cards.

I didn't know what to do with myself. This was exactly why I hated parties. Mum's unwanted words of wisdom popped into my head: 'Most human interaction, such as mingling at a party, can be learned,' she'd said the other day when she'd been trying to get me to go to one of the parties Matilda had been invited to – everyone wanted Matilda at their party. 'You don't need to be shy. Practice makes perfect.'

Thank you, Dr Phil.

I turned to Tom's cousin. I might as well try out Mum's stupid theory, since I was already making a fool of myself by just standing there like an idiot. 'So, what's your name again?' At least the words came out in the right order. That was an improvement on the last party I went to.

He blushed. 'Bartholomew.'

What was this, the Middle Ages? I tried not to smile.

'I know! It's even worse than Caesar. What were my parents thinking?'

'Oh, it's nice,' I lied.

'Most people call me Bart.'

We sat down. After downing half a bottle of sherry, Tom and Matilda started making out. The slurping sounds were deafening. It looked as if they were eating each other's faces off. Bart and I just sat in silence.

I couldn't help wishing that I were more like Matilda. Popular. Confident. Devoid of self-awareness – and, when need be, propriety.

'So …' I said to Bart who had his back turned. I was hoping that something intelligent would automatically follow. It didn't.

Suddenly, someone slumped down beside me.

'Amy ...' The voice was drawling and raspy. I knew it immediately.

'Amy, Amy, Amy ... Lovvvvely Amy ...'

I had hardly spoken to Damien since the Mr Farcy incident. He threw his arm over my shoulder. In his other hand he was holding a huge bottle of vodka. He turned to Bart.

'Who are you?' He didn't wait for an answer but turned back to me and buried his face in the corner of my neck. He stank of alcohol.

'Amy, Amy ... I want to kiss you, Amy.'

'Don't you think you've had enough?' I prised the bottle from his hand.

'Gimmee,' Damien wailed like a child, reaching out his hand for the bottle.

'You're going to make yourself sick.'

'Who caaares,' he mumbled, drooling all over my neck. 'Iss all over anyway. My dad says they'll kill usss all.' He lifted his head slightly and looked up at me. 'Give us a kiss.'

I pushed him off me.

His face sank into a petulant pout. 'Why won't you kiss me?'

The slurping sounds coming from the corner where Matilda and Tom sat, limbs all tangled together, making it difficult to discern where one of them started and the other ended, came to a sudden halt.

Matilda dried her face on the sleeve of her jacket. 'She's saving herself for Prince Harry.'

I shot her my most scorching evil eye.

59

She ignored it. 'Why don't you just get it over with, Amy?' She ran her hands through Tom's hair. 'He's right, you know. We don't know what's going to happen. It could all be over tomorrow. Do you want to die a kiss virgin?'

A shrill laugh spurted from Bart's lips. 'You've never kissed anyone?'

I gave an indignant snort. 'Of course I have. I have extensive experience in sharing saliva.'

'No, you haven't,' Matilda wailed.

I glared at her. Wasn't it enough that Courtney and Louisa were laughing? Did she have to humiliate me too? She had to be drunk.

'I have so,' I lied.

'Okay, tell me, who have you kissed?'

'Kevin.'

'Kevin who?'

'Kevin ... erm ... Tucker.'

'I don't know any Kevin Tucker.'

'You wouldn't. He's not from around here.'

'Oh, so where's he from then?'

'Kentucky.'

'So his name is Kevin Tucker and he's from Kentucky.'

'Uh-huh.' I had no idea where that name had come from. Or Kentucky. I must have been craving fried chicken or something. I tried to radiate nonchalance, but all I exuded was sweat.

'But you've never been to Kentucky. You've only been to Boston to visit your grandparents.'

'Yeah, well, I met him on holiday last year in Spain.'

60

'Oh yeah. And what does he look like?'

'Blond hair. Brown eyes.' At least I didn't say he had white hair, a pointy beard and a stripy apron.

There was a short silence. Then Bart started to snigger. 'I can't believe you've never kissed anyone.'

I wanted to throttle him. Who was he to judge? His name was Bartholomew after all. At least my embarrassment was fixable. He was stuck with his for the rest of his life. And what was the big deal anyway? I'd always had the sneaking suspicion that the big secret no one told you about kissing was that it was totally overrated. I mean, how much fun could sticking your tongue into someone else's mouth really be? I thought about my first kiss that never was, my made-up kiss with Kevin from Kentucky, and I decided the experience wasn't all that different from a real first kiss: faltering, self-conscious and sweaty.

'Was he better?'

Caesar appeared out of nowhere and sat down beside me.

'Excuse me?'

'This Kevin. I hope he wasn't a better kisser than me.'

I stared at him.

He looked at the others. 'I have a confession to make.' Caesar grabbed my hand. The softness of his skin gave me goosebumps. 'Amy and I are lovers.'

I jumped. Lovers? We weren't lovers. And who used the word 'lovers' anyway?

Matilda rolled her eyes. 'You only met each other twenty minutes ago.'

'We were just pretending. We've been secret lovers for months.'

Matilda looked at me and back at Caesar. 'I don't believe you.'

'Oh yeah?' Caesar turned to me, put one hand gently on my cheek and pulled me towards him. He paused and looked into my eyes. His gaze felt as soft as a snow-white cloud on a sunny day. I didn't pull back. Quite the opposite. It was as if a great force pushed me towards him. Like that gust of wind I feared would blow me into the Grand Canyon. My lips touched his and a fire ignited somewhere deep inside me. It wasn't faltering and it wasn't sweaty. It was sweet and tender and real. Sort of.

'Soldiers!' the girl from Andrew's class suddenly shouted. Caesar let go of my cheek.

Someone ran towards the middle of the room, blew out the candle and turned off the music.

Everyone started flinging themselves to the floor. I lay down, and Caesar collapsed beside me, giving me a conspiratorial grin.

'I want a kiss too,' Damien mumbled, half-asleep up against the wall.

'Someone shut him up,' the girl hissed.

I could feel Caesar breathing next to me. His presence was like a drug. It made the world seem brighter, its colours so much more vivid, which made me feel more alive, as if I'd drunk a whole can of Red Bull in one go. I wanted more.

The sound of the soldiers' boots hitting the gravel perfectly in step below us echoed through the empty warehouse. I couldn't resist peeking out of the corner of the window. There were six of them marching in two lines of three. They wore camouflaged jackets and trousers in different shades of grey. Guns with torches attached were sticking out at their sides.

As soon as they were out of sight the candle was lit again and the music came back on.

Caesar smiled at me. 'I hope we can do this again some time.'

Before I could say anything, Matilda jumped to her feet and dragged me up with her. 'We'll take the next shift.'

Reluctantly, I was dragged to the window. It was a long way down and there was no railing – nothing that stood between us and a bone-breaking fall. The height made me dizzy. When I turned around I couldn't see Caesar anywhere. I tried to hide my disappointment.

Matilda grabbed my arm. 'Is it true, about you and this Caesar guy being an item?'

I shook my head.

She let go of me. The focus of the universe was back on her. 'So what do you think about Tom?' She leaned against the door frame, her feet precariously close to the edge.

'He has great hair,' I said, which was the only thing I could think of given that I didn't know him and that he really did have amazing hair.

'I thought maybe you and Bart could hook up. He seems interested in you.'

'Hey!' the girl from Andrew's class called out. 'Stop gossiping and pay attention to what you're supposed to be doing.'

Matilda stepped away from the window ledge. 'I thought there would be more people here. Where is everybody?'

I was left with the responsibility of keeping guard.

'Gone,' said the girl.

'What d'you mean *gone*?'

'Taken.'

'Taken?'

'Yes, taken.'

'Do you mean … like … *taken* taken?'

'Yes, *taken* taken. Haven't you heard? The rumour is they're really keen on teenagers.'

'They're only taking teenagers?'

'Well, not everyone who was going to come has been taken, of course. Many are just cowards who are letting *them* win by not daring to leave their houses. But yeah, some have been taken. By them.'

'By the metallic arm?'

'I don't know. I suppose so.'

'But—'

Matilda was cut off when people started shouting from one corner of the room.

'You're killing our buzz here, ladies!'

I glanced around, but I still couldn't see Caesar anywhere. A draught flooded the room. I wrapped myself tighter in my jacket.

I felt nauseous. I didn't know whether it was my subtle fear of heights creeping up on me, or fear of the lack of something more tangible than air separating me from the height, or the sips I'd stolen from Damien's vodka bottle when he hadn't been looking. The flicker of the candle made the hall seem to move. The music pounded on my eardrums like a symphony played on construction-site tools. The poor sound quality of the battery-powered loudspeakers wasn't doing the substandard playlist any favours.

Lights appeared outside and I jumped back and grabbed Matilda. I was about to warn everyone about the soldiers, but something stopped me. I leaned forward and peered into the darkness. The uniforms. They weren't the grey ones I'd seen before. These were black overalls. The light reflected on them as if they were made from something shiny.

'Hey, guys,' I managed to croak. My throat was dry. 'Guys!' I said again, louder this time. Someone turned down the music.

'There are people coming, but I don't think they're soldiers. Blow out the candle.'

The hall went dark and everyone hurried towards the big window. I held on to the wall to avoid getting pushed out by the crowd gathering behind me. Andrew appeared beside me.

'Hold on to my arm,' he said.

I grabbed it.

'Who is it?' someone whispered from the back.

The uniforms drew nearer. They blended in perfectly with the blackness outside. There were only two of them.

'Shit.' Andrew took a step back. 'Shit.'

He dragged me with him.

'Get away from the window,' he hissed. 'Everyone, get away from the window.'

People started backing away, whispering, 'What? What is it?'

I didn't let go of Andrew. I knew. I knew what he was thinking.

'I think ...' He stopped. 'I think it might be them.'

Some people started screaming. Others ran for the stairs.

'Stop!' Andrew shouted.

No one was listening.

'Do you want to get killed?' he shouted louder.

Everyone stopped and looked at my brother.

He lowered his voice. 'What do you think you're doing? Are you crazy? Have you seen what they're capable of? Have you seen their technology? What are you going to do? Outrun them?'

Someone was wailing. It was Bart. 'You do what you want, guys. I'm out of here!'

He headed towards the staircase but Tom grabbed him by his coat collar, making Bart stumble and fall over.

'Listen to the guy,' Tom told his cousin. He turned to Andrew. 'What do you suggest we do?'

Andrew ran his eyes over the crowd. He started talking really fast. 'I say we stay put, keep quiet and hope they don't find us.'

There was a low murmur.

'Either we all stay or we all leave. If they see people leaving this place, the ones who stay will be served to them on a plate.'

No one said anything. Andrew rolled his eyes.

'Show of hands. Stay or run. Who wants to stay?'

Andrew put his hand up.

One by one, the hands crept up. Everyone was in agreement. Except for Bart.

'Sorry, man,' Andrew said. 'The crowd has spoken. We're staying put.'

Bart grumbled something underneath his breath but followed Tom, who'd started to look for a hiding place inside the warehouse. Given that the hall was just one big, empty space, it seemed unlikely he'd find one.

Andrew turned to me. 'I'm going to keep watch by the window. You go with Matilda and Tom.'

I shook my head. 'I'm staying with you.'

He sighed but didn't protest.

We sat down on each side of the big window. I waved to Matilda, who was crouching in the corner opposite. Tom had his arm wrapped around her. She waved back. Bart slouched next to Tom. The rest of the people were scattered around the room, huddling together in small groups.

I could hear my heart beating.

Andrew was leaning up against the wall, tilting his head forward, edging it towards the window.

I wasn't going to look out at whatever was lurking in the darkness. But I couldn't help myself. I leaned forward.

My whole body went cold.

When it first started, before we saw the metallic arm, I thought about it a lot – what they would look like. I wasn't sure what I expected. Probably skinny, green, lizard-like creatures with protruding black eyes, like the aliens in cartoons. But they looked pretty much like us, with two legs, two arms, a head and a face. They looked so like us that I wouldn't have believed it was *them* if it hadn't been for their complexion.

I'd been able to see them through the dark from all the way up the street. They were pale. Almost white. Their blue eyes sparkled in the blackness. Their eyebrows were perfectly sculpted. Their lips were almost as full as Angelina Jolie's. Although their features were quite delicate, they were both male as far as I could tell. And although one of them was blond and the other had dark hair, they looked really alike. They were almost beautiful in a weird sort of way.

For a brief moment relief washed over me. They had faces! At least they had faces! They weren't the huge, arm-wielding monsters I'd seen in the car park. Heartless. Calculating. Cold-blooded. If they had faces, they had to have ... well, I didn't know, souls or whatever. They had to possess compassion. I felt hopeful. Though I would soon find out that hope was just a manifestation of the lack of information.

A humming sound began emanating from the other side of the hall. It was Bart. He had pulled his knees up to his chest and wrapped his arms around his legs. He was rocking back and forth, mumbling to himself.

'Got to get out of here. Got to get out of here.'

Matilda and Tom were trying to persuade him to keep his voice down. But his chanting only grew louder.

'Out of here! Out of here!'

Out of the window I saw the visitors walk past the entrance to the warehouse. They didn't seem to hear him.

But all of a sudden Bart jumped to his feet and started running across the room. Tom rushed after him, but he wasn't quick enough. Bart hurtled down the stairs.

I held my breath. I remember thinking that this was it. That there would be no tomorrow. I thought about Mum and Dad. They would never know what had happened to Andrew and me.

The visitors had passed the row of warehouses when Bart came running out of the building. He was going really fast. Maybe he would have been able to outrun them. But his footsteps were heavy and the gravel crunched loudly under his feet. The visitors swung around.

It took only a fraction of a second for each of them to pull some sort of cube out of a holster on their belts and aim it at Bart.

The cubes lit up.

'Bart!' Tom came rushing out of the door. 'Bart, watch out!'

A straight line of white light shot from the cubes. Both beams hit Bart and he fell to the ground.

Tom stopped in his tracks. The visitors were looking straight at him. The cubes lit up again, but before they could fire, a metallic arm slid down from the sky towards Tom, who just stood there, paralysed. It stopped level with his eyes, then opened up and sucked him into the void before closing again.

I reached my head as far out of the window as I dared, but I couldn't get a good enough view of what the metallic arm was attached to.

I watched it move over to Bart and swallow his motionless body.

They were gone. Tom and Bart were gone. The visitors turned on their heels and walked away.

It was light outside when we finally plucked up the courage to leave. We walked as quietly as we could past the row of warehouses, every crunch of the gravel evoking the memory of the fate of the two of us who were missing. Slowly, the group scattered. No one said goodbye, the possible finality of the word lingering in the air between us.

Finally, it was just me, Andrew and Matilda. In silence, we kept stepping up the pace until we were running. In my head I was bargaining with the universe: *Please let me live. Please let me escape the metallic clutches of this white-faced, soulless species. If they need to take someone, let them take someone other than me. Someone other than me or Andrew or Matilda. They can have Mr Walnut-face. And Mrs Walnut-face. They're old. They've lived their lives.*

But the universe clearly wasn't listening.

I can't stop thinking about him. Does that mean I love him?

No, don't be silly, Amy. You can't love someone you've only talked to for a few minutes in total. Or can you?

I know what Mum would say: 'Love works in mysterious ways.' But what would Dad say? What would Darwin say?

I realise how inappropriate I'm being, thinking about love when I should be thinking about death and loss and the end of the world. But it's as if I'm not in full control of my thoughts. One minute I'm wondering whether I should do something to help Mum stop crying, and the next I'm thinking about the strange yellow tinge in Caesar's brown eyes. He's like the brain version of pop-up ads – no matter how hard you try to close them and play around with the settings on your browser, they just keep returning: his eyes, his hair, his weird sense of humour.

He's so different from the guys at school, who either ignore you or glance at you and laugh. When he looks at you it's as if he sees you, as if he wants to see the real you and you can totally be yourself around him.

When I think about Caesar it's as if a light is turned on somewhere inside me and for a few seconds I suddenly feel good ... No, not good, better than good ... normal. But I also feel like someone who turned up to a funeral dressed in a hot-pink party dress. I must stop this. I have no right to feel normal with all the devastation going on around me. From now on I'm going to focus on being sad and missing Andrew and Matilda. Besides, thinking about Caesar is pointless. I'll probably never see him again.

6

After the party, everything changed. It was as if the dark cloud above our heads had turned into a concrete roof.

Dad put a padlock on the front door. As if there were any chance we'd be going back out there. And we weren't allowed to take showers any more. He filled the bathtub, along with every container in the house, with water in case the visitors cut off the water supply.

Matilda cried over Tom without a break. I really wanted to cheer her up but there was nothing I could do. Mum said I should give her space; that only time could heal a broken heart.

I didn't think she was only crying for Tom, though. I was pretty sure Matilda hadn't really grasped the seriousness of what was happening until that night. I suspected she was crying for everything else she'd lost.

The only thing I could do was be there for her. While she lay in my bed, crying or sleeping, I sat silently at my desk or on the beanbag by the window, waiting for her to want to talk.

There wasn't much to do. Sometimes I did a bit of reading. Sometimes I just let my mind wander. Mostly, I thought about Caesar. When the electricity was on I spent my time searching the internet for him, without any success. I tried to find him on

Facebook, but there were, like, hundreds of Caesars and I didn't have his last name.

Before, I had found it so unfair that I might die without having been kissed. But now it felt even more unfair to die just when I was starting to discover this new aspect of life. Hate became part of me, like a black shadow in my peripheral vision. I was angry all the time. Who were they to say I couldn't get to know Caesar? Who were they to destroy all our lives?

Boredom soon started to creep up on us. The minutes turned into hours and the hours turned into days until finally it was confirmed. The prime minster was going to give a second statement.

The atmosphere in the living room was surprisingly buoyant as the six of us sat squeezed up against each other on the sofa in front of the telly. It had said on the internet – on all the blogs and also on the BBC website which other than that hadn't been updated for ages – that the prime minister would definitely be on at eight o'clock. We'd only had a tiny amount of soup for supper but as dessert we'd had popcorn made in a real pot from real corn kernels – not in the microwave from who knows what – and the sweet smell of slightly burned butter lingered in the air. Armed with one-liners from her library of self-help books, Mum had managed to coax Matilda into getting out of bed and getting dressed for the first time since the incident at the warehouse. Emma was playing quietly with a kitchen spatula, content after downing a glass of the orange juice from Waitrose. Dad had got his hands on some new old newspapers and magazines and his nose was buried in a Christmas copy of the *Economist*. Andrew was writing a song on his laptop. Mum was doing her nails.

I wouldn't say there was full-blown hope in the air, but mixed with the creamy smell of freshly made popcorn there was at least a whiff of it. I guess we were all thinking it could hardly get any worse. Knowing was better than not knowing, right?

'This guy is pretty cute,' Matilda said about a bald man in his forties who was letting the team from *Cash in the Attic* rummage through a house he had just inherited from his aunt in search of hidden treasures to sell at auction.

I rolled my eyes. 'You're just saying that because of the value of that Victorian vase they just found.'

We were rolling around in a rare fit of laughter when the programme went off air and the screen went blank. It was ten past eight.

Five expectant faces and one drooling, clueless one were reflected in the blackness of the TV screen. No one spoke. We just sat there, staring at ourselves. Five minutes passed. Then the screen lit up.

It was the same studio as last time. Today the prime minister was already sitting at the news desk.

My throat clogged up. I felt as if I couldn't breathe. This was bad. This was really bad.

There were deep lines under the prime minister's eyes. His face was drawn and his skin had a grey tinge to it. As if that wasn't bad enough, he was wearing a *sweatshirt*. It couldn't have been more obvious. The news couldn't be good.

'Dear countrymen,' he began, his voice weak and cracking. He coughed.

75

From the corner of my eye I noticed Dad take Mum's hand and squeeze it.

'I shall make this short,' the prime minister continued hoarsely. 'Right now, leaders around the world are addressing their nations. Despite the combined efforts of governments, peace negotiations with the visitors have not yet been successful. We don't know much, but we do know this: they do *not* come in peace.'

There was a loud rumble in the studio. The prime minister looked away from the camera, over his right shoulder.

His eyes popped as he jumped from the seat.

There was more noise in the background.

He quickly leaned forward, resting his hands on the news desk, and looked back into the camera.

'People!' he shouted. 'Guard your children!'

He glanced again to his side.

'Oh, God,' he mumbled, his legs starting to walk away from whatever was happening off-screen but his hands still firmly set on the tabletop. 'They're after teenagers!' He was speaking really fast. 'Anyone between the ages of fourteen and nineteen is in danger.'

There was some commotion and he looked away.

'No,' the prime minister whispered. 'God, no.'

He straightened up and turned on his heel. He was almost off the screen when a pale figure in shiny black overalls shot into view on the other side of it. Without the slightest effort showing on his snow-white face, he grabbed the prime minister by the back of the neck and dragged him close.

'It's them,' Andrew breathed, looking at Mum and Dad. 'It's a visitor. Like the ones we saw the other night.'

The prime minister's arms and legs flailed wildly. 'They're systematically abducting teenagers,' he squeaked.

The visitor reached for a holster hanging from his belt.

I knew what they kept in their belts. I grabbed Emma and put a hand over her eyes.

From the holster the visitor took a sphere the size of a tennis ball. At first it was black, but then it lit up.

The prime minister started screaming, 'No! Please don't! Don't! I have a family! Don't!'

The ball crackled like burning coal. Tiny little lightning bolts shot out of it as the visitor moved it slowly towards the prime minister's neck.

Matilda slid her hand into mine.

'No!' His face was elongated with fear; his mouth hung open; his eyes were wide and staring.

The ball was closing in on him.

'Please!' he cried like an animal stuck in a trap. 'Please, don't!' They were sharp cries. Raw. I felt them bore into the pit of my stomach.

The visitor's long, white fingers tightened their grip on the prime minister's neck.

He winced. He stopped struggling. But suddenly he swung his head around to face the camera.

'Fight!' he growled. 'Fight them! Don't let them take our youth!'

The visitor pushed the ball up against the prime minister's neck.

The light inside the ball turned from yellow to orange.

The prime minister started shaking, first slowly, then vehemently. His head was pulled back and his face scrunched up tight. His jaw clenched and his nose wrinkled. His eyes rolled around in their sockets. Saliva started running from the corners of his mouth. The screen went blank.

Then the lights in the living room went out.

We sat there in silence for a few minutes before Mum got up to light candles.

'Right,' she said. 'Right. I think it's best if we don't start worrying too much at this point. Like the prime minister said, we don't know anything yet. One should not waste one's life worrying about the unknown. "Do not anticipate trouble or worry about what may never happen," a wise man once said. "Keep in the sunlight," he said. That's what we ought to do. Keep in the sunlight of positivity. Maybe everything will be fine. There is no reason to worry about—'

There was a sharp knock on the door.

The lit match fell from Mum's hands on to the floor. She quickly stepped on it. She looked at Dad. He was staring at the front door.

My hand, which was still holding Matilda's, was sticky with sweat. I squeezed it harder.

There was another knock.

'Don't open it,' Andrew whispered.

'Dan? Diana?' said a man on the other side of the door.

The voice was familiar, but I couldn't quite place it.

Dad got up from the sofa. 'Who's there?' he said, one of his eyebrows arching up his forehead, forming the shape of a horizontal question mark.

'It's John,' the voice whispered back. 'Anita's dad.'

I couldn't believe it. I let go of Matilda and ran to the door. I looked at Dad. He nodded. I unlocked the padlock and opened it.

There were two figures standing in the dark hallway dressed in dark green plastic ponchos with hoods draped over their heads. A torch shone up into my face. I shielded my eyes.

'Oops. Sorry,' Mr Withers said.

I didn't recognise her at first, but beside him stood Mandira, Anita's mum. She removed her hood. Her long, dark hair fell over the wide shoulders of her poncho.

'Can we come in?' she asked and gave a little smile.

Mum snapped into squeaky hostess mode. 'Oh, of course, come on in, come on in. Great seeing you,' she said, trying far too hard to pretend this was just a normal social call when it obviously wasn't. When had John and Mandira Withers ever been to our house in any capacity other than to pick up Anita?

'Can I get you anything?' Mum continued. 'Water? Or ... erm ... water?'

'No, thank you, we're fine,' Mandira said and glanced at her husband. 'We need to talk to you and Dan.'

'Oh, sure, sure,' Mum said and pointed towards the sofa.

Andrew and Matilda got up.

'Have a seat,' Mum said.

Mandira's eyes shifted between Andrew and Matilda and me. She turned to Mum.

'I think it would be better if we talked in private?'

'Oh, of course, of course. Kids, go and play in Amy's room.' She picked up Emma from the floor and handed her to Andrew. 'Off you go,' she said when none of us showed any sign of leaving.

I turned to Mandira. 'Where's Anita?'

Her face hardened. Her dark brown eyes avoided mine.

'Amy!' Mum snapped. 'To your room.'

I didn't want to go. I wanted to know why Mandira and John were here. I wanted to know where Anita was. And, frankly, I kind of wanted to stay in the same room as Mum and Dad.

'Don't worry,' Dad said and winked at me. 'I'll come and check on you all in a minute.'

I turned and stormed to my room as moodily as I could. Who were they to tell me what I could and couldn't hear? We were the ones in danger. It was me who'd already stared into the hollow darkness of the metallic arm. According to the prime minister, it was us they were after. We had every right to know what was going on.

Matilda grabbed a candle and followed me into my bedroom along with Andrew and Emma. I slammed the door shut.

'I'm sorry,' I heard Mum say through the door. 'Usually she isn't like that.'

Andrew put Emma on the floor, grabbed my laptop and slumped down on my bed.

'Oh, don't apologise,' Mandira said. 'It's understandable given the circumstances.'

I pushed my ear hard against the door.

'What are you doing?' Andrew said without looking up from the laptop.

'Don't use up all the battery,' I hissed. He was watching an episode of *Pretty Little Liars* I'd downloaded that morning.

'How can you watch this crap?'

Matilda put the candle on my desk and sat down on my beanbag.

'Where do you think Anita is?' she said, rolling an empty water bottle that was lying on the floor over to Emma. She grabbed it and squealed. 'Do you think that *they*—'

I raised my hand, my palm facing her. 'Shhh! I'm listening.' The truth was, I didn't want to hear the end of that sentence.

'You sure I can't get you a glass of water?' Mum asked again.

I rolled my eyes.

'Diana, we need a favour,' Mandira said.

'Is everything okay? Has Anita been …?' Mum didn't finish the question.

'Yes.' Mandira's voice was low and breathy. 'Yes, she has.'

'I'm sorry,' Mum and Dad mumbled both at once. 'I'm so, so sorry.'

John cleared his throat. 'I think we should turn to the matter at hand,' he said pragmatically, as if he were in a business meeting.

'Yes, of course, of course,' Mum breathed. 'What can we do for you? Anything. Just name it.'

'It's big,' Mandira said.

'Anything, anything at all,' Mum repeated.

'There is a way …' Mandira paused. 'There is a way to get her back. There is a way to get at least some of them back.'

'That's wonderful news!' Mum chirped. 'How?'

'We've joined the Resistance.'

'The Resistance?'

'The People's Resistance Against the Alien Occupation.'

'I didn't know there was such a thing.'

'They've been gathering strength during the past weeks.'

'That's nice.'

I rolled my eyes again. *Nice*.

'We need your children.'

Mum squeaked. 'What?'

'We need Andrew. Or Amy.'

I snapped my fingers and motioned for Andrew to come over. 'They're talking about us.'

He jumped off the bed and ran to the door.

'Well, Andrew would be a better option. You know how Amy is, all mousy and timid; she's like a little nestling, that girl. Anyway, we need the aliens to take them. Either of them. We need them for bait.'

There was silence. Then I heard a chair scrape against the floor. Mum's voice was as hard as steel.

'Out.'

'Please, hear me out—'

'Get out.'

'Maybe I should have chosen a more sensitive word. A messenger. We need a messenger. We have an ally on the inside. We need to get a message to him in order to get our children back. In order to get Anita back. But the only ones who are getting up there are the people they're abducting. The only ones who are getting in are the kids.'

'You must be out of your mind,' Mum snarled at her. 'Do you really think I'd let you hand one of my children over to the visitors?'

I heard Dad clear his throat. 'I'm sorry, Mandira, but this is absolutely out of the question.'

'We wouldn't be handing them over,' Mandira snapped. 'We'd just give them the message and wait for their turn. They will be taken. There is no escaping it.'

The door suddenly felt cold against my skin. I moved my ear away from it when Mum started shouting at Mandira.

'How dare you say such a thing? Get the hell out of my house! Get out!'

John's monotonous voice began harmonising with Mum's screaming, which made the noise sound like a contemporary choral work composed by a crazy parrot.

'Be logical, Diana. Almost all the kids around here are gone.'

'I don't have to listen to this! Get out!'

'They do this very methodically. It's house by house, neighbourhood by neighbourhood.'

'I said, get out!'

'It's as if they know where everyone lives and how many youths there are in each household. By my estimation, East London won't have any teenagers left by the end of the week.'

'Out!'

Dad silenced the choir. 'I think you guys should leave. We're very sorry to hear about Anita, but we can't help you here.'

Mandira started begging. 'Please. They are going to be taken anyway. This way something good can come of it. This way they'd at least stand a chance of returning home. It might even end the siege. Things might go back to normal.'

There were footsteps. I heard the front door open and Dad say, 'We're very sorry.' Then it closed. I heard the padlock being put back on.

I looked at Andrew. He was staring at the floor, the inner corners of his eyebrows sinking down to his nose in concentration.

'How dare they?' Mum hissed.

'They're desperate. Of course they'll try anything.'

We heard footsteps approaching. Andrew and I jumped away from the door. Andrew landed on the bed, narrowly escaping my laptop, and I crashed down on my desk chair.

Dad came in and sat down on my bedroom floor, followed by Mum. Not knowing we had heard the whole thing, they told us that Anita had been taken by the visitors and her parents were seeing if anyone could help them find her. Dad said that we would, of course, help in every reasonable way that we could. I guessed technically that wasn't a lie.

Mum said that we shouldn't worry. The government would be working on a plan to drive away the visitors. If not the British government then surely the American government. Maybe even the Chinese. She said that we shouldn't worry about the visitors. Of all the teenagers in the whole of London, of all the teenagers in the world, the likelihood of us being abducted was one in a million if not one in a billion. Dad bit his lip. He was always banging on about statistics not being shown the respect of accuracy. Mum went on. 'We're all perfectly safe here in our little flat. Just as safe as we've always been. Very, very safe …'

Mum and Dad left and Matilda and I played with Emma. Although Emma's motor skills didn't even allow her to hold a pencil properly, we tried to teach her how to draw a stick figure. She kept clawing at the paper with her tiny little fingers. Once she managed to get hold of it and sway it dangerously close to our candle. As if things weren't bad enough. We didn't need a house fire as well.

I couldn't stop thinking about what Mandira and John had said. *They are going to be taken anyway.* Was that true? The prime minister had said that everyone between the ages of fourteen and nineteen was in danger. Were the visitors really going to abduct each and every person on the whole planet in that age group? Was there no hope of them missing a few houses? Like our house? Then I remembered the metallic arms. If the visitors were able to reach down from the sky and suck up people like a vacuum cleaner sucked up dust, they'd probably have the technology to do pretty much anything they set their minds to.

The door to my room was open and I could hear Mum and Dad whispering in the kitchen. I tried my best to listen in but without much success. Mum said something about the countryside. Dad said something about it being too much of a risk.

Then the deafening sound of the air-raid sirens drowned out their voices along with my own thoughts. They hadn't sounded since the incident with the metal arm. I grabbed Emma and ran into the kitchen, followed closely by Matilda. Andrew was already there.

'We're staying put,' Dad said and clenched his jaw like he always did when he was about to do something Mum didn't approve of.

Mum sat silently at the kitchen table, staring down at her clasped hands.

The sirens pounded my ears. The intensity of the noise made it really difficult not to react, but I forced myself to stand perfectly still, afraid that if I said or did something, I would somehow be taking sides in Mum and Dad's argument.

'Erm ...' Matilda said, looking at me, 'shouldn't we do something? At least take cover under a table or stand in a door frame or something?'

'That's for earthquakes,' Andrew said and shook his head.

Mum looked up. 'Let's just hole up on the sofa in the living room. Maybe Dad will read us a book. That'll make it all go by fast—'

She jumped from her seat. 'Oh my God! Step away from the window!' She hurled herself towards us and with her outstretched hands started shuffling us towards the door. We scuttled out of the kitchen like a flock of sheep being driven into our fold.

But she might just as well not have bothered. In a building made of ninety per cent glass there is no escaping the outside.

'Holy shit!' Dad said, coming up behind us.

I looked out of the living-room window. There it was. Like a lid on the sky, hovering above the tops of the neighbouring skyscrapers. The source of our captivity. The physical manifestation of the unknown that kept us all under siege. There it was. Right outside our window. One of who knew how many unidentified flying objects that surrounded Earth.

It was as if the sight of it drained the room of oxygen. My arms hung limp by my sides. My legs felt like two sponges that might give in to the weight of the rest of my body at any moment. I didn't have the energy to do anything but stare.

Strangely enough, the vessel looked both outlandish and familiar. It was familiar in the sense that it wasn't far from what I'd seen in movies. It was round. The bottom part was completely flat while the top was curved. The shape of it was like a planet cut in half. Or the top part of a mushroom. What made it feel outlandish, however, was the fact that the sight of it wasn't accompanied by a batch of far-too-salty popcorn and a gigantic cup of cola; there was no assurance that after the closing credits the lights would come on and everything would turn out to have been a cinematic illusion.

From the bottom of the flying object there stretched hundreds of metallic arms like the one we'd seen in the car park. They reached all the way from the sky down to the ground below, where they disappeared around corners and into buildings.

I didn't want to look at it any more, but I couldn't turn away. I focused my eyes on the glass in the window. Our faces were reflected in it, lit up by the candles that were scattered all over the living room. They looked frozen. As if they were made of wax. And transparent. As if we were ghosts.

All of a sudden Mum started running around blowing out the candles.

Our faces disappeared from the glass and I was forced to look at the flying object once again. It seemed to be made of dark-grey steel and it had rows and rows of little dots of light circling it. I wondered whether these were really lights or whether they were windows. Just like the windows of the skyscrapers that used to light up the sky of Canary Wharf before all this.

What would be inside? An army of aliens waiting to rid the Earth of humans so they could have it for themselves? Innocent explorers just wanting to see what our planet looked like? Alien families just like ours but with paler skin and shinier eyes?

We locked ourselves in the bathroom. It was the only room without a single window.

We'd been sitting silently in the dark for at least half an hour when the banging on the door started. At first we thought Mandira and Mr Withers had returned. But we soon realised that it wouldn't be them. Someone was trying to break down the door and we had a pretty good idea who.

'Andrew, Amy, Matilda,' Mum whispered. 'Hide! Now!'

Matilda squeezed herself into the dirty laundry basket. Andrew ran into his bedroom and hid inside his wardrobe. I went into the kitchen and crawled under the sink.

Through a crack in the door of the kitchen cupboard I could see out into the hall. I saw Mum and Dad carrying their big chest of drawers out of the bedroom and place it up against the front door. The panic in their eyes was animal-like.

But no sooner had they let go of the furniture than a loud crashing sound penetrated the noise of the air-raid sirens.

'No!' Mum screamed. Her voice cut through me like a knife.

I heard the wood of the front door being ripped out of the door frame and falling on to the floor below.

Dad rushed into Andrew's room. Within a few seconds he came running back out wielding Andrew's cricket bat.

'Get the hell out of here!' He pointed the bat towards the door. His eyes were wide. 'Get out!'

Then I heard the footsteps and *they* came into view. The sight of them felt like a noose around my neck. There were three of them. They were wearing their black shiny overalls and identical flat expressions on their faces. Their boots creaked as they walked mechanically, neither fast nor slow, towards Dad.

Screaming, Mum ran into the living room and picked up Emma from the floor.

In one swift movement one of the visitors reached out his hand and grabbed Dad by the throat. Then he lifted him up and threw him across the hall. He crashed into the wall before falling on to the shoe rack below. He lay there, scrunched up into a ball.

'Ahhh,' he cried. 'My shoulder! Oh God, my shoulder.'

Mum fell silent. She pushed Emma against her chest and started backing away further into the living room.

The three men split up. One headed for my room, one went into Andrew's room and the third into the bathroom.

I could hear them rummaging through the flat. I really wanted to crawl out of my hiding place. I wanted to be with Mum. I wanted to see if Dad was all right.

There were breaking sounds mixed with the noise of big furniture smashing against the floor. It didn't take them long to find Andrew. With his hands tied up behind his back, he was dragged out of his room and towards the door by one of the men.

Mum started running towards them.

'No! Let him go!'

She was racing past the kitchen when one of the visitors appeared in the doorway of my room. When he spotted Mum approaching he reached for his belt.

'Watch out, Di!' I heard Dad shout.

But it all happened too quickly. The sphere the visitor plucked from the holster on his belt lit up as he pointed it towards Mum. A blue line of light shot out of it and hit Mum in the chest. She immediately collapsed to the floor.

Mum! I shouted silently in my head.

Emma landed on Mum's stomach. She didn't appear hurt.

I waited for Mum to get up. To show a sign of life. But she just lay there completely still, her eyes closed.

Mum. My mum. They killed my mum.

Emma started crying and inching her way down to the floor.

What felt like boiling hot tears were stinging my face.

'Come here,' Dad whispered. Holding his shoulder, his face wrought with pain, he began crawling over to her. 'Come here, Emma.'

The visitor's boots screeched when he turned on the hardwood floor. He looked down at Dad and raised his glass sphere again. It lit up.

I didn't think the visitor would do it. Why would he do it? But he did.

Dad shielded his face. The blue lightning hit him in the stomach.

I stopped breathing. I wanted the world to stop. I wanted everything to stop.

At the same moment the third of the visitors stepped out of the bathroom with Matilda in tow. She was fighting him.

'Let go of me, you creep!'

When she kicked him in the shin he lifted her up from the floor and carried her horizontally under his arm as if she were no heavier than a newspaper.

They were heading for the door. I could hear their voices, soft and flat. Just like their faces. I didn't know what they were saying. I couldn't understand them.

Then I didn't hear them any more. I wasn't sure if they had left. I waited in the cupboard for a while. Emma had stopped crying. She was sitting in the hallway with her back to me. Slowly, the silence morphed into a high-frequency ringing in my ears that felt as if it could split my head open.

I finally crawled out of my hiding place and ran over to Mum. Her face was white. I grabbed her hand. It was freezing cold. I looked over to Dad. He wasn't moving. I tried to hold it in, but I couldn't. I let out a loud scream. It tore at my insides like broken glass.

Emma crawled over to me. Tugging on the sleeve of my jumper, she got unsteadily to her feet and wrapped her arms around my neck. I could feel her wet nose on my cheek.

That was it. It would be just the two of us from now on. We only had each other now.

Mum's hand suddenly moved and I jumped up with shock.

'Mum!' I shouted and knelt back down again. 'Mum! Please, Mum, wake up!'

Her eyes shot open. Her mouth gaped as she struggled for breath. Her chest heaved as she managed to get some air into her lungs.

Gurgling sounds started coming from Dad. I slid over to him. It was as if he was choking. I didn't know what to do so I just raised him up a little and held his head in my lap while he recovered.

Wheezing, he rolled on to his side.

'Andrew?' he breathed.

I swallowed. 'They took him.'

He squeezed his eyes shut.

Mum pushed herself up.

'And Matilda?'

I couldn't speak so I just nodded.

The room was drained of hope. We sat there, on the floor, in silent defeat. Not only had our world been turned upside down, but now there was a huge empty hole in it as well. Nothing would ever be the same again.

Sunday 28 August

I don't know what to do. Mum and Dad refuse to see sense. I tried talking to them but they didn't listen. I made them watch this YouTube video that went viral – it shows a lone car driving along the M25 which is suddenly knocked off the road by a metallic arm – but they still didn't budge. I googled the video of the visitor seizing the prime minister and then I showed them all the others – endless clips of world leaders sitting in TV studios speaking fervently in a foreign language and then being grabbed by a visitor just like our prime minister had been. There was the German chancellor, the president of France, the King of Saudi Arabia. None of them stood any chance against the effortless strength of the visitors. It had no impact on Mum and Dad's decision.

'I'm adamant,' Mum said, not looking at Dad. 'We're leaving London to go and stay with Granny Vera in her cottage in Woodbridge.'

Dad mostly stayed silent. I sensed he wasn't completely convinced that driving to Woodbridge was a good idea. I think he was just saying he was because he feels guilty. He feels guilty about not having been able to save Andrew. I think for him this is more about if I get taken, he can at least tell himself that he tried.

I couldn't help wondering whether Mum and Dad were blind or just stupid. Had they not seen the visitors' vessel outside our living-room window? Had they not seen how big it was? Had they not spotted the hundreds of metallic arms stretching for miles and miles from the sky down to the ground? How on earth did they think they were going to get to Woodbridge? Drive along the A12 as if it were a regular Sunday morning and we were heading to Granny's for her consistently dry roast?

They did however see my point about one thing. 'What if Andrew and Matilda come back?'

Dad came up with the solution. He's going to drive me to Woodbridge since I'm the one most likely to be taken and Mum and Emma will stay behind in London.

I tried to protest. 'The family should stay together.'

But Mum and Dad had stopped listening and had started mapping out the best route.

*

It's the night before Dad is supposed to drive me. I can't let them do this. They would be putting themselves at risk, they would be putting Emma at risk, just to try to save me. To try to save me from something they don't stand a chance against.

There is only one thing I can do. They've given me no choice. I'm taking myself out of the equation.

7

A week after Andrew and Matilda were taken I sent Mandira a private message on Facebook and arranged to meet up. I knew I couldn't go to their house because Matilda had told me it had been empty for some time. Mandira offered to meet me outside my building around midnight. When I got downstairs she was already waiting. She tried to act all calm and collected. But I sensed her anxious anticipation.

'How are you?' she asked, removing her hood. 'How's your family? Is everyone okay?' She was pretending not to know why I'd asked to see her but the hope shimmering in her dark eyes gave her away.

It made my stomach turn.

'They took Andrew and Matilda,' I said, my voice cracking. The cold was biting my fingers. I put my hands in my pockets and felt my keys in one of them. I could still turn back. It wasn't too late. I could sneak back inside where it was warm. Where it was safe. For now.

Her expression didn't indicate even a hint of surprise. 'I'm sorry,' she said, not looking straight at me. 'I'm very sorry.'

She was probably thinking, *I told you so.* She had a right to. Her harsh prediction was etched into my brain. *They will be taken. There is no escaping it.*

She suddenly turned her gaze back to me. Her eyes narrowed. 'How come you escaped?'

Was that accusation in her voice? I looked away. I hadn't really thought about it. But it suddenly did seem strange. Why had the visitors immediately stopped searching the house once they'd found Andrew and Matilda?

'I hid,' I mumbled, staring down at my toes.

I could feel her eyes boring into me. Her stare was heavy with questions. *Why you? Why not Anita? Why not Andrew or Matilda?*

The guilt wrapped itself around my throat. 'I need to get in touch with the Resistance,' I said quickly.

Mandira was silent. 'Why?' she finally said. 'Are you going to help us?'

I didn't know what I was going to do.

'I just want to talk to you, to them.' There was no need to tell her more. There was no need to raise her hopes, promise her something I wasn't able to deliver.

From her pocket she pulled out a dark-green poncho, identical to the one she was wearing, and handed it to me.

'We can't have you drawing attention to us.'

I looked down at my bright red coat.

'Put it on over your clothes. It's the closest thing to camouflage the Resistance have been able to get their hands on.'

The poncho reached down to my knees. It had a strong smell of plastic.

'Let's go then,' Mandira said and headed out of the courtyard. I followed her.

The sky had started to drizzle and I put up the hood. 'Where are we going?'

'You'll see when we get there.'

I stopped. What kind of answer was that? A cold gust of wind slapped my cheek. Could I really trust her? Sure, she was Anita's mum. But I didn't know her – not, like, properly.

Mandira turned around. 'Are you coming?'

'Where are we going?' I asked again, trying to sound as resolute as I possibly could.

'Shhh! Keep your voice down!' she ordered. She took a quick look around. 'You can't know until we get there.'

I wasn't going to let this go. 'Why not?'

She hesitated.

'Why not?'

She gave a soft sigh. 'They're everywhere.' She swept her hair, which was blowing into her face, from her eyes. 'If the visitors capture you before we get there, I don't want to risk you revealing to them the whereabouts of the Resistance. You must understand. It could endanger the entire operation.'

Thick drops of rain started falling from the sky. It sounded like a drum solo was playing inside the plastic hood of my poncho. I wanted to protest. What kind of snitch did she take me for? But I knew there were a lot of ways to get someone to talk, even if they didn't intend to.

'Fine,' I said and headed towards where she stood in the opening of the courtyard.

'Don't worry,' she said and gave a little smile. 'It'll be okay. We've been mapping out the safest streets in London. The streets where we're less likely to run into them. We'll be fine.'

We walked in silence over the South Quay footbridge towards Canary Wharf. The soles of our shoes clicked loudly against the steel. We made our way through Heron Quays DLR station and headed for Reuters Plaza.

'We're going down to Canary Wharf station,' Mandira said and stepped up her pace.

I didn't bother asking why, although I knew it couldn't be to catch the Tube.

We'd almost reached the open glass-and-steel facade which led down to the tracks, where I'd been a million times for the Jubilee line, when Mandira suddenly grabbed my shoulder.

'Shit!' she hissed.

My heart nearly stopped when I spotted two shadowy figures trudging through the dark. I closed my eyes. This was it. Maybe I'd find Andrew and Matilda wherever I was taken. Maybe I would see Anita again. Or maybe ... I hardly ever let myself think it – but maybe they were all dead.

'Who's there?' a voice shouted.

Relief swept through my body and made my knees buckle. Thank God! I opened my eyes. They were soldiers.

The realisation didn't seem to ease Mandira at all. Her fingers were boring into me so hard it hurt.

In a low voice she growled at me, 'We're just out trying to find some food. You understand?'

The two men suddenly raised their guns. 'I said, who's there?' The torches that were stuck to the barrels blinded me. I covered my face with my arm.

'Don't shoot,' Mandira yelled. 'It's just me and my niece.'

They lowered their weapons.

'What the hell do you two think you're doing?' one of the men shouted, his voice rusty and cold. He was the older of the two, his face was covered with grey stubble and he had narrow, bloodshot eyes.

Mandira was still squeezing me hard. 'We're looking for food.'

He gave a low grumble. 'You know you're not supposed to be out. You're going to get yourselves killed. If you needed food, you should have knocked on a neighbour's door and asked for some.'

'I'm sorry, sir,' Mandira breathed and finally let go of my shoulder. 'You're right. You're right. We'll be on our way home.'

'You'd better be,' he said, shaking his head over our lack of obedience and rolling his eyes at the younger soldier, who stood skinny and hunched beside him. He had pimply cheeks and big water-blue eyes. He couldn't have been more than twenty-one.

'Now, get out of here,' the older soldier barked. 'And don't let me see you out here on the streets again while there is still a curfew in place.'

Mandira grabbed me by the collar and started dragging me back the way we came.

'Wait,' a shrill and broken voice called after us.

We turned around. The young soldier was walking towards us. He reached into his pocket.

'Here.'

From it, he pulled out a Mars bar.

'Take it,' he said, extending his hand towards me.

I stared at the chocolate bar and then at the soldier's face. His nose was red from the cold. His cheeks were sunken. I couldn't take his food. Who knew how much he got fed? My bag was stuffed with crackers, cans of baked beans and tuna. I'd eaten two slices of old bread before I left the house. I was fine.

Mandira nudged me towards the soldier. 'Take it, honey, and say thank you to the nice young man.'

I couldn't move. I hated having to participate in this web of lies. I hated Mandira for talking to me as if I were three years old and she were my mother. I already missed my real mother. The one who would never lie and take some poor guy's chocolate bar without even hesitating to think about whether he'd have any more for himself. I hated the cold that was gnawing at my fingers. And I hated the visitors for ruining all our lives. My eyes started to well up.

Mandira pushed me harder. 'Say thank you.'

I reached out my hand. 'Thank you,' I managed through the lump in my throat.

A smile spread across the guy's face, making his eyes twinkle like two blue stars in the night sky.

'Take care,' he said. He straightened his back and hurried over to his colleague.

Mandira and I headed back to Heron Quays DLR station and hid there until the two men were gone. Then we ran across Reuters Plaza and down the motionless escalators leading into Canary Wharf station.

It was strange to see the station so empty. The big, high-ceilinged hall was usually swarming with suit-wearing men and women walking really fast and bumping their briefcases into you as if you were totally invisible. Today it was the other way around. It was as if everyone else had gone invisible.

We scurried across the hall towards the barriers. We didn't need tickets to get in as all the gates were open. When we got down to the platforms I noticed that the glass that closed off the train tracks had been smashed in places.

'Over here,' Mandira said, running ahead of me across the platform.

By one of the smashed holes there stood two Boris bikes. Mandira stopped by the bikes and started pushing them through the hole in the glass. I thought they would fall down to the train tracks but they didn't. The tracks had been covered with wooden planks.

'Why are there bikes down here in the station?' I asked. I'd noticed that the cycle hire outside had been almost empty, which didn't make much sense – it wasn't as if there'd be lots of people needing to rent a bike for an hour or two.

'They've come in handy during the siege,' she said as, crouching on the platform, she let go of the second bike so it crashed on to the makeshift cycle track. 'The Resistance use them to get around. We mostly use them on the Tube tracks. It's much safer to travel underground. We've been working on laying the whole Tube system with planks for a smoother ride.'

Mandira reached into her pocket. 'Here.' She handed me a torch. 'Take this. Only use it in the tunnels. We don't want you accidentally flashing the visitors now, do we?'

I put the torch in my back pocket. Mandira helped me crawl through the hole in the glass without cutting myself.

I bent down to pick up one of the bikes. As I wrapped my fingers around the handlebars I noticed something moving on the plank right next to my hand. I quickly reached for the torch. A faint yellow ray lit up the slightly dirty brown wood.

Immediately, I let go of the bike, which fell on the plank with a hollow, metallic thud, and jumped back. I tried to hold it in but couldn't quite stifle a scream battling its way out of my mouth.

I ran back towards the hole. 'Help me through!' I shouted at Mandira.

'What? What's wrong?'

'Rats!' I shouted, staring around at the creatures that blended in perfectly with the darkness. I felt goosebumps travel down my back and spread across my whole body. 'This place is swarming with rats!'

Mandira gave an annoyed guttural sound. 'I thought you'd hurt yourself or something. Of course there are rats in the tunnels. Have you ever been on the Tube?' she said, the sarcasm tearing at her throat.

She stepped through the hole in the glass. 'They're harmless,' she said and grabbed a bike. 'Well, maybe not harmless exactly; they are, after all, thought to have spread the Bubonic plague. But at this point we have bigger things to worry about.' She swung a leg over the saddle, rested a foot on the pedal and looked over her shoulder. 'Follow me,' she ordered and started pedalling.

I watched Mandira bump along the plank, slowly at first, but soon she'd gathered proper speed.

I directed the torch towards the handlebars of my bike, which was lying all twisted on the plank. A big rat was sniffing at it, its muzzle wet and quivering.

'Shoo,' I hissed. It didn't move. I kicked the bike so it shook. The rat shot away and disappeared into the shadows.

I grabbed the bike and, with the torch in hand, headed after Mandira. Although I could see movement from the corners of my eyes, I tried not to look at the rats lurking in the tunnels. Their squeaks, however, could not be ignored. Each shrill little cry brought to mind their sneaky, black eyes and their dirty, ragged fur.

My clothes were soaked in sweat when Mandira finally stopped pedalling and suggested we take a break. I looked at my watch. The time was one-fifteen. We'd been going for almost half an hour and we'd reached Bermondsey station. We climbed up to the platform and sat down on one of the empty benches. How often during a packed Tube ride I'd wished that the crowd of people would just disappear so I could get some breathing space, not to mention a seat. Now, though, the dream felt like a nightmare.

'You okay?' Mandira asked.

I nodded, too out of breath to speak.

'You'll be surprised how quickly you get used to having to use your own legs to get from one place to the next. You'll be cycling for miles and miles without breaking a sweat before you know it.'

I doubted it but I gave her a smile. 'When ...' I had to pause to catch my breath. 'When did you join the Resistance?'

Mandira lowered her eyes. Her voice sounded hard. 'Right after they took Anita.'

The sweat covering my body suddenly turned cold.

'About two weeks ago. A friend of a friend introduced me to them.'

In the darkness of the tunnel, focusing on the hypnotically repetitive task of pedalling, I'd somehow managed to forget about the reality of things. I'd managed to put out of my mind the whole situation up on the surface along with the consequences of what I was about to do.

'We should get going. If we don't arrive soon, they might not let us into the base for the night and we'll have to sleep down here in the tunnels.'

I jumped to my feet even though my burning thigh muscles begged for a longer break. I wasn't about to spend the night with the rats.

It was difficult to climb back on the bike. It wasn't only my legs that had started to complain but my bum as well. I focused on the pain instead of what lay before me.

After around ten minutes we reached London Bridge.

'Only one more station to go,' Mandira called out to me.

My body may have been relieved but my mind wasn't. *Where were we going? What would happen? Would I ever see Mum and Dad again?* My head flooded with images of the visitors: their creepy, pale skin; their blank, beautiful eyes; their enormous vessels; the sleek surface of their metallic arms.

Before I knew it, we were there. 'Southwark' it said on the blue line that ran through the red circle of the Underground sign.

Together, Mandira and I lifted the bikes up to the platform. We left them there, mounted the stairs and headed out into the night breeze.

It was dark and I could hardly see a thing. I'd been to Southwark often enough and knew what was supposed to be there: a big road, a tall and surprisingly colourful glass building, some old brick houses. I sensed that we were descending slightly, so we had to be heading towards the river. I listened for the murmur of water but there was nothing. I'd always found it strange how a huge river like the Thames could be so quiet.

It didn't take us long to reach the promenade by the river. I loved the bustling South Bank with its slow-walking tourists being pushed out of the way by hurrying Londoners, the noise of buskers and street artists filling the air along with the smell of hot dogs and sugar-coated peanuts sold from rusty carts. This evening, however, like the rest of London, it looked like a ghost town.

'We're almost there,' Mandira whispered, the sound of her voice breaking the enveloping silence like a stone through a glass window.

Across the river, on each side of St Paul's, there was soft light inside some of the buildings.

On our side of the river I could just see the outline of the Tate Modern through the darkness. As we drew closer, I realised how much the square brick building with its tall tower looked like a big hand giving the world the finger.

'Over here.' Mandira took a right and shot ahead of me. I followed her past the rear entrance of the Tate. The windows on the gallery's ground floor had been boarded up with wooden planks.

Mandira turned the corner around the back. I caught up with her by a small door hidden in a crook in the wall.

'We're here?' I whispered, not able to hide my surprise.

'Shhh!' Mandira ordered as she knocked.

A crack opened in the door. 'Password and identification number,' a surprisingly shrill voice demanded.

'Spitfire. Twenty-four of the East London Regiment.'

The door closed and I heard the rattle of a chain before it opened again. Light from inside the gallery flooded out into the street. A tall, stocky man appeared as a silhouette against the bright background.

But suddenly he grabbed the door and tried to slam it shut again. Mandira was already half inside and it hit her in the face.

'Bradley!' she shouted. 'What the—'

'Who's that?!' the man hissed, staring at me with blazing eyes.

Mandira was rubbing her forehead.

'I said, who's that?'

The man was blocking our entrance.

'Don't be an idiot, Bradley, let us in. It's freezing out.'

The man didn't move.

'Bradley!'

'Mandira, you know I can't let an unapproved person into the base.'

A small trickle of blood ran down Mandira's temple from a cut just above her eyebrow.

'Don't give me that procedure bullshit. She's a kid.'

'Rules are rules.'

Mandira pulled the sleeve of her jumper out from under her poncho and started dabbing at the cut. 'Go and get CJ.'

'He's out.'

'Shit, Bradley. Just let us in.'

He lowered his eyes. 'You know how these things work, Mandira. She can apply for entry tomorrow morning. The Collective is meeting at noon. I'm sure they'll be able to consider the application at the meeting.'

Mandira sighed. 'Bradley.' Her voice was softer now. 'These formalities only cause things to drag on. She may be able to help us. You know as well as I do that time is of the essence. I don't want my Anita to spend a minute more than necessary away from home.'

The man shifted on his feet.

'I know you don't want that for your Daniel either.'

He clenched his jaw. 'The only unapproved persons I can let in are prisoners. Is she a prisoner?'

Mandira smiled. 'Sure. She's a prisoner.' She grabbed my arm and pushed past the man.

'You'll have to take her to the holding cell,' he called after us.

'Will do.'

Mandira turned to me. 'Don't worry. It's what used to be the gallery's members' room.'

'And she'll have to appear before CJ tomorrow like any other prisoner!'

'Yeah, yeah ...'

We walked up the stairs all the way to the sixth floor. A guard let us into the holding cell that turned out to be a big room with a bar, tables and chairs, and a huge window overlooking the city. As I was currently the only prisoner, I got the whole room to myself.

Mandira had to go to her own quarters. 'I'll be back in the morning to take you to see CJ.'

The silence fell like darkness on the room.

What was I doing?

I've been waiting in the holding cell for this CJ for three hours now. I'm starting to dislike him already.

I'd only just managed to fall asleep on top of a leather bench using my coat as a duvet when Mandira came to bring me breakfast: porridge made from oats and water – gross.

Mr Withers was with her. He nodded at me.

'He'll be here soon,' Mandira said before leaving.

For the first hour I sat and marvelled at the London skyline bathed in the morning sun. Then boredom set in. There is nothing to do in here. There's no internet and no telly and no books. I've got my phone but it's low on battery so I turned it off. Besides, I bet Mum and Dad are calling me like crazy and I can't talk to them right now. Hearing their voices would only make me run out of here faster than the speed of light. I don't want to change my mind. Or I don't think I do.

I've been trying to distract myself by making up an alternate reality in my head. If there had never been an alien invasion, what would I be doing right now? I'd probably be enjoying the last days of freedom before school started with Matilda and Anita. We'd maybe walk the foot tunnel underneath the Thames over to Greenwich and get some ice cream. Then we'd see a movie, and after that we'd go shopping.

Sitting in a room alone made it easy for Caesar to come back into my mind. Where did he go to school? Why hadn't

I ever seen him around? What would I say to him if I ever saw him again? If things were normal, would we go out?

I can hear voices outside my cell. I can hear Mandira. She's talking to men whose voices I don't recognise. Oh God, what have I got myself into?

8

The door slammed. I looked up from my diary. In walked Mandira and a broad and slightly dishevelled man dressed in a khaki shirt and a camouflage jacket.

The man's stubbled face contorted in horror. 'You've got to be kidding me, Mandira! She's a girl!'

Mandira glared at him, her eyes narrowing and turning into fierce slivers. 'Jesus, CJ,' she hissed through clenched teeth. 'What does that matter?'

'What does that matter?' he growled back, towering over Mandira, looking like a big tree in his forest-green coat. 'Do you realise the enormity of the task, Mandira? Do you?'

Mandira seemed to shrink. 'She's the best candidate we've got, CJ.'

'Well, she's not good enough.'

'Come on, CJ.'

'Show me someone else. Someone other than Little Red Riding Hood over there. What? Was her granny not available?'

'There is no one else,' Mandira said, looking up at CJ, her eyes glistening with moisture. 'This is the *only* candidate.'

'Then we'll just wait until we find someone else.'

Mandira's voice was breaking. 'No one else is willing to do this, CJ.'

I tried to weigh in. 'I can do this,' I said, surprised by the conviction tearing through my voice. I wasn't at all sure if I *could* do this. But I resented the fact that this guy just assumed I couldn't because I was a girl. 'Really, I can.'

CJ ignored me. 'Someone will come forward. Give it time.'

Mandira suddenly snapped. 'Time! Time!' she shouted. 'We don't have the luxury of time. We might all be dead tomorrow! My Anita doesn't have TIME! Your Katie doesn't have TIME. If you don't use her, CJ, I'm out. And I won't be the only one. I'll take the rest of the group with me. People are getting tired, CJ. They're starting to wonder if you're all talk and no action.'

CJ lowered his bushy eyebrows and glared at Mandira. 'You wouldn't.'

Mandira stared right back at him. 'Try me,' she hissed.

He stroked his chin. Mandira didn't blink. 'Fine,' he said and rolled his eyes.

He turned to me. 'Come on then, Little Red Riding Hood. Let me give you the grand tour while I tell you a little bit about the Big Bad Wolf.'

I looked at Mandira. I so did not want to go anywhere with this guy.

'I'll come too,' she said, her face all stiff and her eyes hard. I could see she was a woman on a mission. A mission to save her daughter.

We walked down the black wooden staircase. I'd been to the Tate Modern quite a few times. Mum insisted on dragging the whole family to an art exhibition every couple of months. Dad hated it as much as the rest of us, but when Andrew and I complained he'd tell us off. 'The youth of today,' he'd moan. 'You're so uncouth. So uncultured.'

But it wasn't all bad. In fact the Tate Modern was usually the most interesting gallery out of all of them. Once they were exhibiting a cow that had been pickled in some juice or something and then cut in half so you could see all its intestines and stuff. That was pretty cool.

'They're ruthless, you know,' CJ said to me. 'The visitors.'

Mandira cleared her throat in anger.

CJ lifted up his hands and smirked. 'Just saying.'

'So this is the arsenal,' said Mandira, pointing towards a closed door to one of the exhibition halls.

We walked down another staircase.

'And these are our living quarters.' This time the door was open. The floor was covered with clothes, sleeping bags, cups and plates. A couple of people were sitting on the floor, leaning against the wall. Above them hung a huge oil painting of bright splotches.

We continued down the stairs.

'The Collective meeting starts in five minutes,' CJ said, heading for yet another exhibition hall. 'We'll vote on whether to use the kid or not.'

I'd never told Mandira that I knew she wanted to use me as bait for the visitors and it was starting to annoy me the way she and this CJ just assumed that I was willing to go along with whatever they had in store for me. But what annoyed me more was CJ's lack of faith in me, so I said nothing. I didn't want to give him the slightest reason to doubt me, even though I had no faith in my Resistance abilities myself.

I followed Mandira and CJ into the hall where there were five people sitting around a big table in the middle of the room, waiting for the meeting to start. As we drew closer I realised the table wasn't really a table. It was a big canvas painting propped up on four wooden pillars. I recognised the piece, which had rows of different-coloured spots on a white background. The artist who painted it was apparently really famous. Mum had taken us to see it once, and as we stood there looking at it Dad had said really loudly that some dots on a canvas that he could easily have painted himself was as much art as the mix of scrawl and drool he'd helped Emma produce earlier that morning. Mum had got really embarrassed, shooting people around us apologetic glances and saying that her husband considered his mother's paint-by-number paintings to be art and that the piece was clearly very accomplished and multi-layered ... or something like that.

'Aren't you not supposed to touch the art?' I said, looking at CJ.

CJ gave a snort. 'This useless junk?' he said and plonked himself down on a chair by the makeshift table and made a show of slamming his cup of coffee he'd grabbed by the entrance on to the canvas. The hot, brown beverage spilled over the sides, creating an additional ring on the painting. 'During a war like this you come to see what matters. Art doesn't matter. Why do you think we chose Tate Modern as our HQ? The enemy might bomb the water supplies or the military bases. But an art gallery!

That would be a total waste of ammunition. No one would suspect that an important operation was taking place inside these walls. Nothing important has taken place inside these walls since the building stopped being a power station.'

Mandira sat down next to CJ. I took a seat beside her. As people started drifting into the room Mandira explained to me that every division of the People's Resistance Against the Alien Occupation – and there were many, all over the country, all over the world – elected a central committee called the Collective that organised and coordinated all the operations and handled communications with each other. Soon, every chair around the table was occupied except for one.

'Close the door behind you, Holly,' CJ ordered as a short and rather round woman who looked a few years older than Mum, with long, greying hair and friendly eyes, entered the room.

'What about Ethan?' said a man sitting opposite me, dressed in a checked shirt tucked into surprisingly high-waisted jeans (Matilda would not have approved). 'He's not here yet.'

'He's out,' CJ said without looking up from a pile of notes he was leafing through.

'Out? Out on patrol?'

'Permanently out. I fired him.'

'Fired him?'

'Yes, fired him.' CJ didn't look up from his papers. 'He was weak. Unreliable. A loose cannon. Would have got us into trouble eventually. If you can't stand the heat, get out of the kitchen.'

A low murmur ran through the room like a soft and slightly hesitant gust of wind.

'You can't just fire anybody who doesn't agree with you, CJ,' said the jeans-up-to-his-nipples guy. 'This is a voluntary organisation. There is no hiring or firing. Besides, there is a democratic process in place that should be followed in cases like—'

'Spare me your technocratic, bleeding-heart, holier-than-thou, liberal drivel, Jeremy. This isn't your law practice.'

'But he wasn't even invited to appear before the Collective to state his case.'

'This is war. We haven't got time for this bullshit. In times like these, caution is error. To hesitate is to lose.'

'But we agreed to—'

'I did what had to be done. You elected me as your leader. If you want to evoke a debate on that, that's fine by me. Personally, I'd rather talk about more important stuff. Like how we might finally be in a position to get Operation Alpha off the ground.'

All of a sudden everyone's eyes were on me. My cheeks started to burn. Some of the eyes conveyed the same hope I'd seen in Mandira's face when we'd met outside my house the night before. Others imparted curiosity and yet others the same crumpled disbelief that made CJ frown every time he looked at me.

'Mandira here has stumbled upon a volunteer,' CJ said with a wave of his hand that narrowly escaped Mandira's head. 'Meet Little Red Riding Hood.'

There was silence.

CJ rolled his eyes. 'I know, I know. She's obviously not the ideal candidate. I hesitate to use her. I'd rather wait and try to find someone more suitable. But Mandira's adamant that she'll do. So I think we should just vote on it.'

I couldn't take it any more. I couldn't stand people talking about me as if I weren't there. I raised my hand. 'Excuse me.'

CJ turned to me with an expression of total disinterest, like my input was an unwelcome disturbance. 'Yes,' he grunted.

'Erm ...' The words got caught in my throat. 'Erm ... I ...'

'Spit it out.'

'Erm ... don't you think you should tell me what you want me to do before you start voting? I might not want to—'

'The less you know, the better.'

The muscles in my arms started to twitch and I crossed my hands over my chest as I visualised myself punching the guy in the face. 'In that case, I won't do it.'

'Fine by me.'

'CJ!' Mandira hissed. 'Don't be such a jerk.'

Mandira grabbed my shoulder, her desperation squeezing my flesh and making my whole arm hurt. 'Please, Amy. Don't listen to him. I'll tell you what we need you to do. We need you to be a ...' She paused. 'We need you to be a messenger. That's all. A messenger. We have a contact on the inside of one of the alien vessels. We need to get a message to him. It's a very important message. It could give us our lives back. It could free the kids they've taken. It could free Anita.'

Hearing it said out loud made reality start to sink in. I'd known that the mission involved having to be taken by the visitors, but until now it hadn't seemed real. It felt as if my organs were turning into ice one by one. What had I been thinking? I wasn't Resistance material. I was just a normal girl of average weight, average height, average intelligence and way-below-average physical strength, if my PE reports were anything to go by.

'It could free your brother.' Mandira's face was so tense it could have been made of glass and her wide eyes looked like two dark, dangerous holes in a frozen lake. It felt as if I were drowning in her stare. I tried to loosen my shoulder but Mandira wouldn't let go.

'Sweetie,' said Holly, the woman with the kind eyes who was sitting next to Jeremy, the guy in the high-waisted jeans. 'Sweetie, you can trust us. We wouldn't send you on this mission if we didn't think it was safe. If we didn't think you could do it.' Although her eyes still looked kind, they had a sudden empty intensity to them which reminded me of the glare of snakes I'd recently seen in a David Attenborough documentary.

I ran my eyes across the room. All of a sudden everyone looked like a hostile animal from a wildlife programme. Some stared at me like hungry lions. Others appeared to flash me a set of newly acquired fangs. A man wearing a grey, zipped hoodie and nothing underneath leaned on to the table and gave a wet snort like a bull about to charge. Then I realised it. The raw, animalistic tension in their faces that bordered on aggression; it was loss. They'd all lost someone. To the aliens. They were all here because they knew someone who'd been a victim of the visitors.

'Sweetie,' Holly continued, 'you don't have to worry. We have your best interests at heart.'

The statement felt like a python around my neck. I wanted to run out of there. Run all the way back home. These people didn't have my interests at heart. They didn't care about me. They'd only just met me. They just wanted to use me in a desperate, and probably futile, attempt to get their loved ones back.

All of a sudden I hated them. I hated all of them, their piercing eyes, their grovelling faces. I missed Mum and Dad. I missed Emma. I missed Andrew. I missed the people I knew would always, no matter what, really and truly have my best interests at heart.

'Girlie,' CJ said with a nonchalant toss of his head. His narrow ponytail, pulling together the thin strands of hair that grew on the sides of his head, emphasising the lack of hair on the top, swung over his shoulder. 'If you don't want to do it, you don't want to do it. Personally, I'm reluctant to even consider you as a candidate. We only get one shot at this and no offence but I don't want to be relying on a flaky teenage girl for this crucial mission. The fact of the matter is this: it's going to be tough. It's highly likely to fail. And if it fails, you will be killed.'

A groan of displeasure spread from one person to the next around the table.

'Come on, people. You know this as well as I do. That's the reality of things. This is the reality of the world we live in now.'

I kind of felt like bursting out laughing. Moments earlier I'd wanted nothing more than to punch CJ in the face. But now, out of all the nice, civilised, polite people around the table, I liked him the most. I realised he was the only one being himself. That self might have been a crude, pompous, arrogant brute. But he was honest. He wasn't pretending that he cared about me or believed in me. He was just doing his job, he was just trying to

119

achieve a goal, and he made no apologies about the fact that I was nothing more to him than an instrument to be used to that end.

To my surprise, instead of feeling used or exploited, the realisation made me feel empowered. I'd been given the cold, hard facts and now the decision was mine.

'I'll do it,' I said, leaning forward and giving CJ a determined nod past Mandira, who finally let go of my shoulder.

They might have needed me. But I also needed them if I was to stand any chance of having a normal life; a future.

'All in favour of entrusting Little Red Riding Hood here with Operation Alpha, raise their hands.'

My fate was sealed right there, right then.

Oh, God. I hadn't realised they'd want to do this right away. I kind of thought I'd have a few days to mull things over, maybe even to change my mind. But everything has been set into motion.

It's almost completely dark outside and Mandira and CJ are waiting for me downstairs. I told them I had to pack. I don't know how long I can put this off for. It doesn't take very long to throw a toothbrush and a diary into a backpack and zip it closed.

There's someone at the door. I bet it's Mandira. I can't seem to shake her. It's as if she's glued to my side; she hardly ever takes her eyes off me. I think she's afraid that I won't go through with it. That I'll make a run for it. I probably should.

9

We were sitting around the makeshift table in the meeting room. The whole Collective was there to see me off. They were saying all these reassuring things while not looking directly at me.

'Don't worry, this will be easy.'

'Yes, you'll be back in no time.'

'Maybe by then things will be back to normal.'

The Resistance explained they would give me a small parcel that I was to carry on me at all times. I was to go home and simply wait for the visitors to take me. They said they had it on good authority that the teenagers they were abducting were kept as prisoners on the various vessels that hovered above all major cities on the planet – and many of the minor ones. The Resistance's contact was positioned on the vessel above East London. That was why it was up to the East London Regiment to find a local volunteer. Once I was up there, their contact would find me and collect the parcel.

But suddenly I realised something. I told them about Andrew and Matilda. That as soon as the visitors had found them and dragged them from their hiding places, they'd left the flat as if they hadn't even thought to look for anyone else; to look for me.

'Then it won't work,' Jeremy said as he hoisted up his trousers even further.

CJ didn't seem that rattled. 'Why not?'

'They got what they came for. They won't be back.'

'I don't get it.'

Jeremy pushed his glasses, which had slipped down to the tip of his nose, up so that the frame was buried in his monobrow. 'They're being quite thorough. They seem to know how many teenagers of the right age there are in each and every house. In every flat, in every building. It's almost as if they know whom they are looking for. Once they've got their number, they leave. But they clearly don't know whether they've snatched the right kid or not since they took Amy's friend instead of her without realising it. They think they got what they came for. They won't be back for her.'

CJ stroked his chin. 'I see what you mean.'

I cleared my throat. 'I might have an idea.'

It took a while to convince CJ, but he finally gave in to pressure from the others. My plan was this: if the visitors had an accurate record of how many teenagers there were in every household and they were determined to get them all, I knew of a place they wouldn't have been able to cross off their list yet. Matilda's house. I could go to Matilda's house and pretend that I was her.

We travelled to Matilda's house on Boris bikes, taking the Tube tunnels to Canary Wharf and then the footpaths by the canals. When we passed South Quay station I held back my tears. We were so close to my house. I wanted to go home. I wanted to go home to Mum and Dad and Emma and Andrew.

Then I remembered there would be no Andrew there. I had to keep going.

We cycled without speaking the whole way. We hid our bikes on the tracks and ran as fast as we could to Matilda's.

Her house wasn't far. She lived in one of the big, old apartment buildings next to the station. We rang the bell. Her mum buzzed us in and we made our way up to the first floor.

'Welcome,' Matilda's mum said, so unfazed by our visit that it was as if she'd been expecting us. 'Come in, come in – don't be shy.'

I could hear some sort of humming coming from the living room.

'Come and join us in a prayer; we're just getting started.' She didn't even ask why we were there.

'I was wondering if we could stay in Matilda's room for a bit,' I said, following her along the corridor.

In a circle on the floor sat a bunch of people dressed in blue jeans and white T-shirts. The women wore headscarves that reminded me of women in old black-and-white photos. The men all seemed to be growing beards. They were chanting. All the furniture had been pushed up against the walls. A little girl, she couldn't have been more than five, lay curled up on the coffee table with her arm wrapped around a porcelain doll. It was Matilda's. On the balcony stood a man in a white priest-like gown with his arms stretched out, shouting into the night.

'Sure, honey. Everyone is welcome here. I'll get you guys set up.'

Matilda never talked much about her mum and she almost never invited me over to her flat. Her mum used to drink a lot. But then she found God, or some version of God, and she stopped.

'How's Matilda?' asked her mum as she gave us some blankets and escorted us into Matilda's room.

I stopped in my tracks. I wished the floor would open up beneath my feet and swallow me whole. She didn't know. We hadn't been able to reach her. Just after the visit from the aliens there'd been another blackout. And when the electricity came back on Mum had tried to call her but there'd been no answer.

'I'm … I'm sorry … I'm so, so sorry …' I mumbled, not able to take my eyes off my feet. 'She's gone.'

'Gone?' Matilda's mum repeated after me, her soft blue eyes as clear and unsuspecting as a newborn's.

'Taken.' My voice cracked. 'She was taken. By the visitors.'

'Oh, how wonderful!'

I was sure I'd misheard, but then she ran shrieking out into the hallway. 'Great news, everyone, great news! Matilda's been taken! Matilda's been received!'

There was cheering in the living room.

Mandira's face contorted in horror.

CJ gave a loud snort of amusement. 'Weirdos,' he said and unfolded his blanket, placed it on the floor, kicked off his shoes and lay down.

When Matilda's mum returned Mandira's face had turned red with white splotches; it resembled a slice of pepperoni.

'Why? Why would you say that, Shannon?' she snarled at Matilda's mum. 'Why would you say that it's wonderful?'

'Being one of the chosen ones is a privilege,' Shannon said in a voice that was either robotic or angelic, I couldn't decide. 'It's a great honour to be among the few our Lord Saviour has chosen to settle the rest of the universe.'

CJ was trying not to laugh. 'This just gets better and better.'

'We'd realised long before the prime minister's TV appearance that the visitors had a special role for our youngsters. We were trying to convince them to take the rest of us as well. We tried presenting them with gifts. We have an altar on the balcony, you know. We tried offering them food, artwork, things like that. We tried offering Matilda to them, but she left for Amy's before they came for her.' Shannon smiled at Mandira. 'You know how teenage girls get. They need their friends. It's all about their BFFs.'

Mandira just stood there, gaping.

So that was the reason Matilda had risked her life getting to my house. Her mum and her strange friends had tried handing her over to the visitors! Her mum actually wanted the aliens to take her.

Shannon suddenly turned to me. 'You're welcome to use our altar, Amy. You're welcome to give yourself to Him on the balcony.'

CJ fought a fresh wave of laughter. 'She might just take you up on that,' he said and winked at me.

I couldn't think of anything to say – this was too weird – so I just smiled politely.

I was given Matilda's bed, but I couldn't sleep, partly because of CJ's snoring, partly because of all the questions bouncing around in my head like the little balls on the National Lottery. What would happen? Should I really do this? Could I really do this? And the big one: Was I going to live to see another day?

126

Wednesday 31 August

The house is quiet. The prayer group finally stopped their chanting in the early hours of the morning. Mandira and CJ are still asleep.

I just realised the electricity was on when Matilda's old alarm clock started flashing 00:00 in bright red digits. I jumped out of bed and plugged in my phone. I need it to have some charge when they come for me.

I've downloaded a best-of album of The Smiths. I love The Smiths. Dad used to listen to them all the time. Usually, I don't like anything that Dad listens to. But The Smiths are awesome. I introduced them to Matilda and Anita and sometimes, after school, we'd go to my house and play them on Mum and Dad's fancy stereo and sing along to their songs so loudly that Andrew would come bursting out of his room like an angry tornado saying that we sounded like donkeys during the mating season and telling us to shut up.

My favourite song is 'There Is a Light That Never Goes Out'. I love the lyrics. They tell the story of a person – I feel it's a man – who is driving in a car with someone he is so madly in love with that if a double-decker bus were to crash into them and kill them he would be happy as at least he got to die by his lover's side. Nothing can crush love. It's eternal. It's a light that never goes out.

I'm going to listen to the song when they come for me. If it hurts I will try my best to immerse myself in the soft sound of the music so I won't feel it as bad. And when Morrissey chants, 'There is a light that never goes out,' I will be swallowed up by darkness.

10

I was outside on the balcony. Mandira had pretty much ordered me to go and sit on the altar. The altar was basically Matilda's mum's old kitchen table, covered with an embroidered tablecloth and a whole bunch of statues. There was one of Jesus, one of Buddha and one of an elephant-headed man with four arms.

When I heard the balcony door open behind me I assumed it was Mandira; she was always checking on me to see if 'they'd come yet', as if it would go unnoticed.

'Take me with you,' a man's voice shouted. I glanced over my shoulder to see one of the members of the prayer group rushing towards me. He jumped up on to the altar and wrapped his fingers around my neck. 'Take me with you or I'll kill you.'

I couldn't breathe.

'Take me with you. Take me with you!'

It felt like a gradual slowing of time until CJ came bursting out on to the balcony. He grabbed the man by the shoulders and threw him against the railing.

'If you ever touch her again, I'll smash your head in.'

The man scurried back inside like a defeated animal.

'You okay?' CJ asked.

'I'm fine,' I lied.

'Are you sure you want to go through with this, Amy?'

'Yes,' I lied again.

'Fine, I'll leave you to it,' he said and went back inside, leaving me alone at a moment when I craved company more than anything – even his.

I felt my jeans pocket. The parcel I was meant to deliver for the Resistance was still there. It was the size of a matchbox and made of steel. It looked so unassuming – not like something you'd risk your life for.

A short while later Matilda's mum, Shannon, joined me on the balcony. Her beautiful, long, blonde hair hung over her shoulder in a plait. She looked so much like Matilda it was eerie.

She sat down on the altar and handed me a cup of hot cocoa.

'What are you always scribbling in your notebook, pet?'

'It's a diary.'

She got up. 'I'll be right back.'

She returned with a book in her hand.

'This is for you.'

I bit my lip. I couldn't even say thank you. I managed not to cry until she'd gone back inside. No sooner had the balcony door closed than the tears started pouring down my face. How cruel.

'A diary, just like yours,' she'd said.

The book was *The Diary of Anne Frank*. *The Diary of Anne Frank*! Did she not know how it ended? Did she not know what happened to Anne?

I felt my pocket again. I was so worried I'd lose the little steel box. No one had wanted to tell me what was inside it. I'd tried to open it, but I didn't know how to; it appeared to be welded shut.

It was so small it couldn't contain much more than a piece of jewellery. A ring perhaps? But what would the visitors need a ring for? This wasn't some stupid fantasy like *The Lord of the Rings* – this was reality. Maybe it held a piece of some precious metal the visitors needed and could only be found on Earth. Or a mineral, like a diamond. Then a thought struck me. Was I being sent on a suicide mission? Was I carrying some sort of bomb that would blow up all the aliens – along with myself? Or was it a chemical weapon – a disease that would wipe them all out?

I went over the instruction the Resistance had given me in my head. *Find the Well, wait, Rudolf will come …*

Why was I doing this? Why was I risking my life on a mission I didn't even understand the purpose of? I should just leave. Get up and go back home.

But then my eyes accidentally landed on *The Diary of Anne Frank*, a book about a girl – just a regular girl like me or Matilda or Anita – who spent years hiding away in a few small rooms with her family and then died a horrible death, and I realised something. Something big.

It wasn't as simple as just changing my mind and going back home.

When I'd left home I'd told myself I was leaving for Mum and Dad and Emma. I was taking myself out of the equation so I wouldn't be putting them at risk and splitting up the family. But that wasn't the only reason.

The truth was I was sick of being afraid. And the problem wasn't only the visitors. I'd spent endless energy on worrying about what people like Courtney and Louisa thought of me, on worrying about what to say if I went to a party, what excuse to come up with to get out of going to one. I'd spent endless energy on worrying about not being some imagined right version of myself.

And then the siege started and I understood something: we only get this one life. Just the one. It was up to me to do something with it. In the face of death I got a wake-up call. I didn't want to spend my life hiding away. Not from reality behind a computer screen, not inside my bedroom from some white-faced creeps. A life of hiding was no life at all.

I could have waited for someone else to volunteer to work with the Resistance, someone stronger and braver than I was. But what if no one came forward?

I couldn't just get up and leave. Go home like a scared little dog. I didn't have a choice. Not really. Not if I wanted to have a shot at a normal life – at any life at all. I had to do this.

Friday 2 September

My hands are shaking. My fingers are stiff from the cold on the balcony. But I have to keep on writing. I think this might be the end of the road.

The air-raid sirens have been sounding for almost half an hour. All the people from the prayer group are pushed up against the living-room window, staring at me. The little girl is there, still holding Matilda's porcelain doll. It's petty of me, I know, but I really resent her right now. I resent her for being safe.

Mandira keeps howling through the window, 'Do you see them?' knowing full well that she has the same view as I do. CJ keeps shouting at her to calm down.

I don't need this. I wish they would shut up.

Last night I was reading *The Diary of Anne Frank* when I came upon a passage that made my heart stop. The words were like a speed bump on the page that I didn't see coming: 'I want to go on living even after my death.' I could hardly breathe.

I once visited a museum in Potsdam, Germany, that used to be a prison. Dad is obsessed with war and every summer he manages to drag us on holiday to a place where something horrible has happened. The prison was a detention centre run by the Soviets when Germany was divided into East and West after the Second World War and many people were abused and tortured there. The most horrible prison cells were in the basement. They were tiny and dirty and still smelled of death. But the smell wasn't the worst thing about them. What made it all so real I wanted to throw up was the scratching on the walls. Prisoners had carved messages into the concrete. Some had written their names. Some had only managed their initials. There were poems and drawings and calendars where the dates had been marked off. A survivor, a woman who had been accused of being a spy, had been asked why she had written her name on the wall. I still remember her words: 'We thought we were going to disappear from the face of the Earth. We did it so someone would see it, that's why.'

All along I've been wondering why I'm doing this – why am I writing in this diary? This is the reason. The diary is my wall carving. It's my attempt at living even after my death. It's my attempt at saying, 'I was here.'

When all this is over maybe Mum and Dad and Emma can have it. I want them to know what happened to me if I don't return. I want them to remember me. As long as I am remembered I won't be completely gone.

I don't know how my story will end. Maybe it ends today. Maybe this is going to be my last entry and reading my diary will be like watching a TV show that's cancelled before the makers can conclude their work. Before they can tie up all the loose ends.

Oh, God, I think I can see them. They're coming. They're definitely coming. I'm putting my headphones on ...

There. I'm dancing on the inside. I just love The Smiths. I love Morrissey's voice. It sounds so tragic, yet so reassuring. The narrator of the song is begging his lover to take him out, take him anywhere, away from a place where he doesn't belong. He wants to have fun, meet people, get away from it all …

Shut up, Mandira! Shut the hell up! She's screaming so loudly I can hardly hear the music. She's shouting, 'They're coming! They're coming!'

I want to run inside. But I can't. I have to do this. I know I have to do this. I'm going to do this. Besides, Mandira probably wouldn't even open the balcony door for me.

Okay, the song, I need to focus on the song. They're driving in their car, and there is a double-decker bus, and he doesn't want to go home …

It's right above me now. The vessel. The alien vessel. I can see a door or a hole or something opening.

Is that … is that a metallic arm reaching down from it?

I don't know why I'm still writing, but I just can't seem to let go of the pen. It's slithering slowly, slowly down from the sky. The sunrise is reflected in its sleek surface.

There is a light and it never goes out
There is a light and it never goes out
There is a light and it never goes out

Goodbye, sunrise; goodbye, East London; goodbye, Mum and Dad and Emma; goodbye, Grandma Stacy and Grandpa Jack; goodbye, Granny Vera; goodbye, world; goodbye, life; goodb—

PART II

IN SPACE, THERE IS NO PLACE TO RUN

PROLOGUE

Day Three

I've never in my life been surrounded by more people and yet I've never felt more alone.

The air in here is thick and sticky, as if I'm breathing in glue. It smells of old sweat, like hot dogs fried in bucketloads of cumin. It's the smell of doom.

There are people as far as the eye can see. If I stand on tiptoes it's as if the top of people's heads form a wide desert and the heads are little grains of sand.

My eyes still hurt. The beam was so bright. It was like having lightning strike right into my eyes, like an explosion. And then he was dead.

Of course it's me who should be dead. I guess I am in a way. Dead, that is. We all are. Because of me it's only a question of how and how soon.

I can't face them. I can't face the people I was meant to save. Their future was in my hands. But I failed them. And now, this is our coffin. We've been buried alive and it's only a matter of time until the inevitable happens.

*

I see a spot of red in the crowd. I thought so. It's a T-shirt. An Arsenal football shirt. I know whose shirt it is. It's Simon's. But something's not right.

Oh, no. Oh, no. What have they done? Those bastards. What have they done?

11

Two days earlier

I woke up lying on top of a hard steel stretcher inside a bright metal-clad room. I was connected to wires and tubes and there was an IV buried in a vein in my arm. I was wearing nothing but my underwear. I felt strangely calm.

I tried to sit up but I couldn't. I looked down at my body. My arms and legs were strapped to the bed.

Next to me was another steel stretcher. I squeezed my eyes shut to chase away the fog that clouded my vision. What was that, lying on top of it? Was that …?

Oh my God! I started jerking at the straps that held me down.

'*Help*,' I tried shouting, but my throat was too dry to make a proper sound. *Help!*

On top of the stretcher lay a motionless body.

Help me!

It was a girl. She looked dead. She was definitely dead.

I pulled and pulled and pulled at the straps. They were made of metal and attached to the bed. It was no use.

Breathe, I told myself. *And think.*

And then it all came back to me: the balcony at Matilda's house; I remembered trying not to scream as the metallic arm cut through the cold morning sky. I remembered not being able to move as it approached, and I remembered staring into the blackness of the expanding mouth and sensing what I imagined to be cool, pepperminty breath on my skin. And then: nothing.

I craned my neck as far as I could. A fresh scream gathered in the pit of my stomach like a dark wave on a stormy night. This time there was no stopping the cry escaping my mouth.

'Nooo!'

Next to the girl was another stretcher. And then there was another one. And another and another. I threw my head to the other side. All I could see were rows and rows of steel stretchers and on top of each and every one lay a body.

This could only be one thing: a morgue.

'Let me out of here,' I shouted. Burning hot tears started streaming down my face. 'I'm not dead! I'm not dead!'

Someone appeared by my side. It was a visitor. A female visitor. She jabbed something in my arm. It was a loose wire which looked like it had fallen out of a vein just above my wrist. The tip of it was so tiny I could hardly feel the sting. A strange calm spread from my arm through my whole body. My head felt as if it were filling with cotton wool.

The woman was wearing the same black uniform the visitors I'd seen on Earth had been wearing. Her face didn't look much different from theirs either – pretty and creepy at the same time. The main thing that distinguished her from the visitors I'd seen before and made me assume she was a woman was her shoulder-length, perfectly straight, shiny hair (Matilda would have approved – and asked which hair straighteners she used).

'You'll be joining the others in a minute,' she said. 'You'll be taken to the Camp.'

I stared at the woman, not able to speak. She turned on her heel and disappeared from view.

I was just lying there, inspecting my surroundings with inappropriate calmness, probably because of the drugs or whatever was coming from the wire, when the girl on the stretcher next to me started coughing. Her chest arched upwards. She was gasping for breath.

'It's okay – you'll be okay,' I said to her, even though I knew that she probably wouldn't be; none of us would be okay.

She finally managed to gulp in some air. Her skin relaxed into its proper skin colour.

Suddenly the room filled with coughing and wheezing. Everywhere, boys and girls, just like me, were waking up. The relief made my eyes water. I wasn't locked in a morgue after all. But something told me I might as well have been.

Day One

I'm calling this 'day one' because I have no idea what date it is. I have no idea how long I've been here for. How long was I lying unconscious on the cold steel stretcher? Hours? Days? Weeks?

Technically I don't know where I am either, but I'm assuming I'm on board a visitor spaceship, somewhere not too far from planet Earth.

What I've learned so far is this:

- You can be surrounded by people but still be totally alone.
- The word 'camp' has many meanings, one of which is so horrendous it stretches way beyond the reach of the imagination.
- Cruelty is not a strong enough word to describe what goes on in here.

I'm trying not to get upset about it. I'm trying not to panic. I need to focus on my mission.

I'm doing what the Resistance told me to do. I'm looking for a place called the Well. There I will be met by someone called Rudolf. I've made an X-shaped tear in the left sleeve of my jumper so he'll know that I'm me. That I'm from the Resistance back on Earth.

I put the steel box inside my bra. It feels more discreet than my pocket.

When I asked CJ what was inside it, he refused to tell me. 'It contains the key to peace,' he'd said, not looking me in the eye. 'That's all you need to know.'

I threatened to pull out of the mission if he didn't tell me more, but he just shrugged his shoulders like he didn't care. I think he knew I was bluffing. He knew I'd already decided to do it.

I still have my doubts about the mission, though. But there is nothing I can do about them now. I'm here. And I couldn't go anywhere even if I wanted to.

12

Once the coughing and the wheezing had died down in the vast morgue-like room I'd woken up in, the metal straps on my wrists and ankles clicked open.

The girl next to me wrapped her fingers around the bunch of steely looking threads that were sticking out of her arm and tugged at them as if she were plucking weeds from a flower bed.

I watched people climbing down from their metal beds and getting dressed. Our clothes and possessions lay in a pile next to each stretcher. I suddenly remembered the little box; my mission. I pulled the wires out of a vein in my arm. I ignored the stinging discomfort and jumped down from the bed. I grabbed my jeans. I felt the pockets. Relief shot through me. It was there. It was still there.

I put on my jeans and my yellow spotty T-shirt – the same clothes I'd been wearing when I left home. If this was the last outfit I'd ever wear, I could take comfort from the fact that Matilda would approve. She'd picked it out when Mum took the two of us shopping on her lunch break in the Canary Wharf shopping centre.

I rubbed my eyes. The room felt really bright. My head was beginning to hurt and I noticed a tingling sensation in my stomach as if I had an increasingly frustrated swarm of anxious bees buzzing around in there. The drugs or whatever they'd given me were wearing off.

I knelt down to squeeze my coat into my backpack. The floor seemed to vibrate ever so slightly. I imagined it was because of the engine – we were on a spaceship after all.

The first thing I noticed was the boots. They were black and gleamed like menace in a snake's eye. I looked up. The room was swarming with visitors dressed in black. They marched between the rows of stretchers with the cool demeanour and mindless determination of ants.

Before I could even get up, total chaos had descended. People started screaming. Some were crying. Those who tried to run were grabbed by a visitor and dragged back to their stretcher. Some just stared in shock, others – those who'd never seen a visitor before, I assumed – in hope. But I was well acquainted with the calm creatures in black. And I knew what kind of cruelty their pale, expressionless faces masked. I knew what they were capable of. There was no reason to feel remotely hopeful.

A woman's flat voice cut through the air. 'Please stand on the right side of your stretchers.' She sounded as casual as someone doing the announcements on the Tube. 'Anyone who does not comply will be eliminated.' The mundane tone of her voice might have been as blunt as an old kitchen knife, but the meaning of her words stung like a sharp weapon.

The crying fizzled out, turning into silent despair.

The visitors started to usher us into queues. The woman who'd spoken to me earlier was among them.

147

'Where are we?' I called out to her. 'What's going to happen to us?'

She ignored me. She appeared completely focused on the task of lining us up, her face betraying as much emotion as if her task had been to line the shelves of a supermarket with cans. As it turned out, herding us like cattle to the slaughter would have been a better simile.

A girl's voice rang out: 'Mum, Mum!'

Even though I knew what the visitors were capable of, I didn't see it coming.

'Mum, Mum! I want my mum!'

It could have been any of us; any of us could have lost it. But it was the girl who'd woken up on the stretcher next to mine who was the first to have a meltdown.

What started as a muffled cry quickly turned into full-blown screaming. She was standing in the queue a couple of metres in front of me and I saw her tumble to the floor.

The people next to her pretended not to notice as they shuffled away. I wondered whether I should go to her, try to calm her down. Maybe recite some of Mum's self-help quotations.

The girl's calls gradually turned into unintelligible screams.

A pair of visitors, walking side by side and perfectly in sync, started to approach her. She put one hand over her mouth. But she couldn't stop screaming. It looked as if she was trying to catch her own despair.

The visitors looked calm. They travelled at a leisurely pace. They didn't look menacing at all.

They stopped in front of her. They stood there for a few seconds, studying her.

One of the visitors put his hand into the holster on his belt. He took from it a glass sphere. He pointed it towards the girl. Not even then did I think to be worried. It lit up. From the sphere shot the sparkling red ray of light. It hit her in the chest.

The girl crumpled to the floor. She lay perfectly still on her back. *Maybe she's just asleep*, I thought, her body half-frozen, like Mum and Dad when the visitors came for Andrew. But then I noticed the dark spot on her T-shirt. Right above her heart. It spread peacefully across the white fabric – red, like a rose opening up from a bud. It was blood.

I held my breath. I couldn't move. They'd killed her. They just killed her.

While the visitor put the sphere back in its holster, the other one bent down and grabbed the girl's hair. Then they turned on their heels and walked back the same way, dragging the girl behind them as if she were nothing more than a bag of rubbish that needed to be taken out.

This had been a mistake. I should never have left home. I should never have contacted the Resistance. I didn't want to die. No one should die at fourteen.

The girl in front of me in the queue was wearing pyjamas. Her only possession was a tattered teddy bear which she held tightly to her chest.

I suddenly wondered if I had a photo of Mum and Dad and Andrew and Emma on my phone. I couldn't remember when I'd last taken a photo of my family.

The queue started moving. We were led out of the morgue-like room. No one dared to protest. No one dared to even make a sound.

I had no idea what to expect when I stepped out of the room. What greeted us was some sort of hard nothingness. It was a corridor made of chrome-coloured steel. There were no screws in the walls, no skirting boards down by the floor and no mouldings by the ceiling. All corners were rounded. I felt as if I were taking a walk in one of the minimalistic, Scandinavian-design chrome bowls Mum liked so much that appeared to have no function other than to stand empty on every surface in our living room.

The air smelled of absolutely nothing. The silence had an exaggerated nothingness to it.

Then we turned the corner. It was another corridor but this one was swarming with people – visitors. They were walking around, neither fast nor slow, with quiet dignity, like pale ghosts floating numbly through the air, their black overalls shining with unworldly perfection. Some were walking alone, some in groups, but everyone just looked straight ahead without even glancing our way. It felt as if I'd just stepped on to a busy but strangely silent high street without any shops.

We walked along identical maze-like corridors for what felt like for ever. The queue was held in line by a horde of visitors with flat expressions. Every time anyone showed signs of slowing down, a visitor appeared beside them, towering over them with indifferent menace.

It all felt so unreal, as if this couldn't really be happening to me – as if I were floating above reality, observing it from a distance. I watched the people in the queue put one foot in front of the other, their bodies stiff with fear, as if this were just a movie or even a dream – when you're dreaming you're there without really being there.

I squeezed my palms into fists. I had to clear my head. I had to focus. I had a job to do.

I was trying to imagine where they were taking us in an effort to prepare myself for whatever would come next when we suddenly came to a halt. We were there. We'd reached the Camp.

Nothing could have prepared me for what I saw.

They say that after a while you can get used to anything. Mum says it all the time, particularly to Andrew when he complains about the unbearable hardship that is his curfew, and sometimes to me when I tell her I can't bear another of her celebrity-inspired meals made from quinoa and kale, which are meant to eliminate wrinkles and turn her into Gwyneth Paltrow. But I'm starting to have doubts. I think whoever Mum is quoting is wrong. How can you ever get used to something like this?

The Camp. What can I say? When I think of the word 'camp', I think of summer camp – girls with impeccably shaped legs wearing shorts that are barely distinguishable from knickers, running giddily around in mud and then sitting down by a campfire to roast marshmallows. Or I think of a holiday camp – rows and rows of wobbly tents and smugly parked caravans and people wearing non-weather-appropriate attire, sheltering from the rain and trying to convince themselves that they're having fun.

But then there is the other type of camp. The type that you never think about because it's just too awful to comprehend.

13

A door opened in one of the steel walls. The queue started moving again. The girl with the teddy bear clutched to her chest was drawing away. But I couldn't move. It was as if my legs had turned into two concrete blocks.

A visitor grabbed my shoulder. I could feel how cold his skin was through my T-shirt. 'On with you,' he said as he pushed me forward with the heel of his palm.

I tumbled through the doorway.

It took me a few seconds to get my bearings. When I did, I couldn't believe what I was seeing. Seconds earlier I'd been in a place defined by odourless order and spotless steel walls. But suddenly everything had changed. Entering the Camp was like entering another world. But not only that, it was also like going back in time. I suddenly felt freezing cold. This was a place and time in history no human being ever wanted to revisit.

The Camp was crowded with people. This time not with visitors, but humans.

We'd studied the Second World War last year at school. I didn't do well in the final exam. I could never remember which battle was which: the Battle of El Alamein, the Battle for Brittany, the Battle of the Bulge (which sounded to me like something you read about in *Heat* magazine, involving eating less carbs and doing five thousand sit-ups a day). But what I never forgot was the photos. The photos of the concentration camps. The camps Hitler set up where millions of people were imprisoned and killed.

Everyone has seen the photos of the concentration camps. They're horrible. But the photos I was thinking of weren't the ones that made Anita cry during history class. They weren't the ones of the skulls and bones found in mass graves. Those were awful. But there were worse. Far worse. For me the most horrifying photos from the Second World War were the photos of the inmates in the concentration camps while they were still alive. Before they became skulls and bones in mass graves. I'll never forget the faces. Men. Women. Children. They all had the same expression. Their eyes looked kind of hard and soft at the same time. They were stony but still full of hope. There was cold determination in their hollow cheeks. Uncompromising pride in their clenched jaws and raised chins. They were cold and they were starving, but some managed to smile. But there was no hiding it. I always wondered whether they knew what was coming. Despite their brave faces, their desperate efforts to cling on to their humanity, to cling on to life, there it was. Fear. No, not just fear. Soul-destroying terror.

These faces were here. In the Camp. Not the same faces obviously, but the people in this cramped, foul-smelling space camp had the same expression as the people in the concentration camps during the Second World War.

I couldn't see the visitor who'd pushed me anywhere. In fact, I couldn't see any of the guards who'd escorted us to the Camp. With a swish the Camp door closed behind us.

I ran towards the door. But where the door had been there was only a steel wall.

What now? Were they just going to leave us here? Weren't they going to tell us anything about what was going to happen to us?

I scanned the crowd for the girl with the teddy bear, but I couldn't see her anywhere. The people from the queue were slowly melting into the Camp crowd, like drops of water into the sea.

'Wait!' I called out to no one in particular. 'Shouldn't we stick together?'

But they were gone.

I took a breath. *Come on, Amy, focus.* I started making my way through the crowd. As I squeezed myself past people who didn't pay me the slightest attention I noticed something. Their age. Everyone in the Camp was young. I remembered the prime minister's words, what he'd said on the telly before the visitors got the better of him: 'Anyone between the ages of fourteen and nineteen is in danger.'

That sounded about right. The Camp appeared to be some sort of prison for all the kids the visitors were snatching from Earth.

I tried to make eye contact with those around me, but it was as if people refused to meet each other's eyes in here. If someone accidentally glanced your way, they looked through you, not at you. In a way it felt a bit like being on the Tube. You were lost in the crowd. Just one of many. Nothing special.

How many people were locked up in the Camp? Thousands? Tens of thousands?

I was getting tired. Noticing two girls sitting on the floor, I decided to join them. Maybe they could tell me something about the Camp. Maybe they could tell me what was going on. Maybe they could help me find the Well.

'Excuse me,' I said as I sat down. Judging by their matching pyjamas they were sisters. 'Have you been here long?'

Neither of them answered.

I tried again. 'I just arrived so I don't really know my way around. Do you know of a place called the Well?'

They didn't look up.

I noticed they were holding hands. I felt a sting in my chest. It had to be nice to have someone like that. Not to be alone. I wished Andrew were here. I missed him. I missed his frown. I missed him obsessing about his hair. I missed shouting at him to turn down his music. I missed him never eating the strawberry chocolates in Mum's box of Quality Street that we sometimes sneaked into when she wasn't home because he knew they were my favourite, even though he liked them too.

I wondered if he was in here somewhere. I wished I could go and look for him. But I didn't have the time. I could feel the little steel box the Resistance had given me inside my bra; a hard, cold reminder – literally – of the mission I had to carry out. I had to find this Well.

156

I suddenly noticed I was starving. 'Where can I find food?' I asked the sisters without expecting an answer. They didn't disappoint. Silence.

Then I remembered the Mars bar the soldier had given me when I'd travelled with Mandira to the Tate Modern. I ripped off my backpack. I'd never wanted a chocolate bar more in my life. If the soldier had been there, I would have given him the biggest hug in the history of mankind.

I grabbed the bar from the bag. I was about to tear it open when someone shouted at me:

'Are you crazy? Put the chocolate away.'

But it was too late.

A guy in a bright-orange tracksuit, twice my size, came rushing towards me at the speed of a tiger. He grabbed my throat with one hand and started clutching at the chocolate bar with the other. I didn't know why but I didn't let go.

A girl, looking like a peacock with blue and green highlights in her hair, flew at me. She scratched at my face with long, purple nails as she too tried to prise the bar from my tightly clenched fist.

'Hey, she can't breathe!' It was the same voice as before; it was the guy who'd told me to put away the chocolate bar. 'Stop it.'

My attackers didn't pay him the slightest attention. A fist flew into my face.

'Stop it.'

The tiger guy finally noticed the peacock girl. As he realised he had competition, he let go of my throat and instead grabbed the girl by the hair. It turned out her multicoloured highlights were extensions. The extensions came loose. The tiger guy lost his balance. With his fists full of blue and green hair and an expression of horror on his face, he tumbled to his knees, landing on top of me.

The peacock girl chirped with delight. But her victory was far from being sealed. She reached out to snatch the bar from me, but as she did so her legs got tangled with mine and she fell, landing face down on her rival.

I gasped in pain. With the two of them on top of me, my ribcage was buckling under the pressure of their weight.

'Get off her!' the mystery voice called out.

I managed a peek from the bottom of this human pile. The voice belonged to someone wearing a big, red T-shirt. He stood hovering over the three of us as we rolled around, knotted together, in an awkward fist fight.

Despite his lack of success he wasn't giving up. 'Hey, look out,' he shouted. 'The Capos are coming.'

Suddenly, the burden on my chest lifted. Before I'd even managed to get to my feet the tiger guy and the peacock girl had disappeared into the jungle of humans.

I stood there, frozen in shock. What had just happened?

'I'd put it away if I were you.' It was the guy in red.

I was still holding the mangled chocolate bar. With fumbling hands I put it in my pocket.

The guy was wearing an Arsenal football shirt. His hair was red. Matilda would have deemed the shirt unfitting for his light-pink skin tone. 'Amy, you never wear red and pink together,' she'd once said while we were trying on clothes in Topshop and

I'd picked out a pink top and a red miniskirt. 'They go together like love and granny pants.'

The guy started to walk away.

'Wait!' I called out. I meant to say thank you but a question flew out of my mouth instead. 'What is a Capo?'

The guy looked me up and down. 'You're new here, aren't you?'

I didn't answer.

'You need to be more careful.'

'Why is everyone so ...?' I couldn't finish the sentence. A lump was forming in my throat. 'Why is everyone so mean in here? Why don't people look at you? Why does everyone just ignore you?' My eyes started to water.

The guy's cheeks turned red and he looked away. 'There, there. There's no need to ... you know ...'

His embarrassment almost made me laugh. 'Cry?' Funny how afraid guys seemed to be of anyone showing emotion. Andrew was the same. So was Dad. The poor guy looked so helpless I almost wanted to give him a hug. Instead I stretched out my hand. 'Hi, I'm Amy.'

He smiled with relief. 'Hi, I'm Simon,' he said and we shook hands. I'd finally made a friend in this cold, unfriendly prison.

We sat on the floor. Discreetly, I took out the chocolate, opened the wrapper and tore the bar in two. I gave one half to Simon.

'Thank you for saving me.'

He shrugged as he examined his piece. 'They would have let you go as soon as they'd got the chocolate from you.'

159

'Why? Why would they attack someone just for one lousy bar of chocolate? Don't they give you food in here?'

'We get food,' he said as he sniffed the chocolate. 'Oh God, it smells good.'

'Then what? Does it taste bad?'

'Worse.' He gently touched the chocolate with his tongue. 'It tastes of absolutely nothing.'

'Nothing? How can nothing be worse than bad?'

'You'll know after you've been here for a while.' He shoved the whole piece of chocolate into his mouth and closed his eyes as he chewed slowly, slowly. When he finally swallowed, he opened his eyes again. 'Thank you.'

A ripple went through the crowd. People were shuffling towards us, their movements as synchronised as leaves blowing in the wind. Screaming erupted in the distance. No one seemed to pay much attention.

'What's going on?' I couldn't see anything.

Simon's eyes appeared not to focus. I guessed he was still thinking about the chocolate. When he finally faced me, his expression had turned hard. 'This is why.' He sounded angry.

'Why what?'

'Why no one looks at you in here. Why people just keep to themselves.'

The shouting grew louder: 'Keep your hands off me, you white-faced freak.'

I stared at Simon. 'I don't understand.'

'Why bother making friends if they're gone the next day or the day after that or the day after that or the day after that—?'

160

'Or the day after that.' The screaming fizzled out. I sighed with relief. 'I got that part.' I tried to work out the right question to ask. 'But what I don't get is … what I don't get is …' I didn't even get what it was that I wasn't getting.

Simon bowed his head. He didn't seem too keen to talk about things. His red fringe fell across his eyes. He was shorter than me but I thought he looked about the same age.

He finally pushed back his fringe. 'The Red Stacks are out.'

'The Red Stacks?'

'There's a Collection in session. Every day the visitors come in here, grab a bunch of humans and take them away.'

'Where do they take them?'

'To the Selection Lab. They're put through some sort of tests or something. I don't know what the tests are for, but those who are taken never return to the Camp.'

I was starting to feel slightly nauseous again. 'If they don't return, how do you know where they're taken?'

'Because of the Capos.'

'The Capos?'

'Their official title is Camp Administration and Peacekeeping Officers. It's Capo for short. They're meant to maintain order within the Camp. Some of them assist in the Selection Lab. But what they really are …' Simon sucked in his lips as if he were trying to swallow them. But it was anger he was trying to swallow. 'They're really just plain old traitors,' he snapped. 'They're supposed to be one of us, they are humans after all, but instead they're working with the visitors. They're bloody collaborators.'

I noticed that smell again. The smell of old sweat and human misery.

'See those two guys over there?'

I could only see the back of their heads. They were tall, one was wearing a leather jacket, and they were standing opposite a girl half their size. She was clutching an empty water bottle.

'See the red band on their upper arm?'

'Yes.'

'That means they're Capos.'

The guy in the leather jacket snatched the water bottle from the girl. Then the two of them walked away laughing.

'Hey!' I didn't mean for my indignation to become audible – it just happened.

Simon pinched my arm. 'Don't. You'll get into trouble.'

'Why? Will they report me to the visitors?'

'They don't need to. They can make your life unbearable in so many other ways. They'd probably start by confiscating your possessions. Then they might pound on you just a little. The Capos are in charge of serving food, so they might let you starve for a few days …'

Enough said. It was only an empty water bottle after all. I didn't look at the girl. 'How do they decide who becomes a Capo?'

Simon shrugged his thin shoulders. His Arsenal shirt looked at least a size too big for him. 'Some are chosen by the Red Stacks. Some volunteer. The Capos are selected based on their capability to show brutality. So they're basically what we call bullies back home.'

162

Even though Simon telling me about Camp life was awful, I suddenly felt upbeat. The reason was simple: I wasn't alone any more. I had made a friend.

I noticed something warming on the palm of my hand. Damn. I'd totally forgotten about the rest of the chocolate bar. My stomach was rumbling. But it didn't matter. I reached out my arm.

'Here, you have it.'

Simon stared at the chocolate. His eyes were narrow and his mouth hung open slightly. I could see how much he wanted it. But then he shook his head. 'No,' he said. 'You should eat it. It might be the last thing to ever bring you pleasure.'

'We'll split it,' I said, and I wouldn't take no for an answer.

My mouth was stuffed full of sugary joy when a thought popped into my head. It was a long shot. There was no way it could be that easy. 'Do you know what the Well is?'

Simon swallowed. He raised his eyebrows. 'Yeah, of course.'

Day Two

I'm finally here. I'm finally where I'm meant to be. I found the Well.

It's this gigantic steel tank, many metres wide, reaching from floor to ceiling. It has taps all over and people keep turning up and drinking from the taps, which appear to have motion sensors. Most people just put their mouth under a tap but a few have containers they put the water in. Probably something they'd been holding when they were abducted. A toothbrush holder. An empty Coke can. I have a half empty bottle of water in my backpack. I'm realising that a thing with no value down on Earth can hold immense value in space.

So I'm just waiting. Waiting by the Well with Simon. Just as Mandira and CJ told me to. It's funny how the Resistance knew about the Well but didn't mention anything about it being inside a prison camp.

I'd been waiting for about an hour when something that sounded like a school bell started ringing. Everyone around me got to their feet and began walking in the same direction.

'What's going on?' I asked Simon.

'They're serving food.' He stood up. 'Shall we go?'

I couldn't leave my post. What if Rudolf turned up while I was gone? He might think I hadn't made it and the mission would be ruined.

People were starting to return with small bowls of what appeared to be some sort of porridge – really white porridge – which they ate with spoons shaped like tiny shovels.

'I can't. I can't go,' I said. 'I have to stay here.'

Simon squinted. 'Why can't you go?'

I tried to come up with a believable lie but nothing came to mind. 'I can't tell you.'

'Suit yourself, but I won't be able to pick up food for you. There's only one bowl per person.'

Simon returned with one bowl and two spoons.

'Here you go,' he said, handing me a spoon. 'You can have some of mine.'

'That's okay.'

'Take it. Before I change my mind.'

Although my stomach was happy to receive the food, it turns out Simon was right: the taste of nothing is in a strange way worse than a bad taste of something.

Simon told me that food is only served once a day in here. The porridge has the perfect nutritional balance to keep us going for that long.

When Simon got to the Camp it was almost empty. He's been here from the start. At first the people here tried to find out why they were being brought here. They tried to ask the visitors, but Simon said they almost never talk to humans. They made a couple of unsuccessful attempts to escape the Camp through the sewage system. But they didn't get very far – it turns out there really is no point escaping the Camp as you're still stuck inside a spaceship.

Nevertheless, I've been unable to get the sewage system out of my mind. Hearing about it made me want to hurl. Not because of Simon's description of the squishy texture of the human excrement that covered the drainage pipes they crawled through. The sewage system made my stomach turn because it made me realise something: there is no Plan B. If this Rudolf doesn't show up, that's it. I'm stuck here. We all are. Because in space, there is no place to run.

Where is Rudolf? Did I misunderstand the plan?

14

I was sitting on the floor up against the Well – Simon was taking a nap next to me – when a guy in a black T-shirt with a photo of The Killers on it staggered towards me holding a big bucket. He put the bucket on the floor under a tap and turned it on. The noise the water made when it hit the bottom was a wonderful break from the breathy silence. I listened to the crashing sound and imagined it was a drumbeat and I was listening to music on my phone (which had long before run out of battery). I rested my eyes on the T-shirt. I hadn't thought about him for at least half a day. I tried not to think about things that made me sad. I tried not to think about things that reminded me of home. Of how things used to be. But seeing the T-shirt made me lose my resolve. Andrew had a T-shirt just like that.

'Amy!'

For a second I thought it was all in my head. I was sure I'd started imagining things. I'd wanted to go and look for him but I had to stay by the Well.

'Amy!'

The T-shirt was approaching me.

Not for a minute did I think to look up, to take my eyes off the deliberately scruffy-looking band members to see who was wearing the T-shirt. Not for a minute did I think it could be the same T-shirt I'd once stolen from Andrew's room, an endeavour that ended in a shouting match and resulted in him buying a padlock and a chain for his wardrobe.

'Amy! Amy!' Someone grabbed my shoulders, lifting me to my feet.

'Andrew?' I'd thought I'd seen him here yesterday. I couldn't take another Andrew mirage, another disappointment. 'Andrew, is it really you?' I said, sounding like a character in a bad school play.

'Of course it's me,' he said, rolling his eyes and throwing his head back to get his overgrown fringe, hanging limp across his forehead, out of his eyes – there were clearly no hair products in space. 'Who else would it be?'

And then he did something he hadn't done since I was five and I'd fallen off my bike and fractured my wrist. He wrapped his arms around me and squeezed me so hard his heart tickled my cheek.

He smelled of home. For a second I thought I might cry. But I knew it would only make him uncomfortable and ruin the moment, so I restrained myself and buried my face in The Killers.

'I'm sorry,' he whispered into my hair.

I looked up at him. 'Sorry?'

His face was a bit paler than usual and I thought I could detect a light shade of grey underneath his eyes.

'I'm sorry they got you too.'

I loosened my grip on him. Should I say something? They hadn't got me. Not really. I wasn't like the rest of them. I wasn't like the rest of the people in the Camp. I wasn't a victim. It felt as if I was lying to him.

'We should have done it,' Andrew said as he let go of me. He put his hands in his pockets and scrunched up his nose in his I'm-Andrew-and-I'm-so-cool-that-I-can't-be-bothered expression, pretending there never was a hug. I went along with it.

'Done what?' I said, crossing my arms over my chest in an effort to mimic his coolness.

'We should have listened to Anita's mum. We should have listened to Mandira. At least that way we might have stood a chance.'

It just jumped out, like a feisty frog I was struggling to hold in my mouth. I couldn't help it.

'Andrew, I did it!' I lowered my voice. 'I went to Mandira,' I whispered. 'I'm working for the Resistance.'

'You're what?'

Just behind Andrew I noticed something speeding towards us. 'Shhh!' I whispered.

No sooner had my brain registered what my eyes could see than a voice I knew as well as my own ripped through the air. 'Oh my God! Amy!'

All of a sudden I was lying flat on the floor. I was laughing and shouting in pain at the same time.

'Careful! You're about to break my arm!'

Matilda was right on top of me. She'd jumped on me from a distance I'd thought impossible for anyone who wasn't a long jumper. She pinched my cheeks, shrieking deliriously, 'Oh my God! It's so great to see you.'

Then I heard a voice I'd feared I would never hear again. 'Hi, Amy.'

Ever since we became prisoners on our own planet I'd tried to remember when I'd seen her last. What we'd been doing. Where we'd gone. Was it when we went to Westfield to buy some neon tights? Or was it outside Haslam's?

Matilda rolled off me and I scrambled to my feet. 'Anita! Oh my God, Anita!' Her thick black hair wasn't as shiny as usual. 'I thought you might be dead.'

She flinched. I felt my cheeks go red. With our continued existence under threat it was probably insensitive to say the word out loud. Dead. Everyone in here was trying to ignore the precariousness of the situation. I sure was. The only thing you could do so as not to lose your mind was to fake some sort of normality. Establish a routine. Mine went like this: circle the Well twice in the morning; sit down and think about who would be the next character from *EastEnders* to get amnesia; do ten lunges and ten sit-ups; go over the plot of a movie, scene by scene, picturing the actors and their surroundings in my head; eat once a day; try to stay awake when everyone else lies down on the floor to sleep so as not to miss Rudolf. Acknowledging the possibility of death only messed up your routine.

Looking down at my yellow Converse, I decided that life was too short for wasting time on being embarrassed. 'It's so great to see you!'

Anita smiled. 'Did you ever manage to upgrade your hard drive?'

That was it! That was the last time I'd seen her. I'd dragged Anita along to PC World to buy a solid-state hard drive. I was going to install one for her as well if it worked.

I shook my head. I couldn't believe I'd forgotten. We'd gone to PC World and then we'd stopped at McDonald's and shared a large portion of fries. It's sad what you take for granted when things are fine.

'Nerds!' Matilda said, then turned to Andrew. 'How can a trendy guy like you have such a dork for a sister?' She howled with laughter at her own joke. Then she linked an arm in mine. 'I'm so happy you're here. These two lovebirds are driving me crazy.'

'Lovebirds?' I looked at Andrew. He was blushing. Anita stared at her toes.

'Let's go,' Matilda said and pulled at my arm. 'We've set up camp not far from here. Tom's waiting for us. Did I tell you Tom is here? It's really cosy, our little camp. Well, considering ... We've got a blanket and a pillow and some mugs and this lovely bucket so we only have to fetch water every few days – don't forget the bucket, Andrew – and I traded my watch for mascara, lipstick and tweezers so we should be able to do something about this washed-out face of yours.'

'Wait!' I said and jerked my arm loose.

Matilda stopped.

'I can't.'

'You can't?'

'Yeah, I ... I can't.'

'You can't as in you have other plans? You have other plans ...

inside this hellhole where nothing ever happens and no one has plans EVER?'

'Kind of.'

'And would you mind sharing those plans with the rest of us?'

I glanced quickly at Andrew. The movement was barely discernible, but he was shaking his head.

'I can't.'

'You can't?'

I couldn't look at her. If only I wasn't such a bad liar, I could have made something up. I just nodded my head sheepishly.

'All right then. Amy's travelled all the way up here from planet Earth but she has more important things to do than to hang out with her friends.'

She was offended. And confused. Of course she was. I would have been too.

'Let's go. I promised to pluck Chantelle's eyebrows. Those eyebrows won't pluck themselves, you know. And Andrew, I'll do yours as well. All men should pluck their eyebrows – like David Beckham does. We may be descended from gorillas but there's no need to look like them.'

'You mean apes,' Anita said.

'What?'

'You mean apes. We're not descended from gorillas. We're descended from apes.'

Matilda stared at Anita as if she were crowding her head with information as uninteresting as the colour swatch numbers of different shades of grey. 'Whatever.' She turned on her heel. 'Let's go.'

Anita proceeded to follow Matilda but stopped when Andrew said, 'I'm staying.'

I couldn't tell if Anita looked at him surprised or accusingly. Were they a *couple*?

'I want to talk to Amy.' He handed the water bucket to Anita.

She stood there looking as if she were about to split in two down the middle, not knowing which one to follow – Andrew or Matilda.

'You go with Matilda,' Andrew said. 'I'll be back in a bit.'

'See you later, Amy,' Anita said, rearranging the water bucket, resting it on her hip as if she were holding a baby.

I watched them walk away. They were out of sight, swallowed up by the crowd, but I could still hear them bickering.

'Give me the bucket,' Matilda snapped.

'Why?'

'You'll only drop it.'

'I'm not going to drop it.'

'Oh, as if you weren't going to drop the bowl with the celebratory jelly Amy made me on my last birthday.'

'That was an accident!'

'Exactly my point. Give me the bucket.'

For a brief moment I was back in East London; I was home.

Andrew grabbed my arm. 'Tell me everything.'

And I was back in the Camp.

Day Three

This was all a big mistake. What was I thinking? How did I ever believe I could possibly be of use to the Resistance? I'm not Resistance material.

In school we were told about how civilians joined underground movements to fight the Nazis during the Second World War. Like Sophie Scholl who distributed anti-war leaflets at her university in Munich. She was executed by guillotine for her actions, along with her brother.

These were seriously strong and brave people. I am neither of those things. I can hardly do a single push-up. And I still prefer to have my bedside light on when I go to sleep to fend off the dark.

I want to go home.

15

I told Andrew everything. I told him how I'd contacted Mandira, how I'd been to the headquarters of the Resistance, how I'd gone to Matilda's house so the visitors would take me. I showed him the steel box and told him about Rudolf.

I was mid-sentence when I was suddenly interrupted: 'There is a Resistance?'

Shit. I'd forgotten about Simon. He'd woken from his nap.

'You can't tell anyone!'

Simon put his hand on his chest. 'Cross my heart and hope to—'

'Who's that?' Andrew snapped. He looked Simon up and down with a disapproving frown. I knew why my brother appeared to take an instant dislike to Simon. It was because of his shirt. He loathed Arsenal. Andrew was a Tottenham man. Just like Dad, who'd lived in Tottenham when he first moved to the UK from the States and had supported the team ever since. Mum hated football. 'Do they have to play *every* weekend?' she'd cry when Dad and Andrew were watching a match on TV, as if they had some say in the Premier League's scheduling.

'Hi, I'm Simon,' he said with a smile. He seemed oblivious to Andrew's menacing glare. Men and their testosterone.

Andrew turned back to me, ignoring Simon. 'How is this meant to work exactly?'

'How is what meant to work?'

'This mission.'

I repeated the part about Rudolf.

'But what will it achieve?'

'What do you mean?'

'You hand over the steel box. Then what? Will the siege end? Will the visitors go back home? Will they be destroyed? What?'

'Erm … yes.'

'Yes, what? Will the aliens leave Earth?'

'I suppose so.'

'And what about us? Is someone coming to pick us up?'

'I'm not sure … I think … I think …' My head was starting to throb. The air felt thicker than usual. Suddenly, I couldn't see properly; it was as if everything were covered with grey mist. I peered at the people around me, a sea of people, grains of sand, a whole desert of them. The bigger the desert, the more insignificant the grains. I remembered the concentration camps in the Second World War. In our history textbook it said that eleven million people died in the camps. A rough number. That's what the lives of the people who'd been killed in the gas chambers, shot, starved to death or worked to death had been reduced to. A faceless number – and a rough one at that.

What were we to those down on Earth but a number? A drop in the ocean. A few grains of sand in a desert. Why would anyone save us? They were too busy saving those who hadn't been taken. They were too busy saving themselves.

The faces of people around me suddenly looked so thin. Their cheeks so hollow. And their eyes. Their eyes were dark, like empty sockets.

'No!' I heard myself shout.

Andrew jumped and hit his elbow on one of the taps on the Well. Some people looked up and glanced my way, their gaze detached and shrouded in embarrassment, as if I were just another person freaking out.

I wanted to shout at them: 'I'm not just having a plain old meltdown. I'm not just another grain of sand.' I'd seen quite a few since I got here, quite a few besides the girl who was killed by the guards in the morgue. Yesterday, a girl started banging her head against the tank of water that was the Well. No one had interfered. After a while she just stopped and walked away. And once I'd seen a boy collapse to the floor crying. But my breakdown wasn't like that. I wasn't screaming just for myself. Mine wasn't the only demise I was facing. Mine wasn't the only life I was responsible for. Humanity's future was in my hands. Their future was in my hands.

'Breathe,' Andrew said, grabbing me by the shoulders.

Simon quickly handed me my water bottle. 'It will be okay.'

'How?' I shouted at him. 'I have no idea what I'm doing. I'm not cut out for this. I'm no Sophie Scholl.'

'Who?'

'They should have chosen someone else. Someone strong. Someone brave. Not someone ordinary.'

'Amy, get yourself together,' Andrew mumbled. He seemed embarrassed, sounding like Dad trying to get Mum to calm down

177

during one of the many panic attacks she had whenever Grandma and Grandpa were expected for a visit.

But Simon wasn't rattled. 'It will be okay. We'll help you. You're not alone in this any more.'

I managed a deep breath.

Simon put his hand gently on my shoulder. 'I haven't seen you sleep at all since you got here. Why don't you have a little time out? You and your brother should go and catch up with your friends. I'll stay here and wait for this Rudolf guy to show up. We can take shifts.' Simon made an X-shaped tear in the left sleeve of his Arsenal T-shirt, using a pin he wore with the Arsenal logo. 'There. Now he knows who to talk to. Just give me the box and I'll keep watch.'

I tried to protest. But Andrew joined Team Simon. 'It's a great idea,' he said. He seemed to have forgiven Simon for wearing the wrong shirt.

Simon smiled. 'It's a plan then.' Something like hope twinkled in his eyes. Or was it pride? 'Come back in the morning and the next shift is yours.'

I handed him the steel box. Even though we'd only been friends for two days I trusted him completely. Andrew gave him a manly, bordering on Neanderthal-esque punch on the shoulder. Then we were off.

Andrew led me through the crowd to where they'd set up camp.

Matilda noticed me approaching. 'Oh, so the very busy Amy Sullivan has decided to grace us with her presence,' she said, turning back to the magazine she was reading. It was old – a summer special with the headline 'Fat Celebrity Beach Bodies' on the cover.

Tom was there. I smiled at him. I was glad he was alive.

'Hi,' he said.

'Don't talk to her,' Matilda hissed.

We both ignored her. 'Bart?' I said, unable to form a proper sentence around the question I wanted to ask.

Tom shook his head, looking down at the floor. 'We haven't seen him.'

'Maybe …' I said, trying to sound hopeful.

'Yeah, maybe …' Tom said, smiling unconvincingly with only one corner of his mouth.

Matilda dug her fingers into the magazine cover. 'I said, don't talk to her.'

'Oh, don't be like that,' Anita said. She was lying on the floor beside Matilda on a blanket beneath a piece of sheet they'd turned into a tent. It was held up by stacks of porridge bowls, using them as poles. Inside the tent I could see a couple of cups, some magazines, a book and some toiletries. It was very cosy, considering.

'Where did you get all this stuff?' I asked, ignoring Matilda's haughtiness.

'We traded for it,' Anita said, raising herself up to her elbows. 'I got a book, a cup and tweezers for Matilda for my iPhone. Andrew got the magazines for his wallet.'

I crawled into the tent and sat down beside Matilda. She slammed down her magazine.

'I know something's up!'

I glanced over at Andrew. He had sat down just outside the tent and was whittling a piece of wood with a kitchen knife. He shook his head.

Matilda wasn't giving up. 'You might as well tell me. I'm going to find out anyway.'

'Shit!' Andrew exclaimed and stuck his finger in his mouth.

'I told you to be careful with that,' Anita said, jumping to her feet. She grabbed a toilet roll they'd clearly nicked from one of the Camp toilets and started wrapping paper around Andrew's finger.

'What are you doing?' I asked once the drama had subsided – it turned out the kitchen knife was as sharp as a stick.

'I'm making a bow.'

'A bow? A bow as in a bow and arrows?'

'Yep.'

'Why?'

'Just because,' he said, returning to his carving. 'You never know.'

'You never know what? That you'll be selected for the Space Olympics archery team? That Robin Hood will call with a vacancy in his group of Merry Men?'

He ignored me.

Matilda started pestering me again. 'You have to tell me what's going on. We're meant to be best friends. Does that mean nothing to you?'

I grabbed one of the magazines and started reading about celebrities who'd performed the heroic deed of venturing out without make-up on. It got her off my back.

It felt good to take my mind off things. It felt good to be surrounded by friends. It felt good not to think about Rudolf. It felt good not thinking about becoming a grain of sand in a desert, a faceless number, one in eleven million.

Soon they started to dim the lights. It looked like sunset with the slightly wrong shade of orange tint to it. In space there was no difference between night and day but the visitors seemed to artificially create the passing of time with lights. I wondered if there was a difference between night and day on their planet or if they were doing it for our benefit only.

Where did they come from? They had to come from a planet of some sort, a planet so far away human telescopes couldn't spot it. Or maybe they weren't from anywhere. Maybe they were just drifters in space, living on board their spaceships, stealing teenagers from planets all over the universe to … to what? What did they want with us? What did they need us for? What were the basic needs of any organism? They needed food. Air. Water. Were we food to them? Like hyenas to a lion? Were we a source of water? Maybe they drank blood. Like vampires. Or, since the human body was sixty per cent water, maybe they intended to extract all the water from our bodies and dry us up until we became shrivelled like raisins.

No. That didn't make any sense. The Well. They were supplying us with more water than they'd ever be able to extract from us.

The light was almost out. Matilda and Anita were already asleep. The Camp was completely silent except for the sound of Andrew whittling his bow. I was so tired I could hardly keep my

181

eyes open. I lay down on the hard steel floor and used my backpack for a pillow. Under the rhythmic sound of a blunt knife scraping a piece of wood I fell into a dreamless sleep.

Everyone was still asleep when Andrew and I headed for the Well. Simon was wide awake.

'No news,' he said and handed me the steel box. 'Did you manage to get some sleep?'

'Yeah, thanks,' I said and gave him a well-deserved smile. I was feeling so much better than the day before. Maybe things would turn out okay after all.

The next second I saw someone approaching us. I immediately knew it was him. He was dressed in black overalls and had a pale face. He looked like all the other visitors I'd seen; he looked like the visitors at the party at the warehouse; he looked like the visitors who'd taken Andrew and Matilda; he looked like the visitors who'd led us from the morgue to the Camp.

He stopped a couple of metres away from the Well and started glancing around. I should have been afraid of him, he was one of them after all, but I wasn't. I was so sure that I just walked up to him and said, 'Rudolf?'

He didn't answer immediately. He looked at me closely. He had two weapons tucked tightly in holsters on his belt, one round, one triangular. The colour of his face reminded me of a thin layer of snow on a dirty road: white with a hint of grey in it when looked at closely.

His eyes were big and blue with the slightest tinge of purple and they constantly emanated bewildered amusement, as if he was on the verge of asking a question but always thought better of it. I couldn't tell his age. He could have been twenty and he could have been fifty.

'Yes. I'm Rudolf.'

I couldn't stop staring. His English sounded so … English.

'You're from the Resistance, right?'

I tried to take my eyes off his weirdly wrinkle-free face that made the Photoshoppers at *Vogue* seem inadequate at their job.

'Yes, I'm … I'm Amy.'

He glanced over to Andrew and Simon who were standing behind me, staring.

'I'm … I'm Andrew,' my brother mumbled, stiff as a rabbit caught in headlights. 'And this is Simon.'

Rudolf didn't seem interested and turned his gaze purposefully back to me.

'I understand you've got something for me.' His every little expression, his every movement, his every word oozed confidence. I immediately felt as if my job was done, as if a heavy load had been lifted. Rudolf would take care of things from now on. I'd passed the baton and it was in safe hands. As I reached into my pocket and wrapped my fingers around the hard steel box I was lightheaded with relief. This was it. We'd be free. We could go home.

But I knew something was wrong before he opened his mouth. There was suddenly something on his face that resembled a frown. No, not a frown exactly – the visitors' faces didn't seem to be capable of a wide range of expressions. It was more that the colour of it changed slightly. As if the thin layer of snow had melted and more of the grey of the dirty road beneath it became visible.

'Run,' Rudolf suddenly whispered from the corner of his mouth. He was looking at something over my shoulder.

Instinctively, I turned around. At first I didn't see anything unusual. Just a mass of teenagers with frightful looks on their faces wondering whether they'd ever see home again. But then, suddenly, a gap opened in the flood of people. The word 'run' was buzzing around my head. But my feet were stuck to the ground.

Along the pathway that had formed in the crowd marched a group of five masked men. They were wearing shiny overalls similar to Rudolf's. But theirs weren't black, theirs were grey and they wore black balaclavas that completely covered their faces.

I took a small step back. As I did I noticed hazel-brown eyes with a yellow autumnal tinge peer through one of the balaclavas. They looked so familiar.

'Run,' Rudolf whispered again.

The guy with the eyes suddenly stopped. He squinted. *It couldn't be. It just couldn't be.*

He stood there frozen for a fraction of a second. Then he grabbed something from his pocket. He reached out his arm. I recognised the high-pitched whizz all too well.

Rudolf's fingers dug into my shoulders.

'I said, run!'

I stared into the hazel eyes. They widened as the sphere-shaped weapon lit up.

'Shit!' Andrew shouted.

Rudolf pulled me up. It was as if I were flying. My feet weren't touching the ground and I could almost see all the way to the furthest part of the Camp. The next thing I knew, he had dropped me back down behind him so he stood between me and the masked men.

'There are others!' he hissed. 'On the outside. You need to—' But he didn't get to finish. Bright light hurt my eyes. Rudolf cried out in pain when the white beam from the sphere hit him right in the chest.

People around us started screaming.

Rudolf stumbled. 'Find them,' he heaved as he crumpled to the floor.

Everyone was crawling over each other as they tried to get away.

I stood there staring down at Rudolf. He was completely motionless. His body was all crooked. One of his legs was at a weird angle and his arms were spread to the sides as if he had been crucified. His black overalls looked like a deflated bin bag. His head was turned. His eyes had lost their bewildered amusement and stared empty into space. He was dead.

Before I realised it I was running. I hacked through the crowd, flailing my arms with my fists clenched. I could hear Andrew and Simon breathing hard behind me.

I thought I heard someone shouting out my name in the distance. *Amy! Amy!* But it couldn't be. It just couldn't have been him.

'Faster,' Andrew ordered.

I tried to obey but I was already moving as fast as I could. And besides, why were we running? There was no place to go. There was no point. Rudolf was dead. It was over. Our one and only chance of getting home was gone.

Day Four

Losing a friend is like losing a limb. That's what Mum said after her friend Erika died from cancer. She said, 'The loss of a friend is like that of a limb; time may heal the anguish of the wound, but the loss cannot be repaired.'

I feel as if someone has reached into my chest and squeezed my heart until it exploded. I think I'd rather have lost a limb. How could they do that? Haven't they taken enough from us? Isn't depriving us all of joy, happiness, freedom and hope for a future enough?

I hate them. I hate them with every fibre of my being. I hate them so much I'm shaking. I can hardly hold my pen. I wish they were all dead.

I know what Mum would say. She'd say it's not worth it. 'Forgiveness is the virtue of the brave,' she once told me. 'Holding on to anger is like grasping a hot coal with the intent of harming another; you end up getting burned.' I think she read it on Twitter.

But I don't agree. I think forgiveness is overrated. I think forgiveness is stupid. I'll never forgive them. Stuff forgiveness. Revenge. Revenge is what I need to feel better. If I ever get out of here, I will do everything I can to make sure they suffer.

16

I don't know how long the three of us had been running for when we finally came to a standstill. We'd lost the masked men in their grey overalls a long while ago, but we'd kept on going anyway, hurtling through the crowd like hunted animals through a forest.

We made our way back to our makeshift camp in silence. There was nothing to say.

'Where have you been?' Matilda asked when we arrived. 'And who are you?' she said, looking Simon up and down. She turned to me before he could answer. 'What are you up to? I insist that you tell me.'

I let Andrew tell Matilda, Anita and Tom what had happened. About my assignment. About the Resistance. There was no point in trying to keep it a secret. The mission had been blown. There was no cover to break.

'It's okay,' Anita said. 'It's not your fault. It wasn't an easy task. It was a long shot.'

'She's right,' Matilda said, and Tom, Andrew and Simon repeated it after her like monotonous parrots.

But I could hear the disappointment in their reassurances.

'Who was he?' Matilda asked. 'This Rudolf.'

I shrugged. 'I don't know.'

'Why was he going to help us?'

I shrugged again.

'Is there no one else …?'

Andrew, Simon and I looked at each other.

'I mean, there must be someone else. If he was willing to help us, there must be someone else who is ready to do that as well.'

Andrew raised his eyebrows as if he was asking me a question.

I looked away. I couldn't stand the hope in his eyes. There was nothing we could do. It was over.

'There might be,' Andrew said, and the optimism in his voice spread like fairy dust over the group. They stared at him like kids at Christmas waiting for Santa Claus to arrive.

He shouldn't have. He shouldn't have raised their hopes like that.

'There are others,' Andrew whispered as the group leaned in. 'That's what he said. That's what Rudolf said before he … before he, like … died. He said, "There are others. On the outside. Find them."'

'Forget it.' I lay down on the floor and pretended to be asleep. I didn't want to talk to anyone. I hated this place. I felt as if I were stuck in a coffin. Buried alive deep in the ground.

After an hour my back couldn't take any more of the steel floor. I sat up, bowing my head, hoping to be left alone. It was too much to ask.

'Cheer up,' Matilda said. She was playing a card game with Tom. He'd got the deck of cards from some girl in exchange for his socks. Now he was sitting barefoot on the floor, displaying toenails that were in serious need of cutting.

I ignored her.

Andrew, Simon and Anita arrived from the Well with the bucket brimful with water.

'What are you playing?' asked Anita, sitting down beside Matilda. Her hair was wet. She must have washed it in the Well. What I wouldn't have given for a shower. A proper shower. With soap. And hot water.

'Poker.'

Andrew took a seat so close to Anita that if he'd sat any closer he would have been on top of her. I still couldn't believe they were an item.

'Can we play?' he said, putting his arm over Anita's shoulder in a cool, casual yet affectionate way.

It bugged me that they were together, although I wasn't quite sure why. It made me feel more alone somehow. Was it because it was my brother or because I was the only one in our group without a boyfriend now?

'Sure,' Matilda said. She gathered up the cards that were scattered on the floor and started shuffling. 'I was losing anyway.' She stuck out her leg and kicked me in the shin. 'Come on, Amy. Join us.'

'I'm not in the mood.'

'Come on.'

I couldn't take it any more. 'How can you just sit there playing cards? How can you act as if nothing is happening?'

Matilda exuded patience. 'Just because we're not thinking about things twenty-four seven, it doesn't mean we're acting as if nothing is happening.'

'Aren't you angry? Aren't you angry about what's going on? About what's being taken from us?'

189

Matilda put the cards down. 'Yes, Amy, I'm angry. Yes, I'm scared. Yes, I realise that every day up here could be my last. But that doesn't mean I'm not going to squeeze as much pleasure, as much fun, out of a crappy situation as I possibly can.' When she looked up at me her eyes were simmering with certainty. She looked so confident. So sure of herself. She reminded me of Mum. 'At some point you've just got to get on with it.'

'On with what?'

'Life.'

I stared at her. The voices of the people in the Camp all mixed together sounded like the murmur of waves, or the constant sound of traffic. It was the background noise to our new life.

Matilda suddenly grinned at me cheekily, as if everything she'd said, like her profound speech, had only been a frivolous joke. 'Come on, Amy.' She grabbed the deck of cards. 'If you don't join us, I'll turn this into strip poker. Now that's a sight you don't want to see. I haven't shaved my armpits for almost a month. Soon I'll be able to plait the hair under there.'

I couldn't help but smile.

'Fine,' I grunted and shuffled over.

We played for torn-up pieces of toilet paper. It only took five rounds for Matilda to lose all of hers.

'You know what they say: if you're unlucky at cards, you're lucky in love,' she said, reaching out and pinching Tom's cheeks as if he were a little baby.

'That's not how it goes,' Anita said. She scooped up her winnings and added them to her rapidly growing pile of toilet paper.

'Yes, it is,' Matilda said, rolling her eyes. Her shoulders sunk tiredly towards her hips as if she were losing patience with a petulant child.

'No, it isn't. It's the other way around.'

Matilda glanced at Tom, then at me and then back at Anita. 'The other way around?'

'Yeah, the other way around. Lucky at cards, unlucky in love. That's how it goes.'

'That's what I said!'

'No. What you said was unlucky at cards, lucky in love.'

'It's the same thing.'

'It's not the same thing. It may have the same implication, but it is not the same thing.'

'It's so the same thing!'

'It's not!'

'Oh my God, whatever!'

Suddenly, I started laughing. I laughed so loud people nearby began turning around. But I just kept on going, laughing even harder as the astonishment on my friend's faces morphed into concern. After a while, a wide smile swept across Matilda's face and she started laughing too. And then Anita joined in. Andrew and Tom looked at each other, swapping self-conscious little smiles, before joining in as well, quietly at first, then with the fervour of an overcompensating comic. We were like a choir of hysterical monkeys screeching out of tune. More and more people started staring at us, but we just kept on going. We must have laughed continuously for at least ten minutes.

Slowly, the laughter faded out. We sat in silence for a while. 'What are we going to do?' Matilda finally said.

No one answered for a minute.

'I don't know,' Andrew said finally, staring down at the floor. In the aftermath of the manic laughing fit the quietness was as sombre as a funeral. 'But we have got to do *something*.'

Anita slipped her hand into his.

Something inside me snapped. 'There is nothing we can do!' I yelled louder than I'd intended. But it was as if the volume button on me were broken and I couldn't turn my shouting down. 'Can't you see that we're stuck? We're stuck in here.'

'But—' said Matilda.

'There's no but,' I shouted at her.

She tried again. 'But the others – Rudolf said there are—'

'Don't you think I've thought about that? Don't you think I've tried to come up with some solution, some plan, to get out of the Camp, to find those *others*? After all, it was my responsibility. It was my responsibility to save you all. But there is nothing I can do. There's nothing anyone can do.'

But Matilda had never been easily quieted. 'What about the sewage system? Simon was just telling me this lovely, not at all boring story about the sewage system. We can get out of the Camp through the sewage system. We can at least *try* to find the others.'

'The sewage system! Are you out of your mind? So what if we got out of the Camp through the sewage system? It's not as if we could just waltz around the spaceship looking for whoever Rudolf was talking about. We don't exactly look like visitors, if you haven't noticed. Face it. It's over.'

I waved my hand to emphasise the finality of my statement, and accidentally knocked over the water bucket.

Everyone jumped to their feet as water spilled everywhere. Tom quickly gathered up the cards to try to save them from damage. Matilda grabbed the magazines.

'Sorry, guys – I'm so, so sorry.' Here I was trashing their hope of returning to their old lives along with ruining what little gave them pleasure in their new ones.

Anita had grabbed a toilet roll and was trying to stop the water from reaching the tent. 'Don't worry about it,' she said, too busy to look up.

I felt awful. I bent down to help her, but slipped and hit my elbow on a cardboard box we used as a table. A piece of kitchen foil wrapped around an old greeting card fell from the top of the box into the puddle.

'My mirror!' Matilda exclaimed.

What was wrong with me?

Simon helped me to my feet. 'I'm going to fill up the bucket again. Do you want to walk with me to the Well – take a five-minute break?'

'No, I need to help clear this mess up.'

I quickly picked up the foil. It was soaking.

'Okay.' He squeezed my arm tight.

I dabbed the foil with my T-shirt.

'See you in a bit,' he said and let go of my arm. He turned on his heel. 'And remember: don't sweat it. It will all be okay.'

I growled as the foil ripped in two. I tried to push the two pieces together. Maybe Matilda wouldn't notice. But there was no point. The greeting card was soaking wet. The mirror was ruined.

When I finally looked up, Simon was gone, swallowed up by the crowd like a drop of rain by the sea.

I hadn't said goodbye to him. I never said goodbye.

Day Five

I don't know if I'm doing the right thing. Should I? Shouldn't I?

They said they'd do it. They said they're on board with my plan. They said they trust me. But they shouldn't. I have no idea what I'm doing.

I'm so nervous I feel like throwing up. If they get killed, it's my fault.

I miss Earth. I miss my laptop. I miss the internet. Making decisions without being able to do a bit of googling first is hard. Although . . . I suspect not even Google could help me with the dilemma I'm facing right now.

17

Simon had just left for the Well when the screaming started. It originated quite some distance away, but it was loud enough for Matilda to forget about her foil mirror.

I craned my neck, trying to see over the crowd. 'What's going on? Is there a Collection in session?'

Andrew straightened his back. 'I don't know.' He and Tom were squeezing the water from the edges of the sheet that made up our tent. It had got wet during the great spillage. 'It sounds different to a Collection. Rowdier somehow.'

A guy came running through the crowd – a boy really – wearing big glasses and a *Star Trek* T-shirt. He looked far too young to belong in here.

'They're protesting! They're protesting!' he shouted like a travelling information service.

Andrew just managed to grab hold of his shirt before he disappeared back into the crowd.

'Wait. What are they protesting about?'

'The food,' the boy said, his legs still moving. 'The Capos are trying to keep a lid on things, but the situation is seriously out of control. Some have got beaten up pretty badly.'

I handed Anita a porridge bowl. I was drying them and she

was stacking them up to reform the makeshift tent poles. 'Why are they protesting about the food?'

Anita shrugged.

Matilda snorted. 'Have you tried it?'

'It's no Gourmet Burger Kitchen. But at least we don't go hungry.'

'You'll understand when you've been in here a bit longer.'

Andrew let go of the boy. We finished cleaning up, rearranging what hadn't been ruined by the water on to cardboard boxes inside the tent.

The screaming grew louder. A rumour circled the Camp, like the whistling of the wind. People were saying that the Capos hadn't been able to handle the situation by themselves. They'd got the guards, known as the Black Stacks, to help them. The Black Stacks were shooting at the protestors.

Twenty minutes later, the Camp had gone quiet except for a few quivering whispers of uncertainty. It was over.

Where was Simon? He should've been back by now. I decided to head for the Well to look for him.

I recognised it immediately. The shirt. Something dark and burning began to boil in the pit of my stomach, like lava inside a volcano about to erupt. It could, of course, have been another Arsenal T-shirt; his probably wasn't the only one on board – a lot of people supported Arsenal, as unimaginable as it was to Tottenham supporters like Dad and Andrew. But there it was, small and weathered, perched right underneath the Arsenal crest – 'Right over my heart,' he'd said – the pin his grandfather had once owned. He'd been so proud of it. 'It was my grandad's. I'm the third generation of Arsenal supporters in my family.' It was gold and had a picture of the Arsenal cannon on it. 'We're called the Gunners,' he'd said as he held out the heirloom with a crooked smile on his face. He would never have parted with it.

He'd been my first friend in the Camp. He'd shared his food with me when I was starving. I knew something bad had happened to him.

I ran without thinking towards the guy wearing Simon's T-shirt. He was big and hairy, probably one of the older ones in the Camp. But I didn't think. I just grabbed him by the shirt.

'Where did you get that? Where did you get that shirt?'

The sleeves of the shirt stretched over his big, muscly arms. He clearly worked out – he probably could have ripped me off him and thrown me across the room with one hand. But he didn't. He just stared at me with the same astonishment as if I'd been a rabbit that had popped out of a hat.

'Why?! Why do you have Simon's shirt?'

'Simon?' His voice was husky, as if I'd just woken him up. 'Who's Simon?'

'Simon! Simon! The guy who owns the shirt you're wearing.'

'Oh.' He looked down at his feet. 'I … I … like, found it,' he murmured, his gaze fixed on his shoes.

'You found it? You found it where?'

Then I noticed it. I let go of the shirt. As a reflex I backed away.

Just underneath the pin there was a hole in the T-shirt. Black burn marks covered the edges. Scattered around the hole were small stains of blood. They were smudgy, as if someone had tried to wash them out. I looked at the greying gold pin Simon's grandfather had once owned. 'Right over my heart,' he'd said.

I knew he was dead.

I stood completely still, my mouth wide open. My eyes were wet.

The guy wearing Simon's T-shirt finally stopped staring at his toes and looked up.

'What?' he said. He scratched his hairy face as if he was looking for something for his hands to do other than hang limply down by his sides, sticking out of a dead man's T-shirt. 'It's not as if he has any use for it any more.'

I wanted to jump on him, bury my fingers in his face and rip his stupid beard off; or, better yet, remove it hair by hair with Matilda's tweezers. I wanted to throttle him with my bare hands. But I knew it wasn't him I was mad at. He wasn't the one I hated with every cell, every atom, every proton and every neutron of my body. No. It was them. The visitors had done this. The Black Stacks had killed Simon. Put a hole in his Arsenal shirt, right by the pin that had been worn by three generations of his family with massive pride. Now, there wouldn't be a fourth.

I suddenly felt my eyes dry up. The dark and burning matter in the pit of my stomach had made its way to the surface. When you place drops of water on hot lava they boil until they evaporate. My tears had evaporated on the flaming magma that was my hate for the visitors. They were evil. Pure evil.

I knew I had to do something. I wasn't going to let them win. At least not without a fight. I'd make them pay. I'd make them pay for what they did to Simon. For what they did to all of us. If it was the last thing I did.

When I got back to camp I called a group meeting.

Matilda barely glanced up from where she'd buried her head in Tom's neck. They were lying on the floor all tangled together like a chocolate twist pastry. 'Since when have we needed group meetings?'

She was in one of her moods.

'Please.'

'I'm busy.'

I looked at Tom.

He just shrugged his shoulders, knowing full well that nothing good could come of crossing Matilda's volatile side.

Anita got up from where she'd been sitting on the floor, watching Andrew make an arrow for his bow using a wire coat hanger. She joined me inside the tent.

'How are you going to shoot the arrow?' Matilda raised herself up on her elbows. 'You don't have a string. Without a string your bow is nothing more than a stupid stick.'

I studied Andrew's craftsmanship. Judging by the crooked and blunt arrow, the lack of string was the least of his problems.

'Is it that time of the month then?' Andrew said as he wrestled the hanger, trying to make it straighter.

Anita squealed. 'Andrew!'

'Sorry. Sorry, Matilda. Didn't mean it. The bow is all set. Anita is going to give me a piece of hair.'

'A piece of hair?' Matilda wrinkled her nose with the same intensity as when she watched me change Emma's poopy nappy.

'Yep.'

Andrew had never been one to elaborate.

'Like from her head?'

'That's usually where hair comes from.'

'Why?'

'Told you. For string. That's what people did in the olden days. I read it in a book once.'

'No, I mean, why would you do that, Anita? Why would you be willing to cut off a chunk of your hair for your boyfriend's stupid project? Why would you do that to your hair? You'll have a bald spot, you know.'

'She won't have a bald spot. We'll cut it from somewhere you can't see. And I don't need that much.'

Matilda had clearly not yet got all the frustration out of her system. 'Why are you doing this? It is so pointless.'

Andrew didn't bother looking up. 'No reason. It's better than just sitting around doing nothing. Doing something is better than doing nothing.'

'Exactly!' I seized the chance. 'Which brings me to the group meeting. We have to do something.'

Matilda sneered. 'Sounds good. Why don't you make a cheese grater out of that cardboard box over there?' She pointed towards one of the crumpled brown boxes we used as a shelf.

'I mean about the situation. My mission. Simon is …' I couldn't finish the sentence. The bastards. 'I don't know how, but I'm going to complete the miss—'

Suddenly, a deep, thundering voice came crashing down on us like the angry voice of God. The whole Camp shook.

'Humans of Earth.'

Matilda grabbed hold of Tom as if the floor had opened up beneath her and she were about to fall into it.

'I will make this short,' the voice said again. Its force felt like an electrical current running through my body. I noticed some people staring at the ceiling. I looked up. Above us hovered projections, some sort of holograms of a visitor's face, the same projection again and again. It was like watching TV without the screen.

'I am the president of Pronax.' The visitor's voice rang out simultaneously from all the flying holograms, making it sound like a talking choir. While he looked almost the same as the rest of the visitors, his face had a certain mummified quality to it that made him appear older than the ones I'd seen before. His skin was tight but it didn't seem to have much flesh underneath it. His lips were so thin they were almost non-existent and his hair was a coarse tangle of grey. He kind of looked like an old Hollywood star who'd had one too many facelifts.

But his voice was anything but frail. 'I was aware that humans are a treacherous little species and now I'm being told that you are an ungrateful one as well.'

I looked over at Andrew. I wanted to scoot over to him in order to feel less alone, but I couldn't move.

'You repay our hospitality with rudeness and violence. Some of you are protesting about the nourishment we offer you. You should be grateful for receiving our perfectly balanced porridge instead of the nutritionally questionable, greasy substances you call food. The insolence. We should let you starve. It would serve you right.'

The visitor paused. The Camp was as quiet as a dead man's grave.

'We Pronaxians are an honourable species, far more honourable than you Homo sapiens. Unlike humans, we honour every section of the Code of the Union. And when it comes to your treatment we've actually done more than the Code requires. We've gone above and beyond – we've provided you with better nourishment than is required during intergalactic imprisonment; we've not imposed on you any of our own customs and laws. In fact we've generously let you set up your own society, managed by an elite group of your own people.'

Was he referring to the Capos?

'But our patience is wearing thin. My men will be employed to keep the peace.'

A sharp whisper echoed through the Camp.

I moved closer to Andrew. 'Is that bad?'

'They're the Red Stacks,' he said, his head still turned up to the ceiling as he focused on one of the presidential heads. 'They're even worse than the guards.'

The sound of discontent was drowned out by the president. 'All disorder will be met with force. Anyone disturbing the peace will be eliminated.'

There was a thud, white noise, then nothing. The president of Pronax had disappeared into thin air.

The silence was broken by Matilda stamping her foot. 'Great! The Red Stacks. That's just what we need.' She stomped towards our tent, threw herself down on the floor and grabbed one of the old and now slightly damp magazines.

I stared at her. Of course. That was it! That was exactly what we needed.

'You've got it,' I whispered.

Matilda was shaking her head. 'Taylor Swift is having another of her social media rows.'

'Matilda, you've got it!'

'These public celebrity rows are so stupid that you've got to love them.'

I clenched my hands into fists. 'I know what we have to do.'

Day Six

It's really early. The camp is dark. Everyone is still asleep except for a few Capos walking around, keeping watch. And us. We're getting ready. We're getting ready for our shift.

This is it. Soon my job will be done.

18

The others hated my idea. But I finally managed to persuade them. Deep down, they knew that we didn't have a choice.

I pretended to be confident. I pretended to know what I was doing. But I hadn't got a clue about anything. I could only hope I wasn't leading them all to their deaths.

The next time there was a Collection, we ran towards the screaming. It wasn't easy. Like fish swimming upstream, we had to fight our way through the crowd of people running in the opposite direction. They were running away from the Red Stacks.

Dozens of visitors had encircled a large group of people who looked as helpless as sheep in a fold.

Some of those imprisoned were screaming, some were crying and some were just standing there in a daze of confusion and shock.

But the visitors weren't the ones I'd seen before. Yes, they were as pale as snow at the North Pole. Yes, they were wearing luminous overalls. But there was something different about the creatures closing in on the helpless flock of detainees. First of all, they weren't wearing the standard black overalls but red ones, making the visitors look like burning flames ready to devour anything in their path. And their eyes – there was something different about their eyes. Beneath the apathy which appeared to be a general feature of the species rippled something else – something that looked like ruthlessness.

'Come on,' I called out to Andrew, Matilda, Anita and Tom who was lagging way behind.

I knew we were running out of time. Like a group of synchronised ballet dancers, the Red Stacks reached into the holsters hanging from their belts, took out glass spheres and pointed them towards the ceiling. A white beam of light shot diagonally from each sphere. The beams joined in a point high up in the air, forming a teepee-like structure above people's heads. The visitors began to lower the structure, moving it towards the ground by pointing the spheres downwards. It was a cage made of laser bars.

I ran as fast as I could towards it. With all the strength I had, I squeezed myself in between two visitors and into the circle. One of them looked down on me. I thought he might try to stop me. But he didn't seem to care if he had one more prisoner to take away.

'Hurry!'

Andrew and Anita entered the circle holding hands. The cage was only a metre from the floor.

Matilda threw herself down and crawled underneath it.

Tom was about to follow her when he suddenly stopped.

Matilda reached out of the circle and grabbed his arm. 'Come on, Tom.'

What was he doing? He didn't have to come. None of them had to come. I'd said I was perfectly capable of doing this by myself. But they had insisted on coming with me. They'd said it would increase our chances.

Matilda pulled Tom towards her. He slid across the floor.

He'd just reached the inside of the circle when the laser bars hit the floor. We were locked in.

The cage started moving as the Red Stacks began making their way through the Camp, still pointing their spheres towards the floor. We had no choice but to move along as the laser bars pushed against those standing at the back of the cage.

We were led through the Camp. Those on the outside stared at us. The horror on their faces reflected my deepest fear: Were we being marched to our deaths?

We came to the Camp door. Visitors dressed in black were guarding it. They made sure no one escaped as our cage was manoeuvred through the big hole in the wall. The door closed behind us. We'd entered the unknown.

The corridor looked the same as last time: clean, cold and steely. And, like last time, groups of visitors in black walked along it, looking straight ahead as if in their own world, not giving us a second thought.

But suddenly the uniformity was broken. A large group of visitors dressed in grey overalls walked past us. I was admiring the strange illumination of the fabric when I realised something. Their faces. The faces of the ones in grey. They weren't pale. They didn't look like visitors at all. They looked ... they looked *normal*. Human.

'Hey,' I managed to croak. 'Hey, guys!'

No one answered. No one so much as glanced my way. They disappeared around the corner.

I grabbed Andrew by the shoulder. 'Did you see that?' Had I been imagining the colour on their cheeks? 'What was that?'

'I don't know.'

Then I remembered. Rudolf. Rudolf's killers had been wearing grey overalls.

I almost keeled over. I felt as if I'd been punched in the gut. Had his killer been one of us? Had his killer been human?

We came to a halt. We were there.

A giant door opened up in one of the walls, like the mouth of a dark cave. It was the Selection Lab. It was empty. We were pushed inside. The door closed behind us and the laser bars disappeared into thin air. The cage was gone. But no one moved.

The Red Stacks walked away. The room was so bright I had to shield my eyes. I glanced around. I couldn't see much for the crowd.

We'd only just started making our way through the group of people standing up against each other like sardines in a can when visitors in black swarmed in.

They started moving us around. With the efficiency of a casino card dealer, the crowd was divided into ten groups. There were around twenty people in each group. By locking arms Andrew, Matilda, Anita, Tom and I managed to stay together.

Each group was lined up to form a perfectly straight queue. I raised myself on tiptoes. I couldn't see what we were queueing for. The harsh lights were reflected and magnified in the empty steel surroundings. The sole presence of visitors in black was enough to keep the dozens of ex-Camp inmates in check. Except for one.

'Hey, you! Yes, I'm talking to you, you butt-ugly alien weirdo.'

Of course this had to be the person standing right in front of me in the queue.

'Ever heard of tanning salons?'

He was slurring. I pinched his shoulder. 'Are you trying to get us all killed?'

He turned around. 'Mind your own—'

My old life hit me like a fist. 'Damien!'

'Amy!' He stepped forward to give me a hug, but somehow his legs got tangled up. I just managed to catch him before he hit the floor. He stank of something that reminded me of Granny Vera's medicine cabinet.

'Are you drunk?'

He smiled a drooly smile. 'Oh, lighten up.' He gave a dismissive wave with his hand, which accidentally hit me in the nose. He didn't even notice. 'I just had a bit of cognac. I'd thought it was my dad breaking down the living-room door to stop me drinking all his good stuff, but it was them coming to get me. White-faced party poopers.' He laughed at his own attempt at a joke. 'So where are we exactly?'

He'd clearly just got here.

But I didn't get to explain. A dark shadow fell over us. A visitor in black grabbed my arm. Without a word he started pulling me away.

'Hey!' I shouted. 'Hey, let me go!'

The visitor stopped. He stared at me, slight surprise breaking through the emptiness in his silver-grey eyes, as if he was thinking, *What's the big deal? You're all dead anyway.*

'It has been requested that you move to a different queue.'

His grip was firm without hurting me. 'Requested? Requested by whom?'

He turned on his heel. The question-and-answer session was clearly over.

'No, wait! My friends! My friends, can they come too?'

The visitor glanced at Andrew, Matilda, Anita and Tom, who stood huddled together behind me. He shrugged his shoulders.

'I'm coming too,' Damien said, running after us, his legs barely holding him up.

The visitor dropped us off in a queue two rows over. Then he was gone.

'What was that?' Matilda asked.

I shook my head. 'I have no idea.'

The queue moved a few steps every couple of minutes.

Anita came up to me. 'I think what you're doing is so brave.'

'Don't be stupid …' I mumbled. 'I'm the least brave person I know. Anyone would do the same. It's only what needs to be done.'

'That's not true. Don't sell yourself short. You've always had the tendency to sell yourself short.'

I heard a sigh behind me. 'Who says that?' It was Matilda. 'Only old ladies and second-rate psychologists use the phrase "sell yourself short". I feel as if I'm stuck in an old people's home.'

Anita and I looked at each other from under our brows. We tried not to laugh.

Quietly, we waited our turn.

211

And then we were there. There. It couldn't have been more unassuming. It was a big steel desk. A glass plate stuck out of the middle like a non-reflective mirror. I felt as if I'd been queueing up for something as mundane as the post office.

But then I saw him. He was sitting on a steel chair behind the desk, wearing grey overalls.

I had tried to shake the feeling. I'd tried to banish the thought. And for a time I'd been successful. But there was no denying it. It had been him behind the balaclava. The person with whom I'd shared my first kiss had tried to kill me.

'You.' My voice was a whisper.

He was staring right at me. His face was expressionless. His dimples were barely visible.

'It was you.'

Caesar's eyes darkened.

Matilda stepped forward. 'Hey, I remember you! You were at the party down by the docks.'

Andrew's face hardened. He'd realised it too.

Anger soared through me. 'It was you who killed Rudolf.' I lost all self-control and began shouting. 'And you tried to kill me!'

Caesar pretended nothing was happening. He put his hands on the steel table. It lit up with something that looked like a touch-screen version of a keyboard. He started tapping it.

'Hey, I'm talking to you!'

The anger had filled me with a certain fearlessness. I felt as light as a hot-air balloon floating high above both the events and their consequences. Then a familiar voice rang out and it was as

212

if I'd burst. Totally deflated, I came crashing down, back to reality.

'Amy!'

Was that joyous spite I detected?

'Always nice to see you, Amy.'

Why her? I'd always found it hard to speak around her. I had to force myself to open my mouth. 'Hello, Courtney.'

She was standing next to Caesar, wearing a white T-shirt, a denim skirt and a smirk. Around her toned upper arm was a red band.

I flinched. 'You're a Capo?'

Louisa appeared behind her. Even in space they came as a pair. 'We both are,' she said with coy enthusiasm, as if I'd just paid them a compliment.

Caesar growled at them. 'Get on with it, you two.'

Louisa rushed past the desk, towards me.

There had to be at least twenty identical desks inside this steel hall they called the Selection Lab. Behind each one there stood a person wearing a grey uniform and two Capos wearing normal clothes. The queues in front of the desks were getting shorter.

Louisa took me by the arm and led me to a stool. 'I promise, it won't hurt.'

I sat down. 'What won't?'

The next thing I knew, Courtney had jabbed something that looked like a steel ballpoint pen into my arm. I was too shocked to react. She held it there for a few seconds. A small light lit up at the tip.

'Got it,' Caesar said, looking hard at the glass plate sticking out from the desk. It was some sort of computer screen. Symbols I'd never seen before ran across it.

Courtney removed the pen-like instrument.

'What is that?' I shouted.

'We're testing you.'

'Testing me for what?'

Courtney didn't answer.

The screen went blank for a few seconds. When it lit up again it showed a number in red: 2.

Courtney pulled me up off the stool. 'I'll take her.'

Behind us there were three steel doors in the wall. I could see Capos dragging people who'd been tested towards different doors. Once there, the door slid open and the Capos pushed the prisoner inside. Then it closed again, like the mouth of a lion that'd had a bellyful.

Caesar suddenly jumped to his feet. 'Wait!'

Our eyes met briefly before he quickly looked away.

'It's wrong,' he said, straightening his back, his tall presence casting a long shadow over Courtney.

She stared at him. 'What is?'

'The result. The result of the test is wrong.'

She wrinkled her nose and shot up her lip in that annoying, disrespectful way she always did when she was about to give one of our teachers a hard time. 'How can it be wrong? It's never been wrong before.'

Caesar snapped at her. 'Well, it just is. Take her to room three.'

Courtney had never been good with orders. 'But the computer said two.' Her voice sounded as thin and nasal as ever. God, she was annoying. 'I think I should just take her to room two.'

Caesar's eyes widened. His face turned red. He looked like an angry bull ready to charge. 'It's not your job to think. Disobedience will not tolerated. You take her to room three right now or I'll have both you and your friend stripped of your status as Capos.'

Courtney shrank, her shoulders curling down to her waist.

Louisa clearly wasn't about to lose her prestige. 'I'll take her!'

Matilda pushed in front of Andrew and Anita, who'd been standing behind me in the queue.

'We're coming with her.'

'You need to have your test first, sweetie,' Louisa said, smiling as if she were the receptionist at a doctor's.

Matilda ignored her. 'Come on.' She dragged Andrew and Anita towards me. Then she grabbed Tom by the arm.

Courtney stepped in her way. 'You're not going with your loser friend. It doesn't work like that.'

Matilda rolled her eyes. 'Oh, stop being such a cow. Amy's not a loser. And you're going to regret being so mean to her when she becomes the one to save humankind and bring us all back home.'

My jaw dropped down to my chest.

'She's on a secret mission, you know.'

'Matilda!' I couldn't believe her. She'd just said it. *A secret mission.*

Courtney looked me up and down. She narrowed one eye as if she was trying to determine whether I was capable of such a task. Before she could make her final judgement, Caesar pushed her out of the way. He took me by the arm.

'She's right. Only one goes through at a time.'

'No!' Matilda grabbed hold of his grey uniform. He shook her off with ease, curling his lip in bemusement.

But I'd had an idea. 'You're wrong.' I stomped my foot for effect. 'We *are* going through together.'

Caesar stared at me. One eyebrow shot quizzically up his forehead. 'No, you're not.'

I tried to sound authoritative even though I was about to throw up from nerves. 'If you split us up, I'll call over one of your pale, black-clothed friends over there and tell them what you did. I'll tell them about Rudolf. I imagine that hiding your face means the same thing wherever you are in the universe. If you have to hide your face, you're doing something you're not meant to do.'

Caesar scanned the hall. Then he growled at me, 'Fine. You and your friends come with me. But you'd better come quietly. And hurry.'

He turned and headed for the doors.

We ran after him. Matilda pulled Tom along. He appeared to be half-frozen from indecision.

Andrew patted me on the shoulder. 'Good job.'

Damien appeared beside me. He'd clearly decided he was one of us. 'Is it true you're on a secret mission?'

I ignored him.

We stopped in front of one of the doors – the one furthest away. I turned around and saw Courtney and Louisa staring at us. I wasn't sure if it was annoyance or bewilderment that creased their faces. I wanted to laugh. I *won*. I'd got my way. I'd put my foot down and got my way. I felt so victorious. I felt as if I was capable of anything. For a moment I thought I could totally do this. Of course I could successfully complete a secret mission for the Resistance down on Earth. I was Amy Sullivan, saviour of the universe … or humankind at least. But then the door opened.

Day Six – evening

I still smell of dead chicken. The lights are dying out. I'm waiting for everyone to go to sleep.

I know I shouldn't do it. I know I shouldn't go. But I am. Just this once I am going to do what I shouldn't. Because someone is lying. Someone is messing with me. And I need to find out who.

19

Room three was a cold and empty steel chamber the size of a fridge at the butcher's. Lambs to the slaughter. That was what we were.

Caesar pushed us inside.

I turned towards him. 'What's going to happen to—?'

The door closed. He was gone.

The silence made my ears ring. We all just stood there looking at each other, waiting for something awful to happen. The Nazi gas chambers popped into my head.

I almost cried with relief when a second door opened at the back of the room. Two guards in black luminous uniforms walked inside. At least it wasn't a gas chamber if they were inside too.

They made us form another queue. The visitors seemed to love their queues. Then they led us out of the room and into a corridor.

'Where are you taking us?'

'To the kitchen,' one of them said.

I was sure I'd heard him wrong. But I hadn't.

It was in fact a kitchen.

'You'll be stationed here during the day,' one of our visitor escorts told us. 'The shift starts at six-thirty and ends at nine.

Failure in pulling your weight will result in an appropriate punishment according to the law of the Code of the Union.'

In between chrome-coloured cabinets, worktops and giant sinks stood kitchen staff dressed in grey overalls. Grey. It was the same uniform Caesar had worn. The uniform of Rudolf's killers. The uniform of those who looked like us, who looked human, but didn't seem to belong to us.

The visitor shouted something incomprehensible. It reminded me of the cry of a donkey. What was that? A language?

One of the kitchen staff in grey came running – a girl with a long, red plait falling over one shoulder. She had an angry frown on her freckled face.

She answered the visitor back. My heart stopped. She emitted the same donkey sounds as the visitor. How could she speak this strange language that sounded like something a mixed breed of whales, horses and humans had come up with?

'The Defects run the kitchen. You'll answer to them.'

Defects? What was a Defect? Was that the name the visitors had given us humans?

I stared at the girl. Who was she?

Her eyes met mine. They were burning with annoyance. 'What?' she hissed.

Andrew stepped forward to get a better look. The others were huddled in a group behind us. They were whispering.

'Silence,' the visitor thundered. His dark eyes reminded me of the black mouth of the metallic arm that'd brought me here. 'We Pronaxians do not look kindly upon disobedience. We respect order, the foundation of efficiency and longevity. According to section six of the Code of the Union I am not allowed to tell you to do the same. But it would serve you well to bear our beliefs in mind.'

The visitor turned to the girl. 'Get them started.'

The girl's shoulders sank as she sighed. 'This is our threshing machine.' She pointed towards a steel monstrosity the size of a car which looked like a bottle that had been tipped over. She touched the bottleneck. 'This is where the grain comes out. Unlike humans, Pronaxians only eat porridge from a special grain grown on—'

The visitor in black barked, 'Efficiency!'

'Yes, sir. You don't need to know that. It's not important to the task at hand. Not important … Okay, over here we have the rations we got from Earth this morning.'

She pointed towards a big pile of stuff on the floor. I could see what had to be hundreds of cans of garden peas. There were raw, whole chickens and what looked like prawns. There were eggs, some sort of red meat, a few loaves of bread and a mountain of tomatoes.

'You'd better get to it then.'

We just stood there, staring at her.

Andrew was the first to form the question. 'Erm … get to it?'

The girl frowned. 'Putting together tomorrow's menu. Then starting on today's dinner. You know, for the Capos.'

So the food was for the Capos. That was why people were willing to betray their own kind. There was something in it for them.

The girl studied us. 'You were tested in the Selection Lab,

221

right? Only those who show a genetic predisposition to the appropriate talents are rewarded with kitchen duties. You know how to prepare food, right?'

Matilda started laughing. 'Prepare food? Are you kidding me?'

The girl hesitated. 'The last group I had couldn't handle the pressure. If you don't have the skills needed, I will have to send you back.'

I felt panic rise in my chest. None of us had any experience with cooking. Andrew and I could hardly make toast. Matilda considered adding boiling water to Pot Noodles cooking. Anita's signature dish was frozen lasagne and Tom … well, I didn't know about Tom.

From the corner of my eye I saw Anita pinch Matilda in the back. 'Of course we do,' she said and shot her a stern look. 'We've all shown exceptional talent for food preparation. Come on – let's get started.'

We began rummaging through the pile of food, doing our best to look like the specialists we were meant to be.

'I think this selection is very well suited to a hearty casserole,' said Anita, holding a head of lettuce.

Last time I checked, casseroles did not contain lettuce. 'You're absolutely right, Anita,' I said, raising my eyebrows knowingly. 'And then we could make pea *foie gras* and *coq au vin à la crème brûlée* with a dash of *escargot gravy*,' I added without understanding a single word of what I was saying, hoping the French I'd learned from the menu in a Paris hotel room our family had once stayed in would add an extra authority to my acting.

222

Andrew frowned. 'Pea liver pate? Chicken in red wine with vanilla custard and a dash of snail gravy?'

Oops. I stared at the food, trying to remember dishes I'd seen people make on *MasterChef*. I was feeling pleased with myself. We'd successfully completed the first part of our plan. We were out of the Camp. But that was only the beginning. We didn't exactly have time for leisurely cooking. We had our mission to attend to. But we also needed to come up with realistic recipe ideas so our cover wouldn't be blown, otherwise we'd be sent straight back to the Camp.

I was deep in thought, trying to figure out how the bread, the eggs and the peas could somehow constitute a dish, when I felt someone standing next to me. I thought it was Andrew. I started thinking out loud.

'French toast with peas? Is it just me or does it sound like something you'd feed to a zoo animal?'

'Don't do it.'

I dropped the peas. It wasn't Andrew's voice.

'I know what you came here for. I know what you and your friends are planning. Don't do it.'

I turned around. The yellow tinge to his brown eyes was exaggerated in the fluorescent lighting. His face was hard.

I tried not to show my fear. I tried to muster some defiance. 'What are you doing here?'

Then I saw them, Courtney and Louisa, standing by the kitchen entrance. The girl with the red plait was giving them her introductory tour.

'I had myself and my team transferred to kitchen duties.' He

223

smiled a crooked smile. He was obviously pleased with himself. His smile faded. 'Don't do it.'

'Why the hell should I listen to you?' I hissed at Caesar. 'You tried to kill me.'

'Amy, things aren't the way you think they are.'

'So you didn't try to kill me.'

'That's not what I mean.' He grabbed my arm.

'Let go of me or I'll scream.'

His fingers dug into me harder. 'You don't know what you're doing.'

'I'll scream, I swear. I don't think the guards in black will be happy with you interrupting my work. It isn't very efficient. You're not being very obedient.'

I didn't have to follow through.

'What is going on over there?' It was one of the visitors who'd brought us to the kitchen.

Caesar's back bent like a straw in a storm. He uttered something I didn't understand. It took me a while to realise what it was. I felt like throwing up. Who was he? *What* was he? A human who spoke the alien language? A visitor who looked like the people on Earth?

Even though I couldn't understand a word of what he was saying, it sounded like an apology. He gave a submissive nod to the guard. Then he walked towards the threshing machine where he started feeding white wheat-like straws into a funnel.

After that everything happened faster than we'd dared to hope.

I'd prepared myself for the prospect of having to work in the kitchen for weeks, months even, before we'd manage to get hold of any of 'the others'. My plan to find Rudolf's associates was simple: now that we were out of the Camp and had access to the people who made up the ship's crew we would simply ask around. It sounded so uncouth. If this had been a movie, my strategy would have been something more sophisticated, more complicated, more exciting. But this was reality – cold, bland reality.

There were visitors in black going in and out of the kitchen all the time. They were our target. Rudolf had been wearing black. Not grey. Not red. Black.

I made an attempt. 'Rudolf, do you know Rudolf?' I asked a woman with hypnotically beautiful blue eyes accompanied by a blank expression. She ignored me.

We'd been in the kitchen for no more than an hour when Matilda found him. She beckoned us over.

We gathered around the pile of food. The visitor Matilda had tracked down pretended he was checking out our provisions.

'You've got it?' He looked almost identical to Rudolf. His greyish-white skin. The shiny blue eyes. The flat expression.

Tom, who'd been of little use when we were making the recipes and hadn't approached a single visitor in search of Rudolf's associates, suddenly sprung to life.

'It's her!' He pointed towards me. 'She's got it.' The words shot out of his mouth like a burden he'd been trying to get rid of.

The visitor turned towards me. I wasn't sure but I think he attempted a smile.

I didn't move. Something told me not to move.

'So, you have something for me? You have something for the vice-president?'

Don't do it. Caesar's words bounced around in my head like unruly butterflies. *You don't know what you're doing.*

I studied the visitor. 'What do you mean the vice-president?'

'The Splinters. Do you have the thing for the Splinters?'

The Splinters. Why did I have the feeling I'd heard that name before?

The guy seemed to be getting agitated. 'We don't have much time.'

'Give it to him,' Tom hissed a little too loudly. Another visitor turned around and craned his neck.

'I …' I swallowed. 'I don't have it.'

What I'd interpreted as a smile disappeared from the visitor's face. 'You don't have it?'

Automatically, I touched my pocket where the steel box from the Resistance was carefully tucked, wrapped in toilet paper. 'I have it. But I don't have it on me.' I was a bad liar. 'I, um … I left it in a safe place.'

The visitor growled ever so slightly. 'Bring it tomorrow. To your shift. I'll meet you here.'

I had to ask: 'Why?'

'Why what?' said the visitor.

Tom shot me a dirty look. 'She'll bring it. We'll bring it.'

I ignored him. 'Why are you helping us?'

The thud of feet marching in perfect step filled the kitchen.

The visitor spun around. 'Shit.'

Through one of the sliding doors flooded an army in red. The president's men. They walked in a straight line with the determination of blood coursing through a vein.

'Shit, shit.'

I was taken aback by the level of emotion in our visitor's voice. What did he have to be afraid of?

He started scurrying away from us. 'You don't know me,' he hissed from the corner of his mouth. 'We've never met, do you hear? You don't know me.'

We were escorted back to the Camp after our shift. We would be picked up again tomorrow morning for our next one.

Courtney and Louisa joined us in our little tent. As Capos, each of them had got a small plastic container of food. It turned out simple kitchen staff didn't enjoy the same privileges as Capos.

Louisa shared hers with the rest of us. Courtney ate hers alone.

I told them about my mission. About the Resistance back on Earth. As Capos it wasn't unlikely that they had some inside information. Maybe they could help. We had nothing to lose.

I asked them about the tests in the Selection Lab. What was inside room one and two? They had no idea.

'What about those … what are they called? Defects, yes, the Defects – what are they?'

Courtney stuck a whole potato into her mouth. She answered while chewing. 'Some say they're humans who were abducted from Earth as babies and raised by the Pronaxians. Some say they're aliens from a planet far away which looks exactly like

227

Earth. I think they're just the same creepy aliens as the white-faced ones who've had plastic surgery to look less creepy and more normal.'

Louisa handed me a piece of chicken. 'You have the last bit.' She was smiling at me.

I stared at her. Why wasn't she being a cow?

Tom reached out his hand. 'I'll take it.' He jabbed the chicken into his mouth.

'Tom!' Matilda exclaimed.

'What?'

I shrugged my shoulders. 'It's okay.'

The events of the day were a soft muddle sloshing around in my head. I told the others about Caesar. About his words of warning. I didn't know what to think. Should we be more careful about whom we trusted? Could we really trust the visitor who'd said he was Rudolf's associate?

'Why are we even discussing this?' Tom moaned. 'You should have given him the box.'

I ignored the icy accusation in his voice. 'But what if Caesar is right? What if things aren't what we think?'

Tom sighed. He chewed his words as if he were talking to a stubborn child. 'He tried to kill you.'

There was no arguing about that.

Eventually, we agreed on Rudolf's friend being the safer bet. It was the Resistance back on Earth that had got us in touch with Rudolf and we knew we could trust the Resistance. We just had to take our chances and hope that Rudolf's friend really was his friend.

Day Seven

Last night was a mistake. I shouldn't have done it. I shouldn't have gone.

I'm trying to write in my diary, but I can't see anything. Aren't they going to turn on any lights in here? Are they just going to leave me alone in the dark to rot?

I'm afraid. I'm so afraid.

20

Our shift in the kitchen started at six-thirty on the dot. We were split into eight groups, each consisting of one human and three Defects – it was a move to make our work more efficient. Yesterday, we'd decided on making French toast for breakfast, prawn and garden pea salad for lunch and chicken for dinner. My group was in charge of dipping the bread into the egg mixture to make the French toast. Then Andrew's group took the bread and fried it on a giant griddle. The task was tediously repetitive. We were like a human conveyor belt. Matilda's group was in charge of chopping the tomatoes for lunch. Tom opened the cans of garden peas and handed them to Anita, who rinsed them under water. Courtney, Louisa and Damien had started preparations for dinner.

There was no sign of Rudolf's friend. I didn't think anything of it at first. It was early. No one woke up at six-thirty unless they were forced to. But when he hadn't shown by midday I started to get worried.

'He'll come,' Anita whispered in my ear as she walked past me on her way to the loo. There were no breaks other than loo breaks.

Breakfast had been served successfully and I'd been moved on to dinner. I was gutting and cutting up chickens – no supermarket pre-prepared chicken pieces here – when I felt a slight shiver. I turned around. Caesar was standing behind me. I had not heard him coming. I tried to hide my surprise. This place gave me the creeps. I quickly turned back to my work.

Caesar moved closer. I could feel his breath on my neck. He was supervising the whole thing and he'd been walking between the groups, suggesting improvements to 'maximise speed and minimise waste' as he so annoyingly put it. But apparently he wasn't there to criticise my butchering skills.

'He won't come,' he whispered.

I squeezed my fingers around the spongy chicken intestines. I told myself I didn't know what he was talking about. But I did.

'He won't be back here. Ever.'

I felt as if the chicken were squeezing my intestines, not the other way around. It was all my fault. I had two lives on my conscience. Two visitors had been eliminated because of me. First I'd got Rudolf killed. Then his friend.

Fear and rage muffled my voice. 'It was you, wasn't it?' I turned towards Caesar. 'You were one of the masked men who killed Rudolf. In the Camp.'

Caesar didn't answer.

I wanted to jump on him and claw out his eyes. 'You killed his friend as well.'

Caesar lowered his gaze. 'We didn't need to. The president's men took care of that.'

The air was filled with the smell of chicken blood and animal carcasses – the smell of death. A lump formed in my throat. 'They were helping us.' My vision became cloudy. I wasn't sure if it was rage or tears. 'They were our only hope. They were helping us.'

Caesar looked up and narrowed his eyes like an animal ready to attack. 'Don't be so stupid.' His face was flushed. 'They weren't helping you. They were helping themselves. They were using you.'

My heart was racing. He was lying. He'd tried to kill me. I turned back to the chicken and rammed my knife deep into the pink flesh.

Caesar took hold of my arm. 'Come, let me show you something.'

He began dragging me towards one of the sliding doors.

I dug my heels into the steel floor. I tried to wriggle myself free. He was a killer. He was going to kill me.

He must have seen the panic on my face and he rolled his eyes. I noticed how smooth his skin was. 'You'll be fine.'

I didn't believe him. I made myself as stiff as a tree trunk so he couldn't pull me any further.

Caesar sighed. A lock of hair fell across his forehead. His hair was really shiny. 'All humans, come with me,' he shouted. He whispered out of the corner of his mouth, 'I can't do anything to you with all your friends there, can I?'

One of the visitors in black guarding the doors said something that sounded like a horse choking on hay. Caesar answered in the same manner. The visitor stepped away from the door. I wasn't sure about Caesar's logic, about him not being able to kill me with my friends there, but I followed him anyway.

Andrew, Matilda, Anita, Tom, Courtney, Louisa and Damien – the rest of the humans in the kitchen – put down their tools.

232

The sliding door opened and we followed Caesar out of the kitchen.

I studied his face, his sharp jawline, his light stubble, the cute little dimples on his cheeks I always wanted to touch. 'What did you say to him?' I asked, reminding myself of the fact that Caesar wasn't even human. Or was he?

'That it was time to chop you all up for the human stew we're making.'

I could feel the blood drain from my face.

Caesar let out a sudden laugh. 'Just kidding. Wow. I didn't think you were this serious. I said I was going to show you the new rations in the cold rooms so you could start coming up with tomorrow's menu.'

My cheeks turned hot from relief and embarrassment.

'Hurry, we don't have much time.'

We followed Caesar down quietly busy corridors. He nodded towards some of the people wearing grey uniforms with normal non-visitor-like faces, but he carefully avoided looking at the ones wearing black. They ignored us completely.

He finally stopped in front of a small door that was almost indiscernible in the steel wall. He laid the palm of his hand flat on the door. The wall lit up around his fingers. The door opened with a soft swishing sound.

I was immediately struck by the smell. It wasn't especially strong, but it reminded me of something. It took me a while to realise what. It reminded me of people. Of life. It reminded me of home. It reminded me of Earth. I could swear by it – it was the smell of sweat and dirty socks.

'Where are you really taking us?' I asked, but Caesar just stepped into the darkness beyond the sleek steel wall. The rest of us looked at each other.

I noticed Tom wince and his lips part questioningly, like when a fish sticks its head out of water, as if asking: *Should I really be doing this? I am a fish after all*. 'I really don't think ...' he began.

I raced through the door after Caesar. I didn't want another one of Tom's debates. The others followed and Tom gave a sigh of superior indignation. He thought he was so smart. He was always saying to Matilda, 'It's *whom* – it's *whom*.'

At first I didn't see a thing. It was dark and we were walking along a narrow corridor or some sort of tunnel. But it wasn't long before we heard voices and light started penetrating the darkness.

Caesar stopped and turned to us. 'I'm taking a giant risk. You shouldn't be here. So don't do anything stupid.'

None of us replied.

'We cannot be seen by the security services. Can I trust you?'

He looked directly at me. I opened my mouth but closed it again. I didn't owe him anything. I had no idea who the security services were, but I wasn't going to give him any assurance. It was up to him if he wanted to trust us or not. I didn't care.

'I'll take that as a yes.'

He kept on walking, leading us towards the light. Anita caught up with Andrew and took his hand. Tom put an arm around Matilda's shoulders. Courtney, Louisa and Damien walked in step behind me. Who did I belong to? (Or was it whom?) Each of the people I'd been closest to – Matilda, Anita, Andrew – had someone else in their life to go through this with. A sense of loneliness hit me. I tried to shake it off. How silly. I had bigger things to worry about.

The tunnel came to a sudden end and we stepped on to some sort of balcony. A huge, bright space opened up. It was almost as if we were standing in a Roman amphitheatre, though one made of steel. I could see rows of balconies in the distance, each on top of the other.

Caesar grabbed the barrier and leaned over it. I sensed it was a long way down. We could have pushed him off the balcony easily and made a run for it. But there was no point.

'Take a look,' he said. 'This will be your life.'

Matilda stepped forward. She'd never been afraid of heights, as her frequent use of stilt-like stilettoes demonstrated.

'If you do what you came here for, Amy, this will be your life.'

I wasn't sure if Caesar saying my name like that was meant to be menacing or his way of showing concern.

Matilda was staring down on our fate. I tried to read her face, but it gave no hint as to whether it was a good fate or a bad one. Not that I couldn't venture a guess. I followed Matilda to the brink and lowered my eyes without really wanting to.

They looked like ants from so high up. Grains of sand in the desert. The distance may have reduced them in size, but it didn't dampen the impact of their situation. I could sense their discomfort, their claustrophobia, their utter misery.

Then Andrew stepped forward and leaned over the balcony railing. One by one, the others followed.

I could hear children crying. I could hear laughter, singing, fighting, talking. It was the sound of life. But what kind of life?

Several metres below us was something that looked like a battery farm for chickens. But instead of chickens there were people. It was as if the floor of the Roman amphitheatre had been tiled with people. Some were wearing grey overalls like Caesar. Some were wearing normal clothing. They stood there, squeezed up against each other, with nowhere to go. My head filled with horrid images from a documentary I'd seen on chicken farming. Their brittle bones, their crooked legs, their broken beaks.

It was similar to the Camp we were kept in. But worse. More crowded. Bleaker. More permanent somehow.

Caesar's voice was as cold and sharp as an icicle hanging precariously on an eave. 'This is the Colony. This is my home.' Again he directed his words at me. 'And it will be yours if you do what you're planning.'

I could hear Louisa sniffing.

The smell of old – no, ancient – sweat was making me feel sick. A lump formed in my throat.

Louisa started crying – full-blown sobs. 'I want to go home.'

'Shhh,' Caesar ordered. 'Don't let the security services hear you.'

Of all the possible endings to my story, of all the things that could go wrong – failure to complete my mission, pain, death – I'd never imagined such a mundane demise. I'd never imagined the possibility of just rotting away – not hungry, not in pain, not uncomfortably – in a room in space. I couldn't think of anything worse.

Tom saw it differently. He sounded as if he'd just won the lottery. 'So they're not going to kill us!'

His exuberance was like a contagious disease that spread at the speed of light. 'Yeah! You're right!' Courtney exclaimed, hanging on to his words as if they were a lifebelt. 'They're not going to kill us.'

Anita nodded her head as eagerly as if it were an Olympic sport. 'We're going to be okay – we're going to be okay.'

Louisa kept on wailing. Damien put his arm around her. 'Dude, stop crying. They're not going to kill us. We're going to live.'

Caesar's eyes sparked with what appeared to be anger. 'Not being dead doesn't necessary mean that you are alive!'

Damien looked at Caesar, as confused as if he'd been explaining quantum theory to us in Chinese.

Caesar took a deep breath. 'Okay. Okay. Let me show you something else.'

We followed him along the balcony. It was so big it would have taken us an hour or two to walk the whole circle. I detected some movement on the other side. I peered into the distance. Were those—?

I didn't finish my thought as Caesar threw himself to the ground. 'Down, down! It's the security services!'

I tumbled to the ground like an obedient dog. The others did the same. I had hardly touched the cold steel floor when I thought, *I don't take orders from him*, and prepared to stand up again.

'They will punish you too.' Caesar's soft brown eyes were like a sedative to my willpower. 'The Red Stacks won't only punish me – they will punish you as well.'

I lay back down.

Caesar started crawling across the floor. 'In here,' he said, turning into a tunnel-like corridor, similar to the one we'd arrived through. In the safety of the shadows he jumped to his feet. 'Hurry.'

There was nothing else for it – we ran after him.

I bumped into him when he stopped abruptly and I started to blush. As I stepped back, he laid his palm on the wall and it lit up around his fingers like before. A door opened to a tiny box room.

We stepped inside. The door closed and the box started moving. We were in a lift.

I had no idea whether we'd gone up or down, but when the door opened again sombre darkness greeted us.

'Don't worry, the Red Stacks hardly ever come here,' said Caesar when Louisa refused to get out of the lift.

'Why?' I asked.

'The grief. They find it so aesthetically displeasing.'

The air smelled strange. Like pungent flowers. Or incense.

'What is this place?' said Andrew as we followed Caesar down another corridor.

'You'll see.'

Caesar stopped. He reached into a holster on his belt. I panicked. Nothing good had ever come out of one of those holsters.

'Watch out!' I called. 'He has a weapon.' I swung back around towards the lift.

'Don't be stupid,' Caesar said. 'If I was going to kill you, you'd be long dead by now.'

I cleared my throat, trying to pretend my tiny outburst hadn't happened.

In his hand he was holding a thin, square piece of what looked like glass, the size of a mobile phone. It lit up and he pointed it towards the wall like a torch.

'Here they are.'

We huddled together around Caesar. I couldn't make out what we were looking at. It was as if the wall had been covered in some sort of scribble. Like something Emma would produce if she was handed a pen.

'What is this?' I asked and accidentally brushed up against Caesar's arm. Or was it accidental? Sometimes I felt a strange urge to touch him. When I wasn't fearing him, I wanted to feel his hair, stroke his skin.

He pointed towards a scratching of what appeared to be an artistic representation of a tangled mess.

'These are the names of my parents. Hebuda and Mikmar.' Caesar moved his finger. 'These are their dates of birth.' More mess. 'And these are the dates of their deaths.'

Something that sounded like a desperate sob suddenly echoed through the dark corridor. Was this a trap? The darkness was like a blindfold. I grabbed Caesar's arm, ripped the light from his hand and started flashing it every which way.

Louisa shouted out, 'There's someone there!'

I gasped. Along the corridor stood people. They were touching the wall, quietly stroking the scribbles, ignoring us.

'What are they doing?' I yelped. Everyone was dressed in grey overalls like Caesar's.

'Amalgamation of souls.'

'Amalga-what?'

'Some of us believe the soul is situated in the palms of our hands. They're trying to become one with the dead. This is what you would call a cemetery.' Caesar grabbed the light back from me. 'Well, as close as. Technically, this is just another corridor; the ship is a big maze of corridors. And there are no remains here, just names carved into the steel. Your body is let loose into space when you die. Or, in most cases, not when you die, but when your time is up.'

When your time is up? What was he talking about? He wasn't making any sense. Why couldn't he just make sense? I was sick and tired of all this. This was my life. I had a right to know. I had a right to understand what was happening; what was going to happen to me. Something inside me snapped like a dried-up twig.

'What!?' I shouted. 'What do you want me to do? Can someone just tell me what to do to make things right?' One of the mourners shushed at me.

Caesar put a hand on my shoulder. 'Show some respect.'

I shook him off. 'If anyone thinks they can do a better job ...' I reached into my pocket and pulled out the little steel box the Resistance had given me. 'Take it – just anyone take it.'

The yellow in Caesar's eyes appeared to eliminate the brown. They looked like the eyes of a panther ready to attack.

Andrew rushed towards me. 'Snap out of it, Amy.' He grabbed my hand and closed my fingers over the box, then closed his own over mine.

'We're all scared,' he said, looking into my eyes. 'None of us knows the right answer. None of us knows what to do. You're not alone in this. We're in this together.' He squeezed my hand. 'The only thing we can do is our best. We can't do any more than that.'

The darkness made his cheeks look hollow and his eyes sunken. I almost laughed. I was going to tell him that he sounded like Mum quoting one of her self-help books. But I didn't get a chance to. Behind us there was a soft swishing sound. A door to a lift started opening in the wall. A strip of light fought the darkness of the corridor like a Chihuahua barking at a bulldog. The door had only opened halfway when someone wearing grey overalls came running out, shouting in the visitors' language.

'*Hrwakaka sumatra krawata.*'

'Shit,' Caesar said as the footsteps of the mourners filled the corridor. They were running. There was shouting. 'We need to get back. Now.'

Caesar headed towards the lift the man in grey had come out of, but a group of people shot in front of him.

'What? Why?' Andrew said, letting go of my hand.

'The Red Stacks are coming.'

'But you said they never—'

'They usually don't.'

Caesar started running along the dark corridor. The rest of us followed like trembling shadows. We didn't have to go far. Caesar stopped and touched the wall, opening a door to another lift. All over people dressed in grey were doing the same. How many lifts were there? We hurtled inside. The door closed. Silence.

241

I turned to Caesar. 'Who are the Red Stacks exactly?'

'The president's security services. I don't know what they were doing down there. They're usually not that bothered with the Ten Pillars of Perfection. They usually turn a blind eye ...'

'The Ten Pillars of Perfection?'

'A body of laws the Defects must live by. Most of the sections outlaw futile emotions.'

'Futile emotions?'

'Sadness, fear, hate. Grief. And love.'

The lift door opened. We were back in the corridor where we'd started. The kitchen was right opposite. I recognised it from all the other half-hidden doors on the ship as it was the only one that had a window. A small crack allowed the smell of chicken burning to drift out. A couple of white-faced visitors in black overalls walking past eyed us with flat expressions. I couldn't see any Red Stacks.

'Where are the others?'

Caesar looked both ways, as if he were crossing the street, before heading towards the kitchen. 'The others?'

'The people from the cemetery. The people like you.'

'Most of them aren't allowed up here. They don't have security clearance. Most of the Defects are only allowed in designated areas.'

'But you? How come you're allowed up here? I've seen more like you walking the corridors. Are you not ... *a Defect*?'

'We're the lucky ones. We're genetically undesirable.'

Every time I asked Caesar a question it was as if he gave an answer to a totally different one.

We stopped in front of the kitchen. Courtney sniffed the air. 'They're ruining the chicken.'

Tom moaned. 'I'm hungry.'

Matilda rolled her eyes. 'Really, Tom, is that all you're thinking about?'

Caesar was blocking the kitchen door. 'I beg you. Hand the box over.'

I put my hand in my pocket and squeezed the box from the Resistance.

'Please, Amy. You don't know what you're doing.'

I studied his face. His cheeks had a rosy tint to them. A small scar separated one of his eyebrows. His lips were slightly cracked.

'What are you?' I looked over my shoulder at the white-faced visitors who were turning the corner. 'Are you one of them?'

Caesar lowered his eyes.

'Give me the box. We can help each other.'

'Are you one of them?'

'Just give it to me.' He took a step towards me but before his foot had touched the ground Andrew jumped in front of him, grabbed his shoulders and pushed him back.

Caesar slammed into the kitchen door. 'Chill, man. When are you going to realise that I'm trying to help you? When are you going to realise that if I wanted to harm you, if I was going to stop you with force, you'd all be dead already.'

I pushed myself up against Caesar and narrowed my eyes, hoping to give him a taste of what being cornered like a helpless animal felt like. 'Just tell me, are you one of them?'

Caesar tilted his head to one side. I stood so close I could feel the heat from his body. I liked how he smelled of honey and lavender.

'I am, and I'm not. It's complicated.'

Suddenly, the door to the kitchen opened. A visitor in black was standing in the doorway. His eyes widened slightly before he started hissing in his strange-sounding language.

Caesar lowered his head and answered something back as meekly as a servant in *Downton Abbey*. He turned to us.

'You're needed to cook the chicken.'

For the rest of the day I stood by the griddle and watched pink flesh turn white.

At the end of our shift Caesar and two visitors in black accompanied us back to the Camp. I was at the rear of the group. Caesar was walking behind me. With every step I could feel him draw closer. I put a protective hand over my pocket that contained the little steel box.

We were almost there when he leaned forward and whispered something in my ear. I couldn't believe what he was saying. But at the same time, I could believe it. None of the others noticed. None of the others heard. If they had, they would have gone mental.

Day Eight

Is it a new day? I don't know. It might still be yesterday. It's difficult to tell in here.

It's funny how quickly your eyes get used to the dark. But the spirit ... the spirit never gets used to being locked up.

He betrayed me. I can't believe he betrayed me.

I don't know what I'd do without my diary. Writing in this keeps me sane.

I wonder what the others are doing. Are they worried? Are they looking for me? Maybe they've already given up on me. Maybe they think I'm dead.

21

My original plan was to wait until everyone was asleep. The lights in the Camp had started to dim. One after the other the members of my small group, my space family, started to give in to the fading light. Matilda and Tom fell asleep in each other's arms, bathed in the red glow from the fake sunset. Courtney, Louisa and Damien, who'd moved in with us without asking, played poker until they couldn't see the cards properly. Damien was snoring loudly within minutes. Anita seemed to be waiting up for Andrew who was working on his bow again, but when the shiny imitation of the Moon and the stars as seen from Earth replaced the Sun she gave up and went to bed.

I was sitting by Andrew's side, watching him work. I didn't know he was aware of me being there until he suddenly said, 'I'm not sure we should stick to the plan.'

'Huh?'

'I'm not sure we should be putting all our efforts into finding another Rudolf.'

I held my breath, then breathed out in a controlled stream. 'Okay.'

'I mean, how do we know we can trust them?'

So I wasn't the only one having doubts. 'The Resistance.' I hesitated, then added, 'The Resistance back on Earth was working with them.'

'Yeah, but did they have all the facts? Could they be a hundred per cent sure this Rudolf guy and his associates were really helping us? I mean, what is it that you're doing here? What is it the Resistance wants you to do exactly?'

I flinched. I should have insisted on being told what my mission was. I should have demanded to know.

'I mean, have you tried opening the box?'

'No, Andrew. I haven't tried opening the box,' I barked at him. 'I've been too busy doing my nails and waxing my legs. Of course I've tried to open the box! Do you think I'm completely stupid?'

I squeezed my lips closed. I couldn't wake the others. I needed them asleep. But he was right. This would have been so much easier if we knew why I'd been sent up here. I *had* been stupid.

We sat in silence for a while. When Andrew showed no sign of going to bed I made up an excuse.

'I'm not tired. I'm going to take a walk.'

Andrew didn't seem to find it at all suspicious. He just nodded and continued working on his bow. I grabbed my backpack and left.

When I got to the Well I sat down on the floor. I was cold and tired. Working a twelve-and-a-half-hour shift in the kitchen had been hard. Although working was definitely better than sitting around doing nothing.

As I waited I kept thinking, *I shouldn't be doing this. I should go back to the others.* But I knew that this time I wasn't going to do what I should do.

And there he was.

'Well, hello there, Miss Amy,' he said as I got up. 'How are you doing this fine evening?'

He sounded nothing like the guy I'd been dealing with during the day. He sounded like a jolly seventeenth-century farmer who'd stumbled upon a time machine. I frowned. 'Why are you talking funny?'

'I didn't realise I was. I was trying to sound endearing.'

'Well, stop.'

'All right, Miss Amy. Your wish is my command.'

I was trying not to let the cuteness of his dimples affect me. 'What? What do you want?'

'I told you. I just want to – what do you call it? Hang.'

That was not exactly what he'd whispered in my ear on the way back from the kitchen. He'd said, 'Meet me tonight. By the Well. When the lights are out. I want to talk to you. Just you as you. And me as me.'

'I'm not handing it over.'

'I'm not asking you to.'

'I don't even have the box with me,' I lied.

'I just want to spend time with you. I just want to get to know you. As if everything were normal. As if we were two people who had just met.'

'People. You're not human, are you? Are you even a person?'

I was taken aback by the hurt on his face. 'Of course I'm a

person. Even he is a person.' He pointed towards one of the guards in black standing in the distance, half-asleep against one of the Camp doors. 'The fact that I'm not a *Homo sapien from the planet Earth* doesn't mean that I'm not a person. That doesn't mean I'm not a person who deserves the same respect as all of you.'

I felt my cheeks go red. 'Sorry.'

'No, I'm sorry.' Caesar looked as if he'd shrunk a little bit. 'Maybe I'm not a person. We don't even have that word – *person* – in my language. It's just that we Defects are constantly being told what we're not. We're not enough of this and not enough of that.'

Silence. I didn't know what to say and I was embarrassed by his anguish. I wanted to ask him what a Defect was but I sensed it was a sore subject. I finally cleared my throat. 'How come you speak English so well?' I said, trying to change the subject.

A dimply smile. 'We were made to learn it before we came here. Along with a host of other human languages. English is easy compared to a lot of them.'

'How many do you speak?'

'I don't know. Maybe twenty.'

I was gobsmacked. I only spoke one. One and a half if you counted the few words I knew in German.

Caesar put his hands energetically on his hips, making him look like a farmer now too. 'So. What do you want to do?'

'What do I want to do?'

'Yeah, like, if you were down on Earth and you were meeting up with a guy, a guy from another town, let's say, a really charming and funny and endearing guy, what would you do?'

I couldn't help smiling. 'I don't know. Maybe sit down with him and just have a chat. Make him tell me a bit about himself.'

'Okay. Let's go.' Caesar turned on his heel.

I hesitated.

'I promise not to make a stew out of you.'

I knew that I shouldn't go. But it was the dimples. I couldn't help myself.

The guard let us out of the Camp without a word. 'I already told him we have some kitchen business to attend to,' Caesar said. We walked the ship's maze-like corridors for a while. They were mostly empty.

'Where is everyone? Is it really night-time?' I always thought they were faking it in the Camp for our benefit.

'There is no night and day in space.'

'I know that!' I didn't want him to think I was stupid. 'What I mean is, is it night-time now where you come from?'

'I don't know. I haven't been there for so long. But there is night and there is day. Just like where you come from. Or at least there was.'

We turned the corner into what seemed to be a dead end. Caesar walked too purposefully towards the steel wall blocking our way for it to be a barrier. He touched it. It lit up, making his fingers appear orange. The door to a lift opened. How he found his way around the ship's many identical hallways I would never know.

We stayed silent for the duration of the lift ride. I was both nervous and excited. Andrew would have gone out of his mind if he knew that I'd left the Camp. Matilda would have felt betrayed.

250

Not because I was putting everything at risk: myself, the box from the Resistance that I was carrying in my pocket, the whole mission. She would have been pissed off because I didn't invite her along. Tom would have started an annoying debate on hedonism versus self-restraint. Anita would have stayed silent, Courtney and Louisa would have pointed out that I was not dressed for a date and Damien would have kept on snoring.

I felt Caesar's eyes on me and began to blush. The lift was slowing down. This was a much longer ride than the one we'd taken earlier in the day. When the door started to open I couldn't help stepping back. Caesar put his hand on my shoulder gently.

'It's okay. You're safe.' His eyes sparkled, the yellow and brown burning, dancing like autumn leaves in the wind. I did feel safe.

So I did it. I stepped out of the lift. I can't really describe it. The feeling. It was like being swallowed up by a large beast. But at the same time it was like being set free. It felt like the beginning and the end. It was everything and nothing. I thought I'd seen it. On TV. In Hollywood films. In documentaries. Technically, I knew what it looked like. But I hadn't really known. I so hadn't.

I tried to say something, but the only sound that came out was, 'Oh.'

Caesar laughed. 'Impressive, don't you think? You never get used to it.'

Impressive didn't even begin to describe it. The vast beauty. The graceful emptiness. This was space as I'd never seen it before. This was space as no human had seen it before – except maybe for astronauts ... and maybe not even them. No astronaut had stood under a glass dome the size of a football field bathed in the soft darkness of the seemingly endless universe. No astronaut had been able to look up at the shiny stars, planets and galaxies that peppered it like sequins on a velvety cocktail dress, as naturally as standing in a field looking up at the unhindered sky. And then there was Earth – home. A defiant splash of colour. A cotton ball streaked with blue nail polish.

I couldn't look down. I was walking and staring, walking and staring and suddenly—

'Watch out!'

It was too late. I bumped into something so hard it felt like being hit in the stomach. I almost keeled over but managed to grab hold of whatever it was that had stopped me in my tracks. I took a sharp breath and looked around, trying to get my bearings.

'Are you okay?' Caesar rushed to me.

They were everywhere, sticking out of the floor as far as the eye could see. Rows and rows of waist-height square columns. I straightened myself up. I ran my hand over the top of the column. It lit up. It was the size of the seat of a chair and made out of white plastic. It felt warm to the touch.

'What are they?'

'They're the incubators.'

'Incubators?' I stared into the light and noticed a shadow moving around inside the column. Was that …?

'This is where new life is grown.'

I pulled my hand back. The light went out.

'Don't worry. They don't bite. They probably don't even have teeth yet.' Caesar grinned.

252

I didn't think it was funny at all. My mind was filled with images of pale-faced visitor babies dressed in black onesies with murderous glints in their perfectly shaped newborn eyes. 'Are we allowed in here?'

'Of course we're not. But I tweaked my authorisation a little. When I'm not working in the Selection Lab or doing the kitchen shift I'm maintaining the servers in the server room.'

I'd once accidentally caught a glimpse of the TV show *One Born Every Minute* while channel hopping. The sight of a new life entering the world was the most disgusting thing I'd ever witnessed. Until now. 'I think we should get back.'

'Back to your prison?'

I didn't answer.

'Let's sit down. Let's have that chat.'

He was right. Going back to the Camp didn't sound very appealing.

'Please.'

'Fine.'

We sat down on the cold steel floor beneath the dark infinity of the universe. Caesar leaned against an incubator. It lit up. I could see the outline of a foetus the size of a melon inside.

'Oh, sorry.' He moved away from the white plastic column. The light faded and the baby disappeared. Caesar drew his legs up under him. 'So, what do you want to know?'

I laid the palms of my hands flat on the floor. What did I want to know? I looked up. My eyes were drawn towards Earth. It looked so fragile this high up. Like a little marble ball, hard but brittle. I wanted to know everything, but also nothing. Knowing nothing meant that I could still have hope. Knowing nothing meant that I could convince myself that this wasn't over – that Earth, my home, had a future. But knowledge … knowledge was the great destroyer of dreams and delusions.

'What are you?'

'Don't you mean *who*?'

'No. No, I mean what.'

'We went over this. I'm a person. Just like you.'

'I'm aware of the fact that you're a person. We've established that. But what is a person?' I sighed. How could I put this? 'If you accidentally cut yourself, say on the chopper in the kitchen, would you bleed?'

'What?'

'If you cut yourself, would you bleed?'

Caesar recoiled. 'Of course I'd bleed. Everyone bleeds.'

'You and your people invade our planet, break into our homes, hoover us up as if we're this insignificant dust that needs to be got rid of—' The words got caught in my throat. But I wasn't going to cry. 'So for all I know you could be a robot; underneath that skin you could be made of steel – you could be a lizard preparing to eat me for supper. You know all about me – well, maybe not me personally, but you speak English and you've been to Earth – yet I know nothing about you.'

There was silence. My heart was jumping around in my chest.

The black universe above us was reflected in Caesar's eyes. They looked cold and hard. But suddenly it was as if light penetrated the darkness. He smiled. 'A green lizard? I know I'm no … what is he called again? George Clooney. But—'

'George Clooney! He's seriously old.'

'Tom Cruise.'

'Eww ...'

'Prince Harry, then.'

'Closer.'

'Okay, someone you find attractive. But a lizard?'

Our eyes met. We stared at each other in silence and then, at the exact same moment, we burst out laughing. I laughed so hard, tears started running down my face. I laughed so hard, I could hardly breathe. We laughed and laughed. At one point Caesar laughed so hard his nose made a snorting noise and we laughed even harder. After a while our laughter began fading out. We looked at each other in silence again.

Caesar was first to speak. 'I'm sorry. I get where you're coming from. I tend to forget that Earth hasn't gone through the Enlightenment; that you're not part of the Union.' His eyes shone like little yellow-brown suns. 'Let's start again. Hi. I'm Caesar. But Caesar is just my Earth name. We all got to choose an Earth name before we came here. My real name is Katrakak.'

'Katra ...' I tried.

He smiled. 'Call me Caesar. I like Caesar.'

'Hi, Caesar. I'm Amy. Nice to meet you.'

His presence had a sweet softness to it. Like sponge cake.

'So, where are you from, Caesar?'

Was that sadness on his face? Whatever it was, he tried to smile through it.

'I'm from a planet called Pronax. It's not that far away actually. Only around fifty million light years.'

'Oh, only fifty million light years – that's nothing.'

He laughed. 'It's all relative, I guess.'

'So what brings you here, Caesar?'

His face was taken over by the shadows he'd been trying to hold back. He looked pale in the blue glare of Earth, which hovered above us like a nosy intruder.

'You.'

'Me?'

'Not you personally. Humans. The people of Earth. More precisely, the young people of Earth.' He fell silent. Then he reached into the holster on his belt and pulled out the thin piece of glass he had used as a torch in the cemetery. It reminded me of a smartphone. He touched the glass and a photograph appeared on it like it would on a screen.

'This was my house.' He handed me the gadget. It was so much lighter than my smartphone. And the clarity of the image was incredible. The photo was of a white, windowless house that looked eerily similar to the incubators. In front of it there stood a man and a woman. I touched the screen and the photo popped out of it. It hovered above the glass pad in 3D. Just like the president's head had that day in the Camp – a hologram.

I couldn't hide my amazement.

'I guess your technology doesn't do that then.'

I tried touching the house with my finger but it went right through it. I pointed towards the man and the woman. They looked strangely normal. If it weren't for the weird box-shaped house behind them and a strange orange glow in the sky, they could have been normal people back on Earth. 'Who are they?'

'Mum and Dad,' Caesar said. 'Back on Pronax. Before ...' He fell silent.

'Before what?'

'We thought we were lucky. We feared they'd leave all the Defects behind.'

Caesar reached over and tapped on the glass pad. The photo of his house disappeared and a 3D re-creation of a planet jumped up from it. It looked a bit like Earth seen from space but it clearly wasn't Earth. There was more white and less blue and green.

'Our planet is dying.'

'Dying? Why?'

Caesar shrugged his shoulders. 'We don't know. It just seems as if its time is up. Its core is going cold. We tried to revive it. We tried reigniting it with a nuclear stimulator. It's what you on Earth would call an atomic bomb. But it didn't work. If anything, it made things worse. They think it accelerated the process.'

'Why can't the core go cold?'

'It affects the atmosphere. When a planet's core cools it can no longer generate a magnetic field. Without the magnetosphere to protect it, the planet's atmosphere is gradually stripped by solar winds and eventually there is no air to breathe. That's what happened to your neighbouring planet, Mars. It used be quite habitable some billion years ago. There was water and air. But then its core went out, the magnetic field disappeared and the atmosphere was blown away.'

I realised I should pity Caesar and his people. What a fate, having to leave your planet – it wasn't like losing your house; then at least you still had ground under your feet. But I didn't feel pity. Anger swelled inside me like a river during a rainstorm. 'So, your planet is dying. And you plan to steal ours.'

Caesar flinched as if the thought had never occurred to him. 'No. The president would never do that. He would never break the Code of the Union; he would never take a planet that is already inhabited by others. He follows the rules to the letter. He's honourable.'

'Honourable.' The word shot out of my mouth like spit. 'Following the rules doesn't automatically make you honourable. How is it honourable to abduct people from their homes and lock them up in a prison camp in space?'

Caesar lowered his eyes. 'You're right. You're right. Honourable is the wrong word. He's a rule follower. He's predictable. That's what I meant.'

'Then what?' I was shouting. 'What do you want with us?'

Caesar put his hands up like a criminal being confronted by a police officer'. 'It's them. We Defects have no say in this. It's the Corrects. They want you.'

'The Corrects? The white-faced ones?'

'Yes. They need a backup plan. If the worst comes to the worst, this isn't sustainable.' He was waving his arms around in a gesture that looked as if it was meant to tell me something.

I just stared at him.

'This. The incubators. The continuation of the species. Our planet is dying. We have to find a new home. No one knows how long it will take. Maybe a few years. Maybe generations. But while we're searching, energy is in limited supply. And it takes a lot of energy to grow a whole living and breathing organism. If we don't find a viable planet to live on soon, there won't be enough energy to sustain the species.'

I noticed that there wasn't actually silence underneath the glass dome as I'd thought. I could hear a faint humming sound, like the noise our fridge made at home. It came from the incubators. 'So it isn't just your planet that's dying – it's you.'

Caesar hugged his knees to his chest. 'I guess you could say that.'

I wasn't sure if it was the humming, the overwhelming vastness of the universe above us or the incomprehensible information flow clogging up my brain, but I was starting to feel faint. I tried to shake it off. 'I don't get it. What has it got to do with me?'

'It turns out that perfection comes at a price.' Caesar sighed. 'At first they didn't care. They couldn't see how it mattered.'

The dizziness was turning into a headache. 'You're really not making any sense.'

'I know. I'm not very good at this. I'm trying to work out where to start.'

'The beginning. Start at the beginning.'

'Okay. The beginning. I'm starting at the beginning. Hmm … I guess it all began generations ago. It's difficult to say exactly when – the change was gradual – but most would agree that there was a turning point around five generations ago, in the time of my great-great-great-grandparents, when they discovered the Elixir.' Caesar looked at me, his eyes like big question marks asking whether I was following.

I nodded.

'Okay. A long time ago life on Pronax wasn't that different from life on Earth, from anywhere in the universe really.'

It took at least a second for the implication of his statement to sink in. But when it did, it felt like an explosion inside my brain. 'There are others?! Like you? Like us?'

'Of course there are. All over the universe. Like us. Totally different from us.' Caesar furrowed his brow. 'What – you didn't think you were alone, did you?' He laughed.

I blushed. 'No,' I lied.

'Sorry,' Caesar said. 'I didn't mean to laugh. Although we're not the same, we kind of are. Our origin is the same. We're all from the same beginning. We all have our origin in the Big Bang. Therefore it's logical that we evolved in similar directions. There are some regional variants because of different living conditions. For example, the people on planet Zootra have short arms and long necks because their forefathers foraged food from trees using their mouths rather than their hands.'

I frowned. 'Like giraffes?' Dad was always banging on about how natural selection had caused the giraffe to evolve a long neck so they could reach the nourishing leaves highest up in the trees.

'Kind of. And some have longer legs because their forefathers had to deal with uneven planet surfaces.' Caesar straightened his back. 'Let me just show you.' He reached for his glass pad. 'I have some photos.' He tapped the pad. 'This is me, Mum and Dad on Celestina.' They were sitting on what appeared to be a sandy beach. The photo was old. Caesar looked around seven years old. 'Even though it's a bit far from Pronax, two solar systems away, a lot of us go there for holidays. It's warm, it has two suns and the atmosphere is high in nitrous oxide so you feel really relaxed.' He tapped the pad again. 'And this is Evity.' The photo was of a snow-white cornfield under a blood-red sky. 'Dad took it. He was a Grower. Evity is the bigger of the two nutri-planets, Evity and Graze. They're the planets where the grains are grown for the porridge we eat. No one lives there, of course. You couldn't. It's too warm and the atmosphere is almost unbreathable.' He tapped the pad once more. 'And here we're back on Pronax. I'm standing at the foot of Mountain Esha.' The ground was covered with red gravel and brownish moss. 'It's just outside my town. I often went there for a hike when I had the time.'

Shadows fell across his face. 'I'm told things first began to change with the Corrections. It started out innocently enough. They were only small genetic tweaks really. At first they only did it to eliminate certain diseases. Those who were having a baby and could afford it bought a DNA editing treatment for the embryo.'

'Editing?'

'A small modification to the embryo. It's like cut and paste. They used a pair of molecular scissors to cut the DNA and then inserted new pieces of genetic code at the site of the cut. That way they could cut out the heritable diseases coded by mutations in the DNA. But it wasn't long before they started to use the technology for other purposes – other treatments began to pop up. More and more babies were genetically modified for beauty, intelligence, strength, mood.'

'Mood?'

'People were made less susceptible to feelings. Sadness, anger, grief, love, happiness. Too many ups and downs were considered to reduce the quality of life. Some were even defined as a disease. Uninterrupted contentedness was thought to be the perfect state.'

'Wow.'

'The aim with the genetic tweaks was to correct what was wrong with our species. Bring us closer to perfection. Well, bring *them* closer to perfection.'

'Them?'

'The Corrects. It didn't take long. Maybe a generation or so. *We* became *them* and *us*.'

'So you and the Corrects, are you not the same?'

'We used to be. Before the Corrections started we used to be the same species. Now ... I don't know. Since the Elixir, I don't know. The separation started early on. From the beginning of the Corrections we lived in a two-tiered society. Only those who could pay for treatment had Correct children. Those who were poor had to have children the old-fashioned way and hope they would turn out okay.

'You could easily see who were Corrects and who were Defects – people who hadn't been genetically altered. The Corrects were all super-pretty – their skin was perfect, their teeth were straight, their eyes were big. Slowly, they began to resemble each other. But it was considered a good thing. Among the Corrects, everyone was equal. Equally pretty, equally smart, equally content.'

I wondered whether Caesar could tell one Correct from the other.

'Breeding between the Corrects and the Defects was banned. It was said to slow the evolution towards perfection.'

Caesar sighed. 'And then they found the Elixir and the gap widened even further.'

'The Elixir?'

'The reason you are here is that they found the Elixir. Or what they thought was the Elixir.'

The word made me feel cold.

'I don't know when the search for the Elixir started. But all of a sudden everything began to revolve around eternal life. Most hereditary diseases had been eliminated, but people still died. They hadn't cured old age. They hadn't cured death. Suddenly, people became obsessed with quantity.' Caesar grimaced.

'What's wrong with quantity?'

'Nothing,' he snapped. 'As long as it isn't at the expense of quality.' He narrowed his eyes. 'Imagine a life that has been stripped of everything but function. Imagine living for the sole purpose of breathing.'

'I don't understand.'

'What gives you pleasure? What do you like doing?'

'I don't know … I like playing computer games. Listening to music. Reading.'

'And what is the function of those things?'

'What do you mean?'

'What do they achieve?'

'Nothing. I just like them. They're fun.'

'Exactly!'

'Exactly what?'

'That is exactly my point. The things that make life worth living don't have any function.' His words were burning with passion. 'The Corrects had obtained beauty, intelligence, the eradication of disease, pain and heartache. They'd come as close to perfection as you'd think possible. But no. It wasn't enough. They got greedy. The final frontier had to be conquered. They were hell-bent on prolonging life, no matter the cost. First they started tampering with the food. Normal food – vegetables, meat, fish, food like you eat – suddenly wasn't good enough.

'It was long before my time, of course, but I've been told we used to enjoy food.' His eyes met mine. 'Like you, we used to sit around the dinner table with friends and family and eat and talk and laugh. Instead of food they invented the porridge-like goo, perfectly balanced for longevity and health. No one laughs and talks around the dinner table while eating tasteless goo.

'Then it was the extracurricular activities. I'm told that everyone used to have hobbies. We used to play games, read texts, watch plays, make music. But most of them made way for activities designed to increase health: individually designed exercise programmes, sleep, hours spent in oxygen tanks. You've seen them in the corridors – the Corrects – how they walk, neither fast nor slow, as if they're just floating through the air with nowhere to go?'

I nodded.

'Because of technological advances, the Corrects only have to work a few days a year. Defects are used for all manual labour. Walking has been deemed the optimal exercise for longevity. So the Corrects spend most of their lives walking the ship's corridors at the exact speed of five kilometres per hour.'

264

Caesar's shoulders slumped. 'I guess for them, giving up the things they liked wasn't that difficult. Enthusiasm was one of the emotions that had been deleted from their DNA. We, the Defects, were meant to live like them, according to their values. But for us it was hard. We had to fight our urges, our instincts, our genetic faults every day. It was impossible. We kept on doing things we liked, but discreetly. Of course it wasn't that discreet. So they came up with the Ten Pillars of Perfection. The laws of the Ten Pillars were meant to improve the lives of the Defects – they were meant to give us what they had. Long and balanced lives, free of emotional ups and downs, uninterrupted contentedness.

'And then they found the Elixir. It's kind of ironic. My great-great-great-grandmother was on the team of scientists that discovered it. Back then, the division between the Defects and the Corrects hadn't reached its later heights. There were still Defects who were on an equal footing with the Corrects – who were just as smart, just as capable. If she'd only known the implications of her discovery.'

I realised I was holding my breath. I quickly breathed in. 'What happened?'

'They were doing experiments on quinshasas. It's an animal that in Earth terms looks a bit like a mix between a monkey and a rat. They discovered that if they removed the reproductive system from the body of a quinshasa and replaced it with hormone implants, the aging process would slow up to fivefold. It turned out the reproductive system was a ticking time bomb. It was the part of the body that determined when the organism didn't serve a purpose any more. When it had done its part in preserving the species and was needed no longer. That was it. That was the Elixir they'd been looking for. The key to eternal life.'

I wasn't sure I understood. 'So how … I mean, if you remove …'

'Cloning,' Caesar said, as if reading my mind. 'That's how they kept the species going. Technically, they didn't need the reproductive system. Scientists had long since discovered cloning. So the Corrects started having their reproductive systems removed, and when they wanted to have children they just had little clones of themselves made who were grown in incubators.'

'So can they really? Live for ever?'

'No, not for ever. But pretty close. The clones – the new generation of Pronaxians – were genetically tweaked so they were created without a reproductive system. The natural life expectancy of a Defect is around 150 years in Earth time. A Correct can live for up to 750 years.'

My anger soared again. *What an ungrateful group of people.* Here they were with their good health, beauty, amazing technology and long lives invading a planet inhabited by a far more primitive species and abducting them. Didn't they have enough?

'I still don't get it,' I snapped, taking my rage out on Caesar. 'I still don't get what this has to do with me. What this has to do with young people living on Earth.'

Caesar squirmed where he was sitting on the floor as if getting to the point was physically painful for him. 'As I said, they need a backup plan.' He paused. 'We, the Defects, are one half of their backup plan.' Was he embarrassed? 'You're the other.'

No. I refused to believe he was saying what it sounded like he was saying.

'There are thousands of Pronaxian ships cruising the universe looking for a new settlement, a new planet. This could take centuries. These incubators ...' He looked around the room at the perfectly white, square columns sticking out of the floor. 'This might be the last generation of Corrects. We don't have enough energy to grow them any more. Not until we find a new home. And maybe not even then. Pronax was extremely rich in energy sources. We might not get that lucky again.'

I felt dirty. Used. Violated. I wanted to get up and run. Run as fast as I could. But I knew it was useless. I'd realised it as soon as I'd got here: in space, there is no place to run.

So I tried to keep calm. I heard Mum's voice in my head: *Panic is just a state of mind. You control your own thoughts. Calmness is a choice.* How I missed her.

'After the Elixir, the Defects became second-class citizens. We were made to live in separate neighbourhoods from the Corrects. We weren't allowed to do jobs that required intellectual thinking; we were only thought to be capable of manual labour. We were meant to abide by the Ten Pillars of Perfection. But we had always been free.

'A few weeks before Pronax was scheduled to be abandoned, all Defects were rounded up and locked up in Camps on the escape vessels.' Caesar took a deep breath. 'We didn't know why we were being held like that, but we were happy to be there. The Corrects controlled everything on Pronax: the government, the resources, the space fleet. We'd been sure they would just leave the Defects on Pronax to die. So sure in fact that there had been a few attempts to steal ships from the fleet by groups of Defects. But then …' Caesar started shaking his head as if he doubted his own words. 'They didn't give any explanation. It wasn't until we'd left Pronax that we found out the reason they took us with them. Why they chose to save us.' Caesar lowered his eyes. 'They saved us for the same reason they abducted you. Our lives are no longer our own. We are to become the saviours of the Pronaxian race.'

I was finally starting to put two and two together and getting something resembling four. But I was still hoping my calculations were wrong. 'What do you mean?'

'The Corrects are no longer capable of breeding naturally. They can't have children without massive technological interventions. You know what happens to species that can't reproduce.'

I wasn't sure if I was meant to answer.

Caesar's eyebrows sank. 'They die out.'

I suddenly remembered the pandas. They were on the news all the time. As they were facing extinction, people working in zoos all over the world were trying to get them to mate. Apparently, their efforts weren't very successful because the pandas kept in captivity weren't interested in procreating.

'Without technology and the energy to power it there is a danger Pronaxians will become extinct. But there is one hope: the Defects. This small underclass of people who never had the means nor opportunity to obtain perfection is the only hope to keep the species going.'

I'd seen the Camp the Defects lived in. Caesar's home. It looked and smelled worse than a cage in a zoo. I couldn't help wondering whether the Corrects would be more successful than the zookeepers in their efforts.

'How can they do that? How can they be allowed to do that?'

'Sacrificing the individual for the whole is perfectly legal on Pronax. It's a common practice among societies all over the universe.'

In a way, I could understand. Desperate times called for desperate measures and facing extinction was as critical as a situation could get. 'I guess it makes sense …' I started to mumble but Caesar interrupted me.

'No, it does not! It doesn't make sense at all! What's the point? What's the point of living just for the sake of breathing? They've taken all enjoyment out of life. Nothing has any value unless it prolongs life in some way. But isn't it better to live properly for a hundred years than to hardly live for a thousand? There is no point in just existing. You might as well be dead. They might just as well be dead.'

I didn't care for being shouted at. None of this was my fault. I shouted back at him.

'And how is this my problem?'

Caesar fell silent. He didn't look at me when he spoke. 'They did calculations. There aren't enough of us. There aren't enough Defects. We aren't genetically diverse enough. They need more.' He looked up. 'They need you.'

I couldn't help it any longer. I scrambled to my feet. Deep down, I'd known. Ever since he'd started his weird speech on reproduction, I'd suspected this.

'So what? Are they just going to pair us up and … and …?' I didn't want to finish the thought. 'Are they just going to make me hook up with someone at random and … and …'

'Well …' Caesar hesitated. 'Not everyone is eligible.'

When I didn't think things could get any worse, they did.

'You know the tests in the Selection Lab?'

'Yes.'

'And the three doors …'

I felt cold.

'The test was to determine through which door I was meant to send you. Door one is for the breeding programme. Those eligible are paired up with a compatible Defect. Door three, the one you went through, is for those who aren't deemed eligible for breeding because of a genetic flaw – or what the Corrects consider a flaw – but have shown applicability for certain work, such as kitchen work. Like me. I didn't qualify for the breeding programme. So I work. Not many do qualify for work. Most things are automated on board the ship, so they don't really need that many workers. Only a handful of humans have qualified: a few for kitchen duties and a few to help out at the medical bay where they're being trained in midwifery.'

He stopped.

I stared at him. 'And door two. The one I was actually meant to go through.'

He didn't look at me when he answered. 'Elimination. Door two is for elimination.'

I started shaking.

'Amy, sit down.'

I was backing away. 'This isn't happening. I'm dreaming. Any moment I'm going to wake up in my bed, at home, in London, on planet Earth ...'

'Amy.'

'No, this isn't happening. You're not real. You're just in my head; this is all in my head. I'm just having a nightmare.'

'Amy, stop.'

Little did I know the nightmare had hardly begun.

Day Nine – I Think

I've lost all sense of time. I guess that's what happens when you're locked up in a prison cell surrounded by nothing but complete darkness.

I've been thinking about what Caesar told me. I've been thinking about the Pronaxians. How their society got split in two. I'm not sure which group I'd rather belong to – the beautiful, eternally content Corrects or the ordinary, emotional Defects.

On the one hand, it would be good to be rid of disease. And I get why it would be beneficial to erase the emotional ups and downs of life. But depriving people of experiencing love? Is that a price worth paying?

Caesar saved my life. I was meant to go through door number two. When he ran the test on me in the Selection Lab, the result was TWO. The result was elimination.

I'm so confused right now. Did he save me because he has feelings for me? It is possible. He isn't a Correct; he's a Defect. He can experience all the same emotions that humans do.

But if he has feelings for me, why did he betray me? Why did he have me locked up in here?

Maybe he doesn't have feelings for me at all. Maybe I imagined the chemistry we had. Maybe he just saved me to get his hands on the little steel box he so coveted.

22

No matter how loudly Caesar shouted at me, ordering me to calm down, I couldn't stop panicking. Adrenaline was gathering inside me like a tornado threatening complete destruction.

It only took four words for everything to change. Four magic words stopped my meltdown and turned the tornado into a light summer's breeze. 'We *can* get out.'

I stared at Caesar. *What?*

'There is a way.'

I had to force myself not to start jumping up and down. There was a way! There was a way!

'If you give me the box you brought with you from Earth, there is a way.'

The happiness drained from my heart like water from a kitchen sink. I felt empty. Of course there was a catch. I put my hand in my pocket and wrapped my fingers around the box.

'You can trust me, Amy.'

The void inside me was filling up with anger. What kind of gullible idiot did he take me for?

'We're in the same boat.' Caesar suddenly grinned. 'Or spaceship rather.'

I narrowed my eyes, feeling like a tiger protecting her cubs. There was nothing I wouldn't do to safeguard my mission.

'You can save your breath. I'm not giving you the box. And besides, even if I did, it would be of no use to you. It's impossible to open. I've tried.'

Caesar wrinkled his nose. 'It's not meant to be opened.'

'What do you mean?'

'It isn't a box.'

The steely edges of the box, or what I'd taken to be a box, were digging into the palm of my hand.

'Really, Amy, what do you know about the situation? What do you know about the reason for you being sent here?'

I didn't answer.

'Do you think it's sensible to do something you don't understand the consequences of?'

Rage rushed through me. I wanted to slap him. 'You try it! You try having your life ripped from under you. You try having your head overflowing with questions. *Why? Who? What?* You try being who knows how many hundreds of thousands of kilometres away from home, flying around space in a vehicle that up until a few weeks ago only existed in movies.'

Caesar's face fell. His skin turned pale. Suddenly, I could see how the Defects and the Corrects had once been the same people.

'I'm sorry,' Caesar said, starting to walk towards me.

'Stay back!'

He didn't listen. 'I'm really, really sorry.' He stopped right in front of me and took my hand. 'I was being stupid. I should understand, shouldn't I? If anyone should understand, it's me, a

Defect. I know how it feels to be made to leave your home. I know how it feels to not be the master of your own destiny. You start clutching at straws.'

I didn't look at him but I didn't pull away either. Was I clutching at straws?

'Let me show you.'

His grasp was warm.

'Give me the box and I'll show you. I promise to give it back. That is, if you still want it back after you know the truth.' He squeezed my hand. 'Amy, I think whoever sent you here doesn't have your best interests at heart. I think whoever sent you here is using you.'

He was lying. He had to be lying. The Resistance had the same interests as me. I squeezed the box that wasn't a box. Someone was lying. Either it was the Resistance or it was Caesar. The rational part of me said it had to be Caesar. Of course it was Caesar. But doubt had already started to cast its long shadow over my conviction. How could he be lying? His skin was so perfect and his dimples were so cute. *Amy, looks can be deceiving*, I told myself. But I couldn't ignore this instinct I had. When Caesar looked at me with his brown-yellow autumn-like eyes it felt like an embrace. He was actually looking at me, whereas CJ and Mandira and the rest of the Resistance always looked *through* me. I'd told myself it was a grown-up thing. Grown-ups often looked through people younger than them. As if they didn't matter. As if they weren't worth noticing. Kids – what did they know? But it was more than that. It was something else.

I had to do it. I had no choice. I removed my hand from my pocket. 'Here. Take it.'

Caesar stared at my open palm. 'Are you sure?'

I nodded. I wasn't. I wasn't sure about anything. Caesar might well steal the box. But this was the only option I had if I wanted to have any hope of knowing the truth. I told myself that if he did steal it, I would just run after him and grab it from him. *Yeah, right.*

He didn't take the box from me but reached into his belt for the glass pad.

'What are you doing?'

'Put the cube on the pad.'

'Where?'

'Just anywhere.'

I carefully placed the steel box on to the shiny glass surface. The screen lit up. I jerked my hand back. The box stuck to the pad like a magnet to iron. All of a sudden letters mixed in with illegible scribble began to scroll up the pad's screen.

'What is this?'

Caesar stared at the pad. 'The files are being downloaded.'

'Downloaded?'

'From the cube. This is the information you were meant to hand over to the Splinters.'

'The Splinters. Who are the Splinters?'

'They didn't tell you anything, did they?'

I watched the letters rush across the pad. After a few seconds the screen went black again. Caesar removed the box and put it in the holster on his belt. I considered demanding that he give it back but I was in a hurry to see what was on the pad. Caesar touched the screen. What appeared looked underwhelming. Black letters on a white background, just like a Word document. The top part of the page was written in English, the bottom half in the Pronaxian scribble I recognised from the cemetery wall.

Caesar buried his nose in the pad.

'What does it say?'

Caesar didn't answer.

'Let me see.' I tried grabbing the pad from him but he was holding on tight.

'Just as we thought,' he mumbled to himself.

'What?'

'Those bastards.'

'What? What? Tell me?'

Caesar looked up. 'Sorry, sorry. Okay. If you hand the box over to the Splinters, you will be sealing your planet's fate.'

I just stared at him.

'You will be personally responsible for its future. And it will be a bleak one.'

I didn't know why, but I felt dirty.

'See for yourself.' He handed me the pad. I had to force myself to accept it.

The heading of the document said: 'Surrender treaty between the People's Resistance Against the Alien Occupation of Earth and the vice-president of Pronax'. I read it again. Surrender treaty. Surrender treaty. I tried to spin the meaning of the phrase in my head. It didn't say who was surrendering to whom. But I wasn't even close to buying my attempt at self-deception.

Below the title there was a list of legal-sounding promises:

1) The People's Resistance Against the Alien Occupation (hereafter called the Resistance) agrees to unconditional surrender to the Splinter Group of Pronaxians Devoted to the Rapid Discovery of the New Fatherland and the Overthrow of the President (hereafter called the Splinters).

2) The Resistance agrees to join forces with the Splinters under the leadership of the vice-president in their permanent occupation of planet Earth. It agrees to disclose all details in their possession of military significant locations on their planet (see Appendix A for details) and details of the varied governments scattered across the planet's many countries (see Appendix B), and to aid the Splinters in their rapid overthrow of those governments (see Appendix C for the first steps).

3) In exchange for the aforementioned, the Splinters agree to free from captivity 16,238 of the abducted youths from Earth who, once back on Earth, will be exempt from the Pronaxian breeding programme (see Appendix D for list of chosen youths).

Then came the signatures. There had to be at least a hundred, one from each division – the head of each Collective. There it was, the signature from the East London Regiment. Charles Johnson. It was CJ. CJ had signed off on this. I couldn't believe it.

There was a sour taste in my mouth. I wanted to throw up. *Permanent occupation.* I had thought I was on a mission to fight an alien invasion. But no. Quite the contrary. CJ and Mandira had sent me on a mission to surrender to the visitors. They had sent me on a mission to hand over planet Earth to an alien species.

I was a traitor. I was a traitor to my country. I was a traitor to my people. I was a traitor to my planet.

'Are you okay?'

What had I done?

'You don't look so good.'

'The Splinters ...' I could hardly talk. 'What are they?'

'They are a group of Corrects loyal to the vice-president.'

'Who's the vice-president?'

'No one. We don't really know. His identity is kept hidden for security reasons. Rumour has it that the vice-president is working on undercutting the president of Pronax. It is said that the vice-president doesn't think the president is willing to go far enough in securing his species' future. The vice-president thinks the president should ignore the Code of the Union, take Earth with force, exterminate the human race and turn it into a permanent home for the Pronaxians to live. But the president will never go against the Code. He won't break a single law of the Union. So, the vice-president and the Splinters are working to undermine him. They intend to overthrow him. Then they'll be in power and they'll be able to do whatever they want.'

The list. Suddenly, I had to see the list. I scrolled down. Appendix D. The names were in alphabetical order. I selected the letter S. There were hundreds of people on the list who had a last name starting with S.

John Salisbury, London.

Gerhard Schaaf, Munich.

Karen Sigurjónsdóttir, Reykjavik.

Adeline Simoneaux, Lille.

There were names from all across the world.

There it was. Sullivan.

There were two Sullivans on the list.

Alexander Sullivan, New York.

Catherine Sullivan, Salt Lake City.

At first I was sure I had overlooked it. I remembered Mandira and John's' visit to our house. Before Andrew and Matilda had been taken. Mandira wanted to use me or Andrew as bait for the Resistance. She'd said that we would be taken anyway. She'd said that way something good could come out of it. She'd said, 'This way they'd at least stand a chance of returning home.'

My name had to be on the list. I'd done what they'd asked. They had to have put me on that list.

'Amy, I think you should sit down.'

I clicked on the letter W. I noticed it straight away.

Anita Withers, London.

My palms were sweating. The pad slipped from my grasp. Those lying, cheating traitors! It wasn't hard to put two and two together. The Resistance had sold us out. Instead of fighting the enemy, they'd done a deal with them. A really selfish and shortsighted deal. To get their own kids back they'd promised to help the visitors conquer Earth. They'd betrayed us all and they'd made me complicit in their treachery. And they hadn't even bothered to put me on their bloody list.

It suddenly all made sense. Their furtive looks. Their unwillingness to give me details about the mission. The way they always looked through me when they spoke to me.

My cheeks were burning hot. They weren't going to get away with this. I wasn't going to let them. *We can get out.* That was what Caesar had said. I quickly turned to him.

'There is a way. You said there is a way.'

He nodded. 'Yes. There is hope.'

'What kind of hope?'

'The hope of freedom.'

I'd been promised that before. 'For you or for me?'

'Hopefully, both of us.'

I'd come here to save Earth, I'd come here to save humanity along with all the kids who'd been abducted, but I'd found out that I'd been deceived. There was no plan to save the planet, to save our collective home. There wasn't even a plan to save all the kids who'd been taken – only a few of them. There was no common cause. There was only self-interest. Everyone was just looking out for themselves.

I couldn't save Earth from the white-faced aliens who had besieged our planet. But I could save it from the traitors among our own. I could save it from the Resistance. There wasn't a chance in hell I would hand over their surrender deal to the Splinters.

And then there was us: me, Andrew, Matilda, Anita, Tom and all the kids who'd been so cruelly snatched from their lives and locked up in a prison in space. We had to look out for ourselves. Like everyone else, we had to save ourselves.

I had a chance and I was going to take it. But this time I wasn't going to behave like a gullible idiot. This time around I was going to be in charge.

'Okay, what do we need to do?'

Day Ten

No one has been into my cell for what feels like days. Logically, though, I know it hasn't been days. Probably only hours; a guard brought me a bowl of porridge and a glass of water this morning. But solitude distorts the sense of time.

I'm trying not to imagine what they're going to do to me. Writing helps me keep my mind off it.

I had such high hopes when Caesar and I walked out of the glass dome, leaving the creepy incubators behind. I felt so empowered. So in charge. Everything was going to be fine. We didn't know how exactly, but we would figure it out.

Then suddenly the place was swarming with Red Stacks.

I was about to run, to try to make a break for it. But Caesar grabbed me by the T-shirt. The neckline dug into my throat.

'As I was saying,' he barked at me, his face hard and his voice angry, 'you are under arrest.'

I stared at him. What?

He wasn't looking right at me.

Had this all been a trap?

The Red Stacks said something to Caesar in their incomprehensible language.

Caesar nodded in response. He looked me straight in the eye. 'The president's men will be taking over from here.'

Then he just walked away.

*

So I ended up here, in a cell full of darkness so condensed that I can almost touch it.

I'm tired – which is strange because I've hardly moved for hours. I've been lying on the floor trying to imagine what my life would be like now if there had never been a siege; if there had never been any visitors. I would be starting school. Year 10. I would be sick with dread as usual at the start of the school year, worrying about what latest trend I didn't pick up on over the summer that would give Courtney and Louisa a reason to criticise me. 'Oh, look at that – she's wearing leopard-print socks. Doesn't she know that leopards are so last season? This year it's zebras.'

Mum would be giving her start-of-the-year self-esteem-boosting speech. 'Be true to yourself, Amy, love; you're perfect as you are.' And I would be rolling my eyes so hard I'd get a headache.

If I woke up right now and discovered that all this – this cell, the siege, the visitors – had only been a bad dream and my old life was still there waiting for me, I would ignore Courtney and Louisa and I would give Mum a hug and tell her I really appreciated her cheerleading tendencies.

Shit. I can hear something. Voices. Someone is coming. I hope this isn't it. I hope this isn't my last entry; that this isn't the end.

23

When the door to my cell opened I had to shield my eyes from the brightness pouring in. It was as if they'd resigned themselves to the prospect of never seeing light again and had forgotten how to respond to it.

Once I'd recovered I could see two figures in red standing in the doorway. The president's men. In a flat voice one of them ordered me to come with them.

I felt numb as we walked in silence along empty corridors. Empty corridors; as empty as their perfectly sculpted eyes reflecting their empty lives. That's how Caesar had described the Corrects. Quantity instead of quality.

I glanced at my captors. In their red overalls the visitors' complexions seemed to be bordering on purple.

We stopped in front of a steel wall that looked like a dead end but I knew from experience would be a door. One of the men put his hand on the flat surface, which lit up. With a swishing sound the door slid to the side.

'You do not address the president unless invited to do so,' one of the men said.

'The presid—'

I was cut off by a strained, husky voice coming from deep inside a big steel hall.

'You're a girl.'

I knew the face. I'd seen it once before. Then as a hologram, a hovering head in the Camp, threatening to kill anyone who 'disturbed the peace'. There he had looked like a living, breathing mummy. In person, he looked even older.

'Should I feel offended?' The president cleared his phlegmy throat, sounding like a congested toilet being flushed. 'I should think I was an opponent worthy of your strongest. Then I find out that our infiltrator is of the sex that you humans regard as inferior.'

I don't know what came over me. The words just started shooting out of my mouth. 'Girls aren't the inferior se—'

'What did I tell you?' the guard hissed and squeezed my arm. 'I told you not to—'

The president waved a hand that looked so veiny you would be forgiven for thinking he was actually inside out. 'Wait outside.'

The two men left the room as quickly as bullets leaving a barrel.

'I will get straight to the point,' the president said. He was sitting behind a steel desk. His chair started moving with a soft electrical buzzing. It turned out to be on wheels. It was a wheelchair. Well, at least the steely space version of a wheelchair. He steered past the desk but stopped at a safe distance away from me.

'I need their names and the details of your plan.'

I stared at him. His eyes were turning yellow and bloodshot.

'The names of your co-conspirators. The traitors on board my ship and your collaborators back on Earth. And I want to know your intentions.'

His voice sounded detached. There was no hint of emotion. It was just as if he were asking me to pass him the salt.

I don't know what happened. Maybe it was his strangely calm manner, his frail looks or just that I had lost my mind, but I didn't hesitate. 'No,' I said, so firmly I made myself jump. I had no idea where that no came from. I usually wasn't courageous. Quite the contrary. I'd always tried to get out of PE on the days we were meant to jump over the vaulting horse. And sometimes I'd pretended I needed to go to the bathroom just so I'd have an excuse not to run into Courtney and Louisa in the corridors at school.

To my own amazement, I didn't stop there. 'How do you even know that I'm an infiltrator? How do you know I'm not just one of the kids you've been snatching from Earth like some ...' I couldn't think of a strong enough word. I tried again. 'Like some ... like some pervert.'

The insult didn't register. 'It doesn't take much for a Defect to talk.'

That shut me right up. So he had betrayed me. Caesar had betrayed me. This hadn't been some sort of a misunderstanding.

Why? Why would he do that? Why would he do that after I promised to help him? After we'd agreed to work together? I needed him; I needed the Defects. But the Defects needed me as well. I was speechless.

'You only need to show them the electrical heart-stopper – it's a device that stops the heart beating; the pain is excruciating –

286

and the secrets come spilling out. Believe me, no one can keep a secret in the presence of the heart-stopper.'

'You can't,' I just managed to utter. All my cheekiness was gone.

'Oh, don't worry. You won't have to suffer the heart-stopper. No, no. I always abide by the Code of the Union.' He breathed in and stuck out his chest ceremoniously. 'Organisms shall only ever have to endure punishment within the cultural boundaries of their own species.' He breathed out. 'So legally I can only use methods that you humans use yourselves to get you to talk.'

My legs almost buckled from relief. What could he do to me then? Imprison me? I was already in prison. This ship was my prison. Space was my prison. I wasn't going to tell him anything.

'It's actually you, your people, who don't abide by any rules. Who don't honour legally binding agreements. You're one of the most abhorrent species I've come across in my very long life.'

'Abhorrent! Abhorrent! Who are you calling abhorrent?' I seemed to have got my mojo back.

The president shook his head. 'Like this. You don't even respect your elders.'

His comment only encouraged me. 'At least we don't go around the universe abducting people from other planets to use them in some disgusting breeding scheme.' My stomach turned as I recalled the details of what Caesar had told me.

'From what I know of humans I'm confident in saying that you would if you could.'

'No, we wouldn't. We would never do that.'

An expression crossed his face that I couldn't put my finger on. Was it a hint of a smile? 'You poor humans.' Maybe it was scorn. 'After your treachery, your gullibility is your greatest weakness. Why do you think you're here? I'm no scoundrel. I abide by the Code. You're here because your leaders, your governments, agreed to your handover.'

I wasn't going to buy into his mind games. 'You're lying.'

'You believe what you want. But I have no reason to lie to you.'

It couldn't be true. It wouldn't make any sense. 'Why would they do that?'

The president shrugged his shoulders. 'As with everything else. It was a trade agreement.'

I went cold. Dad was always talking about business controlling the world. It wasn't governments that decided our fate. It was money. It said so in the *Guardian*. I tried not to let my doubt show. 'No, no. I don't believe you.'

'In their defence, they didn't have much choice.' The president's shiny red uniform, the same as his men wore, creaked as he rearranged himself in his chair. 'It's years since we discovered our planet was dying. Pronax. Our home. As soon as we found out, we realised we needed to backtrack. We needed to reverse our evolutionary path. If we were going to be homeless, we wouldn't have access to enough energy to reproduce with the scientific accuracy we'd become used to, and unfortunately we were no longer equipped to do it the old-fashioned way. We searched many solar systems for a match, for people who bore enough genetic likeness to us to be able to help carry on our species. Then we encountered planet Earth and the Homo sapiens who lived there.'

'So you just decided to take us. Remove us from our homes and imprison us.'

'Of course not. We approached your governments. We asked for their cooperation. It wasn't forthcoming.' The president raised his grizzled eyebrows, so long they fell like the branches of a weeping willow across his eyelids. 'But then we got lucky. A plague of Vulgars hit your galaxy.'

The word gave me the creeps even though I had no idea what it meant.

'The locusts of the universe: mindless single-cell organisms that travel our world in swarms of quadrillions and wreak havoc wherever they land. They set upon planets and strip them of all energy sources such as gas and oil, all plants and vegetation such as grass and wheat, as well as water, until nothing is left and the planet becomes inhabitable for a species like humans.'

'And how was that lucky for you?'

'We possess a pesticide that kills them. You needed something from us. We needed something from you. We sprayed your planet for you and saved it from imminent destruction. In return you had to give us one million humans between the ages of fourteen and nineteen. It was a large enough group to start again as a species, but small enough so as not to affect the survival of the human race.'

I suddenly remembered the prime minister. That was what the prime minister had said on TV. *They're after the children. Anyone between the ages of fourteen and nineteen is in danger.* He knew. He'd been in on it.

289

'We had a contract. Your leaders signed it. They even gave us a list of which individuals to take and where they could be found. But when it came to delivering, they said they'd changed their minds. They said they couldn't. It would look bad. Politically. The people wouldn't stand for it. They wouldn't get re-elected.'

Re-elected. The word felt like a punch to my eardrums. Had that been their biggest worry?

The president shrugged his thin shoulders. 'So you see, I'm only taking what is rightfully mine.'

I could see his point. This frail, expressionless, allegedly perfect version of a man who looked like a melted waxwork from Madame Tussauds had a point. But I didn't care. Our leaders, our politicians, had sold something that wasn't theirs to sell. My life was mine. William Davidson, or whoever had brokered the deal, had no right to me or any other human being.

'The Code of the Union stipulates that interplanetary contracts are binding as long as one party is a member of the Union of Galaxies. You respect the Union. It's been in existence for longer than your planet has been inhabitable. Its founding members are the first planets that came into existence.'

'I don't care about your stupid Union,' I snapped. 'You can tell yourself that you're honest, that you're honourable, because you follow some Code. But it isn't fair. It isn't fair to just abduct people from other planets whenever you feel like it.'

The president groaned as if my voice were causing him physical pain. 'Fair. I forget what a primitive people you humans really are. The sense of fairness is just a feeling. And what's more, it's a feeling based on an artificial moral compass. It's fiction. It's air. It's nothing. What is fair? It's a decision, not some inherent truth.' He shook his head, thin locks of hair sweeping across his dry forehead as quietly as feathers. 'When you become part of our society we have to do something about these feelings you humans are so obsessed with. We have to ingrain in you the Ten Pillars of Perfection. The Defects used to be like you. We've been quite successful in getting them to control their emotions with the structure from the Ten Pillars.'

'So you think,' I mumbled.

The president didn't hear me. He touched a small glass pad on the steel arm of his wheelchair and started backing away from me. 'There is nothing wrong with what we're doing. This is a common practice throughout the Union. It is the duty of one species to save another from extinction if at all possible. You should know; you try to save animals from extinction on your planet all the time.' He frowned. 'Note, in most cases you are responsible for their plight; yet you only seem to want to save the cute ones, like the panda bears. You never save the ugly ones. You didn't even lift a finger to save the Yangtze River dolphin, which looked like a worn-out piece of pink soap with piggy eyes. That one was never going to make it on to anyone's T-shirt. In that, as with everything else, you let feelings control you.'

The pandas, this dolphin. I studied the president's skull-like face. 'How do you know so much about us?'

'So much? We do our homework, of course. Don't you think we do our homework when it comes to choosing a species to carry our genes into the future? You're too emotional, too selfish, too naive, too hung up on how you are feeling instead of how you can maximise what you've got. You're not perfect, far from it. But you will have to do.'

'Maximise what we've got.' I was pretty sure where he was going with this. 'You mean prolong our lives?'

'Yes, of course. Life is the only thing an organism really has. Everything else is illusion. Distraction.'

I remembered how frustrated Caesar had been when he'd told me about the Corrects' obsession with quantity. His irritation seemed to have rubbed off on me. 'That's not true,' I snapped at the president. 'Living isn't just breathing. Living is experiencing, enjoying, having fun just for the hell of it. You shouldn't just live life, you should *feel* life. You should feel all its different dimensions; you should feel happiness, sadness, elation, grief. Love.'

The president's face scrunched up into a ball of indignation. 'Love! You mean the disease?' He shook his head. His cheeks appeared flushed. If I hadn't known better, I would have thought that he was *feeling* something – something like frustration. 'I forget that I'm talking to a primitive,' he said as if to himself. He looked at me. 'It's been thousands of years since love was recognised as a disease.' He was speaking patronisingly slowly. 'Like mental illness; like depression or addiction. First the Darthonians, one of the oldest species in the universe, invented medication that controlled it. Once we started to perfect ourselves genetically on Pronax, love was one of the first diseases we eliminated from our genome.'

So it was true. The Corrects really didn't believe in feelings. Even though Caesar had explained to me the world of the

Corrects – their obsession with efficiency, their preference for quantity over quality – I hadn't been able to imagine it to be so absolute.

I stared at the flesh-deficient old man. I felt like Alice in Wonderland. I was falling down a rabbit hole. But the place I was going to was so much worse than the world of a mad tea party and a foul-tempered queen. The life that awaited me was like living death. I wouldn't be allowed to feel; I wouldn't be allowed to have meaningless fun; I wouldn't be allowed to fall in love, have my heart broken, experience joy, sadness, boredom, excitement. The only two things that mattered would be breathing and procreating. That was it. That would be my life as a member of the Pronaxian society. I and the rest of the abductees would be turned into mindless animals. Or worse: eliminated for our 'flaws'.

The realisation was like a big, heavy stone tied around my ankle. I was trying to keep afloat, I was trying to swim, but in fact I was sinking into a deep, cold, dark ocean of despair.

The president turned his wheelchair around and drove back towards his desk. 'Anyway,' he said, situating himself behind it, 'I have better things to do than debate the menace that is love with an evolutionarily inferior organism. My men tell me you were sent here to aid the Splinters in their efforts to overthrow me. I want you to tell me everything. What is their plan? Is it true that my vice-president is orchestrating it? Whom are the Splinters working with back on Earth? What is your mission on board my ship?' He leaned forward, placing his elbows on the desk.

I might as well have told him everything. My mission on board the ship had turned out to be a deception – I wasn't here to end the siege; I wasn't here to save planet Earth. And my collaboration with Caesar and the Defects was clearly over before it had even begun, as he'd obviously sold me out. If I obliged, maybe the president would go easy on me – maybe he would show some mercy. I should just have done what he asked.

But I didn't. 'I have nothing to say to you.'

I don't know the reason for my defiance. Maybe I felt that the only thing I had left was my free will so I'd better hold on to it. Or maybe I thought I had nothing to lose; he'd already told me he wouldn't be using his torture device, his heart-stopper, on me. He'd already said he was abiding by his precious Code, so there was nothing he could do to me that was worse than what he and his people had already done; he had long since taken my freedom away from me.

I was wrong.

Characteristically, or rather for genetic reasons, he did not show surprise. 'All right then,' he said and started tapping on his desk with his fingers as if he were playing the piano. Suddenly, a hologram of Earth popped out of the table. 'Let's see what measures we have at our disposal.' He did some more tapping. The hologram disappeared. It was replaced by a two-dimensional white square with a logo on it. I jumped. The colours. Blue, red, yellow, green. I recognised the logo. It had been a big part of my everyday life before everything changed, before the siege. It was Google. The president of Pronax was browsing the internet.

He started nodding his head. 'Yes, yes, I thought so. This will be easy.'

He was looking at websites. I was standing behind the holographic computer screen so everything appeared the wrong way round to me – I couldn't read what he was reading. But it wouldn't have mattered if I'd been sitting beside him at his desk. He was scrolling down the pages so quickly I would never have been able to keep up. The Pronaxians had to be cognitively superior to humans. No human could read that fast. Was he really taking everything in?

I recognised some of the websites. Wikipedia. BBC News.

The president finally looked up from his floating computer screen. 'You humans, like so many of the more primitive people of the universe, sure are a ruthless species.'

The phrase 'Look who's talking' almost shot out of my mouth but I stopped myself.

'As I've explained to you, in accordance with the Code of the Union I can only subject you to punishment used by your own species on your own planet. I must admit, I am almost spoilt for choice. You humans are certainly creative in your cruelty.' He kept on scrolling. 'Wow. This I haven't seen before. An electric chair. How interesting.' He peered at the screen. 'It says here that a condemned person is strapped into a wooden chair. Then various cycles of electrical currents are passed through the body in order to cause fatal damage to the internal organs. How ineffective. How brutal. How fascinating.' He scratched his chin. 'Hanging. Yes, I've seen that before. It's a common practice on Harac.' He shuddered. 'Haracians. Frightful little species.'

I was starting to feel lightheaded. I wished I could turn off my brain with a switch. I needed to stop thinking. The horror. The cruelties we humans were responsible for. Torture, murder, war, genocide. The images in my head – things I'd seen on the news, read in history books – were like weeds in a flower bed spiralling out of control and suffocating everything else. The fact that the president respected the Code didn't get me off the hook at all.

He was immersed in his research. 'Waterboarding. Seen that. Nail-pulling. Basic. Finger-chopping. Interesting. Oh, wait. Here is another one I haven't seen before. The guillotine. Wow, look at this. What a primitive way to carry out beheadings. A frame, some weights and an angled blade. No wonder it sometimes took many attempts to chop their heads off. Why didn't you just use a butter knife?'

Was that an attempt at humour or was it a threat?

He kept on reciting evidence of human cruelty as if it were a shopping list. 'Guns, knives, bombs. A gas chamber. How strange. Who are those Nazis?'

The blood rushing to my head was causing my ears to ring. The door opened behind me.

The president looked up from the computer screen. His thin lips parted as he drew a quick breath. 'What are you doing here? How did you get into my chamber?'

That was the last thing I remember.

Day Eleven

I woke up alone in a bed with dirty linen, inside some sort of cubicle defined by sheets hanging from rusty poles. My head was throbbing.

It wasn't my prison cell. I could see my backpack lying on the floor by my bed.

'Hello.' My throat was dry and the word felt like a razor blade making its way out into the world.

That was when Caesar's head popped through the curtains.

'Great! You're awake.'

I have no recollection of how I got here. I'm told that I was saved from the president's chamber by an underground army of Defects. Apparently Caesar arranged the rescue mission. He said he hadn't betrayed me. He said that when we bumped into the Red Stacks he had decided to pretend I was an escapee from the kitchen team and that he had been out looking for me so he could hand me over to the security services. He said he was sorry but it was the only thing he could think of to prevent them from arresting us both.

I don't know if I believe him. I don't know if I trust him any more.

The Defect army 'disabled' the Red Stacks in front of the chamber (I don't want to know what 'disabled' means). Then Caesar used his tweaked authorisation to open the door and throw some sort of sleeping-gas canister into the room. It knocked the president out cold – and me too.

Caesar carried me all the way back to the Colony, the home of the Defects – and the humans who have so far been paired with Defects for the breeding program. I can't remember any of it.

God, it stinks in here. I can hear murmurs beyond the curtains – people's voices buzzing softly like bees in a hive. It is the sound of Defects – and humans – going about their everyday business.

I'm just waiting. Caesar told me to wait. He was going to get Stephanie.

I have this niggling dread in the pit of my stomach. Maybe it's just the sleeping gas wearing off, but I can't shake the feeling that something awful is about to happen. That soon, this will all be over.

24

Stephanie, it turned out, had a personality as pleasant as the Spanish Inquisition.

'*Hrwakaka ta puwakamana*,' she hissed.

Her black hair snaked over her shoulder in a ruffled plait. Anger seemed to be a permanent fixture on her face.

'Don't be rude,' Caesar said. They were standing over my bed as if they were visiting a patient in the hospital. 'Speak English in front of Amy.'

Stephanie rolled her eyes. 'I don't trust her. She looks like a snitch.'

I wanted to get out of bed, but I still felt groggy.

'Are you sure she didn't disclose our plans?'

They were wearing identical grey overalls.

'Stephanie, chill. I told you: we got her out before she could be made to talk.'

'You know that if she squealed on us we're as good as dead?'

They were talking about me as if I weren't there. The frustration gave me the strength to sit up. 'I didn't squeal on you. I'm not a snitch.'

'We know you're not,' Caesar said, smiling at me, almost paralysing me again with his perfect little dimples.

Stephanie kept on ignoring me. 'I don't understand why we need her. Why do we want this to be a collaboration?'

'You know why.'

'I really do think you're exaggerating her importance. I mean, she's human. What is she good for? She's barely more intelligent than a quinshasa.'

I remembered the rat-monkey animal Caesar had told me about in the incubator room.

Stephanie's black eyes were burning like coal. 'You couldn't find a cockroach down there to join forces with?'

Was she seriously comparing me to a cockroach?

Caesar sighed. 'Stephanie, we've been over this. It's too much of a risk to go it alo—'

Stephanie didn't let him finish. 'I don't trust her. The others agree with me. I think we should get rid of her.'

I had to do something, say something. 'He's right.' I had no idea where I was going with this. 'Caesar's right. You do need me.'

'Yeah, yeah, yeah – I've heard it all. We need a human ally; we need someone on the inside, someone who can offer us protection, blah, blah, blah. Until you give me something concrete, I'm voting that we go it alone and I'm urging the others to do the same.'

'There is something!' I squeaked, feeling like a helpless mouse about to be eaten by a big, angry cat. 'I can offer you something concrete.'

Caesar and I had talked about it. In the incubator room. We were sure that we would be able to help each other. We just didn't know exactly how. But when I saw the president browse the internet an idea had started to form in my head.

Stephanie scowled at me. 'What?'

I opened my mouth but quickly closed it again. No. I couldn't show her my cards. Not yet.

The Defects had a plan. Caesar had told me about it on our 'date' in the incubator room. They wanted to break free from the clutches of the Corrects. From their breeding programme. From the prison that was their life. They wanted to live. Properly. Not just exist the way the Ten Pillars of Perfection dictated they did. So they were going to make their escape.

'We've been planning this ever since the Corrects stumbled upon Earth,' Caesar had said. 'We immediately knew this was our chance. We look enough like humans to be able to blend in. If we were able to get to Earth, we could just disappear into the crowd.'

But the vice-president and the Splinters were a threat to their plan. The Splinters were working on overthrowing the president, taking Earth for themselves and killing off every single human being except for those they needed for the breeding program. The Defects needed humans to be able to hide, so they needed to stop the Splinters.

But fighting the Splinters on board the ships wouldn't work. That would reveal the Defects' plan of escaping. They had to foil their mission discreetly. That was why Caesar and Stephanie and a number of Defects from all the ships surrounding Earth had travelled to Earth.

Their plan had been to eliminate the Splinter's collaborators back on Earth – the Resistance. They'd got to Earth as stowaways, hiding on vessels transporting Corrects who were working on securing what they considered to be rightfully theirs – one million teenagers.

That was when I'd met Caesar for the first time in Waitrose.

Inside the incubator room Caesar had told me how the final escape would go off. The Defect army had weapons. A lot of them. Breaking out of the Colony would be easy. The tricky part would be getting off the ship. But there was a way.

Aboard every alien ship there were thousands of small shuttle-pods that were used for short excursions, deliveries between the different vessels of the fleet and maintenance work. Caesar said that stealing them would be difficult but definitely doable.

'If we get them all, there will be room for all the Defects and more than half the humans on board this ship,' Caesar had said. 'On board *every* ship. This isn't just us. We're working with the Defects on board all the ships surrounding your planet. If we work together, all the continents of Earth will get at least some of the abductees back.'

It was a no-brainer. Of course I'd help him. Of course I'd work with the Defects. I ignored the 'half the humans' part. Some would have to be left behind. I'd face that dilemma if and when it came to it.

But there was one problem. Although the visitors had destroyed a lot of weapons and military equipment down on Earth, they'd never be able to get it all. The people on Earth were starting to fight back. They didn't stand a chance, of course. But the shuttle-pods weren't built with military use in mind. A single shot from something as primitive as a bazooka could destroy one.

The Defects knew this for a fact. A group on another ship had got hold of a couple of shuttle-pods and tried to escape to Earth. They'd been shot down shortly after entering Earth's atmosphere.

That was where we came in. The humans.

'Is there anything you could do to help?' Caesar had asked. 'Do you have any idea how we could land on Earth without being attacked?'

'I don't know,' I'd mumbled, chewing on my lip as I tried to think of something.

'Do you know what locations are of military importance on Earth – what locations would be used to attack the shuttle-pods? You could help us avoid them.'

I shook my head.

'Or could you somehow talk to your governments? Negotiate with them?'

I almost laughed out loud. I imagined myself giving the prime minister a call.

'Hi, this is Amy Sullivan, for William Davidson.'

'And what is this in reference to?'

'Oh, I just want to convince him to give a group of aliens safe passage to Earth and then accept them into our society.' He didn't even like immigrants from foreign countries living in the UK. And they were human.

We had left the incubator room without a plan.

Stephanie was rolling her eyes at Caesar. 'She hasn't got anything. She's useless.' She turned on her heel. 'Get rid of her.'

I scrambled out of bed. I wavered slightly but the sleeping gas had almost worn off. 'I do have something. I have a solution to your problem. But I need the others.' I turned to Caesar. 'I need you to get the others. My brother. Matilda. Anita.' I had no guarantee that the Defects would still consider this collaboration once I'd given them what they needed. I had no guarantee that they wouldn't just leave us here to rot. If they betrayed us, if they didn't keep their promise to save the humans on board the ship along with themselves, I was at least going to make sure that Andrew, Matilda, Anita and I were in a position to get on one of the shuttle-pods, with brute force if necessary. But for that to happen I needed them with me when I did what I was going to do.

'No,' Stephanie said.

'Fine,' I said, shrugging my shoulders, trying to play it cool, all the time feeling as if I was about to throw up. 'Then I won't help you.'

'Do I look like I care?'

Shit. She was calling my bluff.

Caesar touched Stephanie's arm softly. A strange emotion resembling anger exploded in my chest. Were they a couple? 'Stephanie—'

'It's too risky.'

'But we've got no choice.'

Stephanie growled at him. Then she laid her hand on his. She looked him straight in the eye and gave a hint of a smile. 'Fine.'

Andrew, Matilda and Anita jumped on me with the enthusiasm of newborn puppies. I fell backwards on the bed. They'd clearly thought I was dead.

'I knew you were fine; I knew you were okay,' Matilda repeated too many times for it to be true.

'What were you thinking?' Andrew shouted at me. He sounded angry, but I knew he wasn't. He was just in shock. Dad did the same thing. He shouted at us when he really cared. 'Whatever possessed you to just leave like that?'

I shrugged sheepishly. I didn't think answering 'a cute guy' would quiet the situation.

My little cubicle felt crowded. Caesar and Stephanie were having a hushed discussion by the foot of the bed in their secret language. Tom, Courtney, Louisa and Damien stood back, looking at their toes.

Caesar had asked if I'd wanted him to bring them *all*. 'The fewer, the better,' he'd said.

I have to admit, I was tempted. I was tempted to say, 'No need.' Of course I had to save Tom, for Matilda's sake. And Damien was harmless. But Courtney and Louisa. How often at school I had fantasised about the two of them disappearing into thin air. How often I had wished I'd never have to see them again. A part of me, a big part of me, wanted to leave them in space to rot. But when it came to it, I couldn't.

'We need to act quickly,' Caesar said, shifting into English. 'From what you told us, Amy, the president still thinks that you're here to work with the Splinters. But it won't be long until he realises that it was the Defects, not the Splinters, who saved you from his chamber. And then it won't be long until he finds out what we're up to.'

Tom was the first to protest. 'What we are up to? Since when are we working with this guy?'

Ungrateful bastard. Surprisingly, Damien joined him, putting his hand on Tom's shoulder. 'I'm with my mate here.'

Tom nodded. 'Thanks, bud.'

What was this? Some kind of a male bonding session?

Courtney and Louisa moved closer to Tom and Damien. 'We think we should just stick to the plan and do what the Resistance back on Earth wanted us to do,' Courtney said.

I felt as if my head was about to burst from frustration. 'Stick to the plan!' I should have left them to rot. 'There is no plan!' I shouted. 'There is no Resistance. There are only traitors!'

Tom sighed. 'I know you have the hots for this guy but—'

'Now, you listen to me, you idiot. The Resistance back on Earth sold me out. It sold all of us out. They didn't send me here to save Earth. They sent me here with a contract that states that they're going to help the visitors conquer Earth. They sent me here to betray the human race.'

Tom shook his head. 'No.' He didn't believe me. 'I mean, why? Why would they do that?'

'To get their kids back. I have a list. List of kids who will be set free in exchange for the Resistance's cooperation.'

I could see the hope burn like hunger in his eyes.

'No, you're not on it, Tom. You're screwed with the rest of the human race.'

I gave Anita a dirty look. It wasn't her fault she was on the list. She didn't even know she was on it. But I couldn't help myself.

'None of you are on the list, okay.'

306

They didn't need to know about Anita. They'd only resent her for it. And she definitely didn't need to know. I couldn't have anyone thinking there was another way out of this.

'What then?' Tom growled, as if somehow this were all my fault. 'What is this great plan of yours?'

I told them everything. I told them about the breeding programme. I explained that we were a part of the Corrects' plan to save the Pronaxian species, to make it possible for them to procreate naturally again. I told them about my encounter with the president; about the deal he did with our governments back on Earth; about how the human leaders went back on their word. Finally, I told them about the shuttle-pods; that we were going to help the Defects escape the Corrects and get to Earth. In return, they would take as many of us abducted humans with them as they had room for.

'I don't know,' Tom said, swinging from side to side as if physically weighing up his options. 'I mean if we join the Defects, we might get back to Earth.' He shifted on his feet. 'But something might also go wrong and we'd get killed.' He swung back again. 'If we don't join the Defects and stay aboard this ship, yes, we would have to go along with the Corrects' plan for us, but we would definitely live.'

Caesar snapped. 'You wouldn't.'

'I wouldn't what?'

'Live.'

Tom flinched.

Caesar's impatience coloured his cheeks. 'You're not tall enough. And you.' He turned to Courtney. 'You wouldn't make it either. They don't want gapped teeth to become a part of the Pronaxian race.'

Courtney started blushing. I couldn't help smiling. I'd never seen her properly embarrassed before.

Caesar reached over to Louisa and touched the red Capo band on her arm. 'And none of the Capos would measure eligible. The Capos are chosen from the most violent of your species, the most self-centred and cruel. The brutality is tolerated by the guards in your Camp because it is an integral part of the Camp system – it turns prisoner against prisoner; divide and conquer as you say. But the Pronaxians would never want those attributes to become part of their new generation.'

Louisa began to sniffle.

Caesar sighed. 'They were never going to use all of you. They're going to weed out those who don't fit the bill. They want to keep the species as genetically flawless as possible. That's why I didn't make it.' He pointed at the dimples on his cheeks. 'Shortened facial muscles that cause dimples are actually a genetic defect. That's what they're doing in the Selection Lab. They're screening for genetic defects.'

I wanted to reach out and touch his face. How could something so cute be a flaw?

'What ...?' Courtney said but the question got stuck in her throat.

Caesar finished it for her. 'What happens to those who aren't eligible?'

Courtney nodded.

'I showed you the cemetery. You would just become another name on a steel wall. That's what happens to those who are sent through door number two in the Selection Lab.'

Andrew had been silent but suddenly he threw his arms in the air. 'And what? They just … they just kill you?'

'They don't use that phrase. It's not what you humans call "murder" when it's for the good of the species. It's not murder when efficiency dictates it. As far as they're concerned, your time is just up.'

The muscles in Andrew's neck bulged under his skin like angry waves on a stormy sea. 'How?'

'Space will be your killer as well as your grave. You're put into the airlock chamber. Then they just open the door. Once you're sucked out, it's pretty quick. You're not able to breathe. You lose consciousness in around ten seconds. You're dead in two minutes.'

Death by vacuum. We'd all seen it in movies. Heads exploding. Bodies freezing – turning into popsicles in seconds. Tom's face was pale. They all seemed pale. Like living corpses. There was a sour taste in my mouth. Maybe that was exactly what we were.

Caesar lowered his eyes to the floor. 'That's what happened to my parents. After we left Pronax, the Defects were categorised into three groups: Breeders, Workers and Drains on Resources. Mum and Dad were unlucky. Mum had worked as an underground singer at home on Pronax and Dad was a Grower – close to what you would call a farmer. The Corrects don't believe in music and there were plenty of farmers. Mum and Dad's skills weren't needed. They weren't considered eligible for the breeding programme. Too old, they said. So their time was simply up.'

I put my hand on Caesar's arm. Tom gave me a sharp look. But I didn't care.

Caesar leaned towards me ever so slightly. 'All the Defects were screened in the Selection Lab. Just like you humans. I wasn't eligible for the breeding programme. Genetically undesirable, they said. But I got lucky. I was sent through door number three. Genetically, I have an aptitude for technology. I worked as a programmer at one of the centres for communication on Pronax. So they put me to work. I got a post with the Department of Palm Identification and Security Clearances. I was moved to the Selection Lab because of the strain that was on it following the abduction of all you humans.'

I suddenly understood what Caesar meant when he'd said he had 'tweaked his authorisation' when we sneaked into the incubator room. His work made it possible for him to go wherever he wanted. He manipulated their technology. He was the space version of a techie.

'I changed my station to "kitchen" by hacking into the ship's servers once you'd been stationed there so I could—'

'This is so boring!' Matilda suddenly exclaimed. She slumped down on the bed. Her hair fell softly over her shoulders in loose and surprisingly shiny waves. You could see how naturally smooth her skin was now that she didn't have access to all her make-up. Neither space nor this deadly ordeal could diminish her perfection. She would have definitely been eligible for the breeding programme.

'I'm sorry.' Caesar moved away from me. The heat from his body lingered on the palm of my hand. 'Am I tiring you with this talk about your imminent demise?'

'Yes, you kind of are.'

Anita gave a loud sigh and Matilda made a point of ignoring her, turning her head theatrically in the other direction, her hair fanning out almost in slow motion as if she were a Greek goddess with PMS. It felt so much like the good old days that I nearly started crying.

Matilda leaned back in the bed. 'I mean, if we're all about to die a horrible death or, worse, become sex slaves for some ugly alien race, why are we standing here chatting? I just want you to get to the point.'

'I was getting there—' Caesar started but Matilda wasn't in a tolerant kind of mood.

'So, if I understand you correctly: those Splinter guys are going to turn us into breeding machines and—'

'No.' Now it was Caesar's turn to interrupt. 'The Splinters are working with the vice-president. It's the president who intends to turn back the clock, back to when our species was capable of breeding naturally. He's what you humans would call the good guy in all of this. He's honouring the Code.'

Matilda's indignation sprayed out of her nose. 'The good guy! The guy who has besieged our planet, abducted us, imprisoned us and is going to use our reproductive organs to his own advantage is the good guy.'

'If you think that's bad, you're really not going to like what your supposed allies, the Splinters, have planned.'

'How can it be worse?'

'Try taking over your planet and wiping out the human race.'

The curtain of the cubicle suddenly opened. The screech of the steel rings scraping against the rusty poles sounded like the end of the world.

A Defect, wearing the usual grey overalls, stepped inside. His face was covered with sweat and his breathing was heavy, as if he'd been running.

He said something in the visitors' language. I knew by the hurried tone of his voice that it wasn't anything good.

Stephanie ran up to the new arrival and hugged him hard.

'Who's that?' Andrew said to me.

I'd never seen him before.

'It's Adam,' Caesar said. He looked worried. 'Stephanie's boyfriend.'

I felt a light explosion of relief in my stomach. 'So Stephanie isn't, like, your girlfriend?'

'She's my cousin.'

Andrew wasn't interested in Caesar's relationship status. 'What is he saying?'

'They're on to us. The president and the Red Stacks. There has been a leak.' Caesar walked over to Adam. 'Who was it?'

Adam glanced at us before switching to English. 'It was Harry.'

'Who's Harry?' Andrew asked.

'One of the lieutenants in our army,' said Adam. He turned back to Caesar. 'I told you that you couldn't trust him.'

Caesar buried his face in his palms. 'How much does the president know?'

'Everything Harry knew. He knows that we're trying to find a way to escape. He knows about the weapons we've collected. He knows we want to get to Earth.' Adam looked at me. 'He knows that a human was sent here to work with the Splinters.'

So that was how the president knew about me.

Caesar looked up again. 'So they don't know about the shuttle-pods. If it was only Harry, then they don't know about the shuttle-pods.'

Adam shrugged. 'I guess not.'

Caesar quickly turned to me. 'Amy, what is your idea? We have to move fast. We have to act now. We have to leave before the president works everything out.'

I could feel everyone's eyes on me. I began to sweat. 'So ... erm ... what I was thinking was ...'

Stephanie let go of her boyfriend and cleared her throat unnecessarily. 'We don't have all day.'

Matilda gave Stephanie an icy glare. 'Then why are you interrupting?'

Stephanie physically retreated, as if someone had just thrown a punch at her. She clearly wasn't used to being talked back at.

'The internet,' I finally managed to say. 'I saw the president browse the internet. Our internet. The one we have back on Earth.'

Caesar nodded. 'We have access to almost every known information source in the universe.'

'I need access to the internet.'

'Okay,' Caesar said, his lack of enthusiasm causing me some worry. 'Why?'

In the incubator room, when Caesar had asked if we humans could help the Defects, he'd suggested that we somehow disable

313

the weapon systems that were used to attack the shuttle-pods. He also suggested we could contact the human leaders to negotiate a safe landing on Earth. If this had been a blockbuster starring Tom Cruise, we would have made a bomb and blown something to smithereens. But I knew neither of those things would work. I had another idea, though. It wasn't explosive. It wouldn't have worked in a Tom Cruise film. And it would never have made it as the plot of a political thriller. But maybe, just maybe, it was mundane enough to work in reality.

'My plan is simple. I'm just going to announce our arrival.' I paused for effect. 'Via the internet, I am going to tell everyone on Earth that we're coming. I'm going to let them know that we'll be arriving soon – the humans who were abducted. I'm going to explain to them that we'll be travelling in small shuttle-pods, and that they're not to shoot.'

I must admit I was rather proud of myself. I thought it was a good plan. But the feeling of triumph didn't last very long.

Stephanie's indignation made her sound as if she were choking on her vocal cords. 'Really. The internet. That's your great plan. Why didn't we think of that?'

My embarrassment manifested itself as burning sensation on my cheeks.

'So, what are you going to do? Send an email to your leader?'

I couldn't face her. I turned my gaze to my toes. 'Not exactly. I mean, I don't even know if there still are leaders back on Earth. They might all be dea—' I couldn't say the word. 'I was going to make the information go viral. On social media and in chat rooms and stuff like that.'

'Viral? Like the cat videos you humans enjoy watching so much?'

I could feel I was starting to look like a very ripe tomato. 'Not just that. Maybe we can contact the media outlets that are still operating too – there are probably a few left.' I didn't know why I was being so defensive. I didn't have to be. I knew what I was doing. If I knew one thing, it was computers – the internet, YouTube, chat rooms, alternative reality computer games. That had been my life.

'This is our best chance,' I said, daring myself to look up and face Stephanie. 'If everyone knows we're coming, the people will never allow armies or governments or whatever to shoot us down.'

Matilda touched my arm. 'I actually think that's a good idea.'

Saying that Stephanie didn't sound convinced was an understatement. 'Good idea! Why do you think you had to come here? Why do you think the traitors who sent you here didn't just send the surrender treaty via what you call email or whatever?'

Caesar clenched his jaw. 'There's no need to be so harsh, Stephanie. She doesn't know. How could she know?'

'Know what?'

Caesar's eyes glistened. I couldn't tell if he was disappointed or scared. 'Why do you think Adam is here?'

Was that an existential question? I frowned in concentration. 'I don't know. Why are any of us here? I'm not sure if I believe there is an inherent purpose to life.'

'No, I mean why is he *here*? Inside the sick bay, this cubicle? I have a communication device in my pocket. A phone, you'd call it. He could have called me and told me the bad news.'

'I suppose ...'

'But he didn't.'

'Okay ...'

'For the same reason the Splinters couldn't communicate with your Resistance electronically.'

'I have no idea what you're talking about.'

'Haven't you wondered why the Resistance sent you here?'

'I know why they sent me here. They sent me here to betray humanity.'

'Yes, but why did anyone have to come here? Why didn't they just send an email?'

'Oh, I see where you're going.'

'Every device that is used for communication aboard this ship, every device that is used for information technology, is monitored.'

'Monitored? Like, someone is listening in?'

'It's more advanced than that. Each and every word, spoken or written, every search term, is run through a computer program that determines its level of threat.'

'Level of threat?'

'It calculates the probability of subversiveness. They did it on Pronax as well. Ever since the second uprising.'

'There was an uprising?'

Stephanie rolled her eyes. 'You didn't think this was the first time we've tried to break free, did you?'

I ignored her. So did Caesar.

'The Defects have been revolting ever since the Corrects started imposing their values on us, ever since they came up with the Ten Pillars of Perfection. We've tried to establish a separate community from them. A group of Defects even tried to leave Pronax to find a new home. But we haven't been successful.'

'But you can do something about it. You can bypass the computer program. Like you tweaked your authorisation.'

Caesar was shaking his head. 'It isn't possible. It isn't just a software problem. It's a hardware problem. You'd have to remove a tiny chip from the device, but if you tried that, you'd trigger an alarm – and that would give the president's security services, the Red Stacks, your exact identity and location. You wouldn't stand a chance.'

So this was it.

'I told you they'd be useless,' Stephanie said, shaking her head at Caesar. 'I told you they were just monkeys in clothes. This was stupid. They are stupid.'

'If anyone is stupid, it's you.' Matilda was rummaging in her back pocket.

'Excuse me?' Stephanie looked at Matilda as if she were a riddle she couldn't solve.

'You're totally stuck inside a box.'

'Stuck inside a box?'

'You need to get your backside out of that freaking box.'

Anita took it upon herself to translate. 'She means you need to think outside the box.'

'That's what I said.' Matilda produced something from her pocket.

At first I didn't realise what it was. The object was so out of context my brain just couldn't register what my eyes were looking at.

'This is what I'm talking about,' Matilda said, waving a small tube-shaped container as if it were a magic wand.

I stared at it. It wasn't. It couldn't be.

Anita was clearly as baffled as I was. 'Is that … is that … mascara?'

Day Eleven

I can do this, I can do this, I can do this, I can do this ...

We were ready to go. We'd put on grey overalls, just like the ones the Defects wore, so as not to raise suspicion as we travelled around the ship.

'Won't they see a difference?' Anita asked.

'If they looked, they would,' Stephanie said. 'But they hardly ever look at us. We're invisible to them. We're considered as significant as specks of dust.'

We were just leaving when a Defect poked his head inside the curtain. His cheeks were flushed.

'Hrwukataka lamasaka tuka.'

'English, please,' Matilda said, as if she were controlling this whole operation.

Caesar squeezed his eyes shut. 'Oh, no.' He opened them again. 'How many?'

'The number stands at thirty, as far as I know. But it's increasing fast.'

Matilda slammed a hand on to her hip. 'Can someone please explain what's going on?'

Caesar ran his fingers through his hair. 'The Red Stacks. They've started arresting our soldiers.'

'Your soldiers?'

'The Defects' secret army. The team of people who were meant to get us out of here.'

The new guy interrupted him. 'You have to go, Caesar.

You too, Stephanie. Harry has clearly ratted on us all. We have to hide.'

'Hide!' Caesar was pulling his hair so hard his forehead looked like it had been Botoxed. 'Where would we hide?' His eyes were wide. 'No. We have to leave. We have to set the plan in motion. We have to get as many shuttle-pods as we can and leave right now.'

'But what about the landing issues? No one is willing to take the chance that the humans won't shoot us all down.'

'We may have a solution to that.' Caesar turned to Stephanie's boyfriend. 'Adam, you go and send the signals to the other ships. Tell them we'll be leaving in two hours.'

Matilda pulled a face. 'I thought you couldn't communicate.'

'It's a light signal. It's primitive. Stephanie and I will go and tell the army to set things in motion.' Next he turned to me. 'You have an hour to complete phase one of the operation. Then you have an hour to complete phase two.'

I was going to say we needed more time. I was going to say it wouldn't be possible. But I knew there wasn't an alternative. Either I did my part or this would be the end.

25

The smell in the Camp was exactly the same as when I'd left it five days earlier. It stank of peppery sweat and human misery.

Caesar said he'd come and get us in an hour.

Matilda led the way. The rest of us followed.

Tom was whinging. 'This is too risky. Does anyone else think this is too risky?'

He seemed to have lost the support of Damien and Courtney. No one answered.

We were making our way through the dense crowd when Louisa came up to me. Just Louisa. Not Courtney, which was strange. Usually they were like conjoined twins who shared their free will. 'Is it certain that we are going to get a seat?'

'Yes,' I said, just to get her off my back.

'It's only fair that we have priority. I mean, we're helping. We're making this happen.'

I tried to ignore her. I was busy working out how I was going to do this.

'Amy.' She touched my arm. 'I know this is your mission, and I know we haven't always been the best of friends ...'

She trailed off. Saying that we maybe weren't 'the best of friends' was an understatement. I remembered the time Courtney

321

and Louisa found a dog poo on the school field and hid it in my bag when I wasn't looking. The whole class thought it was hilarious when I pulled out a handful of shit instead of my notebook. I tried to laugh it off, but I was mortified. After class I went to the bathroom and cried. Anita found me and, without saying a word, cleaned my bag for me and walked me home.

Louisa was starting to dig her fingers into my arm. 'You have to take me with you back to Earth. It wasn't me. I mean, it was me, but it was Courtney really. She made me do all those things.'

'Don't worry about it,' I said, even though I wanted to slap her.

Matilda stopped. 'We're here.'

How she knew, I had no idea. We were somewhere in the Camp. It looked like every other spot – crowded with people who ignored you.

'What do we do next?' Andrew said.

'I guess we just wait,' Matilda answered.

'But we only have an hour.'

'I am not a magician, Andrew. I can't make people appear out of thin air.'

But we got lucky. Matilda started waving. 'Greg, hey, Greg! Over here!'

A short boy around our age, who would in a less politically correct era have been described as fat, put a finger up to his lips and shushed Matilda.

Matilda hunched her shoulders. 'Sorry, Greg, sorry.'

The plump little boy came over. It was difficult to believe that this was supposedly one of the most powerful humans inside the Camp.

'What can I do for you today, Matilda?'

'We're in a hurry. We need our phones back.'

Greg was what Matilda called a broker. Apparently he was known as the go-to guy around the Camp. If you needed something, he either had it or he could get it for you – for a fee, of course. He had sold us the sleeping bag.

'No can do.'

'Come on, Greg. Give me just one of them back. I only need one.'

Greg folded his arms across his chest. His stomach was poking out from under a black V-neck T-shirt. He had a gold chain around his neck and his ash-blond hair was combed back. He looked like a children's version of a gangster.

'Even if I wanted to, I couldn't. I've traded them all.'

'All eight of them?'

'There's a surge in demand. Apparently people are using mobiles to play a new game. It's inspired by air hockey. They use the phones both as pucks and mallets. It's fun. You should try it. There's going to be a tournament. Anyone can take part.'

'I'm good.' Matilda's voice sounded strained. She was getting worried. So was I. 'What about laptops? Do you have any laptops?'

Greg's brow lifted. 'I actually just got one in.'

'Great!' Matilda turned to us and did a silent phew. She turned back to Greg. 'How much?'

'It doesn't come cheap.'

'How much?'

'What have you got?'

Matilda produced the mascara from her pocket.

Greg snorted. 'You've got to be kidding me.'

'There's more.' Matilda rummaged through her pockets and handed Greg a hairpin with a flower on it.

'This isn't nearly enough. What about the sleeping bag? Do you still have the sleeping bag?'

Matilda shook her head. We'd checked. It had been stolen while we'd been gone, along with most of our accumulated possessions, leaving the tent almost empty.

Matilda looked at us over her shoulder. 'A little bit of help, please. Has anyone got anything of value?'

I removed my backpack. There was hardly anything in there. I still had my house keys. I handed them to Greg.

He held them in the palm of his hand and studied them as if he were an antique dealer evaluating priceless jewellery. He put them in his pocket. 'What else have you guys got?'

Damien stepped forward and handed him a crumpled five-pound note.

Greg scowled. 'Is that meant to be funny? Are you making fun of me? I don't have time for this.'

Matilda grabbed Greg's arm. 'Sorry, Greg. Don't leave. Damien here is just a bit slow. He didn't mean anything by it. He hasn't realised yet that money doesn't have any value in space.'

Anita found a button in her pocket, Courtney handed over her necklace, Louisa offered half a packet of tissues and Andrew took off his belt. Tom reluctantly offered Greg his watch after Matilda forced him to. But nothing seemed to be enough to buy us that laptop we so desperately needed.

I saw Caesar approaching. The hour was up. How could the hour be up?

'Are you ready to go?' he said, glancing over his shoulder to see if he was being followed.

I suddenly remembered something. 'What about this?' I said to Greg with my arm still inside my backpack. I pulled out the copy of *The Diary of Anne Frank* that Shannon had given me. I'd totally forgotten that it was still there.

Greg wrinkled his nose. 'It won't do.'

Andrew turned on his heel and ran.

Caesar sighed. 'We need to go. Now.'

I snapped at him. 'We can't.'

'But we have to.'

I stared at him, not knowing what to do.

Andrew returned with one of the few things that hadn't been nicked from our tent: his handmade bow and arrows.

Greg's interest had been piqued. 'What's that?'

'A bow. And some arrows.'

'Does it work?'

Without a word, Andrew placed the arrow and drew back the black string made from Anita's hair. He pointed it upwards and released the arrow, which shot high up in the air.

Greg was impressed. 'Wow.' He turned to Andrew. 'The laptop is yours. I'll take the bow and arrows and the rest of the stuff.' He glanced at me. 'You can keep the book.'

We left the Camp. I could only hope that this would be the last time I'd see it.

Day Eleven

We have been betrayed. I can't believe this is happening.
How can this be happening?

26

Everything seemed to be going fine. No, not just fine. Perfectly according to plan.

We'd been able to move freely around the corridors in our grey uniforms. The visitors in black didn't suspect a thing. Fortunately we hadn't come across any of the particularly scary Red Stacks.

Caesar had let us into a room that was full of steel boxes with blinking lights on them – a server room. Apparently they were all over the ship as everything was run by computers. Even the toilets had little chips in them which determined when to flush and with how much force.

'How can we connect the laptop to the ship's systems?' I asked Caesar. We didn't have a cable or anything. And besides, what kind of USB cable would be compliant with alien technology?

'I have a universal adapter. It can connect any device from anywhere in the universe to anything I want to.'

The server room was hot and stuffy. We were sitting in a circle on the floor. The light had a deceitful green hue to it which made everyone look really drawn, as if they had aged thirty years. My heart was beating fast. Even though Caesar said that connecting the laptop to the internet would be the easy part, I was nervous. What if it didn't work? I was also worried about the program that monitored all the devices on board. Caesar said it wouldn't be able to detect our laptop. It relied on hardware that was placed inside the devices during the manufacturing stages. Hence the need to connect to the internet through a device that was made on Earth and not on Pronax. But what if he was wrong? If the program detected our laptop despite everything and it did a calculation on the probability of us doing something subversive, the result would be a deadly one hundred per cent.

The universal adaptor looked like a thin metal thread. It would have fitted through a needle. Caesar slipped it into the USB port. It was far smaller than the usual cable but somehow it didn't fall out.

The door to the server room opened. Stephanie slipped inside.

'Everyone's ready. We're just waiting for the go-ahead.'

Caesar got up and started walking around while holding the computer.

'What are you doing?' I asked, not completely trusting that he wasn't going to disappear with the laptop and leave the rest of us in the lurch.

'I need to plug it into the system.'

Damien snorted. 'You'd think that things would be wireless here in the future.'

Caesar knelt before one of the metal boxes. 'This isn't the future, this is space, and most things are wireless.' He placed the laptop on the floor and plugged the other end of the cable into the server. 'Devices need to have a certain hardware built in to be compatible with our systems wirelessly. And last time I checked, Earth hadn't yet acquired cytosol technology.'

Damien looked like a child who had just been told off.

'There.' Caesar waved me over. 'We have a connection. Do your thing.'

I could hardly believe it. This had been too easy.

I sat down and placed my fingers on the keyboard. The familiarity of the smooth plastic sent me back to my room on the Isle of Dogs. How far away it seemed. Not just literally, but emotionally. It felt as if it belonged to a different life, in a different lifetime.

I opened a browser. My main aim was to target all the chat rooms I knew of. But I couldn't help myself. It was like a reflex. I began by typing in Facebook.com and logging in.

There wasn't much activity on my feed. Maybe it was because the blackouts had got worse. The routers didn't work if there was no electricity – no router, no internet. But maybe the reason was more ominous. Maybe the internet connection wasn't the problem. Maybe the problem was that most of my Facebook friends had been taken.

I began writing a status:

People of Earth. My name is Amy Sullivan. I'm on board one of the alien vessels surrounding our planet. Soon a fleet of small shuttle-pods will enter Earth's atmosphere and seek to land. On board, there will be humans. The kids they've been abducting. I ask you not to shoot. Please, please, please don't shoot.

I pressed 'Post'.

Caesar was hovering over me. 'Is that it?'

I shook my head. 'No. We need to do more. This needs to spread.'

I copied the Facebook message and started entering chat rooms. I pasted in the message. Again and again I pressed ctrl v. I could only hope that someone was there to read it.

I decided to try more traditional outlets as well. I opened my email. I was going to send an email to the BBC.

My inbox was filled with spam. But my heart twisted inside my chest. In between offers for protein powder and penis enlargements there were emails from Mum and Dad. Poor Mum and Dad. They were frantic. I quickly scanned the subjects.

'Where are you?'

'Please come home'

'We love you'

Caesar got up to talk to Stephanie. I grabbed the chance and opened one of the emails from Mum. I typed as quickly as I could: 'I'm okay. I'll hopefully be home soon. I love you.' I pressed 'Send'.

I felt guilty and relieved at the same time. I felt relief over the fact that whatever happened I had managed to tell Mum and Dad that I loved them. I had said goodbye. I felt guilty for not offering Matilda, Anita and everyone else the chance to do the same. But there just wasn't time.

'How much longer?' Caesar said from where he stood next to a frowning Stephanie.

I sent off my email to the BBC. 'I don't know,' I said, opening one of the chat rooms to see if there had been any response.

Shit. I tried to hide my shock. I tried to keep my panic from showing. It didn't work.

'What?' Andrew let go of Anita's hand – they had been holding hands the whole time, which really annoyed me; I wanted him to be by my side but I didn't want to have to ask. He sat down next to me. 'What's wrong?'

I didn't answer. I was still reading.

Andrew leaned forward, his nose almost touching the screen. It didn't take him long to realise the severity of the situation. He grabbed his hair and pressed his lips together so hard the skin around his mouth turned white.

'Can someone please explain what's going on?' Matilda shouted.

It had never occurred to me. It just hadn't.

I began reading out loud the comments to my post.

'Ha, ha, very funny,' wrote someone who clearly thought it was a joke.

'I bet you're one of them,' another one said. 'I bet this is a trap; that you're an alien pretending to be a human. If you dare come close to our planet, we'll shoot you down, you white-faced freak.'

This was bad. This was really bad.

The others knew it. Louisa started crying. Courtney began shouting at her, 'Shut up, shut up, shut up!'

Of all the things that I imagined could go wrong, I never thought that the people back on Earth, my fellow human beings, wouldn't believe me.

Anita rushed over, slumped down beside Andrew and buried her face in his neck.

Damien started laughing. A frantic, psychotic laugh.

Tom's reaction was as predictable as rain at Wimbledon. 'I told you so! I told you this was a bad idea!'

Matilda snapped, making a popping sound like a twig breaking in two. 'I can't take this any more. I can't take this negativity. I can't be with someone who is always nagging. Nagging, nagging, nagging.'

Tom's face crumpled, along with his ego. 'I can't be with someone who's got her head in the clouds all the time.'

'Fine. We're over.'

'So over.'

'That's what I said. Over.'

Stephanie began waving her arms in the air. 'Can everybody please calm down? It's like a zoo in here.'

Caesar pushed Andrew out of the way and sat down next to me. 'There must be something we can do. I mean, we can convince them that this isn't a hoax, right?'

I began typing again.

```
FrizzyAmy: This isn't a trap, guys. Please believe me. I
was taken by the visitors. We have help on the inside.
We're making our escape in about an hour's time.
AwesomeDude: Yeah right.
Linda97: Get out of the chat room. You're annoying the
hell out of me.
```

I needed to do something. I needed to convince them that I was me; that I was human. *But how?*

I had an idea.

```
FrizzyAmy: Ask me anything. Ask me something only a human
would know. Like the capital of the UK or something.
```

AwesomeDude: . . . What is the name of the pub in EastEnders?

I did a victory lap in my head.

FrizzyAmy: The Queen Vic!
Linda97: This is silly. Have you seen the visitors' weapons? Have you seen their technology? If you were one of them, it wouldn't be very hard for you to find out the capital of the UK or the name of some stupid pub in a stupid soap. You'd only need access to Google.

She was right. But what could I do? How could I prove that I was a human stuck in space? I could do a video of the server room and upload it to YouTube. But they'd only say it was a fake; that it was staged.

I checked out the other chat rooms I'd posted in. What little was left of my morale plummeted. They were all saying the same thing. No one believed me.

My eyes suddenly stopped on a familiar nick. NY152. It was the annoying, arrogant guy in New York. The one I sometimes played against in World of Warcraft. I'd had many battles with him over the years. His avatar was an exceptionally ugly orc. I'd only defeated him once. I sometimes chatted with him online afterwards. He gave me patronising tips on how to improve my performance.

I could only hope he remembered me.

FrizzyAmy: Hey, NY152. We met in World of Warcraft.

333

NY152: Oh, hi, I remember. Your sense of humour is as bad as your virtual sword skills. People don't seem to be appreciating your joke.

FrizzyAmy: It's not a joke.

NY152: It's not?

FrizzyAmy: No. I've been taken. We're making our escape. But people don't seem to believe me. They think that I'm not me. That I'm an alien pretending to be human. But I'm not. I'm me. I really am me.

NY152: Okay.

FrizzyAmy: How can I prove that I'm me?

NY152: I don't know …

FrizzyAmy: I told them to ask me a question only a human could answer but they said if I was an alien I could google it.

NY152: I can see where they are coming from.

FrizzyAmy: But you know me. Sort of. You believe me, right?

NY152: I don't know …

FrizzyAmy: I could turn the camera on so you can see that I'm me.

NY152: I've never seen you in person. I've only seen your avatar.

FrizzyAmy: Oh yeah …

Shit. This wasn't working.

NY152 *typing* . . .

Ny152: I've got an idea. I know a question that only you know the answer to. It can't even be googled. If you are who you say you are, if you are indeed FrizzyAmy, you can answer this question. If you can't …

FrizzyAmy: Ask me. Hurry up.

NY152: the only time you got the better of me playing WoW was during a battle that took place on the continent of Pandaria. What combination of weapons did you use to bring about my demise?

I jumped when Caesar interrupted me. 'Do you know? Do you know?'

'Know what?' Stephanie asked.

Caesar began explaining to the others what was going on.

I squeezed my eyes shut. I had to get the answer right. This was it. This was the moment our fate would be decided. It was a question of life and death. Literally.

I placed my fingers on the keyboard. I was pretty sure I remembered it correctly.

FrizzyAmy: Draconic Avenger, a two-handed axe, and the Legionkiller, a crossbow.

I waited. Every second felt like a whole day. I started doubting myself. Maybe it was the wrong answer. Or maybe NY152 had gone offline. Maybe he had been taken by the visitors and I would never get my confirmation.

His reply finally came.

NY152: CORRECT! I believe you. I'll help you spread the word in all the chat rooms. And on Facebook as well.

I was about to tell the others the good news when Tom started whinging again. 'I need to go to the bathroom.'

'There isn't a toilet in here.' Caesar rolled his eyes. 'Can't you just hold it in?'

'I need to go to the bathroom,' he repeated like a big kid.

'Just find a quiet corner then.'

'I'm not a dog.'

Stephanie growled from frustration. 'I'll take him.'

They left the room.

I told the group that NY152 had confirmed my identity. Relief filled the room like a spring breeze.

'What do we do now?' asked Caesar.

I shrugged my shoulders. 'I don't know. I guess we just wait a bit and see if the others accept the confirmation from NY152. The only thing we can do is to wait for the word to spread.'

I started browsing the internet. The BBC's website seemed to have some recent updates. I scanned the headlines.

'Forest fire in Epping started by a visitor's laser gun'

'Metallic arm kills seven in car on the M11'

'Study shows two thirds of teenagers in the UK are now missing'

I don't know why I did it. I really didn't expect anyone at the BBC to be monitoring their inbox right then. But I pressed refresh anyway.

The force of hope exploding in my chest made it hard to breathe.

'It's here!' I shouted to the others. 'There's an article about us.' I started reading it out loud. 'Contact has allegedly been made with one of the missing teenagers abducted from Earth in recent weeks. The girl, who is believed to be from East London, stated in an email to the BBC and in several online chat rooms that the children of Earth will be returning home in the next hour or so. The abductees, who are thought to be prisoners in the alien vessels besieging Earth, will be travelling by small space shuttles.

'The authenticity of the claim has not been completely verified but the source is believed to be credible. In the last few minutes the interim UK government has been contacting governing bodies around the world to let them know about the development. Armies are on standby but are under orders not to shoot.'

There it was. Our safe passage back home. This couldn't have gone any better. Everyone in the server room started cheering and hugging.

'I knew you could do it,' Anita said as she high-fived me.

'We're going home,' Louisa cried, wrapping her arms around Courtney.

'You're a genius, you,' Damien said as he ran over and planted a wet kiss on my cheek.

'She is – I've always said so,' Matilda added, punching the air.

Caesar got to his feet. 'It's not a guarantee, but it's definitely better than nothing.'

We were preparing to leave the server room when the door opened. It was Stephanie. Just Stephanie. She looked pale and her hair was all out of place.

'I'm sorry,' she said. Were those tears in her eyes? 'I'm so sorry.'

Day Eleven

The Defects had been so careful in their planning. They'd never communicated anything about their escape electronically. Everything was discussed face to face in hushed conversations so their interactions wouldn't be picked up by the computer program that monitored all telecommunication devices on board. Communication between Defects in different ships was done with light transmissions that resembled the Morse code we had back on Earth.

But it only took one traitor to sabotage everything.

27

'I'm sorry,' Stephanie was still saying as we ran along the ship's corridors. The lights in the ceiling were flashing purple. The ship's alarm had been turned on. How could he have done this to us?

'He came out of the bathroom and just started shouting something about handing himself in. Something about telling the president everything in exchange for immunity. I didn't know what to do. I should have shut him up. I should have broken his neck. But I panicked when I saw the Red Stacks coming. I couldn't think of anything else to do but run.'

'Down here,' Caesar ordered as he turned the corner.

I had no idea where we were going. None of us did. We were just following Caesar in the hope he knew what he was doing.

He finally stopped. 'Stephanie, go and tell the army to set off the bombs.'

'Bombs?' I didn't like the sound of that.

'They're only smoke bombs with mild sedatives in them. Our plan was to set them off by the quarters of the Red Stacks, to slow them down once they realised we were stealing the pods. Thanks to your friend, we will have to use them much sooner than we intended.'

He turned back to Stephanie. 'And make sure Adam and the others are ready to storm the pod rooms.'

I suddenly realised something. 'What about us? What about the humans in the Camp? You're not leaving us behind. Don't even dream of it. I'll stop you. I'll start screaming. Like Tom. I'll draw the attention of the Red Stacks. Either we all go or no one goes.'

Caesar looked at me with such hurt in his brown eyes it made my heart sting. 'Amy, I'd have thought you'd trust me by now.'

I couldn't look at him, but I didn't back down. I did trust him. Or I thought I did. But I wasn't taking any chances.

Caesar sighed. 'Legions of our soldiers have already charged your Camp. It shouldn't take them long to overpower the guards. There aren't that many of them. They weren't expecting anyone to come and rescue you, as your species barely has the capability to exit your atmosphere, let alone conduct warfare in space. Defects are being led out of the Colony as we speak. Your people will be joining them on their way to the pod rooms.'

The corridor we were standing in was empty. Caesar placed his palm on the steel wall, which lit up. A door opened. 'And if you don't trust me, there are practical reasons for why we wouldn't betray you. We need you. You're our entry ticket. Our plan requires your species to believe that there are humans on board the shuttle-pods. The best way to do that is simply to have humans on board. It will also make it easier for us after we land to leave the pods and disappear into the crowds. As your people are busy greeting the humans, we Defects can quietly disperse and go and find ourselves new homes.'

We followed Caesar into the room. 'Stephanie, go already,' he hissed, taking his anger with me out on her.

'I'll go with her,' Damien cried out. 'To keep an eye on things. Make sure that the humans get seats on the pods.'

'So will I,' Courtney was quick to add.

'Me too!' Louisa predictably yelled.

Stephanie rolled her eyes. 'Fine. But no more. I can't have a herd of you slowing me down.'

I didn't know if they were offering to go to secure the interests of their fellow human beings, or if they were simply making sure they got seats for themselves on one of the shuttle-pods. They were gone before I could ask.

The room we were in was the size of a broom cupboard. It had a steel chair and a steel table with a computer screen sticking out of it like in the Selection Lab.

'Where are we?' I asked.

Caesar laid his palms on the table, which lit up with a touchscreen version of a keyboard. The symbols didn't look anything like the letters of the alphabet I knew. He tapped the keyboard and the screen lit up.

'This is an access point,' Caesar said. 'One of the places where the ship's different systems can be controlled.'

I was leaning over Caesar's shoulder, looking at what was happening on the screen. Andrew, Matilda and Anita were hovering on tiptoes behind me, trying to catch a glimpse of something that offered hope.

I didn't want to interrupt Caesar. I knew whatever he was up to, time was of the essence. But I couldn't take it any more. 'What are you doing?'

He stared at the screen and mumbled, as if to himself, 'The

fleet's grain repositories. This is the access point to all the grain repositories.' He was typing and talking. 'There is no central command aboard our ships. Everything is controlled through different access points.' His voice turned into a monotonous drone. 'Efficiency through division of labour. Security through distribution of power.'

I wondered what I'd asked. I tried again. 'The grain repository what?'

'I'm activating my program.'

'What are you talking about?'

He quickly looked up with something that was either surprise or scorn on his face. 'You didn't think breaking out of here would be enough; you didn't think it would be that easy, did you?'

I just stared at him.

Caesar sighed. 'Just think. It's obvious.'

'What is?'

'If we manage to escape this ship – if we manage to get to Earth – don't you think the Corrects will just come after us? Let's say you make it back to your home, you snuggle up in bed, happy that you're reunited with your family – how long do you think it will be before there's a knock on your door, before a metallic arm slides in through your window and sucks you back up here?'

No one answered. I felt empty. Out of breath. Stupid. How had I not thought of that?

Matilda recovered the quickest. 'So what are you going to do? Let me guess. You're setting a time bomb. When we leave the ships they will all explode into a thousand pieces and kill all the white-faced arseholes.'

She clearly still hadn't realised that we weren't stuck inside a Hollywood film but a real spaceship.

Caesar appeared offended. 'I am not a monster. I'm not going to wipe out all the Pronaxian Corrects.'

Matilda rolled her eyes. 'Sorry, Mr Sensitive.'

I didn't understand Caesar. He'd killed people before – human and alien. But the thought of wiping out the monsters who had imprisoned him and killed his parents appeared to offend him.

He turned his gaze on me. 'What? Why are you looking at me like that? Not all of them are bad people. Some of them do bad things. But that doesn't give anyone the right to punish them all. I don't agree with their values and I don't want to live by them. But I'm not wiping out every life form in this universe I don't agree with. That would make me even worse than them.'

The room was getting hot. Anita stepped in to cool the situation. 'You're quite right,' she said in her mediator voice. 'So what is the plan?'

Caesar's eyes lingered on me. I stared back at him. I imagined his palm on my cheek. I imagined me caressing his fingers. I remembered our kiss back at the warehouse party. He smiled at me as if he knew what I was thinking. I couldn't help blushing.

He turned back to the screen. 'What I'm doing is buying us time. I'd already laid the ground work. I'm taking control of the fleet's grain repositories. They're huge storage rooms aboard each ship where the food is kept. They carry grain that will last the whole population of each ship for up to ten years.'

I felt hope beginning to buzz in my stomach. 'What are you going to do?'

'It's simple. I'm going to open up all the shutters and let the grain be sucked out into space.'

Andrew started nodding. 'That's good. That's actually brilliant.'

Matilda looked perplexed. 'I don't see the difference. Why not just bomb them? How is it more humane to let them starve to death?'

'They won't starve to death. There are emergency rations kept in different places on board every ship. But they will have to leave immediately to get to a nutri-planet in time.'

The hope was spreading from my stomach to my limbs like little bees travelling through my veins. 'How much time will it buy us?'

'Maybe a year in human terms.'

A wall of disappointment stopped the bees in their tracks. 'So they will be back. In a year.'

'I don't know. Maybe. Maybe not. Maybe they'll move on. Go somewhere else. Maybe they'll find a planet with enough energy to keep the species going without us, a planet that can sustain their technology. Maybe they will be able to start using the incubators again and forget all about us.'

'That is a big if.'

'That's the best we've got,' Caesar said, tapping away at the keyboard. He began mumbling to himself again. 'Okay. This is good. I'm in. I'm inside the system. Okay. Now I only have to activate my program and …'

The silence felt like eternity. The words that broke it felt like a sledgehammer to the soul.

'Oh, no, no.'

Anita buried her face in Andrew's arm. Matilda looked at me and slipped her hand into mine.

'No, no, no.' Caesar was tapping away frantically. 'I can't believe they did that. I can't believe they're on to me. They found it. They found my program. They've removed it.'

I leaned forward, looking at the screen. It was empty except for five softly drawn symbols that flashed in red in the top left corner. 'That's okay. You can just install it again.'

Caesar reached into one of the holsters on his belt and produced his pad. He started tapping it with one finger, hitting it much harder than necessary.

'No, I can't. I can't. They've surrounded the control station with some sort of firewall.'

'What kind of firewall?'

'I don't know. I've never seen it before. It looks as if it's connected to the monitoring system. It detects the device that is trying to gain access and automatically blocks it.'

Matilda squeezed my hand. 'But you can do something. You must be able to do something.'

Caesar slammed his fists down on the table. 'There is no way around it.'

I let go of Matilda's hand. I slid my backpack off my shoulder, unzipped it and pulled out the laptop.

Caesar looked at it, unimpressed. 'I know what you're thinking. But I don't know how to work it.'

'I know how to work it.'

'It's so primitive.'

'Sometimes all you need to dig a hole is a spade.'

345

'But this is only an access point. We'd need to go back to the server room to plug directly into the system.'

'Then we'll go to the server room.'

'But thanks to your friend we're not exactly safe there.'

'We'll be quick.'

'I don't know …'

'We have nothing to lose.'

Caesar was looking at the others. But where he had expected to find confirmation of his doubts, there was only hope.

Just as we were about to leave the access point, a group of Red Stacks ran past the room. Caesar managed to close the door just before they saw us.

'We're running out of time,' Caesar said. 'They must have cleared the corridors of the sedatives. They're probably going to the pod rooms to fight the army. We can only hope that the shuttle-pods have started leaving the ship.'

We waited until the coast was clear and then got back to the server room unnoticed.

We plugged in the laptop.

'Do you have another one of those cables?' I asked.

Caesar pulled one out of his holster.

'Great. Now plug the pad into the laptop.'

I opened the editor. I had done some coding before. Once I'd created a computer program that pinged every time a new cat video was posted on YouTube. And once I'd programmed an app for Matilda's phone that added blusher to people's cheeks in all the photos she took. It made everyone look like a dishevelled

clown, but it worked. However I'd never done anything like this.
I started typing.

```
function sendToDevice(request){
var output = [];
```

'I'm creating a program that turns the laptop into a mirror,'
I explained to the others. 'The laptop will mirror every action
on the pad. But the system will think it's coming from the
laptop.'

'That's brilliant,' Anita exclaimed. She'd actually helped out a
bit with the blusher app. 'So the commands that are given on the
pad won't be detected by the monitoring system because the
laptop doesn't have the hardware that alerts it. We'll be able to
bypass the firewall.'

Matilda squealed. 'Who would have thought that all those late
nights cooped up in your bedroom with only a sad little laptop
for company would one day save the human race?'

I kept on tapping, ignoring the insult.

```
if(result !=='undefined')
return result;
```

'There.' The screen of the laptop turned white. 'Activate the pad.'

Caesar swiped it with one finger. It turned from white to
black. So did the screen of the laptop.

'It worked,' Andrew said with obvious disbelief.

'Try logging in to the grain repository system,' I told Caesar.

He started typing. 'I'm in!'

I felt satisfyingly smug. 'Okay. Reinstall the program.'

I followed what Caesar was doing on his pad on the laptop screen. There was a bit of a lag.

'Almost there,' he said.

The lag grew bigger. The laptop fan was blasting away.

'I'm installing the program,' he said, placing the pad on the floor. He looked down at the illegible white signs on the black background. 'It says it's going to take a few minutes. I guess the laptop is slowing things down. It doesn't possess the same computational capacity as our technology.'

We were just sitting there, staring silently at the devices, when the door to the server room opened.

The sight felt like long, treacherous fingers wrapping themselves around my throat.

'You shit!' Matilda's face was red with anger.

It was Tom. And he wasn't alone.

I stared at him. I hadn't really believed Stephanie when she'd said he'd betrayed us. That he had done it on purpose. That he had started screaming. That he had wanted the Red Stacks to pick him up. I thought it was a misunderstanding.

It wasn't.

'I told you so. They're planning an escape!' Tom was shouting. 'Now it's your turn. I want to see the president. He owes me a ride home.'

His hands were tied together with something that looked like rope made of steel. Tom really had decided to try to save himself by selling out the rest of us.

The two Red Stacks who were holding Tom, each by one arm, seemed as surprised to see us as we were to see them.

Caesar, Andrew, Matilda, Anita and I jumped up all at once.

One of them spotted the laptop. 'What's this?' he said in the poshest English I'd ever heard. 'What's going on here?'

He didn't wait for an answer. He let go of Tom and started reaching for something tucked away in the holster on his belt.

I immediately knew what it was. 'Watch out!' I screamed. 'He's grabbing for his gun.'

He pulled out a sphere that fitted perfectly in the palm of his hand. It lit up. But he didn't aim it at us.

'No,' Anita shouted. 'The laptop.' She leaped forward. 'He's aiming for the laptop.' Anita clutched his arm. The weapon fell from his hand and bounced twice on the floor before the light inside it went out.

I grabbed it.

'Shoot him,' Matilda shouted.

The sphere wasn't lighting up.

'You control it with your mind,' Caesar called out.

But the Red Stack had got his bearings. He reached out for Anita, pulled her up against his body and wrapped his arm around her throat.

She started choking.

'Let her go!' Andrew screamed, running towards them. But he didn't get far.

The other Red Stack let go of Tom. He stepped in front of Andrew. His movements were so quick he looked like a biological jet engine. He lifted one hand as if he were about to wave away a small fly. It seemed as if he'd hardly touched him, but Andrew went flying through the air. He slammed against the hard metal surface of one of the servers by the wall opposite the door. His scream cut through the air and my soul. As he collapsed to the ground I saw that his head was bleeding.

There was a soft tingle in the palm of my hand. The sphere gave a little glow. I tried to focus my mind. I tried channelling all my fear and all my hate from my mind to the weapon. The light increased. It seemed to be working. The sphere was buzzing. I didn't know how, but I knew it was ready.

Anita's eyes were shut. Her face was turning blue.

I raised my arm and aimed for the Red Stack's head.

But suddenly Anita opened her eyes. Their fiery focus contradicted the blueness of her skin. Her lips parted. The choking sounds turned into words.

'The laptop,' she croaked.

The Red Stack who had attacked Andrew was rushing across the room.

'Save it. Save them all. Save mankind.'

I didn't think. If I'd had time to think, I would have acted differently. I wouldn't have let my instincts take control. Dad would blame Darwin. I blame myself.

I swung my arm to the side. The Red Stack was still running towards the laptop. But I had a clear aim. I focused my mind. I thought about the visitors. How they had ruined all our lives. I thought about all the parents who were grieving for missing children. I thought about Mandira, about how mean and ruthless sorrow had made her. I thought about Mum and Dad and Emma.

Did they still have hope, or had they given up on ever seeing me and Andrew again?

The sphere went off. A clear blue beam shot out of the weapon in a straight line. It hit the Red Stack in the back.

He crumpled to the ground, just a few centimetres away from the laptop. Lying dead still, in his red overalls he looked like an animal carcass ready to be shipped to the butcher's. I didn't know if I had killed him. I hoped I hadn't killed him. I hadn't wanted to kill him.

I couldn't worry about that now. I had to save Anita.

I spun around. I was reaching out the hand that held the sphere when I heard a soft snapping sound – almost like a twig cracking, but not quite as hollow. It was more like a wishbone breaking in two.

I didn't realise what had happened until Matilda started screaming.

I stood there with my hand reaching out in front of me. I felt my face drain of colour.

Anita's head was resting horizontally on the Red Stack's arm. Her eyes were wide but empty. Her mouth was open. Blood trickled from her nose, down her cheek and on to the Red Stack's sleeve.

'He broke her neck.' Matilda started crying.

Andrew was trying to get to his feet but he couldn't find his balance.

The Red Stack looked down at Anita. She looked so small in his arms. Almost like a child.

Without showing the slightest expression, the Red Stack let go of her body, and it tumbled to the floor.

I tried to convince myself that she wasn't dead. I tried to tell myself that we could fix her. Things weren't always as bad as they seemed. You could cure the most horrendous diseases. You could restart a heart that had stopped. What else ... what else ...

I didn't notice him approaching.

Caesar called out to me. 'Amy!'

The Red Stack was marching towards me. I aimed the sphere at him, but I couldn't focus. He grabbed my arm, twisted it and ripped the weapon from my hand, then pushed the sphere up against my throat.

'No!' I heard Caesar call out as I felt the object heat up on my neck.

This was how I was going to die. I closed my eyes. At least I'd tried.

But suddenly I couldn't feel the hot patch any more. There was a thud. I opened my eyes. The Red Stack was lying on the floor by my feet. I looked up. Stephanie stood in the doorway, holding a triangular weapon. Damien stood next to her, his mouth open in surprise.

My legs gave in and I collapsed to the floor. The room smelled of burned flesh. And blood. I felt as if I was about to throw up. I crawled on my hands and knees over to Anita's body.

'Anita.' I tried shaking her. 'Anita.'

I'd always imagined death to look peaceful. Death was like sleep, except you would never wake up. I was wrong.

Anita's face was frozen in contorted terror.

'Anita.' I touched her bloodied cheek. It was still warm.

Stephanie growled. 'What are you still doing here? We need to go.'

Andrew crawled to us. He placed two fingers on Anita's neck to check for a pulse. His eyes watered. He shook his head.

Caesar knelt down by the laptop. 'There was a problem.'

'What kind of problem?'

'With the grain repository system. But the upload is almost done.'

'Then what are you waiting for? Let's go.'

Caesar got up. He gently touched my shoulder. 'We need to go.'

I ignored him. I took Anita's hand in mine and lay down beside her. This was my fault. I'd made the wrong choice. I shouldn't have listened to her. I shouldn't have listened to my instincts. I should have saved her. To hell with the rest of the kids on board. To hell with mankind.

Andrew put his palm over Anita's eyes to close them. It did nothing to diminish the panic in her expression. She was gone, but the horror of her final moments would be there on her face for ever and ever.

Andrew staggered to his feet.

'Amy,' he said, his voice breaking. 'Get up.'

The skin of Anita's palm was soft. It hadn't been hardened by time, by life. No one should die this young. No one should die before having really lived.

'Amy,' Andrew said again, 'we have to go.'

I closed my eyes and pretended I wasn't there. Nothing would ever be the same again. Even if by some miracle we got back to Earth and, by an even bigger miracle, the visitors buggered off and preyed on some other species somewhere else in the universe, things would never really be the same again. I would never again go for an ice cream with Anita and talk about the latest developments in the world of microprocessors. I would never again watch Anita and Matilda argue about which invention was more important, the mass-produced computer or mascara.

'Help me,' someone whimpered in a corner of the room. It was Tom. He was cowering behind one of the servers. He reached out his arms. 'Help me get the handcuffs off. There's a tool in his belt. A key or a fob or something.'

Matilda steadied herself. She dried her face with the back of her hand. Then she started running towards Tom.

'You disgusting coward! You traitor.' She jumped on Tom, who fell backwards to the floor. 'It's all your fault.' She threw herself on top of him and began hitting him in the face with clenched fists. 'You killed her, you bastard. You killed my friend.'

Caesar rushed over and grabbed Matilda by the wrists. 'This is not the time or the place.'

Matilda fought him, but no matter how hard she punched the air, Caesar didn't let go. She finally gave up, her whole body collapsing in sorrow. She leaned her head on Caesar's chest and started crying again.

He wrapped his arms around her. 'It's okay,' he said, stroking her hair. 'It will be okay.'

'What do we do with him?' Stephanie asked, gesturing with her head towards Tom.

I let go of Anita's hand and sat up. I couldn't believe she was even asking. 'We leave him here, of course.'

Now Tom started crying. 'I'm sorry. I'm so, so sorry. I didn't mean for this to happen. Please don't leave me here.'

Andrew was heading over to the dead body of one of the Red Stacks. 'This one?'

Tom nodded.

Andrew bent down and started rummaging through the Red Stack's holsters.

'What are you doing?' I shouted at Andrew.

He pulled out a small glass pebble. He lifted it up for Tom to see. 'This one here?'

Tom nodded eagerly.

Andrew started towards Tom.

'Andrew! You're not doing this, Andrew.' I got up and followed him. I grabbed his arm and tried wrestling the pebble from his hand.

'We can't leave him here.'

'He just killed Anita. He just killed your girlfriend.'

'And when we're all safely back on Earth I'm going to make him pay. But I don't want his death on my conscience.'

Tom reached out his arms towards Andrew.

'Andrew.'

'I know you, Amy. I know you won't be able to live with yourself if we just leave him here.'

He placed the pebble inside a hole in the middle of the handcuffs. They lit up slightly before the steel turned soft and they fell to the floor like a piece of rope.

'Let's go,' Stephanie said.

Caesar helped Matilda to her feet, then turned to Stephanie. 'What's the situation?'

'It's going surprisingly well. We managed to free the Colony and the Camp without too many casualties. Most of the pods have already left. The bad news is that there isn't going to be room for everyone.'

I glanced over at Anita's body. My legs were about to buckle when, suddenly, Damien was by my side. He linked arms with me, giving me the support to stay on my feet.

'Courtney and Louisa are saving us a seat,' he said. 'They're doing it kicking and screaming. Literally.'

Damien somehow looked more alive than ever.

'You should've seen them.' He began steering me towards the door. 'Courtney punched a guy right on the nose. I swear, she smashed it into a million pieces. And Louisa pulled another girl's hair so hard she came tumbling down right when she was about to get into one of the pods. That one is ours now. And you should have seen the soldiers. They slaughtered those prissy Red Stacks and the rest of the white-faced freaks as if it were nothing. As if they were just stepping on a bunch of ants or something.'

We were in the doorway. Andrew, Caesar, Matilda and Stephanie were right behind us. I stopped. I was about to turn around – Anita, we couldn't go without Anita – when Damien pulled gently at my arm so I was forced to keep on going.

'When we get home, Amy, I'm going to take you on a date. Like a proper date. I'm going to take you somewhere fancy. Somewhere posh. Like Nando's.'

I almost laughed. Maybe things would get back to normal. One day.

Day Eleven

Last Night I Dreamt That Somebody Loved Me
This Charming Man
Please, Please, Please, Let Me Get What I Want

Stop Me If You Think You've Heard This One Before
I Want the One I Can't Have
Heaven Knows I'm Miserable Now

I Started Something I Couldn't Finish
What Difference Does It Make?
Well I Wonder

A poem by Amy Sullivan made up of song names by The Smiths.

28

There was chaos in the corridors. There was smoke everywhere. The purple lights were blinking manically. The alarm was screeching. We ran past a couple of seriously wounded Red Stacks. Some dead visitors in black. And one dead human. A girl. She was wearing pyjamas with a clown print on them. I tried not to look too closely.

Stephanie was leading the way. Damien was still by my side.

'I'll see you in the pod room,' Caesar said suddenly and turned the corner in the opposite direction.

'What?' I stopped. 'Where are you going?'

'Back to the access point.'

'Why? You said the upload was done.'

'Yes, my program is reinstalled. But I haven't released the grain. I can only gain access to the repositories through the access point.' He turned on his heel. 'But don't worry. The rest is easy. I'll be quick.'

'I'm coming with you.'

Andrew grabbed my shoulder. 'No, you're not.'

Caesar turned back. 'He's right. There's no need. You need to secure yourself a seat on one of the shuttle-pods.'

I shook Andrew off me. 'I'm coming with you. I need to make sure everything goes according to plan.'

'I've got it under control, Amy. Go with your brother. I'll see you later.'

Andrew tried dragging me away.

'No. This is my responsibility. Just as it is yours. I was sent here to save everyone. I was sent here to save Earth.' I hesitated. Technically, I was sent here to betray Earth. 'I came here to do my part. I'm doing it. I'm seeing it through.'

Andrew let go of me. 'Then I'm coming too.'

'Andrew, no. You can't come. Go with the others.'

'I'm coming.' He started following Caesar.

'Andrew, you're not coming. Think about Mum and Dad. If I don't …' I didn't want to think about any what-if situation, but Andrew was forcing me to. 'If things don't go according to plan, there's no need for them to lose both of us. It's important one of us gets back. Someone needs to explain things. Tell them what happened; why we did what we did. Why I left.'

Andrew didn't say anything. He didn't need to – he looked as if he were about to split in two.

Matilda moved over to him and took his hand. 'Amy needs to do what she needs to do. If anyone can save Earth, it's her.'

Tom cleared his throat from over where he was stooping next to Stephanie, whom he probably considered the least likely one of us to strangle him.

Matilda growled at him with such ferocity that saliva sprayed from her mouth. 'You don't have a say in anything any more, you little shit.'

Caesar shifted on his feet. 'You should hurry. Before it's too late.' He turned to me. 'Let's go then.'

I smiled at Andrew and Matilda. 'It's going to be okay. I'll see you guys in five.' I followed Caesar down a corridor, feeling as if I'd just told a lie.

Getting to the access point was easy. There was very little smoke in the corridor we took. There were no dead bodies to step over.

We'd just reached the access point when an existential crisis I didn't realise I was having presented itself.

'I feel so dirty,' I said.

Caesar was sitting down by the steel table that had the glass computer screen sticking out of it. 'I know. They don't let us take baths either. Water is rationed. It's easy for them to be strict about it; their skin is partially self-cleaning due to genetic engineering.'

I winced. 'I don't mean that. I feel dirty on the inside somehow.' The screen lit up. 'Because of the Red Stack. I didn't mean to kill him. Not really …'

Caesar started tapping on the keyboard. 'You shouldn't feel guilty. It was self-defence. It was self-preservation.'

I tried to hold it in. This was neither the time nor the place for a meltdown. But the question just shot out of my mouth. 'But then why isn't it okay when they do it?'

'When who does what?'

I was very aware that I sounded screechy, bordering on hysterical. 'If that was self-preservation, then me being here, me being taken, is also self-preservation. The president is just trying to save his people, his species. How is it different?'

Strange symbols were flashing on the screen. 'I don't know.'

'You don't know?'

Caesar sighed. 'I don't know everything.'

'How can you not know everything with all your technology – with your gadgets and genetic modification?'

'Technology usually raises more questions than it answers.'

'If you and your species don't know everything, then who does?'

'Everything isn't black and white, Amy. Sometimes there aren't any answers. Sometimes there is no right and wrong.' He took a breath. 'Almost there, I'm just waiting for my program to upload the command.'

I didn't mean to but I couldn't help it – I began hyperventilating.

Caesar jumped up from his chair.

'I'm okay, I'm okay – keep doing what you're doing … this is silly …' The room started spinning. Or was I spinning? I closed my eyes. It made it worse. I wobbled. Caesar managed to catch me before I tumbled to the floor.

'Sit down. Put your head between your knees.'

I did as I was told.

'Okay, breathe. Slowly.'

He was stroking my back. Up and down. Up and down. With his other hand he gently brushed the hair from my face. I imagined a field. Green grass. We were lying on our backs under a blue sky, watching clouds pass by. Our arms were touching. We were on Earth and everything was back to normal. There had never been a siege. There had never been visitors. There was just me and him, him and me, and neither of us cared what lay beyond Earth's atmosphere.

I opened my eyes. The room had stopped spinning. I looked at Caesar. He was staring at me, his autumnal eyes wide with worry. I smiled. He was worried about me. We were in the middle of an epic escape, but there he was, worrying about me.

I couldn't help myself. I reached out and placed my palms on his cheeks. His skin was soft with a stubbly edge to it.

Caesar moved closer.

'Maybe …' I hesitated – what if he didn't feel the same? But I decided to just go for it. 'Maybe, when we're back on Earth, I could ask Mum and Dad if you could, like, live with us. While you look for a place or whatever.' I was blushing. 'You could have my little sister's room if we moved her cot into Mum and Dad's.'

Caesar smiled back at me. 'I would love that.'

My skin tingled. He did. He did feel the same.

Caesar leaned forward. His smile was crooked. Expectant.

This was it. This was the moment. Our other kiss didn't count. The one at the warehouse back in East London. It had only been for show. This was different. This was for real. This was going to be my real first kiss.

I was going to remember this.

I ran my thumb gently over Caesar's lower lip. He placed his hands on my waist and pulled me closer.

He raised his eyebrows. 'Maybe you'll take me out on a date when we get to your planet. Maybe even to this place called Nando's.'

I laughed. 'Yes, maybe.'

'Amy, I really like you—'

I couldn't hold back any more. 'Stop talking.' I leaned closer. Our noses touched. I could feel his breath on my skin. I could feel the warmth from his lips on mine. His fingers were digging into my waist. I liked it.

I closed my eyes. This is it. *This is going to be my first—*

My whole body stiffened when a screeching noise blasted out from the computer. It sounded almost like an ambulance siren.

Caesar let go of me, jumped to his feet and ran towards the computer.

'Shit.' He was typing on the touchscreen keyboard.

'What is it?' I got up.

'Shit, shit, shit.'

'Did it fail? Did the program fail?'

He sank in his chair. His voice was a whisper. 'No.'

'Then what?'

'It worked. The hatches to the grain repositories of all the ships in the fleet have already started to open. Soon the grain will be sucked out.'

'That's great!'

He didn't answer. He was frowning. Why was he frowning?

'You should be ecstatic. You did it. We're going to get out of here. We're going to drive the visitors away from Earth. We're going to be safe. You should be happy.'

'I should be.'

'But you're not.'

He dug his fingers into his hair and pulled at it. 'I made a mistake.'

'I'm sure you didn't. Every program has small bugs in them. You said it worked. That's the only thing that matters.'

'It's not a bug.'

363

'Then what is it?'

'I don't know. Stupidity. Sloppiness. Selfishness.'

'What are you talking about?'

'I made a program that opened the hatches.'

'Yes.'

'But I didn't make provisions for them to close again.'

'So?'

'My program doesn't close hatches, it only opens them.'

I was getting really confused. I tried again: 'So?'

'The grain repository is sixty per cent of the size of each ship. Do you know what happens when such a large part of a ship gets depressurised? When so much of its atmosphere gets sucked out in one go? The hull will breach. The ship will disintegrate. Break apart.'

'For the third time: so?'

'They will die.'

'Who will?'

'Everyone on board. Everyone on board every ship of the fleet will die.'

'Oh God.' I didn't know what else to say.

Caesar was rubbing his face.

'I need to fix it.'

I thought I might throw up. 'But we're running out of time.'

'I know, I know,' Caesar hissed at me.

'Sorry.' I took a deep breath.

'I can't believe I didn't realise …'

But I could. I'd done some coding. I knew a lot of programmers online. They all had one thing in common. They all approached their work one problem at a time. Building a computer program was nothing like building stuff in the physical world. If you built a door in the real world that opened, by default it closed as well. But when coding, nothing happened on its own. You had to think of every minor detail. Every function in a program required its own line of code. To open a door, you needed to write code. And if you wanted that same door to close, you needed to write more code. It turned out computer programmers were the same across the universe.

Caesar looked as if he might faint.

'We'll fix this,' I said. 'Don't worry about it. You can write another program. Or just add a few lines to the old one. Then we'll go back to the server room and I'll help you install the changes and—'

'No,' Caesar said sharply. 'This is my mistake. I'll fix it. You should get going.' He got up from the computer. 'Come on. I'll take you to the pod room. Then I'll come back here and finish this.'

'No!' Why *wasn't he listening to me*? 'I'm seeing this through. We're in this together. I told you. This is not just your thing. I have a responsibility too.'

He tilted his head to one side and lowered his brows. Just like Dad when he wanted me to 'stop behaving like a child' (even though when it came to staying up late on school nights I was always considered a child).

'It's too risky,' Caesar said with a theatrical sigh. 'What if we're too late? What if your pod leaves without you? There's no way of knowing what the president will do to the humans who are left on board. When there aren't enough of you to see through his plan of saving the Pronaxian race, he'll probably just throw you out into space. The last thing you'll see before your body swells up to the point of exploding and you die is the inside of an airlock. Is that what you want? Really, is that what you want?'

I so wanted to punch him in the face. 'Stop trying to scare me into obedience!'

'Then stop being so stupid.'

'You stop being stupid.'

'No, you stop being stupid.'

'No, you stop being stupid.'

'No, you stop being ...' He fell silent. A smile crept over his face.

I laughed. This was so stupid. 'Let's get on with it.'

Caesar pulled out his pad and started tapping it.

'We can do this,' I told him. 'We can do this; it's no problem. You'll fix the program and I'll help you with the laptop and ...'

He wasn't listening. He was lost in his coding. I sat down on the floor and waited.

Day whatever ...

There is darkness around me and there is darkness inside me. I feel so guilty. But what could I have done? I did everything I could. Didn't I?

29

It was all going so well. Or so I thought.

I was sitting there confidently, doodling in my diary, when Caesar said, 'Almost there.' I closed the diary and began returning my things to my backpack. I was giddy. Almost happy. I was going home. Then he added, 'Shit.'

My heart sank. 'What? What's wrong?'

His fingers were skidding furiously over the keyboard, like tiny, helpless creatures trying to wriggle their way out of restraints. He finally stopped typing. 'Nothing. It's done,' he said. There was a hollow lack of conviction in his voice.

'You sure?'

'Yeah. Absolutely positive.' He sounded more cheerful now. 'And not only that. I have some good news.'

Finally, some good news.

'There's no need for us to go back to the server room.'

'Oh.'

'I managed to bypass the monitoring system.'

'How?'

'By duping it. It was actually quite brilliant.' He grinned. 'But it is of course known throughout many galaxies that I am a brilliant guy.'

'How?'

'By creating a sort of denial-of-service attack and overloading it. And a man-in-the-middle attack. And some other things.'

I had no idea what he was talking about. But I just assumed that was to be expected. That this was some Pronaxian computer speak. I looked at the screen. It was blank.

'Let's go,' he said, opening the door.

I followed him out into the corridor. There was no one around, but the air smelled of smoke.

'Bollocks,' Caesar said, sniffing the air. 'They've reached the final stages.'

'What? Is it over? Are we too late?'

'Not necessarily. But the army is on the defensive.'

'How do you know?'

'They've started using fire to fight off the Red Stacks. They're down to the most primitive of their weapons. That means they're out of ammunition. They're out of energy bolts for the stunners.'

'The stunners?'

'You know. The small glass shapes the Corrects use to kill.'

'What a nice name for such a horrible thing.'

'We can only hope that the shuttle-pods are still able to leave.'

We started running. The smell of burning grew stronger. I was just thinking how lucky it was that the corridors appeared to be empty when the steely scenery took a dramatic turn.

I tried not to gag. The floor was covered with bodies. Dead bodies.

Caesar didn't hesitate. He began tiptoeing his way between them, carefully stepping over lifeless limbs and pools of blood.

'Come on!'

I had no choice but to follow.

Most of the dead were wearing red or black overalls. Some of them had a clean wound right by their heart. They'd been killed with a stunner. They were the lucky ones. Others had experienced a far more painful death. They looked like skeletons made of coal. They'd been burned to a crisp. The pain they'd felt at the moment of death was etched onto their gaping, blackened faces.

Lives were fragile wherever you were in the universe. One minute you were there and the next—

Something snapped underneath the sole of my shoe. Shit. I'd stepped on someone's fingers. Someone's dead fingers. I felt sick as my body began to ooze cold sweat.

I couldn't take this. I couldn't go any further. Caesar. Where was Caesar?

My eyes glanced over the battlefield that separated us. There he was, five metres ahead.

'Caesar, I can't—'

I stopped as Caesar stumbled to his knees. I thought he'd bumped his foot on a corpse. But he hadn't.

'Caesar, are you okay?'

He was kneeling beside one of the bodies.

I forced myself to keep on going.

He was mumbling something to himself. 'No, no, no.'

Just one step at a time.

'No, no, no.'

I caught up with him. I didn't want to look, but I made myself do it.

I almost didn't recognise him. I'd recently realised that dead people looked nothing like themselves. Maybe it was because they *weren't* themselves any more.

'Stephanie's going to be devastated.'

His mouth was open like in a silent scream. There was a small burned hole on his grey overalls, right by his heart. It was Adam. Stephanie's boyfriend.

I didn't know what to say. 'I'm sorry ...'

Caesar laid his palm on his friend's chin. He forced a smile. 'See you in a parallel universe, my friend. Your sacrifice will be remembered, I'll make sure of it.'

Caesar got up. He pretended to scratch his chin, but I was pretty sure he was wiping away a tear. 'It would have been quick,' he said to himself as he walked away. 'That's something.'

That was definitely something. I knew I had to go on. It was either stepping over the dead or dying myself.

We followed the trail of bodies for a few minutes. And then we were there.

'That's the pod room,' Caesar said.

It was the last stop before freedom. Or death.

The entrance to the room was small. Just a normal doorway. What an undramatic passage to the climax of my life.

We stopped on either side of the doorway and peeked through, trying not to be seen. Which would it be: death or freedom?

Inside, there was chaos. On one side of the room stood an army dressed in fiery red. The president's men – the Red Stacks. On the other side was an army of Defects dressed in grey overalls.

The Red Stacks were shooting lightning out of their stunners across the room. The Defect soldiers were brandishing steel sticks that had fire flaming out of them like giant lighters.

I couldn't believe it. The Defects. It looked as if they were winning. The Red Stacks were retreating.

My heart suddenly sank. The fact that the Red Stacks were retreating meant their fighters were all gathered at the back of the pod room, right by the door. There was no way the Red Stacks would let a Defect and a human just walk through their line of defence to join the other side.

I turned around to say something to Caesar, but he was gone – he was running back down the corridor.

I panicked. 'Wait!' I shouted after him, then quickly lowered my voice. 'Where are you going?'

'Wait there,' he whispered back.

I stood by the pod-room entrance, half frozen, not knowing what to do. I watched Caesar disappear down the corridor paved with dead bodies. I turned away. I couldn't bear the sight of death any more. But there was no respite to be had. From inside the pod room echoed the sounds of people dying. Screams, crying, the rumble of fire, thuds of violence.

Where was Caesar? How could he have just left me here?

I was about to go after him when he appeared around the corner. He was pushing a metal container the size of a wheelie bin on wheels. He stopped. I started running towards him. He was bending down, lifting one of the dead bodies into a sitting position.

'What are you doing?'

It was a Red Stack. Caesar started opening the front of the red overalls.

'What are you …?'

He was undressing the corpse.

'What is wrong with you?'

'Stop shouting and help me with his legs.'

'Are you crazy?'

'I'm trying to get us into the pod room. Take his shoes off.'

I bent down and undid the straps on the shoes that were held in place with a magnet. I pulled off the red plastic shoes. The guy was barefoot. His toes looked exactly like any human toes except without hair or imperfections.

'Hand them over,' Caesar ordered.

The Red Stack was now completely naked but for a pair of white pants. Caesar got up. I couldn't believe how callous he was. Didn't it affect him at all that he was stealing the clothes off the back of a person who had once been alive but was now dead?

Caesar started undressing himself. I was too shocked to speak. He stripped down to his pants. I tried not to look, but I couldn't help myself. His abs were seriously toned. He must have worked out. And he wasn't hairless like the Corrects appeared to be. There was a small patch of hair on his chest. It was exactly the right amount.

He slipped his legs into the dead man's overalls. 'A disguise,' he said, zipping it up. He pointed to the wheelie bin. 'Climb in.'

'What is it?'

He opened the lid of the container and started pulling out small clear boxes, each filled with tiny metallic chips the size of fingernails. 'It's an energy storage unit. I noticed it on our way here. It carries energy capsules. Portable energy. Batteries, I guess you'd call them. They were probably meant for the stunners for the fight in the pod room, but whoever was bringing them didn't make it.'

'Why are you dumping all the capsules? Aren't you going to give them to your army?'

'I should. But instead I'm making room for you.'

I just stared at him.

'I'm smuggling you in.'

I finally understood why he had stolen the dead Red Stack's overalls. 'But you don't look anything like them either.'

He shrugged. 'I look more like them than you do. And besides, at least I look like a Defect. Defects are known to have joined the ranks of the Red Stacks. Traitors. The Corrects won't suspect me. Now, get in.'

There was no time to argue. Or come up with a better plan. I started to climb into the wheelie bin, but got ungracefully stuck midway. Caesar had to give me a push on the bum. 'Thanks.'

'My pleasure,' he said.

His dimpled smile was the last thing I saw before he closed the container and I was surrounded by the dark.

A thud and we were on the move. I could hardly feel the ride along the smooth steel floor except for when Caesar stopped pushing the container – I guessed to move dead bodies out of the way.

'Okay, we're there,' he said after a couple of minutes. 'Don't make a sound.'

I could hear that we were in the pod room now. The noise that seeped past the lid of the steel container sounded like a broken stereo playing ten bad dubstep songs at the same time.

We stopped. Someone was speaking in Pronaxian. Caesar answered back in his incomprehensible language. I was sure our journey was over. That our cover had been blown. But then the container started moving again.

The relief was still surging through me when suddenly there was a massive explosion. The container shook and tumbled over. The lid fell open.

Caesar was screaming, 'Run, Amy, run.'

I crawled out of my hiding place as fast as I could. The brightness that greeted me was blinding. I could hear the crackle of fire mixed with desperate screams of horror. All I could see was light and flames and burning Red Stacks running around, waving their hands and trying to put themselves out.

I spotted Caesar. My heart stopped. No. I started running towards him. 'Stop! You're making it worse.'

I ripped the backpack off my shoulder.

'Stay away, Amy! It was a fire bomb. There will be more. Run. Run towards the launching tube.'

The sleeve of his overalls was alight. He was trying to put the fire out with his other arm, but it was only spreading.

I ignored Caesar's orders and started hitting him with my backpack, trying to extinguish the fire. I kept missing because he couldn't stand still.

'Lie down on the floor,' I told him.

He did and I sat on top of him and hit him repeatedly with my backpack. I had no idea what I was doing, but to my surprise, it did the trick. The fire on both his arms went out.

He looked dazed. But as soon as a sizzling whizz filled the air, coming from the other end of the pod room, his eyes seemed to focus again. 'They're lighting another one.' He jumped to his feet. 'Run.'

I was running and trying to get my bearings at the same time. The pod room was huge. Lining the walls, which seemed as high as mountains, were shelves containing square glass boxes. Most of them were empty but a few still held unused shuttle-pods. The room was like the pick-up area at IKEA – if IKEA sold space vehicles.

The pods looked nothing like I'd imagined them. Without thinking much about it, I'd been sure they'd look like small aeroplanes. In fact they looked more like giant golf balls. They were completely round and made from shiny white plastic. Circling each around the middle was a line of black spots. Windows.

'Watch out!' Caesar yelled at me. 'Fire bomb!'

I ducked as a giant ball of flame shot over our heads. *BHAM!* It landed at the back of the room, close to the entrance we'd just come through, and exploded, flooring a large group of Red Stacks who were entering. There was more crying, more shrieking. The noise sounded like the wails of a dying animal lying on a road side.

'Hurry. There's the launch tunnel.'

If this was war, we were running through the middle of the battlefield, unarmed and unprotected. I pushed a Red Stack out of the way. I could only hope he wouldn't shoot me in the back.

I tried to focus my eyes on the army of Defects in the distance. There were no more than ten metres to go. *You can do it, Amy*, I told myself. *You can do it.*

My spirits suddenly lifted. I hadn't expected it. I hadn't noticed them before. Among the Defects I could see humans – kids dressed in jeans and T-shirts and pyjamas. They were helping the Defect fighters to stave off the Red Stacks. Some were holding fire-shooting sticks. Others had formed a shield with their bodies, protecting the human and Defect civilians trying to get on board the shuttle-pods. I felt a surge of pride. I wasn't alone. There were others trying to fight our fight. They were standing up for themselves. They were standing up for us. For a few seconds I felt like part of a team. Of a family.

But suddenly I noticed something else. The bubble of pride burst with an explosion of hurt and anger. How could they?

The humans weren't only fighting alongside the Defects. There were also some fighting beside the Red Stacks. They were fighting against their own people. They were actually preventing us from getting home.

Why? Why would they do that?

I slowed down to get a better look. There were more of them than I'd noticed at first. There was one: a guy wearing dirty joggers and a suit jacket. And there was another one: a girl with her hair in two plaits and a fiery glare in her dark-grey eyes that reminded me of a stormy ocean.

My eyes were suddenly drawn to something shiny on her arm. Something red. I looked for the guy again. He had it too.

They were Capos. Of course they were Capos.

The anger took over all control. Like a raging bull, I turned ninety degrees, away from the launch tube.

I jumped on the girl.

'Why are you doing this?'

A ripple of panic shot across her eyes. But she recovered quickly, pushing me off her.

I lost my balance but steadied myself by grabbing hold of her plaits.

'Ouch!' she shouted.

I pulled on her hair. 'Why are you fighting with the enemy?'

'Let me go.'

'Why are you doing this?'

She was brandishing a glass sphere, a visitor weapon, but she didn't seem to know how to work it.

'Why are you betraying your own people?'

'Fuck you!'

'What did they promise you? A slice of pizza? A warm bed? Protection from pain and sorrow?'

She hit me on the nose with the glass sphere, but my anger completely masked the pain. I only noticed I was bleeding when I tasted the salt on my lips. But I didn't care.

'How can you be so selfish?'

She kept banging my face. 'Shut up! Shut up!'

'You treacherous cow.'

'Shut up, shut up, shut up!'

Someone grabbed me by the arm. 'Amy! What are you doing?'
It was Caesar.

It was as if he'd woken me from sleep; it was as if I'd been sleepwalking.

What was I doing?

Caesar pulled me away from the girl. As we started running again I could still hear her shouting in the distance. 'Shut up, shut up, shut up ...'

Even though I had awoken from my daze of rage, I was still angry. But I wasn't just angry with that girl. I was angry with everyone. Everyone was just looking out for themselves. The Resistance was ready to hand Earth over to the Splinters in exchange for a few of the abducted teenagers. And the governments, the people who were meant to look out for us, were only thinking about the next election. But how were we ever going to beat the visitors, how were we ever going to regain our freedom, if we didn't stand together? The fight against our common enemy was hopeless if everyone was just looking out for themselves.

Caesar and I had almost escaped through the legion of Red Stacks, we'd almost reached the Defect army territory, when I heard someone shout my name.

'Amy!'

I knew the voice. My heart started beating even faster. I frantically scanned the group of Defect soldiers. Their faces were dripping with sweat from the heat of the fire shooting from their torches, the flames reflected in their burning eyes. I couldn't see him anywhere. Had I been imagining things?

'Over here!'

There he was. Andrew. He was battling his way through the crowd of Defect fighters.

I grabbed Caesar. 'Look. They're still here.'

A brief glimpse of relief crossed Caesar's face. It wasn't only me who'd been worried the others would leave without us. He'd acted confidently but he was worried too.

Andrew pushed one of the soldiers out of his way and grabbed my arm. 'We can't wait any longer. We have to leave.'

We hurried after him. Caesar shouted something in Pronaxian and the soldiers began letting us through.

'What's the situation?' Caesar asked.

'We're in the last shuttle.'

'How many will be left behind?'

'I wouldn't worry about it.'

'How many?'

Andrew glanced at me. 'None.'

Caesar frowned. 'That doesn't make sense. There were only just about enough shuttle-pods for all the Defects. Add to that all the humans. I calculated it. There were 1,5073 people who wouldn't get a seat. And that was if we managed to take all the shuttle-pods.'

'Not everyone made it.'

'What do you mean?'

But Andrew didn't need to explain. We'd almost reached the end of the group of soldiers. What lay behind them began to reveal itself.

Way at the back of the pod room, reaching from the ceiling, was a large tube. In front of the tube tunnel was a short queue of the round shuttle-pods. One by one they were leaving the ship via the tube. Strewn across the floor, from the Defect army's line of defence all the way towards the waiting white golf balls, were dead bodies.

My legs stopped moving.

Some were wearing grey overalls. But more were not. Many more of them were wearing the same thing I usually wore. Or not exactly the same thing. But that was what defined us. Like the grey overalls marked out the Defects, diversity identified us. All over the floor lay dead bodies dressed in jeans, skirts, pyjamas, T-shirts, all in different colours, textures and patterns.

Caesar was as shocked as me. 'What happened?' he cried out.

Andrew was trying not to look at the massacre in front of us. 'A variety of things,' he said as if we were talking about something clinical – a lab report in science class or something. 'Many were killed by the Red Stacks when trying to get on board a shuttle-pod.' He paused. 'But some ...' He narrowed his lips as if he were trying to swallow them. 'Some were killed by you people.'

Caesar's face went strangely pink. 'What do you mean "you people"? The soldiers?'

'No. The soldiers were actually trying to calm things down. I'm talking about the other Defects. The ones we were meant to share the shuttle-pods with. Once it became clear that there weren't enough seats, a fight broke out.'

I tried not to let my mind go there. I wasn't going to go there. Not now. But I couldn't help it. How many had died? A thousand? Two thousand? As my eyes wandered over the colourful field of dead bodies, I began visualising their last moments. The horror.

The fear. They thought they were about to escape. What a sinister last twist of fate.

'Amy!' A high-pitched voice from the back of the pod room brought me around like a familiar hug. Beyond the ocean of death Matilda climbed out of the last golf ball queuing for the launching tube. Stephanie was pulling at the back of her T-shirt, trying to stop her. 'Amy, hurry – over here. We're about to leave. You have to get over here right now. I can't bear to lose any more people from my life today.'

That was so Matilda, making everything about herself. I couldn't think of anything more wonderful than the normality of her egocentricity. I began running towards her, stepping over dead bodies as if they were nothing more than pebbles in my way. I slipped in what I was pretty sure was a pool of blood. *Don't look down, don't look down*, I told myself again and again as I kept going. I could hear Andrew and Caesar following behind me.

I was past the bodies. Matilda managed to wiggle herself free from Stephanie's grip. She started running towards me. I had only one aim. I was going to wrap my arms around her and not let go until we reached Earth.

We bumped into each other so hard I lost my breath for a moment. I dug my fingers into her back and buried my face in the crook of her neck.

'Nice to see you too,' she said, squeezing me as hard as an empty toothpaste tube.

Her warmth was like summer sun to a glacier; my emotional resilience began to melt away. 'I was afraid that you guys might have left.'

'Without you, the saviour of the human race? Never.'

I loosened my grip on her and stepped back. I was shaking. 'It's all my fault. I should never have come here. I just made things worse.'

'What are you talking about?'

I'd kept a lid on my feelings for so long – I'd had to – but now all the fear, the anger and the hurt bubbled up to the surface. 'They're dead. Because of me.'

Matilda squeezed my shoulders. 'They're dead because of the visitors.'

My eyes were welling up. 'I shouldn't have raised everyone's hopes. It was a mistake to try to escape.'

'Tell that to all the others. Tell that to the ones who are halfway home by now. Tell that to the ones who will sleep in their own beds tonight for the first time in ages.'

The shuttle-pod behind Matilda began moving forward as the queue got shorter. Stephanie was standing in the doorway. I could see Courtney, Louisa, Damien, Tom and a couple of Defects sitting strapped into white padded loungers which looked like recliners designed for a psychiatric unit.

Stephanie was motioning for us to hurry. 'We're about to leave.'

I swallowed a lump that was forming in my throat. This was no time for a meltdown. This wasn't over. I dried my eyes.

Hand in hand, Matilda and I ran towards the shuttle-pod. We climbed up the short set of steps leading into the golf ball. There were five empty seats. Andrew came in after us.

Stephanie was giving orders. 'Sit down. Quickly. You need to strap yourselves in before we enter the launch tube.'

Andrew and Matilda took their seats.

I was standing in the doorway. Caesar had stopped on the first step and was looking up at me. I reached out my hand.

'Come on now,' I said, smiling at him. I allowed myself, for a fraction of a second, to imagine us going on a date – a proper date – back on Earth, thinking maybe I'd take him to PC World and he could help me pick out an external hard drive and then maybe we'd go for a burger or something. Or maybe noodles if he didn't eat meat. 'You'd better hurry if you don't want to incur the wrath of Stephanie.'

I thought Caesar was about to smile back at me, but his lips twitched into a frown.

'I'm sorry, Amy.'

He was dumping me. I'd been too presumptuous. 'It doesn't have to be PC World,' I said, too flustered to realise that I hadn't even asked him yet. 'We can do something else – whatever you want.'

'I'm not coming.'

'But Stephanie says we're about to leave,' I said stupidly, thinking that he meant he wasn't coming right away.

'I'm not coming at all.'

'I don't understand.'

'I lied to you.'

Sometimes it felt as if we weren't speaking the same language. I had no idea what he was on about.

'I didn't fix my program. I didn't close the hatches to the grain repositories.'

'But you said ...'

'I said I did. But I didn't.'

'But why did you say so?'

'I needed to get you on board a shuttle-pod.' He finally took my outstretched hand. 'You're so stubborn, Amy.' It felt cold. 'We were running out of time. I knew you wouldn't listen to me when I told you that you needed to board a shuttle immediately or be left behind. I knew you would want to help. So I lied to you instead. You're going home. I'm going back to try to fix my mistake.'

I couldn't speak.

Stephanie came up behind me. 'What's going on?'

I turned to her. 'He says he's not coming.'

'Of course he's coming.'

I turned back to Caesar. 'Of course you're coming,' I tried saying, using the same tone of voice Mum used on Dad when he didn't have a choice in the matter: 'Of course you're driving Amy and her friends to the cinema. Of course you're hanging the new bathroom mirror this weekend.'

Caesar let go of my hand. 'Goodbye, Amy.'

Stephanie shoved me out of the way. She glared down at Caesar, her dark eyes glinting with anger. 'Caesar, you're coming. Why aren't you coming? You have to come. This is your thing. You organised this. We need you to come.'

Caesar leaned to the side to look at me. 'Amy, explain to her.'

I couldn't help it. I snapped. 'Explain what? I don't understand what's going on here. Why are you doing this?'

'You know why.'

'To hell with them! You don't owe them anything.'

'Maybe not.'

'They enslaved you. They took your life away from you. They killed your parents. They're evil.'

'I don't like them, I even hate some of them, but I can't let them die. Everything isn't always about good and evil. Sometimes there is no good and evil. Sometimes there are only actions. Whether they're good or bad depends on the perspective. It's like with Tom.'

I glanced over my shoulder. Tom was sitting comfortably in one of the soft, white seats with a happy smirk on his face. My blood started to boil. That coward. Traitor.

'There was no reason for you to not leave him behind. He betrayed you. He almost cost you your lives. But you didn't.'

I didn't know what to say. I hated Tom. Just like Caesar hated the Corrects. But when it came down to it, I would never want to be responsible for his death.

'Amy.' Caesar's eyes were glistening. Were those tears? 'It's been a pleasure knowing you. I hope to get to know you even better. I intend to get to know you better. A lot better.' He smiled his mischievously dimpled smile as he stepped away from the shuttle-pod. 'I will see you again, Amy.'

He turned his back and began walking away. He was about to disappear into the soldiers' battle line.

I couldn't let him do this. I had to stop him. Staying behind was suicide. If he failed in closing the hatches of the grain repositories, he would perish with everyone else. If he managed to fix his program and close the doors, the Corrects would kill him.

Stephanie tried to grab me, but she was too late. I rushed down the steps.

'Caesar!'

Caesar stopped. He turned around. His shoulders dropped.

I caught up with him. His face was stern. He was angry. Or worried. I wasn't sure which.

'Amy, you have to get back.'

This wasn't the end. I refused to let this be the end. 'Caesar, I ... I ...' But I couldn't say it.

'Amy, please go back to the shuttle-pod.'

A war was raging all around us. But I didn't care. For the moment, there were only the two of us. Me and Caesar, Caesar and me. I looked into his beautiful, hazel-brown eyes. There was the yellow tinge that made them look so much like leaves in the autumn. Autumn. I'd always liked autumn. For me autumn didn't represent the end. Even though autumn marked the end of summer, leaves falling from trees and days getting shorter, for me autumn was the season of new beginnings. It was when school started again with the promise of a clean slate and learning new things; I loved the feel of fresh notebooks and the smell of newly sharpened pencils. Autumn was the time of new winter coats and cosying up on the sofa watching new seasons of your favourite TV programmes. This couldn't be the end.

I grabbed Caesar by the hand. 'Why did you do it?'

'Do what?' His expression softened slightly.

'Why did you save me? In the Selection Lab.' *Please don't say it was so you could get your hands on the steel box.*

Caesar lost his fight with his facial muscles and gave a little smile. 'You know why.'

'Do I?'

'It's what we're fighting for.'

My heart sank. So he did it for the box. He did it as part of the Defects' plan to escape to Earth.

'Amy, I—'

'You don't have to explain. I get it. You were just saving yourself.'

'Amy, I—'

'Like everyone else you were just doing what you had to do to save yourself.'

'Amy, would you let me finish?'

I couldn't look at him. Of course. Of course he was just like the rest of them.

'Amy, I think I ...'

I flinched when I suddenly felt his hand on my cheek.

'Amy, from the first time I met you ...'

What was he doing?

'Amy, I'm falling in love with you.'

The rush of emotions felt like a bomb going off in my chest.

'I've been fighting for the right to feel for most of my life. I've been fighting for the right to love. But until I met you, love was just a cause, a hypothetical possibility.'

I looked up at him. I couldn't hold back any longer. I'd wanted to kiss him again ever since the party at the warehouse. I raised myself on to tiptoes. I stared straight into his eyes. Autumn. Time for new beginnings. Our lips touched. Our future flashed before my eyes. I saw us taking a walk along the canals of East London, holding hands as the sun set over the rooftops, its rays reflecting in the glass of the skyscrapers. I saw us snuggling up on the sofa watching *EastEnders*, me explaining the latest amnesia plot to him. I saw us talking and laughing. And I saw kissing – a lot more kissing.

Our lips parted. We looked at each other. His gaze felt like a warm embrace. He made me feel so secure, so content, so happy.

His dimples deepened. 'Love. It's not just a cause any more. It's everything.' He let go of me. The warmth of his embrace still lingered on my skin. 'Never stop fighting, Amy.'

I didn't realise what was happening until it was too late. Caesar turned on his heel. Then he sped into the crowd of Defect soldiers.

What! I rushed after him. 'Caesar!' The crowd was so dense. I couldn't see him anywhere. 'Caesar!' I refused to believe I'd lost him already. This wasn't happening. This couldn't be happening.

I ran randomly in between fighters in grey. 'Caesar!' I'd lost all sense of direction. But I couldn't stop running. I had to keep on running.

Suddenly someone grabbed me by the shoulders. Caesar?

But it wasn't. It was Andrew. He wrapped his arms around me, completely restraining me.

I tried to break free. 'Caesar!'

'Amy, stop it,' Andrew whispered.

'Caesar!'

'We have to go.'

'Caesar!'

'Let him go, Amy. You've got to let him go.'

I couldn't control it any more. I started sobbing. 'Caesar,' I cried into Andrew's shoulder even though I knew there was no point calling out his name.

'Let him go.'

He was gone. *Gone*.

But even if he was gone, I wouldn't be able to let him go. I would never let him go. I had loved him and I still loved him. No one could take that away from me; not a sinister alien species who wanted to eradicate love as if it were a common disease; not time; not space. Caesar would stay with me for as long as I lived.

Day … I Don't Care

I should be happy. Everyone else is. Courtney and Louisa are making plans for the weekend – Haslam's, if the shop is still there, otherwise Westfield – and Andrew is marvelling at the emptiness of space. But I'm not. I feel as empty as … well … the black vacuum outside my window.

We're travelling at the speed of light but you can hardly feel that we're moving.

'How is that possible?' Andrew is asking Stephanie.

Matilda is asking if she can touch her perfectly straight hair.

Tom has the sense to keep silent.

The two Defects in our shuttle-pod keep glancing out of the window at the ever-approaching blue planet. They look as if they're sweating.

We're on our way home. But I can't seem to rejoice in the fact like the others. I know it's a contradiction, but as well as empty, I feel angry and sad and confused. But mostly, I feel guilty.

I keep seeing Anita's dead face. Her broken neck. The blood trickling down her cheek. If I'd only done what the Resistance had asked me to, she would be safe. She was on the list. She had a ticket out of there. But, because of me, because of my decision to change the plan, she died.

I'm getting nauseous. Motion sickness?

I'm going to tell her mum that she was brave. I'm going to tell Mandira that because of what Anita did, humanity has a chance. But I suspect she won't care. I suspect she'd trade the future of the human race in a heartbeat for one more day with her daughter.

And Anita isn't the only one who died because of my choices. I'm trying not to think about all the dead kids strewn across the floor of the pod room. Are their deaths my fault too?

I keep thinking: maybe if I'd only done what the Resistance wanted me to, no one would have died. That doesn't make any sense, of course. If I'd done what the Resistance wanted me to, if I'd handed the agreement over to the Splinters and the vice-president, I'd have handed Earth over to alien forces. Many more people would have died. I'd have been a traitor. If I had to do things all over again, I would do the same.

But what does that make me? Does that make me the same as the president of Pronax? Maybe I'm not a traitor – I didn't sell out my people – but I did sacrifice the individual for the whole. That is his motto. That is what he lives by. That was his rationale for enslaving the Defects and abducting us.

He was only trying to save his species. I was only trying to save mine.

My head hurts. Stephanie is saying that the ride is about to turn bumpy. We'll soon be entering Earth's atmosphere. I'd better put my diary back.

I can feel slight joy now. I will be seeing Mum and Dad soon. And Emma. I'm going to give them all a hug. I'm going to tell them all that I love them. I've never said that to them out loud before.

I am looking forward to getting home. But a part of me – a part of my future, of my hopes and my soul – will for ever be left out here in the harsh darkness of space.

When I used to imagine how my life would turn out, I mostly just hoped for general happiness. Secretly, as a bonus, I also hoped that happiness included meeting a guy I liked.

When this all started, my fear of not having a future, of losing everything, manifested itself as the fear of dying without ever being kissed. But then I met Caesar. Lovely, lovely Caesar with his dimples as deep as the ocean and eyes as fiery as autumn leaves.

But as it turned out, the Corrects were right. Love comes at a price. Because of Caesar, because of love, I'm left with a hole – a big, all-consuming black hole – in my heart.

As I sit here, about to enter Earth's atmosphere, I can't help wondering whether it's been worth it. Would I have traded love for eternal contentedness?

My conclusion is unequivocal: not in a million years.

ACKNOWLEDGEMENTS

Without three amazing women this book would never have landed on bookshelves. Huge thanks to my agent, Sophie Hicks, and my editors at Hodder, Anne McNeil and Polly Lyall Grant, for believing in aliens.

I want to thank Sigþrúður Gunnarsdóttir who took a chance on a clueless debutant ten years ago – an act that defies time and space as the two of us have only aged four years since then. Thank you to Jóhann Páll Valdimarsson and Egill Örn Jóhannsson, a force of nature in the Icelandic literary world.

For all the good times and great advice: thank you to Richard Skinner and the Faber group of 2012.

Thank you to the CBeebies TV channel for watching my kids while I wrote this book.

And to you, dear reader, thank you – as always, you did most of the work.